The

AMISH TEACHER'S GIFT

Love & Promises
Book One

RACHEL J. GOOD

FOREVER
NEW YORK   BOSTON

Copyright © 2018 by Rachel J. Good
Excerpt from *The Amish Midwife's Secret* copyright © 2018 by Rachel J. Good

Cover design by Elizabeth Turner
Cover illustration by Trish Cramblet
Cover copyright © 2018 by Hachette Book Group, Inc.

Forever
Hachette Book Group
1290 Avenue of the Americas, New York, NY 10104
forever-romance.com
twitter.com/foreverromance

First Edition: April 2018

Forever is an imprint of Grand Central Publishing. The Forever name and logo are trademarks of Hachette Book Group, Inc.

The publisher is not responsible for websites (or their content) that are not owned by the publisher.

The Hachette Speakers Bureau provides a wide range of authors for speaking events. To find out more, go to www.hachettespeakersbureau.com or call (866) 376-6591.

ISBN: 978-1-5387-1126-2 (mass market), 978-1-5387-1125-5 (ebook)

Printed in the United States of America

OPM

10 9 8 7 6 5 4 3 2 1

"Memories can be painful sometimes..."

Josiah's grief must have shown on his face. "They can be." To lighten the mood, he gestured toward the flour all over the floor. "And they also can be frustrating, but situations like this create humorous stories later on."

With a bit of tartness to her tone, Ada replied, "Why don't you ask me about this in a few weeks and see if I find it funny?" The quirk of her lips made it clear he hadn't upset her.

Josiah laughed. "I'll be sure to do that." He wasn't certain, though, that he'd ever find the memory of her dabbed with flour comical.

For him, it would stir emotions better left alone.

*To all the parents, teachers, and
caregivers of special children
for your long hours, hard work, and
self-sacrifice*

*And most of all, to all the special
children who bring so much joy
to their families and the world*

Acknowledgments

Thank you to my wonderful Amish friends, who invite me to visit, offer me insights into your lives, and check my books for errors. I'm so grateful for your help.

I especially want to thank the wonderful special needs teachers as well as the Community Care Center teachers and volunteers, who love and care for special needs children. My first tour of the center touched my heart, and when I entered that multi-sensory environment (MSE), I knew I had to include it in a story. The young Amish man in a wheelchair who showed us around answered all my questions, and everyone on the staff was so cheerful and welcoming. Their joy and dedication in providing daycare services to special children and adults was heartwarming.

I hope many people will donate to the wonderful program (Community Care Center, PO Box 65, Intercourse, PA 17534) or attend the benefits. Find out more about the center at http://plaintargetmarketing.com/when-a-community-cares.

Special thanks to my sweet editor, Lexi Smail, and awesome agent, Nicole Resciniti, who made this series possible.

THE
AMISH TEACHER'S GIFT

Chapter One

Ada Rupp balanced on her chair and reached overhead to finish stapling the row of alphabet letters across the front of the classroom. Below her, Mary Elizabeth kept both hands clamped on the wooden chair to steady it. Ada smiled down at her sister. She wasn't sure how much help a six-year-old would be if the chair tipped, but she appreciated her youngest sister's thoughtfulness.

Placing one hand on the blackboard for support, Ada eased herself to the ground, careful not to snag her skirt hem on the stacks of boxes behind her desk. She'd wait to open the boxes and set out the school books until after tonight's potluck.

After Ada's feet were firmly on the newly washed and swept floorboards, her sister blew out a loud breath. Ever since *Mamm* died a few months ago, Mary Elizabeth had been clingy, but as the first day of school approached, she refused to let Ada out of her sight.

Three of the scholars' mothers had cleaned the schoolhouse earlier that week, and today five of Ada's seven siblings had pinned up colorful bulletin boards to decorate the classroom before the singing that evening. Sadie, at age ten, alternated between taking care of the younger siblings and taping words to objects around the room.

"*Danke* for your help," Ada said to her sisters and brothers as she strolled around the room to check all the details. "Everything looks wonderful." She couldn't have done it without them. Usually a few scholars helped the teacher set up, but with all of her students having special needs, Ada was grateful for her siblings' assistance. The room was ready, but Ada wasn't sure she was.

"This was fun," Sadie replied as she taped up one last sign. "It does look nice, doesn't it?"

Desks were fanned in a semi-circle around Ada's desk. Rather than using traditional rows, this would allow Ada to keep a closer eye on all her scholars. Behind the desks, they'd set up rows of chairs for the singing and several tables for the food. Everything was ready—everything except her fluttering nerves.

Drawing in a deep breath, Ada tried to calm the anxiety in her stomach as she went over the list one last time: Lukas and Will—autism; Lizzie—Tourette's syndrome; Emily—hearing impaired, Down syndrome; Nathan—hearing impaired, tantrums.

Although she'd studied books all summer, ever since the bishop asked her to teach at the special needs school, Ada still felt inadequate for the job. Her only qualification had been knowing sign language to communicate with her five-year-old brother, David. She'd learned quite a bit from her studies, but there was a big difference between book learning and real life. What if she couldn't help these students?

*   *   *

As the buggy jolted along the rutted lane, Josiah Yoder glanced over at his *mamm*. "I'm not so sure this was a good idea."

Behind them, his six-year-old son, Nathan, ricocheted from side to side, his screeches echoing in the small enclosed space.

"He'll settle down soon. He always does." *Mamm*'s quiet words could barely be heard over Nathan's screams.

Her reassurance did little to ease Josiah's concerns. In less than five minutes, they'd be at the schoolhouse, and he'd have to face his son's teacher. He'd been dreading this evening, and the closer the day came, the higher his anxiety spiked.

When Bishop Laban Troyer recommended this school, he mentioned this was the girl's first year of teaching. Josiah would have preferred someone more experienced, someone who could handle Nathan's acting out, rather than a nineteen-year-old new teacher. The next nearest special needs school was more than ten miles away if his son proved too disruptive. He'd worry about putting his son on a school bus, but he wouldn't have time to take Nathan there in the mornings before work, which meant his son would have to be home-schooled. Josiah couldn't ask *Mamm* to do that. Josiah, Nathan, and *Mamm* had moved from Ohio to Lancaster two weeks ago so *Mamm* could help his older sister

Linda with her restaurant. From five until ten every morning, *Mamm* baked desserts for the seasonal menu. Caring for Nathan in addition to that exhausted her.

Nathan's screams decreased to grizzling, an indication he was about to fall asleep. From the time he was an infant, the rocking motion of the buggy had soothed him to sleep. It never mattered how rough the road; even jostling and jouncing worked its magic. Tonight, though, Josiah hoped Nathan would be drowsy and calm, but awake, when they arrived.

"Can you keep him from falling asleep?" Josiah asked his mother. Waking Nathan meant dealing with a growling, grouchy child.

Mamm swiveled her head. "Too late. He's curled up on the seat with his eyes closed."

Josiah groaned. Why couldn't his son have waited a few more minutes?

When they pulled into the school yard, several other buggies were already parked. Josiah urged his horse as far from the others as he could. If Nathan woke, he didn't want his son's cries startling the other horses.

After he'd stopped the wagon, *Mamm* touched his arm. "Why don't you go in and meet the teacher? I'll stay out here with Nathan."

"I don't want to leave you here alone. He's hard to handle when he wakes."

Mamm's tired smile was meant to calm him, but it only added to his anxiety. "Don't worry," she said. "You'll know when he wakes and can come help."

Unfortunately, she was right. Nathan's wake-up screams resembled a fire alarm. He and everyone else in the building would know when his son woke.

With a nod of thanks to *Mamm*, Josiah hopped down from the buggy and strode toward the school building. He'd greet the teacher and hightail it out of there.

Before he reached the door, it swung open. The young woman silhouetted in the doorway looked even more youthful and inexperienced than he'd expected. And if the tension lines around her eyes and lips were any indication, she was extremely nervous. Not the best combination to handle his son's volatile personality.

She stepped forward and flashed a bright smile that took his breath away. "Welcome. I'm so glad you've come. I'm Ada Rupp."

Josiah blinked and struggled to put together a coherent sentence. "Josiah Yoder. My son, Nathan, will be in your class."

"Wonderful." Ada's mouth was still stretched into a smile, but it lost some of its brilliance, and the tightness around her eyes reappeared as she peered behind him as if searching for his son.

He gave her an apologetic smile. "Nathan's not with me. Well, he is, but he's not here." His neck warmed, and heat crept into his face. He was stammering like an idiot. "I mean, he's out in the buggy."

"Please bring him in. Most of the other children are here with their families."

"He fell asleep on the drive here, and I don't want to wake him. He's had a long day." Although that was the truth, it wasn't the whole truth, and Josiah squirmed inside. Lying to his son's teacher would not get them off to a good start. Taking a deep breath, he continued, "Actually, I don't want to wake him because he has, um, outbursts. Temper tantrums, I guess you'd call them.

They can be quite violent sometimes. My wife..." He swallowed hard, unsure whether he could keep his words steady.

"I understand." Ada reached out a hand and laid it on his sleeve as if comforting a child, but his reaction to her touch was definitely not childlike. He jerked away, feeling disloyal to Ruth's memory.

The teacher's cheeks pinkened. "I'm sorry," she mumbled.

He regretted his hasty reaction. He hadn't meant to hurt her feelings. "It's all right." His tone sounded gruffer than he intended, and he tried to soften his next words. "I just wanted to introduce myself, but I have to go now." He started to hurry away.

"Wait," Ada called after him.

When he turned to face her, she appeared flustered. She hesitated a moment before fluttering a hand toward the buggies. "Would it be all right if I peeked in at him? So I'll recognize him on Monday?"

Josiah wanted to say she'd have no trouble recognizing him by his ear-piercing squalls, but he held his tongue and only nodded. She'd discover that soon enough. No point in worrying her. She deserved a few more days of peace before school started.

When she stepped off the porch to accompany him, she barely reached his shoulder. Someone that small and slight shouldn't be alone in the schoolhouse with the scholars, especially not if they were all as troubled as his son. Perhaps he should ask if she had an assistant. Part of him wished he could volunteer for the job of protecting her, but that wouldn't be acceptable.

When they reached the buggy, *Mamm* smiled. "I'm

Barbara Yoder, Nathan's grandmother, and you must be the new schoolteacher."

Ada returned the smile. "Yes, I'm Ada Rupp. It's very nice to meet you. I came out to see your grandson." She turned to Josiah.

The blue of her eyes reminded him of Nathan's crystal-clear ones, and the last rays of sunset illuminated the golden highlights in the hair left uncovered by her *kapp*. He almost forgot why they'd come out to the buggy. Mentally he shook himself. This was his son's teacher; he had no business thinking about her looks.

"He's on the backseat," he managed to explain.

She stood on tiptoe to peer inside, and her expression softened. "Oh, how sweet."

Josiah stepped up beside her to glimpse what she saw. He didn't often have an opportunity to view his son like this. Curled up, hugging his green terrycloth rabbit to his chest, eyes closed in sleep, Nathan appeared angelic.

"I'll look forward to teaching him," Ada whispered.

Not once you've met him, Josiah almost said aloud. Maybe he should warn her, though. How could he in good conscience unleash his son's furious outbursts on someone so sweet and innocent?

*   *   *

Ada returned to the schoolhouse, her cheeks on fire. She regretted calling out as Josiah headed across the parking lot. The families in the schoolhouse must have seen her chase after him, but they had no idea his *mamm* had accompanied him because his buggy wasn't visible through the windows. Ada hadn't even started her first day of teaching, and already she'd made a major mistake. Everyone would assume she'd been out there alone with a man—a married man.

Mary Elizabeth hurried toward her. "Where were you?" she demanded.

"Outside meeting one of the scholars." Ada's words came out breathless, and she tried to steady her voice. She had to put Josiah out of her mind.

Her sister's brow wrinkled the way it did before she cried. "I looked all over for you."

Ada tilted Mary Elizabeth's chin up and gave her a warning look. "You promised me you wouldn't cry, remember?"

"I'm not," Mary Elizabeth insisted, although her eyes were damp and she sniffled.

Ada set a hand on her sister's shoulder and drew her close. "I'm a teacher now. I have to do my job." Although her duties didn't necessarily include trailing after Josiah Yoder and requesting to see his sleeping son. Ada tried not to dwell on that thought. Beside her, Mary Elizabeth grasped a fistful of her skirt and hung on tight.

Another buggy rolled into the school yard. The last scholar. With her sister still clinging to her skirt, Ada held open the door but couldn't resist checking to see if the Yoder buggy was still visible. All she could see were puffs of dust in the distance.

Betty Troyer emerged from the buggy, holding a foil-covered casserole dish. Pasting a smile on her face, Ada forced herself to pay attention to the newcomers. Bishop Troyer hitched the horse to a post, before helping his sixteen-year-old daughter, Martha, from the buggy. Then Martha, in turn, assisted her nine-year-old brother, Lukas.

Martha's round face lit with a smile as soon as she spied Ada in the doorway. Holding her brother's hand and waving excitedly, she limped toward the schoolhouse, and Ada responded with a genuine grin. As usual, Lukas never met her eyes.

"*Gut-n-Owed*," Ada said to the family. She also signed it, although with Martha's hearing aids and lipreading abilities, she most likely understood the spoken phrase.

Betty followed her children to the porch. "I'm sorry we're late." Once her children had gone inside, she lowered her voice. "Lukas was in one of his moods tonight and threw a fit about coming. Martha convinced him to get into the buggy, but he brought his comb. I hope he won't cause any disruptions."

"I put two chairs on the other side of the room, away from the crowd. I thought he'd prefer to sit there with Martha, so the singing and talking won't disturb him as much."

"*Danke*. That was a good idea." A long, slow sigh hissed from between Betty's teeth. "That way if he starts flicking his finger along the comb, it may not bother others."

In her studies, Ada had read about stims, the repetitive movements children with autism used to self-soothe. Lukas often ran his fingers along a comb during church services. Stims might not be acceptable in a regular classroom, but she'd allow it in hers. She wanted him to feel comfortable the first few weeks. She'd also set his desk apart from the others to lessen the noise and distraction.

If loud sounds upset Lukas, though, would Nathan's

outbursts be a problem? Perhaps she should have spent more time talking to Josiah to find out about his son's "temper tantrums," as he'd called them. *No doubt*, her conscience warned, *that was the only reason you wanted to spend more time with him.* Ada recalled his twinkling eyes, his reddish beard, his...

Bishop Troyer cleared his throat, and she jumped. "I'm sorry. Did you say something?" she asked, relieved he couldn't read her mind.

"*Jah*, I did." He raised one bushy eyebrow. "You are nervous about tonight?"

"For sure and certain." That was not the only reason for her edginess, though. She gave him her full attention.

"I said the school board met and decided you should have an assistant. Martha will help you." He glanced past her into the schoolroom, a fond smile playing across his lips as his daughter led Lukas to his seat.

"I'm sure she'll be a wonderful *gut* help." Martha would be a hardworking assistant, and she'd be a calming influence on her brother. She'd been several grades behind Ada in school. Because of Down syndrome, Martha had struggled with lessons, but she'd always worked hard until she learned the material. She'd be patient with the slower learners. Best of all, she had a cheerful disposition and loved everyone she met.

"I'm glad you're pleased." Bishop Troyer smiled and stepped into the classroom. "I'll announce it tonight."

Ada convinced Mary Elizabeth to take a seat next to Sadie. Then, fists knotted at her sides and her knees shaky, Ada walked to the front of the room. After swallowing the lump of fear blocking her throat, she gave the crowd a wobbly smile.

"Welcome, everyone, I'm so glad you could come out tonight. I'm looking forward to the school year and getting to know each of the scholars. I hope you'll tour the room and help your child feel comfortable here."

Ada had prepared a longer speech, but having so many eyes fixed on her made her nervous, and her mind went blank. She moved on quickly to the next part of the program. "Why don't we start by singing 'The Finish Line'?"

She hummed to get her pitch, but her voice squeaked on the first notes. Luckily, the crowd soon drowned out her feeble attempts. After they had sung in German and English, Ada invited Bishop Troyer to come forward to share his news.

In a loud, booming voice, he announced, "The school board has chosen Martha Troyer as the assistant for this school."

Martha squealed and clapped at the news, but Lukas shrank back and covered his ears. Immediately, she sobered and leaned toward him. "It's all right," she whispered.

Staring about warily, Lukas lowered his hands, but remained hunched away from the rest of the audience.

Ada hurried over. "Perhaps Lukas would like to sit at his desk while everyone eats." She pointed to the desk that was some distance from the others.

"You'd like that, Lukas, wouldn't you?" Martha reached for her brother's hand and escorted him to the front of the room.

After he sat at the desk, everyone bowed their heads for prayer. Then mothers lifted the lids from the platters or serving bowls they'd brought and set out the drinks.

Ada stepped back until everyone was served. Then she filled a plate and circulated to talk to her students. She'd just taken a bite of a tangy ham and cheese bun when she passed Emily's grandmother Mary huddled together with Betty, their backs to her.

"I'm not sure she's the best choice for teacher," Betty said, "especially not after what happened with her *daed*."

Mary shook her head. "I'll never understand how a child in good conscience could do something like that."

At that declaration, a lump blocked Ada's throat, and she choked. The sound made Mary glance over her shoulder and elbow Betty.

Teary-eyed from coughing and her face burning with shame, Ada croaked out, "Good evening." She forced herself to stand there when all she wanted to do was run and hide. From time to time, she'd overheard people whispering about her, but for the bishop's wife to openly condemn her to another member of the community cut her deeply.

Mary was the first to recover. She waved a vague hand toward Emily. "I'm sure you'll do well teaching sign language. Your brother is so proficient at it."

"And Martha is delighted to be a teaching assistant," Betty added.

"She'll do a *gut* job," Ada said. "I'm looking forward to having Lukas in class."

Betty shifted, her hands twisting the sides of her black apron. "Yes, well…"

Across the room, the bishop beckoned to Ada. "Excuse me," Ada said, and hurried toward him, grateful for an excuse to get away.

The bishop smiled at her. "We passed the Yoders

Elizabeth dissolving into tears about starting school, and David upsetting a glass of milk. By the time Ada had sopped up the puddle and set Sadie to mopping the floor, it was bath time. Everyone needed to be squeaky clean for the first day of school tomorrow. All the freshly ironed clothes were laid out. If only she could organize her own life in such a neat, orderly fashion.

Once she'd *redded* up the kitchen, Ada settled at the table to look over her lesson plans for tomorrow. Sniffles came from the bedroom. She slid the lesson plans into her satchel and hurried to the bedroom. Huddled in a tiny ball, Mary Elizabeth had her face buried in her pillow.

Ada lowered herself onto the bed beside her sister. "What's wrong?"

Her face tear-stained, Mary Elizabeth peeked up at her. "I don't want to go to school tomorrow. I want to stay home with you."

Wrapping an arm around her little sister, Ada pulled her close. "I won't be here. I'll be teaching."

Mary Elizabeth jutted out her chin. "Then I'll go to your school."

Ada sighed. They'd been over and over this. "I have too many students already, and you'll be with Sadie and Grace and Noah—"

"David's going with you." Mary Elizabeth sniffled and gulped back a sob.

Ever since the school board had agreed Ada could take her younger brother with her to the special needs school, Mary Elizabeth had increased her efforts to go along.

"David will help some of the new children learn sign language. You need to learn to read and write."

"I'm good at sign language. I can help you."

Ada smoothed loose strands of hair from her sister's flushed face. "Yes, you could, but I want you to learn new things. And Rebecca is excited about having you in class. She's a wonderful teacher."

"I don't want Rebecca. I want you."

"I know." Ada hugged Mary Elizabeth, whose eyelids were drooping. "Let's talk about this in the morning."

Mary Elizabeth mumbled an *all right* before her eyes closed.

Ada tucked the quilt around her sister and stood. She had no idea how she'd convince Mary Elizabeth when they woke, but for now they both needed their sleep, and Ada had her own worries about tomorrow.

* * *

The sun had barely risen when Josiah stood misty-eyed in the doorway of his son's bedroom. How his wife would have loved to be here today for Nathan's first day of school. He missed Ruth every day, but moments like this—moments they should have shared—sent sharp, swift pangs through his chest. *Why, God? Why couldn't she be here with us? Nathan needs her so much.*

Josiah couldn't let his sorrow cloud Nathan's first day of school. He pushed back the waves of pain and tip-toed into the room to gather his son's clothing. Then he crossed the room to the bed where Nathan lay curled up. His son's chest rose and fell in a soft, steady rhythm. With his reddish-blond bangs feathered across his fore-head, his face wiped free of sorrow, and his stuffed rabbit clenched in his fist, he looked much younger than his six years. Much too young to be starting school.

His throat tight, Josiah braced himself before placing a hand on Nathan's shoulder to wake him. Nathan shrugged off the hand, slid a rabbit ear into his mouth, and chewed on it. Josiah shook his son gently. Nathan's blue eyes fluttered partway open, and he glanced around the room. When he spotted Josiah, his eyes widened and he shrieked.

The high-pitched keening scraped along Josiah's nerves and tore at his already raw heart. He sank onto the bed and wrapped his arms around his son, getting battered by flailing arms and legs. Nathan had always had a temper, but since his *mamm* died nine months ago, he'd become both inconsolable and uncontrollable.

Nathan stilled for a moment and placed his thumb on his chin with his fingers pointing up. Josiah's heart lurched. The sign for *Mamm*. How did you explain death to a six-year-old, let alone in sign language?

Blinking to hold back tears, Josiah first signed, *I love you*, then he followed up with signs for *gone* and *Mamm*.

At the word *gone*, Nathan jerked back and screeched. Ignoring Josiah's signs of love and reassurance, Nathan drew the covers over his head, and his whole body shook with silent sobs. Josiah stroked his son's back through the quilt, but Nathan squirmed away. He refused to allow anyone to comfort him.

Aching to hold and hug Nathan, but knowing it only escalated his tantrums, Josiah waited patiently until his son's sobs turned into hiccuping sighs. Then he lifted the covers to cradle Nathan in his arms. His eyes squeezed shut, Nathan lay limp and boneless, as if the crying had drained all his energy.

Now might be the best time to dress him, a task

that usually spiraled into a daily battle. When Josiah removed his son's pajamas, Nathan's eyes flew open, and he stiffened. Hitting and scratching, he fought Josiah's every effort to put on his shirt and pants. Nathan's elbow smashed Josiah in the ribs, and he winced. A sharp jab caught him in the abdomen. Getting the suspenders over Nathan's shoulders was an even greater struggle. After wrestling socks and shoes onto swinging feet, Josiah scooted out of kicking range and gave them both a break before he began the breakfast tussle.

He was already exhausted, and they still had to deal with school. He prayed he'd have enough energy to do the roofing job he had scheduled today. When Nathan's sobs quieted to moans, he stood, scooped up his whimpering son, and carried him to the breakfast table, dodging flying fists and feet. After plunking Nathan onto the bench, Josiah stepped back and drew in a calming breath.

Some of his friends had recommended spanking Nathan to get him under control, but Josiah sensed Nathan's actions were fueled by grief, not defiance. Punishing him for his inability to deal with a situation he didn't understand seemed unfair. Josiah wished he could find a way to communicate, to explain, to comfort.

If only Ruth were here, she'd find a way to reach Nathan. After Nathan had lost his hearing in Mexico, Ruth had been much too weak during her cancer treatments to teach him many signs, and Josiah had been working two jobs, trying to pay for Ruth's medical bills. After she and Nathan returned home, every spare minute he'd been caring for Ruth. He'd had little chance to learn sign language from her or even get to know his son. Since Ruth's death, Josiah had his hands full with Nathan's tantrums. Even if he found time to learn more than a few basic signs, how could he teach them to his son?

Josiah swallowed hard, pulled the cereal out of the cupboard, filled two bowls, and poured the milk. At least they'd have no struggles at breakfast. Meals were their only peaceful times.

When he reached the table, Nathan grabbed for the cereal bowl, almost upsetting it. With one practiced motion, Josiah slid the bowl between his son's outstretched hands and onto the table. So far so good. Then he set a spoon in the bowl. When Nathan snatched the spoon and started to shovel in the first bite, Josiah tapped him gently on the head. Nathan dropped the spoon, spattering milk on the table, and closed his eyes for prayer.

Ruth had ingrained the habit into him by the time he was two. To remind him when he forgot, she tapped his head with her fingertips. Despite his acting out, Nathan had never once protested the prayers before and after every meal.

As soon as they raised their heads, Nathan dug in, sloshing and slopping the food into his mouth. Later, after Nathan adjusted to his *mamm*'s death, Josiah would worry about table manners. For now, he was grateful for the calm between storms.

After breakfast Nathan began his usual morning routine—the one that always led to his next outburst, the one that broke Josiah's heart. Nathan had done it in Ohio, but he'd continued it here in the new house. His son walked around the kitchen, looking in the pantry, under the table, beside the stove, all places he used to find his *mamm* when she was well. In each place, he signed *Mamm* and *come back*, sometimes as a question, other

times as a statement. He moved into the living room, repeating the signs, and then into the bedroom. He laid his
head against the side of the bed where his *mamm* had lain
ill during the last few months of her life.

His eyes bleak, he signed one final question: *Mamm
where?*

Josiah pressed a knuckle against his mouth to hold
back his own pain before giving his usual answer. As always, he signed, *I love you*, before replying, *gone*.

Glaring, Nathan launched himself in a whirlwind of
fury. Josiah sidestepped the kicks and clamped his hands
over his son's wrists to stop the onslaught of punches.
Catching Nathan around the waist, Josiah headed to the
bathroom for a rushed routine of face washing, tooth
brushing, and hair combing, accompanied by ear-
splitting screeches.

Nathan calmed a bit while they were hooking the
horse to the wagon. Being around animals soothed him,
but as soon as Josiah set him in the wagon and hopped up
beside him, Nathan began another outburst and needed
to be restrained so he didn't fall out. Josiah clamped one
arm around his son to hold him on the seat beside him
and took the reins in the other hand. Nathan yelled and
drummed his feet against the wood. Cars whizzed past,
and many occupants glared at Josiah as if he were hurting his son.

As the wagon jounced over the road, Nathan's
screeches subsided to whimpers. After they'd gone about
a mile, he slumped against Josiah's side, sucking hard on
his rabbit's ear. When Josiah was sure his son was asleep,
he shifted him so he was more comfortable but kept an
arm wrapped around him in case he woke.

Josiah worried about the teacher who would have to deal with his son today. He had a hard time picturing her coping with Nathan's fits.

According to the bishop, Ada Rupp had been caring for her ailing mother and younger siblings since she was nine years old. Now that her mother had passed, she'd been mothering her seven siblings and sewing quilts to help with household expenses. All of that was admirable, but caring for Nathan took a lot of strength. A strength he doubted the pretty young girl possessed.

And he too needed strength. Not only to cope with Nathan's reaction to school but also to remain detached around his son's teacher.

Chapter Three

Shrill screams outside the schoolhouse door startled Ada. She set down the book she'd been reading about autism, and sensing her movement, David glanced up with a question in his eyes. She pointed to the door. Unconcerned, her brother bent his head over his coloring again.

Someone must be dreading school today as much as Mary Elizabeth had this morning. And they'd arrived half an hour early. Ada hurried to the door and opened it a crack to see Josiah struggling to hold his kicking, screeching son. She pushed it open wider and stepped aside, so he could carry Nathan inside.

His cheeks flushed, Josiah offered an apology with a tilt of his head. He tried to set Nathan down, but his son crumpled into a boneless heap on the floor, still shrieking.

"I'm sorry," Josiah said. Nathan's cries drowned out his words, but Ada read his lips. "I wanted to give

Nathan some time to get used to the new situation before I need to leave for work. I didn't mean to disrupt your morning."

When he knelt as if to lift Nathan, Ada motioned with her hand to leave him. "Why don't we give him a little time?"

The distress in Josiah's soft green eyes when they met hers made her want to comfort him. She said with more confidence than she felt, "I'm certain he'll adjust soon enough."

"I'm not so sure."

"My sister Mary Elizabeth had a meltdown this morning about going to first grade. It was heart-wrenching to send her off to school bawling. They usually get over it pretty quickly, though."

"I'm sorry you had such a rough morning, and I've only made it worse." Josiah remained hunched over as if trying to decide if he should leave his son screaming and pounding the floor.

Sinking onto the floor beside Nathan, Ada set a hand lightly on Nathan's back. At first he shied away, but when she maintained her gentle touch, he stopped wriggling, and his shrieks lowered several decibels. A look of relief crossed Josiah's face.

"Don't worry. I can handle him," Ada assured him.

Josiah didn't meet her eyes, but the tilt of his head and eyebrows indicated his uncertainty. "I, um . . ."

The door squeaked open, and Martha peered in. "I came early to help." With compassion brimming in her eyes, she studied Nathan. "Lukas is out in the buggy with *Mamm*. He's afraid to come in with the noise."

Ach, school hadn't even started and already Ada's

classroom was out of control. One having a fit on the floor, the other refusing to come in.

Martha, one hand over her mouth, ducked her head. "I didn't mean..."

"It's all right," Josiah said, setting a hand on her shoulder. "You didn't hurt my feelings." He lowered his voice. "Or Nathan's. He can't hear you."

Martha giggled at his comical expression. Then she turned toward Nathan. "I can help him."

A skeptical look crossed Josiah's face, but Martha didn't notice it. Her attention was focused on Nathan. She sat on the other side of him and placed a hand on his head. When he didn't wriggle away, she laid down next to him on the floor, put one arm over his shoulders, and hummed.

Nathan's cries grew fainter and fainter.

Josiah's eyes widened. "But he's deaf."

Ada stood and placed a finger against her lips to silence him. "He may feel the vibration," she whispered over the thudding of her heart. Whether the sharp staccato beats of her pulse were from tension over Nathan's screaming or from her nearness to Josiah, Ada chose not to examine too closely.

Martha continued to hum until Nathan was sobbing quietly. Then she picked him up, cradled him like a baby, and rocked him while she sang hymns. After a few minutes, Nathan emitted a long, shuddery sigh and gazed up at Martha. He lifted a hand, and a look of fear crossed Josiah's face. He bent over to grab his son's wrist, but Ada tugged his sleeve and motioned for him to wait.

Nathan reached up and stroked Martha's cheek. Her beatific smile made her look like an angel. Nathan returned it with a watery half smile. A frown creased his brow as he studied Martha's face, first touching her lips, next her cheeks, then her throat, as she sang. Squeezing his eyes shut, he pursed his lips and screwed up his face. Strange rumbling noises came from his chest.

He was humming.

* * *

A swift, sharp pain sliced through Josiah. Moisture filmed his eyes, blurring the vision of his son and the young girl into a misty watercolor. His son, who fought being touched or held, was cuddling. And making sounds. His first positive ones.

Nathan had always been fascinated by Ruth's singing, but she'd been unable to sing those last few months. And for the past nine months, Nathan had made no noises other than moans or screams.

His heart overflowing with gratitude, Josiah glanced at Ada, whose eyes were as misty as his. The sunlight streaming through the window turned her hair to spun gold and lit her tender smile. He lowered his eyes before she could read the admiration in them. He should not be thinking like this when he was still in mourning. His mouth dry, he turned his attention back to the miracle unfolding before him.

The bishop's wife stuck her head through the door. "Is it all right to bring Lukas in now?"

"Of course," Ada said. "Thanks to your daughter." She motioned to Martha.

Josiah tore his gaze away from Ada's sweet smile and forced himself to focus on the bishop's wife.

Betty Troyer smiled. "I'm so glad she's doing well as your assistant."

Assistant? This teen girl was Ada's assistant? Yes, she'd done a wonderful job calming Nathan, but what if her humming didn't work the next time?

Josiah cleared his throat. "Do you have other assistants too?"

"Just Martha," Ada said. "And it looks like she'll do a wonderful *gut* job."

"But—" Josiah snapped his mouth shut on his protest. He didn't want to hurt Martha's feelings or her mother's, and he couldn't express concern for Ada's wellbeing.

Ada leaned over to whisper, "It might be best to slip out now while he's not looking. And please don't worry. He'll be fine."

She was so close her sleeve almost brushed his, and Josiah's heartbeat tripled. Although it pained him to do so, he stepped away from her and struggled to take a calming breath before he asked, "It's a half day here too, I assume?"

"We follow the same schedule as the other schools."

Josiah nodded. As they had when he went to school, the scholars had half days the first week of school so they could help with finishing up summer chores. "I'll take time off work to get him." He turned to go, but couldn't resist one last glimpse over his shoulder. First at Martha, who was still holding Nathan, but she had an arm around her brother too. Followed by a quick look at Ada, who'd knelt and was talking to Martha.

Just then the bishop's wife glanced over and pinned him with a pointed look. Josiah gave her a quick wave, turned his head, and rushed to the door. He'd spent so long here he'd be late for work if he didn't hurry, but that wasn't the only reason for his hasty departure. What must the bishop's wife be thinking? He swung into the wagon and urged his horse into a trot, but he couldn't outrace his thoughts.

All morning he struggled to concentrate on his work, but his mind kept straying to the schoolhouse. Images of his son on Martha's lap. Of Ada's smile. Of her leaning toward him to whisper. He shook his head to clear it of those pictures. But other ones soon filled his mind. Nathan throwing fits. The other children crying and backing away. The whole room in pandemonium, and Ada slumped at her desk, head in her hands. Worried she'd be overwhelmed and need rescuing, Josiah asked to take off even earlier than planned and promised to make up the time.

He galloped most of the way to the schoolhouse and sprinted to the porch. He paused and listened before turning the handle, but heard no sounds. Easing open the door, he peeked inside. The teacher's desk had been moved back against the wall. Ada sat on a chair facing the semi-circle of scholars, holding a picture of a cat with the word printed on it. Martha sat on a chair between Nathan and her brother, an arm around each of them. Josiah couldn't believe his son was sitting still and quiet. That was a blessing. Even more wonderful, he was paying attention to his teacher.

Josiah breathed a sigh of relief. He'd spent the morning fretting. Never could he have imagined he'd arrive to find his son calm and interested in the lesson. He'd expected chaos, but the room was silent, except for one girl who was jerking in her chair, flinging her arms in the air, and spitting out a repetitive *duh-duh-duh* sound.

Ada said the word *cat* several times, exaggerating the sounds with her lips. Then she set down the card and, after making a slightly open circle under her nose with her thumb and forefinger, she pulled it out like a cat's whisker. That must be the sign for *cat*.

Josiah found himself imitating her movements the way some of the students were doing, including Nathan, although in his hand, he clutched his terrycloth rabbit. The twitching girl copied Ada, but her arms flew up in the air several times while she was executing the sign, and she made strange clicking sounds. Ada smiled encouragingly in her direction, and then smiled at each scholar in turn. Josiah couldn't see his son's face when Ada nodded at him, but Nathan straightened up and put his shoulders back as if he were proud. Josiah couldn't blame him.

A smile like that was a gift. An encouragement to be his best self. Something Josiah prayed he himself could be.

Chapter Four

Ada was bending to pick up another vocabulary card when a rustling in the doorway startled her. She looked up, straight into Josiah's eyes. Her pulse skittered, and she fumbled the cards. They scattered across the floor, startling the students.

Lukas shrank back in his chair, and Martha removed her arm from Nathan's shoulders to draw her brother close. Nathan's face crumpled, and Ada reached out to pat his knee, hoping he wouldn't start crying. Emily sat placid, a thumb in her mouth, staring straight ahead, lost in her own world, while Lizzie clicked louder and jumped up from her chair, arms flailing. Will flicked at the brim of his hat, which he'd kept jammed down on his head the whole day. She'd allowed him that stim, which seemed to comfort him. He rocked back and forth in his chair so hard the wooden board attached to the desk legs lifted off the floor and banged down with a crash.

Lukas cried out at the sound, and Martha wrapped her arms more tightly around him. Ada cringed, wondering what Josiah must think. The room was dissolving back into its earlier bedlam. She and Martha had spent most of the morning getting all the scholars calmed and seated. Lizzie's head jerked to one side, a sign of her agitation. That tic had calmed earlier, and she'd stayed in her seat, but now her head, hands, and legs were spasming.

Nathan reached a hand toward Martha, who glanced at him and then at Ada with a plea for help. Ada wasn't sure how professional it was to hold a pupil, especially not with his father watching, but Nathan seemed on the verge of tears. Ada picked him up and settled him on her lap, holding him close. He slid a rabbit ear into his mouth and started sucking. His shoulders relaxed as he cuddled against her. The rabbit was working its calming magic again; it had prevented several tantrums earlier today.

Then Ada made the mistake of looking up and meeting Josiah's startled look. Her whole body stiffened, and Nathan's forehead furrowed. He tilted his head and stared at her with a puzzled frown, then followed her gaze to the doorway.

When his eyes latched on his father, he shrank back and screamed. Ada jumped, and he slid from her grasp. Nathan clutched and clawed at her. His cries set off Lukas's howls.

Martha looked at her as if asking permission to take him outside, which she'd done several times earlier to calm him, and Ada nodded. She bent over, struggling to get a grip on Nathan's writhing body. Her ears hurt from the intensity of his screams. Will clapped his hands over his ears and rocked harder, clunking the chair and desk legs in a rapid rhythm reminiscent of horses' hoofbeats.

Josiah burst through the door, thundered across the classroom floor, and swooped down to grab Nathan. His eyes apologetic, he hugged his son close to his chest despite the pummeling fists and thrashing feet. "I'm so sorry," he mouthed before whirling and rushing from the building.

Ada's shoulders sagged. Could the ending of her first day have been any worse? She stood and put a hand on Lizzie's shoulder, hoping it might calm some of the Tourette's tics, and one on Emily's head. Will's mother had warned her he hated to be touched, so she kept her distance as he crashed the chair legs up and down. When the rest of the parents arrived, rather than seeing the calm classroom of a few minutes ago, they'd see two boys screaming outside the building, vocabulary cards splayed across the floor, and two upset children inside. Only Emily remained oblivious to the commotion around her. Even David had looked up from his coloring with fearful eyes.

It was all Ada could do not to burst into tears as Lukas's and Emily's mothers arrived to pick them up. Before they could collect their children, the schoolhouse door burst open, and Mary Elizabeth, eyes streaming with tears, raced across the floor and hurled herself into Ada's arms. The collision almost knocked Ada over, and she grabbed the edge of the desk to steady herself.

Sadie raced in right on her sister's heels. She stopped a moment to catch her breath, then faced Ada. "Mary Elizabeth cried for you all day. She didn't even stop once. Not even when we were on the playground." She paused, then added ominously, "Rebecca wants to speak with you."

Ada barely had time to regain her equilibrium between two screaming scholars exiting and her sisters bursting into the schoolroom before her best friend, Leah, rushed through the door, her eyebrows raised in a question.

"You have two bawling children outside. I hope that means the day went well, and they're sad about leaving you."

Ada's face heated. If only that's what the commotion had been about. "I wish that were so."

"You didn't need to use the first aid kit I packed you, did you?"

"Um, no." Ada didn't tell her she'd been so overwhelmed, she'd forgotten to bring it with her. She'd have to remember it tomorrow. At least they hadn't needed it today. That was a blessing.

"I did wonder if that *daed* was hurting his son."

"You mean Josiah? *Ach*, no, when his son arrived today—"

Leah held up a hand. "Stop by the store tomorrow afternoon to tell me about it. I need to take Lizzie *now*." Coming closer to Ada, she whispered, "Her *mamm*'s in labor."

Ada nodded. Although her friend usually worked in her family's health food store, she also often assisted the Mennonite midwife during deliveries. "I'll pray all goes well."

Leah swooped down, wrapped a friendly arm around Lizzie's shoulder, and then ducked as Lizzie jerked and her arms spasmed. "Sorry, Lizzie. I didn't mean to startle you."

When the little girl glanced up with puzzled eyes, Leah flashed her a reassuring smile.

"Your *mamm* sent me to get you," Leah said. "We need to hurry home. Your *mamm* will soon have a surprise for you."

After Leah hurried the little girl out the door, Ada rubbed her forehead. Her own day had been filled with surprises, some *gut* and many not so *gut*. If she were alone in the classroom, she would have slumped at her desk, head in hands, but instead she blinked back the dampness in her eyes and straightened her back.

* * *

Josiah flipped Nathan so his son's back was against his chest, directing his kicks outward and defusing their impact. It was harder to kick backward, which spared Josiah's legs a battering. He wrapped his arms tightly around his son's body, pinning Nathan's arms at his sides so he couldn't claw or hit, but he couldn't stop his son's animal-like shrieks.

Two young girls, one bawling and the other scolding, had brushed past him, ignoring Nathan's fit. Josiah barely had time to catch a fleeting glimpse of their faces, but the older one, with her golden hair, resembled Nathan's teacher. They must be her sisters. He hoped they weren't bringing more trouble; that poor teacher had already had a rough day, and his son had been responsible for most of it.

Josiah sighed. The girls had pulled their pony cart close to his buggy and left the reins dangling. Ordinarily, an untied pony cart wouldn't be a problem if the animal was well-trained, but Nathan's screeches might startle even a placid pony.

As Josiah hesitated, unsure whether to approach, a girl hurrying into the parking area slowed and examined him with narrowed eyes. Her wide, generous smile suddenly pinched into tightly pursed lips. An older woman stepping out of her buggy on the other side of the playground stopped and stared.

I'm not hurting him, he wanted to assure them, but from Nathan's yelling and flailing, what else could they assume but that his son was being mistreated by a cruel parent?

Josiah turned away, but the fury of the girl's gaze heated his back and flushed his face. With a few long strides, he reached the buggy as she pulled her horse to a halt and jumped out of the wagon. He would put Nathan in the driver's side to avoid startling the pony, and then go around and tie up the cart.

The girl started walking in his direction. Josiah set Nathan in the buggy and shut the door. His son's wails rocked the buggy, and the girl shook her head. She pivoted and rushed into the schoolhouse. Rubbing his forehead, Josiah skirted his buggy, heading for the pony cart. As he rounded the buggy, Nathan slammed himself against the inside with an ear-splitting yell. The impact rocked the buggy sideways toward the pony cart.

His own horse, used to Nathan's rants, only whinnied and stamped, but the pony snorted and shied, turned wild eyes toward the noise, and bucked. Before Josiah could grab for the cart, the pony galloped down the hill beside the school.

"Halt!" he yelled, dashing after the runaway.

Josiah slipped and slid down the slope, choking and sputtering in the dust cloud kicked up by the horse's hooves. The scorched, dry earth puffed around his heavy work boots as he churned up clods of shriveled weeds and desiccated grasses.

As Josiah thrashed along behind, the pony quickened her gait, flapping the reins against her back, whipping her into a frenzy. Josiah, his lungs burning, spurred himself faster and calculated the arc of the swaying cart. It swung in his direction. Closer, closer...

He'd have only seconds. If he missed...

Closer. Almost.

Now!

Diving forward, arms outstretched, Josiah grabbed for the seat back and hung on. Wind whistled past his face and tore his straw hat from his head, sending it sailing as the pony dragged him along. He dug in his heels and leaned back, struggling to keep his grip on the wood, but the pony tugged harder, sending them hurtling faster downhill, his heavy work boots ripping up divots of earth and grass.

The tip of one boot caught on a rock, mashing his toes and jerking him to a stop. The pony's forward movement wrenched his arms, and he pinched his lips together to hold back a cry of pain as he was catapulted forward, feet off the ground. Kicking wildly, he struggled to regain his footing as they crossed a narrow driveway at the bottom of the hill. With all his might, he pulled back on the cart and forced his heels down until they touched the ground. His boots slid across the driveway, scattering sprays of gravel.

With one final full-strength tug, Josiah yanked the cart

sideways, forcing the pony to veer off course and slow to a trot. Another yank brought the reins flying in his direction. Panting, he grasped for them and turned the pony in a tight circle until she stopped.

Then, hand over hand, he eased his way along the reins until he reached the bridle. All he wanted to do was collapse on the ground to catch his breath and rest his burning muscles. But first he needed to soothe the pony. Her flanks were heaving, and her coat was lathered in sweat.

Josiah ran a gentle hand over her withers and whispered, "It's all right, girl. Calm down now. You're safe," until she stopped snorting and tossing her head. Then he guided the pony and small cart back up the hill.

To his relief, Nathan's yells had subsided as his own horse stepped forward and back, rolling the cart in the gentle motion Josiah had often used to calm his son as an infant. But beside the wagon, a crowd had gathered. And in the center stood Ada, frown lines etched into her forehead, one hand on the shoulder of each younger girl standing beside her.

Chapter Five

Leah's scream echoed across the parking lot, and Ada jumped up. Her chair overturned and crashed onto the floor behind her. Will moaned and rocked harder, but Ada's only thought was to get to Leah. Ada started toward the door, but jerked to a stop. Mary Elizabeth stood frozen in place, her hands still gripping Ada's skirt and apron.

"Let me go," she snapped, and her sister's eyes flooded with tears again.

David looked up from his drawing and studied them with worried eyes.

Ada softened her tone. "I need to see what's wrong."

Mary Elizabeth loosened her grip on the skirt, and Ada rushed outside, with her sister dogging her heels. David jumped up from his desk and trailed behind. Across the school yard, Leah stood at the edge of the slope, and Ada arrived in time to see Josiah make a flying leap through the air to snatch the back of the pony cart.

She pressed her hands against her heart, hoping to slow its ragged beating as the pony dragged him for several yards before he pulled the cart to a halt.

Once he'd grasped the reins and had the pony under control, Ada released the breath she'd been holding. She told herself her shaky breathing came from concern for his safety, but an inner voice taunted her that she'd been equally as enamored by his rippling muscles and show of strength as he stopped the runaway pony. She brushed aside those distracting thoughts, along with her guilt at being attracted to a married man, as Josiah steered the cart up the hill. She hurried over to take the reins.

"I'm so sorry," she said. Then, afraid her breathy voice might betray her feelings, she paused and inhaled to calm herself before continuing. "I have no idea why the pony took off like that. She's normally quite docile."

Josiah, his chest heaving, flipped a hand toward his buggy. "Nathan…startled…her," he gasped out.

Ada turned in the direction he'd indicated. The buggy was still and quiet. "Where's Nathan?" She searched the slope and the parking lot.

Josiah, bent over, hands on his knees, sucked in a deep breath before answering. "In the…wagon."

"He's quiet?" Oh, no. She hadn't meant it as a criticism, but it might sound that way to Josiah. She studied his face to see if she'd upset him, but then had trouble tearing her gaze away.

He didn't seem perturbed, though, when he answered. "*Jah*, finally." His laugh ended in a wheeze and a cough. "The rocking…soothes him."

"That's nice." She forced herself to look elsewhere and added hastily, "About Nathan, I mean."

Pressing his hands against his knees, Josiah pushed himself to a standing position. "Sorry, clearly I'm not... as in shape...as I like to think."

"Anyone would be out of breath after chasing a runaway horse." She stopped herself before she added he didn't look out of shape at all, in fact...Her face burned, and she lowered her eyes so he couldn't see her admiration. She had no business entertaining thoughts like that about a married man. Yet her feelings were harder to rein in than an out-of-control pony cart.

Sadie hung her head. "It's my fault. I was in a rush..."

"*Ach*, Sadie, you still should have tied Rosie." Embarrassment added a sharp edge to Ada's words.

Sadie bit her lip. "I won't forget again, but I was so upset about Mary Elizabeth." She lifted her head to glare at her younger sister.

"Enough," Ada warned. Turning to Josiah, she said, "We're grateful to you for..." She stumbled to a halt as she met his intense gaze. A gaze that made her heart flutter, her thoughts scatter. "I, umm..." *What? What did I—?*

A wagon rattling into the school yard jerked her focus from the green eyes fixed on hers. Had Will's mom arrived? *Ach*, she'd left Will alone in the schoolroom!

"Sadie, tie up Rosie," she ordered as she sprinted toward the building. How could she have left a scholar unattended on the first day of school? What would his mother think? Even worse, what if something had happened to him?

But the person emerging from the buggy was Rebecca Zook.

Ada stopped so abruptly Mary Elizabeth plowed into

her. *Ach*, Sadie had said Rebecca wanted to talk to her, but she hadn't realized she meant today.

The bishop's wife pulled in beside Rebecca. Martha, the miracle worker, had managed to calm her brother. Then Martha and Betty turned and waved before driving off.

Ada released a tiny sigh. At least Betty hadn't seen Will in the classroom alone. If she had, perhaps Ada would no longer have a teaching job. A few days ago, Ada might have welcomed that news, but today she'd had a few glimmers of hope, and now she wanted to see if she could help some of these students. It would be a challenge, but she was eager to try.

Suddenly realizing her other siblings weren't on the playground, Ada checked behind her. She'd assumed they'd come with Sadie and were playing outside.

"Mary Elizabeth, where are the twins and Noah and Hannah?"

Rebecca came up behind them. "Don't worry. My brother Jakob offered to take them so we could talk."

Mary Elizabeth tugged at Ada's skirt. "I wanted to go with them to see Sarah's new baby, but I missed you too much." With that, she burst into a fresh spate of tears.

"Oh, Mary Elizabeth." How was she going to handle her sister's clinginess? Right now, though, she needed to be sure Will was safe.

Motioning for Rebecca to follow her, Ada scurried into the schoolhouse with her sister glued behind her like a shadow. To her relief, Will was sitting quietly, staring off into space and flicking the brim of his hat.

Although Rebecca said nothing critical, her look of surprise when she spotted Will added to Ada's shame.

No doubt, Rebecca would never run out of the school-house, leaving a child alone.

Ada didn't want her to think she was totally careless. "I, um, heard a scream, and..."

"*Ach*, these things happen sometimes." Rebecca crossed the room and settled into a chair in front of Ada's desk.

Ada made her way around the desk and sank into the teacher's chair, feeling awkward and off balance, even though she and Rebecca had been friends for years. They'd been in the same buddy bunch at church as teens during *Rumschpringa*, and they all joined the church together a few years later. Friendships like that lasted a lifetime, so Ada hoped Mary Elizabeth's behavior wouldn't cause major problems for Rebecca.

Scooting a wide distance from Rebecca, Mary Elizabeth followed Ada and crawled into her lap. She wound her arms around Ada's neck and hid her face against Ada's shoulder. Ada shifted to make herself more comfortable, but she couldn't ease the discomfort inside.

Despite the tightening in her jaw as she glanced at Mary Elizabeth, Rebecca's words came out calm and polite. "I hope your first day went well."

Ada had no idea how to respond to that. Surely Rebecca had seen the cards scattered across the floor and Ada's lack of judgment in leaving a student in the classroom alone, not to mention the commotion of the runaway pony. It was kind of her to ignore all the obvious mistakes. The few moments Ada had actually spent teaching had gone well, but most of the day... "Martha was a big help, but as much as I'd like to, I'm not sure I will make a *gut* teacher."

"I'm sorry to hear that." Rebecca's sympathetic look made Ada squirm.

The last thing she wanted was pity. "I hope I'll learn to handle the students."

Rebecca sighed. "That can be an ongoing problem, even when you've been teaching for years. Every year, even every day, can bring new challenges."

Ada bit back a sigh. If Sadie had not been exaggerating, Ada could guess the challenges Rebecca had faced today. "I suppose you're referring to Mary Elizabeth."

Rebecca evaded her eyes. Instead, she drew circles on the desktop with her forefinger. "Yes, we did have some difficulties."

Ada had always appreciated Rebecca's forthrightness. For her friend to hesitate this way, Mary Elizabeth must have been a major *schnickelfritz*.

Josiah peeked his head around the doorjamb, and Ada's heart tripped faster. No matter how often she reminded herself he was married, she couldn't control her reaction to his presence.

"I don't mean to interrupt, but I wanted you to know the pony is tied up." He smiled down at Sadie, who beamed back at him before entering the doorway, followed by David. "Sadie did a fine job of securing the reins."

"She usually does," Ada said. "I'm sorry for what happened today."

"I'm the one who should be apologizing. If it weren't for my son—"

Ada cut him off. "Nathan isn't to blame for an untied horse."

"But he did manage to scare the pony into bolting.

Had another buggy been parked beside Rosie, that never would have happened." Josiah made a rueful face. "But that's not all I'm sorry for."

Rebecca's glance bounced back and forth between them, and her eyebrows rose.

Josiah's face colored. "Forgive me for interrupting." He bobbed his head slightly as a good-bye. "I'll see you tomorrow."

Ada lowered her eyes to avoid Rebecca's curious stare, hoping her eyes hadn't revealed the excitement that filled her whenever Josiah appeared.

"You and he aren't—?" Rebecca gestured toward the door.

Not trusting herself to speak, Ada only shook her head. Rebecca must have sensed her interest.

"I hope not, because he's—"

"I know," Ada interrupted. She didn't need to hear her friend say the dreaded word *married*. Josiah's beard made that for sure and certain. *Does she think I have no eyes in my head?*

Rebecca's skeptical look made it clear she didn't believe Ada's denial, but she continued their discussion as if they hadn't been interrupted. "So, as I was saying, I—" She broke off abruptly and glanced at Mary Elizabeth.

Ada nodded. "Sadie, you and Mary Elizabeth need to rub down Rosie. She's all lathered up." She motioned toward the cloakroom. "I keep a basket of rags on the shelf in there. I'm sure there's some clean toweling you can use. And take David with you."

"I don't want to go," Mary Elizabeth howled when Ada set her on the floor.

Turning to Sadie, Ada said, "When you're done, you

can take David and Mary Elizabeth home. I'll be there shortly."

Mary Elizabeth set her lips mutinously and planted her feet. "I want to ride home with you."

Sadie beckoned to her sister. "Want to hear a secret?"

"What is it?" Mary Elizabeth gave her a suspicious look.

"I can only tell you if you come here." Sadie put a finger to her lips and beckoned again.

Mary Elizabeth stomped over to her sister, but when Sadie whispered in her ear, her eyes grew round, and she clapped. "Guess what we're going to do?" she announced.

Sadie put a hand over her mouth. "If you tell, it won't be a surprise."

Looking as if she were about to burst, Mary Elizabeth nodded. Then bouncing along behind Sadie, she headed to the cloakroom. When they came out again, Sadie was carrying the toweling, and Mary Elizabeth handed David his safety vest. The two girls still had theirs on. Her back to Ada, Sadie signed something to David, and he hopped up and went outside with them.

Ada shook her head. Leave it to Sadie to convince Mary Elizabeth to cooperate. She turned back to Rebecca. "I'm sorry for all the interruptions."

Rebecca swiveled to look at Will. "Perhaps we should wait until Miriam comes to pick him up."

Once again, Ada's cheeks heated. She'd not only left Will alone in the classroom, now she was ignoring him. Rebecca had only meant to be kind, not point out Ada's mistake, but it still made Ada feel inadequate. "Of course. Thank you for being so understanding."

Rebecca followed her over as she pulled a chair close to Will's desk. Ada faced him across the desk, careful not to get too close. She'd already discovered what distances made him nervous. "You did a good job today, Will. Would you like a toy to play with?"

A few times that morning, Will had repeated parts of sentences, but now he was silent. Perhaps Rebecca looming over them was making him as nervous as it was making her. She motioned to one of the desks. "You can use one of those chairs if you'd like, Rebecca."

"I'm fine standing," Rebecca said, but when Ada turned pleading eyes toward her, she pulled over a chair.

"I'll get the windmill," Ada told Will. "I know you like that."

She walked to the shelves along the wall and brought back the toy. She set it close to her on the desk and demonstrated pushing the button to make it spin. Then she slowly slid it across to Will.

He cringed away as it came closer, but once she let go and moved back, he reached out a tentative finger and pressed the button. Once he was engrossed in the activity, she bent to pick up the cards that were scattered across the floor, and Rebecca joined her.

"He really seems to enjoy that," she remarked as she handed Ada a stack of cards.

Ada nodded. "I hoped he would. I chose it because it's good for his fine motor coordination, and he likes the repetitive motion."

Rebecca appeared impressed. "You seem to know a lot about how to help him."

"Not as much as I'd like, but I've been reading as much as I can." One thing books couldn't do, though, was to prepare you for the actual classroom. In practical experience with special students, Martha was far ahead of her.

"You've really had a time of it, haven't you?" Rebecca said sympathetically. "Aren't you supposed to have aides?"

"I have Martha, and she does a wonderful job."

"Yes, but shouldn't you have a helper for each student?"

"With the school being new this year, they may still be looking for aides."

"I hope you get more help soon. It's a lot for one person and Martha—no matter how good she is—to handle."

Will's mother dashed through the doorway, looking frazzled. "Please forgive me. I didn't mean to be so late." Miriam headed toward her son. "There was an accident on the main road, so they detoured everyone around. It added several miles to the trip."

Ada sucked in a breath. "It wasn't a buggy, was it?"

Miriam turned toward her. "*Neh*, a big truck overturned, blocking both sides of the road."

So not Josiah, then. Or any of her students. "*Ach*, I hope all is well."

"The driver was not hurt, but the spill is not cleaned up yet."

"I see." Ada started to get up. "Did Sadie leave?"

"*Jah*, the girls and David were just heading down the drive when I pulled in." Miriam gave her a sympathetic glance. "They'll be all right. The detour is well marked, but I can follow them, if you like."

Ada shook her head. "No need for you to go out of

your way. Sadie will figure it out." She hoped. She tried not to imagine her sisters lost on the back roads.

"Of course she will." Miriam glanced at her son and then back at Ada. "And how was Will today?"

"He did *gut*." Aside from banging his chair legs and flicking his hat brim, Will had not had any outbursts. Unlike two of the others.

"He's usually quiet in new situations, but once he warms up, then you must watch out."

Ada cringed, picturing all three of the boys acting out at once. Martha had coped with two today. How would they manage one more?

Miriam knelt beside Will and took one of his hands. He didn't look at her, just continued to push the windmill button with the other hand.

"Come, Will," she said.

He pushed the button several more times, but when his *mamm* rose, he struggled up from his chair. "Come, Will," he repeated, shuffling along beside her. At the doorway, he stopped and blinked in the sunlight, then flicked his hat brim.

"It's all right," his *mamm* said.

"All right," Will echoed, and followed her out the door.

The words *all right* stayed in Ada's mind. If only someone could reassure her everything would be all right. She should trust God, but so often she worried instead. And once she heard what Rebecca had to say, she'd have one more worry to add to her growing list.

Chapter Six

Still hot and sweaty from chasing the pony cart, Josiah was grateful for the slight breeze as he headed down the road. Fields filled with cornstalks rose beside him and touched the pale blue sky, calming his nerves and spirit. He had no idea how his son had wedged himself into the narrow space on the buggy floor behind the front seat, but Nathan was sleeping peacefully, so Josiah left him there. It had been a long time since he could enjoy the beauty of God's creation and a rare afternoon off.

The buggy rounded a bend in the road, and blinking lights up ahead warned of an accident. He tugged on the reins to slow the horse. No point in going any farther; the police would be diverting traffic onto the back roads. It would be faster to turn here and veer off onto the dirt road that ran past Zook's farm.

He clucked to the horse and pulled the reins to head left, but Silver balked. She knew her way home. A car zoomed up behind them, and Josiah quickly steered Silver to the side of the road. It puzzled him why the *Englisch* drove so fast when they'd only need to slam on their brakes up ahead. But sitting by the side of the road gave him time to think.

The teacher's sister, Sadie, would be coming this way with the pony cart. Would the children wait at the schoolhouse to follow Ada, or would they come alone? Maybe he should wait to see. If they were alone, he could show the little ones the shortcut he planned to use. Then they wouldn't have to follow the detour and take a chance of getting lost. If they were following their sister, he'd turn off here and head home. Of course, he wasn't hoping for another chance to see Nathan's teacher. He was only being neighborly.

Cows wandered on a nearby hill, nibbling grass, and Josiah alternated between watching them and checking the buggy's rearview mirror for the pony cart. The sun beat down, heating the buggy interior, and he wiped the sweat from his brow as minute after minute passed and cars zipped by, shaking the buggy. Each time, he held his breath as they passed. He'd almost given up, figuring the girls had gone home a different way, when the cart approached. Josiah pushed aside his disappointment. The children weren't accompanied by Nathan's teacher. He berated himself; he had no right to be thinking of things like that when he was still in mourning.

Hopping out of the buggy, he flagged them down. Sadie pulled behind his buggy. Leaving his door open so his sleeping son would get some air, Josiah tied the horse to a telephone pole. After the runaway cart earlier, he wasn't about to take any chances. Then he walked back to the pony cart to explain.

"A truck overturned ahead, so there's a detour. I can show you a shortcut home."

Although the younger sister had her arms crossed and a pout on her face, both she and Sadie listened carefully. "Where do we turn?"

He was pointing out the left turn they'd take when a tractor trailer rumbled past. The whoosh of wind almost knocked him off his feet. He grabbed for the pony cart to steady it, and Sadie gripped the reins. The roar of the engine and rattling of the truck drowned out all sound.

David, who was sitting behind his sisters, suddenly banged on the back of their seat and pointed toward the cornfield behind Josiah. He rapidly signed some letters, but Josiah could only make out an N.

Josiah glanced over his shoulder in the direction David indicated, but saw nothing except for swaying cornstalks. The wind from the truck had most likely rippled them out of place. As the truck noise faded, Josiah faced the girls again to finish his instructions.

"I'll wait for a large gap in traffic so we can both turn left." He waved to the side road several yards away. "Then just follow me to the driveway past Zook's farm."

David pounded on the back of the seat again and stuck his hands in front of Sadie to sign.

She shook her head. "Not now," she said, and brushed his hands away.

"Oh," Josiah added, "when we turn into the driveway, it'll look like it ends at a farmhouse, but follow me around the barn. There's a small dirt path back there that cuts through the cornfields and runs out to the main road."

After Sadie nodded and adjusted her grip on the reins,

Josiah hurried to his buggy and got in. Amazingly, Nathan remained silent. Josiah waited until three cars had zoomed by, then signaled to Sadie, and pulled out.

Behind him, David was kneeling in the cart and staring back the way they'd come. When the cart bounced over a bump, David almost flipped over the backseat, but he grabbed the wooden slat with both hands and hung on. Josiah sucked in a breath. After the pony fiasco earlier, he didn't want to be responsible for another disaster. He should stop and make sure the boy stayed seated.

The road took a sharp bend, and he spied a safe place up ahead to stop. He was about to signal for them to pull over, when David turned and plopped down on the seat, shaking his head and signing furiously. His sisters paid no attention to him, and Josiah couldn't figure out any of the signs—especially reflected backward in the rearview mirror. Once they stopped, he'd find out what was bothering David, but right now, he wanted to get them home safely.

They turned right and jounced down the rutted dirt lane until they reached the main road. Josiah stopped and walked back to the cart.

"Do you know your way home from here?" he asked Sadie.

She looked around. "I . . . think so."

"You don't sound so sure." He'd better make sure they got home safely. "You live out past the Esh farm, right?" He didn't want to admit he'd driven past there several times, thinking he'd talk to the teacher about Nathan before the first day of school, but never got up the courage to knock on the door. "You can follow me, then."

The relief on Sadie's face showed he'd made the right decision. Behind her, David, his brow creased in a worried frown, was signing. Josiah wished he knew more sign language, but he'd only started learning it after Ruth returned from her cancer treatments in Mexico. They'd both been hoping the Mexican doctors had misdiagnosed Nathan's hearing loss after an infection. Josiah turned his attention to the children to keep himself from spiraling into sadness.

David made a sign he recognized: *corn*, Nathan's favorite vegetable. And one for *cart*. The rest were a blur.

"I think your brother is trying to tell us something," Josiah said to Sadie.

She smiled. "He's excited about the surprise we're planning for Ada."

"She worked hard today." And his son was the cause of most of her work. "She deserves a surprise."

Sadie simply nodded.

"We'll turn right onto the main road then." Perhaps getting Ada's siblings home was one way he could make up for all the trouble he'd caused her today.

When they reached the Rupps' house, Sadie called out a thank-you. Josiah waved and turned the buggy around to head back to his road. All the way home, he relaxed and enjoyed the scenery, but as they approached the barn, his stomach knotted. He dreaded waking Nathan. He delayed the inevitable by unhooking Silver and rubbing her down. Then he walked her to the stall, where a sheet of paper hung on a hook nearby.

After he closed the stall door, he pulled down *Mamm*'s hastily scribbled note:

> *I have to wait tables at Linda's restaurant tonight.*
> *Heat the chicken corn soup for dinner.*

Not only did *Mamm* bake desserts for his oldest sister's restaurant, she also helped out whenever one of the waitresses didn't show up. That meant he and Nathan would be alone tonight. The prospect filled him with dread. *Mamm* usually managed to coax Nathan into his bath and then bed. On nights when she was gone, Nathan often fell asleep on the floor, still dressed in his clothes, worn out after one of his tantrums.

Taking a deep breath, Josiah dragged his feet as he headed to the buggy, preparing himself for an afternoon and evening filled with nonstop screaming. He slid open the buggy door as quietly as he could so he wouldn't wake Nathan suddenly. If he was lucky, he could carry Nathan upstairs to bed, where he'd nap for a while. Josiah pulled his seat forward, bent down, and reached inside to pick up his sleeping son.

The buggy was empty.

* * *

After Miriam and Will left in their buggy, Ada returned to the schoolroom to hear what Rebecca had to say. She bit back the sigh trying to escape. Today had been trying enough. She really didn't need one more burden.

Rebecca was still sitting in the scholar's chair. Instead of sitting beside her, Ada picked up the windmill and replaced it on the shelf, delaying the inevitable. She was already failing as a teacher. Hearing Rebecca's words would add to her sense of inadequacy. Slowly she headed to the chair in front of Will's desk and turned it to face Rebecca.

Her friend cleared her throat. "I don't want to upset you

after you've struggled all day with your own scholars. And you had other problems as well with the pony cart."

Ada had to admit, now that all the children were gone, it was a little less stressful. "I guess you didn't have an easy day either. Sadie told me Mary Elizabeth cried today."

"That's true," Rebecca said. "Scholars sometimes cry the first few days of school, so I'm used to it. But..."

Ada tensed, waiting for her friend to put her concerns into words, but Rebecca remained mute. As the silence stretched between them, Ada tried to find a way to make things easier for her. "You can tell me the truth."

A small sigh hissed through Rebecca's teeth. "In truth, it was *all* morning. And...it wasn't crying. It was wailing. Wailing so loud, I couldn't teach. We didn't have a chance to do any classwork. No one could concentrate."

Ada slumped at her desk. She'd been expecting Mary Elizabeth to act *gretzy*, but she hadn't expected nonstop crying. "What do you think I should do?"

Rebecca glanced out the window. "I really don't know what to suggest. If you weren't teaching, I'd suggest you come in with her for a little while, but you need to be here in the morning, so that won't work."

"I'll talk to her tonight," Ada promised, although she wasn't sure how much good it would do.

"Usually when scholars are disruptive, we can send them home. But with your *Mamm*..."

Ada bit down on her lower lip and blinked to clear the mistiness in her eyes. *If only Mamm were still alive, none of this would be happening.* Mary Elizabeth wouldn't be clinging to her older sister.

Rebecca's eyes filled with tears. "I'm so sorry. I know it hasn't been easy for you this past year." She cleared her throat. "I suppose it hasn't been easy for you while your *Mamm* was ill either, was it?"

Ada's throat closed up. Only a few of her friends realized she'd been caring for her siblings ever since Sadie was born. Most people knew only about the past few years when *Mamm* was bedridden after David was born. And few knew about *Daed*. She hid as much of that as she could, so people wouldn't pity her. Though the previous bishop had counseled her on the final decision, most people were shocked to find out what she'd done. Since then, the gossip had died down, but the disapproval hadn't.

"I didn't mean to bring up sad memories." Rebecca reached across the desk and patted Ada's hand. "Why don't you talk to Mary Elizabeth tonight, and we'll see how she does tomorrow?" She rose. "I think she's jealous David stays with you."

"She could come here if she gets to be too much of a problem, but even if I could handle another scholar, I don't want to reward Mary Elizabeth's crying by giving her what she wants." All the teacher psychology books she'd been reading agreed on that. "But you need to be able to teach."

"*Jah*, it's a hard choice," Rebecca agreed. "Let's see what happens tomorrow. After all, it was her first day."

That was true. And it was Ada's first day too. Maybe tomorrow would be better for all of them.

Chapter Seven

Josiah stared at the empty buggy. Where was Nathan? Had his son climbed out while he was taking care of Silver? At least he'd closed the barn door, so Nathan couldn't have gone far. To get out the regular door, Nathan had to pass Silver's stall, so he was in here somewhere. Searching the barn didn't take long; it normally held only two horses and two vehicles, and *Mamm* had taken one horse and the wagon. Josiah lifted each hay bale and opened equipment and tool closets. Ten minutes later, he'd found no sign of Nathan.

He bellowed his son's name several times, although Nathan couldn't hear. Desperate, he checked inside and underneath the buggy again. But finally he faced the truth.

Nathan was missing.

He couldn't bear even the thought of losing his son so soon after losing Ruth. *Dear God, please help me find . . .* He stopped abruptly. Did he have any right to ask a favor of the God he'd rejected?

No, he was on his own in this. There had to be a logical explanation. How could Nathan have gotten out of the buggy? The doors were too heavy for him to slide open, and Josiah would have heard the sound of them sliding. So where could he have climbed out? The school yard? Maybe Nathan had slipped out during the pony chase. But why hadn't anyone seen him? Josiah hadn't spotted Nathan on the playground, and when he peeked into the classroom, it appeared almost empty. He had to admit, though, that his attention had been so focused on Nathan's teacher, he'd barely noticed the rest of the room. He struggled to recall the details. Another schoolteacher, one *Mamm* had introduced him to last week, had been there, sitting near Ada. And a small boy. Other than that, he was pretty sure the room was empty, but with all his attention concentrated on Ada, twenty children could have been playing in the room, and he'd have missed them.

While he was thinking, his hands were frantically harnessing Silver. "I'm sorry for taking you out again so soon," he said to the horse as he fumbled with the bridle. "But it's an emergency."

If *Mamm* were here, she'd insist on praying, but he was relieved not to face the disappointment in her eyes when she discovered he'd lost his son—and his faith.

* * *

After her discussion with Rebecca, Ada climbed into her buggy, and weariness overtook her. She hadn't realized teaching would be so draining. And they'd only had a half day today. How would she endure the full days that started next week? She had her siblings to care for after she arrived home, and she wanted to read more on techniques to help her students. The tomatoes needed canning, and she'd promised to finish a quilt for the school benefit next month, but when would she find the time?

It seemed her worries piled up faster than dirty dishes in her kitchen, and with seven siblings, she had plenty of those. *Mamm* always said worrying meant lack of faith. *Forgive me, Lord. I know You're bigger than any problem I face. I'm turning them over to You.*

After she'd prayed over each concern, her spirit lightened. She decided to put them out of her mind and enjoy the scenery. Her heart always lifted when she traveled the back roads past the farms. Variegated rows of greens and yellows made the fields look like patchwork quilts spread across the ground.

Ada slowed as she neared the accident site Miriam had mentioned. When she rounded the bend, lights revolved up ahead, throwing off red, yellow, and blue beams and striping the face of a small boy who stood mesmerized at the edge of the road, his eyes and mouth wide as he stared at the fire engines, police cars, and tow trucks. With his straw hat tilted back, he reminded her of Nathan. He was even clutching a small green rabbit.

It *was* Nathan!

She jerked the reins to stop her horse. What was he doing here? And where was his *daed*? He shouldn't be so close to the road without a safety vest. She pulled the buggy to the side of the road and jumped out. Scanning the crowds for Josiah, she sprinted toward Nathan.

When he saw her, his mouth opened even wider. He backed up a bit, and she slowed. She didn't want to scare him.

Stopping a short distance away, she moved her hands in the sign for *Come*. Nathan studied her warily as she repeated the sign. Then he stared at her hands as she did it again.

She had no idea how much sign language, if any, he understood. She'd have to ask his *daed* as soon as she found him. No, better yet, she should schedule a conference with his *mamm*. She needed to stay as far away from Josiah as she could.

Ada had just concluded Nathan hadn't learned any sign language when he took one step toward her. And then another. She smiled to encourage him to continue. When he reached her, he surprised her by slipping his hand in hers and leaning his head against her apron. She stood still a few minutes, while he popped a rabbit ear in his mouth and sucked on it. How different he was from the kicking, screaming child at school that morning. She marveled at his calmness. He didn't seem at all concerned about being separated from his *daed*.

But she needed to get home to her siblings. She didn't like to leave them alone too long. Sadie did her best, but the others often didn't listen when she told them to do their chores. Plus, without supervision, the tomatoes wouldn't get canned before dinner. She inspected the crowds standing on the nearby hillside and gathered along the road watching the cleanup. Only two straw hats in either crowd, and neither one was Josiah.

She hated to disturb Nathan, but she needed to know.

Keeping her fingers wrapped around his, she moved so she was facing him and squatted down. He looked a little downcast. Perhaps he was missing his *daed*.

Ada didn't want to free her hand from his, but she needed to sign. He knew the sign for *come*, so she hoped he'd understand her new message. She set her free hand on his shoulder before letting go of his hand. He shoved more of the rabbit ear in his mouth.

Where Daed? she signed.

Nathan shrank back and glanced over his shoulder nervously. He sucked harder on the rabbit ear, but didn't respond.

Had he disobeyed and slipped away from his *daed*? With his lower lip caught between his teeth, he had that same guilty expression her siblings had when they'd done something wrong. But was that a glint of fear in his eyes? His *daed* seemed gentle with him, but maybe he was different when they were alone.

Ada signed her question a second time. Last time it had taken three tries before he responded, but this time, he answered.

Gone.

Ada wasn't sure what he meant. Surely Josiah hadn't left him here alongside the road. But what could she sign to get an answer?

Nathan reached out and touched the frown lines between her eyes. He must think she was upset with him. She smoothed out her forehead, smiled, and traced a question mark in the air, hoping he'd figure out she was puzzled, not annoyed.

He studied her as if deciding whether or not he could trust her. Then with the rabbit dangling from his mouth, he signed *Daed*. He followed up by pantomiming holding the reins and pointed to her buggy.

If she was interpreting correctly, he was telling her his *daed* drove the buggy. She nodded to show she understood.

He continued by signing *gone*.

Ada shook her head. That didn't make sense. Josiah wouldn't leave Nathan here and drive away.

A hurt look in his eyes, Nathan nodded.

Poor kid. He must think she didn't believe him. She'd have to be more careful with her expressions when she worked with him. Her brother David was used to her, but Nathan took each thing she did seriously. To show she believed him, she repeated his signs.

He pulled the rabbit from his mouth and beamed. So she'd gotten his message right, but she still hadn't interpreted the meaning. Perhaps rather than his *daed*, he was here with his *mamm*. Then it would make sense. She'd noted two or three Amish women in the crowds, but why would any mother leave her child alone by the road?

She signed, *Mamm where?*

His face forlorn, he signed, *Mamm gone.*

Then his eyes welled with tears. They spilled down his cheeks, and he scrubbed at the wetness with his fists.

Ada reached out and embraced him. He cuddled close and sobbed against her shoulder. Poor baby. Something was terribly wrong, and she needed to find out what it was. Maybe his fits were his way of releasing pent-up emotion.

This morning, humming had soothed him, so Ada began a hymn. His sobs quieted, and he pressed his head tightly against her chest. She inhaled deeply with each breath so he'd feel a strong vibration. After a few moments, he reached up shyly and touched her *kapp*, then released a long, shuddery sigh.

Ada had no idea what had caused the cloudburst, and she still had no idea where his parents were. She was positive they weren't gone, but they did not seem to be here, and she couldn't leave Nathan by the side of the road. She told herself she remembered his address from the school records because he was the only student she didn't already know, but her cheeks burned. In truth, she'd been trying to find out more about his *daed*. The house was about four miles down the road from them. Ada would take Nathan there.

After Nathan had calmed, Ada pointed to her buggy and signed the word for *go* and pointed to herself, followed by a question mark.

He must have understood because he nodded. When she set him on his feet and stood, he again clasped her hand. A warm feeling flowed through her. She might not have had a successful day of teaching, but she'd made a heartfelt connection with one of her scholars. And that was a huge success.

Chapter Eight

A block away from where Ada and Nathan stood hand in hand, one of the men directing people around the overturned truck handed his sign to a new worker and started toward them.

"Hey, lady," he yelled as he approached.

Nathan had been smiling up at Ada, but when she tensed, he turned his head and followed her gaze. His hand tightened on hers, and Ada wished she could reassure him, but the man's puffed-out chest and belligerent yell made her edgy.

He waved toward her buggy. "You can't block the shoulder that way. Look at the traffic. It'll only get worse once the schools and early factory shifts let out."

Though Ada tried to keep her voice steady, it had a slight tremor. "We were just leaving."

Growing even redder in the face, the man pointed at Nathan, who shivered and stepped back until he was partly hidden by her skirt. Ada squeezed his hand, hoping to calm his fears.

"Lady, that kid is too little to be out here alone. I don't know what you people are thinking. And why isn't he wearing one of those safety vests like the others do?"

"He was in a buggy."

"Don't lie. I saw him standing over here by himself."

"I'm sorry. There was a mixup and..."

The man talked right over her. "Anyone coulda kidnapped him." He shook his head. "Crazy the way you let kids wander around like that."

"We trust that whatever happens is God's will."

"So it's God's will to let your kids get kidnapped? Like those three kids in the pony cart that was by here earlier?"

Three children in a pony cart rang alarm bells in Ada's mind. Could they have been her siblings? "What did they look like?"

"Hair about the color of yours. The girls had blue dresses and some white thingies tied on their heads." He swished a hand around his head.

Her sisters had on white kerchiefs and blue dresses, but so did many girls their age. Still, if Amish children had been kidnapped, she needed to help.

"Two girls and boy not much bigger than him." The man jerked a finger in Nathan's direction.

Nathan backed up, and Ada wanted to hide him behind her and hold her arms out to the sides to shield him from danger. But Nathan was clinging so tightly to her hand, she couldn't let go.

"The one driving couldn'ta been more than eight or nine," he continued. "That beats all, her driving on a main road like this."

The worries Ada had pushed aside earlier returned in full force. Sadie was ten, but she was small for her age. "So why do you think they were kidnapped?"

"Some man stopped them and motioned for them to follow him up the back road there. I was hoping they knew him, but these days, you never know. I kept an eye on him so I can describe him to the police in case they turn up missing."

A man? Stopping Sadie and Mary Elizabeth? Why would they follow a stranger? Maybe it wasn't her sisters. But she should find out, just in case. "This man, what did he look like?"

"The same as all the rest of you people. One of those hats"—he pointed to Nathan's head—"and them suspender things."

So he was Amish. "You said you could describe him to the police."

"Sure can." The man squared his shoulders. "But what's it to you?"

Ada would care no matter who it was, but it might be her siblings. "I think they're my sisters and brother."

"And your mother just lets them run all over creation with no supervision?"

Ada swallowed hard. "*Mamm*'s dead."

A brief flicker of sympathy flared in his eyes, and his voice was a bit less gruff when he answered. "The man was about yea tall"—he held his hand above his head about six feet off the ground—"and had a reddish beard that came to here." He tapped the bottom of his neck.

That sounded like Josiah. At least she hoped it was Josiah. But why would he take them up this road instead of the detour? "You sure they went this way?" She pointed to the back road off to the left.

"Look, I need to get back to work, but yeah, that's the way they went. If they'd gone through the detour, I might not of noticed. But that road dead ends in about a mile."

"I know," Ada choked out.

"I hope for your sake they're OK, but if they turn up missing, just send the cops my way."

Ada nodded and hurried toward the buggy. Nathan kept up with her. When he climbed up beside the driver's seat, Ada almost protested. What if he had one of his outbursts while she was driving? His *daed* always put him in the back. She didn't have time to insist on that; she had to find out if her siblings were all right.

The minute there was a gap in traffic, she turned left into the dead end. She and Nathan drove to the end of it without spotting any signs of the pony cart. She turned around and headed back. She wanted to stop at home before she dropped off Nathan to be sure her siblings were there. Perhaps the children the man had seen belonged to one of the farms on this road.

She tried to calm herself with that thought, but other fears intruded. How well did she know Josiah after meeting him twice? What if he really had abandoned Nathan by the roadside and kidnapped her siblings? Yes, he was now part of their Amish community, but he'd been living in Ohio for years. What did they really know about him?

* * *

The second Silver was hooked up, Josiah yanked up the barn door, leapt into the buggy, and clucked to Silver.

Once he backed out and turned her around, he urged her into a gallop, leaving the door open behind him. They flew down the driveway. The tractor trailer spill he'd seen earlier would likely be blocking the road, so he turned Silver toward the shortcut. The horse cooperated by going as swiftly as she could. But what if no one was at the school? Ada would make her rounds before locking the building, wouldn't she? She'd notice Nathan unless he'd wandered off.

As they raced toward the blocked crossroad, a sudden thought entered Josiah's mind. When Sadie had stopped alongside the road, David had tried to tell him something. The word he'd spelled started with an N. And later he'd signed *corn* and *buggy*. The small boy had kept pointing to the corn beside Josiah's buggy. Had Nathan gotten out then?

The corn had rippled. Josiah had assumed the truck rumbling past caused the disturbance, but what if it had been Nathan in the corn?

Josiah slowed Silver's furious pace to turn onto the road where the accident had occurred. They had moved the tractor trailer, but the crews were still cleaning the asphalt, and men were directing people around it and onto the detour. A slow but steady stream of traffic flowed in the direction he wanted to turn. Once he got out, he had to cross to the shoulder on the other side.

Drumming the fingers of his free hand on his knee, he prayed for a break in traffic so he could pull out. While he waited, he scanned the cornfields, hoping to catch a glimpse of Nathan. One Amish family watched from the hill nearby, and Josiah caught a glimpse of a small boy about Nathan's height partially hidden beside the mother, and his heart leapt. He stuck his head out the buggy window and craned his neck to see around her, and his spirits plummeted. Definitely not Nathan.

If Nathan wasn't here, and it didn't look like he was, he'd head to the school. But first he'd check the corn rows and ask the people who'd been gathered around the accident.

The cars heading by slowed to a trickle. He waited impatiently for the last car to pass. As the tail end of that car passed him, Josiah nudged Silver around the corner. But down by the cleanup site, a worker flipped the sign from STOP to SLOW. Several drivers on the opposite side of the road revved their engines, and bumper to bumper, the cars inched forward. He'd never be able to cut through.

Hastily, he pulled his buggy onto the shoulder. He tied up his horse, crossed to the center line, and waited anxiously for a gap between cars.

Finally, a lady in a pale blue car slowed. People behind her laid on their horns, but she stopped and motioned for him to cross. With a grateful wave, he raced to the spot where he'd stopped earlier.

Walking up and down the shoulder, he inspected the cornfield, hoping Nathan was hidden among the rows. A group of tourists leaned their heads out of their car windows and held up cell phones to snap pictures of him. He turned his back to the cameras as he checked for footprints and looked down each row.

Finally, he came to a section that looked trampled. He followed the trail of crushed grasses and weeds between the corn rows for a few yards until it dead ended. If it had been Nathan, he'd come this far and turned around. Where had he gone from here?

Josiah hurriedly checked the last few rows, but none had been disturbed. He'd ask some bystanders if they'd seen Nathan. People surely would have noticed a young boy wandering around on his own, especially if he'd been having one of his usual outbursts. The Amish family he'd spotted earlier must have gone inside, so he headed toward the road crew directing traffic and the few stragglers still watching the cleanup.

As he jogged in that direction, the man holding the STOP sign shook a finger at him. "Hey, you the one that left that buggy there?" He flicked his head in the direction of Josiah's buggy. "You're blocking the shoulder."

"I just have a question."

Keeping his eyes on the stream of traffic coming from the opposite direction, the man shook his head. "Drivers have been sitting, waiting their turn. They're impatient. They'll run the buggies off the road."

He crossed the last few yards to the man whose frown had deepened to a glower. "I promise I'll move it. I'm looking for my son. Did you see a little boy anywhere?" He held out a hand, not quite waist high. "He's about this tall with blond hair."

"How can I keep track of all the kids when I need to direct traffic?"

"I know you're busy, but I just thought..."

The man's radio crackled, and an unintelligible voice spoke. He answered in a low growl. Then he glared at Josiah. "I have work to do." He swiveled his head back to the traffic flowing in the opposite direction and counted the cars. "Three...four...red jeep," he mumbled. "All clear." He waited until the jeep had passed, then he flipped the sign to SLOW.

The traffic in front of them lurched to a start. The first driver stepped on the gas and shot past them, shaking the sign.

The sign man yelled after him. "Can't you read? It says *SLOW*." His jaw tensed, and he waved his hand up and down, trying to slow traffic speeding past. "Fools," he spat out. Without taking his eyes off the cars, he grated, "You still here? Get that buggy outta the way."

"I will. But please, can you tell me if you've seen a small Amish boy with blond hair wandering around alone."

"Look," the man said with gritted teeth, "can't you see I'm too busy to look around?"

"I see." Josiah turned to go, but the worker called after him. "Hey, aren't you the guy what took those little kids up the back road? Where are those kids now?"

"At home where they belong."

The man took his eyes off the traffic and studied Josiah with narrowed eyes. "Your house or theirs?"

"Theirs, of course."

Head tilted and eyes narrowed in an *I-don't-believe-you* look, he said, "How do I know you're telling the truth?"

"You don't. But if I did anything to them, would I risk coming back here?"

"Criminals often return to the scene of the crime. Any kids turn up missing around here, I'm giving your description to the cops." A gleam in his eye, he said, "Better yet, I'll just snap your picture."

Josiah held a hand in front of his face. "Please don't. We don't have our pictures taken."

"Definitely guilty. And now you're back for more kids."

"No, I'm searching for my son. I think he got out of the buggy here when I stopped to help the girls." Josiah tried to keep the panic from his voice, but he wasn't successful.

"To help the girls?" the man scoffed. "By taking them down a dead-end road?"

"There's a dirt path leading to the main road in town. It's right behind Zook's barn." He gestured toward the farm in the distance. "We used the shortcut, and I made sure they got home safely."

The man still had a suspicious look in his eye. "Well, be warned. I aim to tell the cops about you if any kids turn up missing."

"So you didn't see a little boy alone earlier?"

"Only little boy hanging around here today belonged to an Amish mom. I gave her a lecture about leaving him alone up there." He stabbed a finger toward the cornfield where Josiah had stopped earlier. "She left him there for at least a half hour."

"When was this?"

The sign man flapped his hand. "Who knows? Maybe an hour ago, maybe less."

That's when Nathan would have been here. Had someone taken him?

Stepping forward and holding up his hand, the man twirled his sign to stop the flow of traffic. He turned to check the cars disappearing past the cleanup site and radioed a message. "You gotta go. You're distracting me from my job. And your buggy's in the way."

"Please, what did the woman look like?"

"I noticed the horse first. All black with this white mark right here." The man rubbed a circle on his forehead just below his hard hat.

A black horse with a white patch? Ada had a horse like that. Had she passed and seen Nathan? She would have stopped if she'd realized he was alone.

"Then she got out and..." The man waggled his eyebrows and leered. "Well, who cares about a horse after that? Even though she had on that crazy all-black getup you Amish wear, she was a looker."

Nausea built in Josiah's stomach. If he was talking about Nathan's teacher...She'd been wearing all black. The bishop had mentioned she was in mourning for her *mamm.* A picture of her standing in front of the classroom popped into his mind. And she definitely was pretty, but this man had no right to sully her purity like this. But as soon as he thought that, Josiah's conscience bothered him. He had no right to judge this man, particularly when he'd been equally attracted to her.

The disembodied voice on the radio startled him. The sign flipped again, and cars flowed by, but Josiah paid little attention to the honking horns and racing motors.

So Ada—at least he hoped it was her—had picked up Nathan. How had she handled him? She was so small and slight. Even he had trouble wrestling his son into the buggy.

"Wait," Josiah said to the man. "How did she manage to get him into the buggy?"

The man shrugged. "Same way as always, I guess. He climbed onto the seat."

"He wasn't kicking and screaming?"

The man gave him a funny look. "Nah, he was docile. Sort of shy, almost."

Maybe this man hadn't seen Nathan after all. "The boy just went with her without fussing?"

The road worker frowned at him. "Why wouldn't he? She was his mom. Leastways, they both had the same blond hair."

Now that Josiah thought about it, Ada's golden hair did match Nathan's. And they both had some glints of red when the sunlight struck their hair. But he couldn't imagine Nathan calmly getting into a buggy. Although, he had to admit, when he'd walked into the classroom earlier today, his son had been calm. But still... "My son's usually, um, feisty."

"Nah, he was a good kid. He stood quietly watching the accident for a long time before his mom showed up." The man lifted a finger, counted several cars behind Josiah, and then mumbled something into his radio.

Josiah supposed the lights and trucks might have distracted Nathan. Actually, when he was alone in his room sometimes, he did play quietly or look at books. It was only when Josiah entered that he started throwing fits.

The man waited until he'd let the ten cars past and stopped the traffic before turning to Josiah. "You sure he's your son?" His leer returned. "Then that broad's your wife, man? If so, you're one lucky dude."

"No, no, Nathan's not her son. He's mine. She's his teacher." At least he hoped it was Ada and Nathan.

"Boy, they didn't have teachers like that back when I was in school. We got these shriveled-up old ladies..."

Josiah was eager to be on his way. After the worker telling him he was too busy to answer questions, he'd certainly turned talkative. Josiah waited until he finished his sentence, then cut in. "I need to go and pick up my son."

"Have fun," the man said. "Oh, by the way, she thought

the girls you took down the road"—he flipped a hand in the direction of Zook's farm—"were her sisters."

"They were." That made him even more certain it was Ada. So most likely the little boy was Nathan. His roiling stomach settled a little, but it wouldn't calm completely until he saw Nathan for himself.

Chapter Nine

When Ada pulled into her driveway, the pony cart was in the barn. Her uneasy stomach settled. Her siblings had made it home safely. She'd hurry in to be sure all was well and remind her sisters to pick the ripe tomatoes while she drove Nathan home.

She climbed out of the buggy, then hesitated. She shouldn't leave Nathan out here alone. He'd already wandered off by himself once. By the time she picked up her school satchel from the back and rounded the buggy, Nathan had already climbed down. He clutched at the edge of her apron the way Mary Elizabeth did when she was nervous or upset.

She squatted in front of him and made the sign for *my* by touching her hand to her chest. Following the sign for *house*, she pointed to the house, then raised her eyebrows in a question.

Some of the nervousness left his eyes, and he nodded.

So he must have understood. She had no idea whether he recognized the signs or if he'd interpreted her pointing, but they'd communicated. That was the important thing.

She reached for his hand and led him to the house. She opened the door and set her satchel on the floor by the coat hooks.

Scrambling sounds came from the kitchen, along with Sadie's sharp "*Ach!* Ada's home."

Somehow that did not sound promising. Ada hurried toward the kitchen. Nathan looked up at her questioningly, but he kept pace with her. When she reached the kitchen doorway, she stopped short and sucked in a breath.

Sadie had mentioned a surprise, but... To say she was surprised was an understatement. Floored was more like it. And speaking of floors, her kitchen floor was completely coated with white powder. Flour dusted the tabletop and counters. And... *Oh, no!* The flour canister lay shattered on the floor. Shards of orange, yellow, and brown pottery lay scattered everywhere. In the center of the mess stood Mary Elizabeth, frosted with flour from head to toe. Even her eyelashes were white.

While Nathan looked around wide-eyed, Ada wasn't sure whether to laugh or cry. But one thing was clear. She'd been worried her sisters and David might not be here. Fears of them being kidnapped had occupied her the whole way home. So this mess paled in comparison to their safety.

"I'm so glad you're alive," Ada said.

Sadie looked at her as if she'd gone crazy. "You're not angry about the mess?"

"Well...I'm not going to say I'm happy about it, but I'm so relieved after hearing that you'd been kidnapped."

"Who told you that?" Sadie demanded.

"A worker at the accident site. He said some man had tricked you into driving down a dead-end road."

Sadie laughed. "The man who tricked us was his dad." She pointed to Nathan. "He showed us a shortcut to get home."

"Josiah showed you how to get home? But that road is a dead end."

"There's a dirt road behind Zook's barn. Josiah took us that way, and he drove the whole way to our house so we could find our way."

"That was nice of him." Now she felt guilty. She'd misjudged Josiah. The whole way home she had been thinking critical thoughts about him, and instead he'd been helping her siblings. Ada laughed shakily. "I'm so relieved to know you weren't kidnapped."

Sadie put her hands on her hips. "*Mamm* always said not getting all the facts straight is how rumors start."

As soon as Sadie said the word *Mamm*, Mary Elizabeth burst into tears. Ada rushed over and pulled her sister into her arms.

"I miss *Mamm*," Mary Elizabeth wailed.

"We all do," Ada said, patting her back.

Across the kitchen, Sadie's eyes filled with tears. *I'm sorry*, she mouthed.

Ada shook her head to let her know she wasn't to blame and hugged her youngest sister closer.

Mary Elizabeth wrapped her arms around Ada's neck. "And I missed you all day." Her voice quavered.

"I know," Ada said. They had to talk about Mary Elizabeth's actions at school today, but now was not the time. First she had to take Nathan home. Then they had to clean this kitchen and can the tomatoes and...

Ada freed herself from her sister's embrace and stood. She brushed at her dress and apron, but only succeeded in smearing the flour into the black cloth. She had white spots everywhere Mary Elizabeth had pressed against her.

A strange sound came from Nathan's throat. A deep, throaty gurgle. He was laughing. It was an odd sound, but he was actually laughing.

Ada stared at him. It was the first time she'd heard him make a joyful sound. Despite the mess, Ada couldn't help smiling. With an exaggerated rueful expression, she swiped at her dress, making him laugh harder. The twins joined in with hearty belly laughs. Sadie snickered, and Hannah giggled. Soon everyone was in hysterics. The harder they tried to stop, the more they chuckled. Even Ada joined in.

Finally, her stomach hurt so much, she held up a hand. "Enough."

The chortles died down to giggles and then to occasional snorts.

Sadie sobered and glanced around the flour-coated room. "I'm sorry, Ada. We wanted to make cookies to surprise you."

"I see. You for sure did that."

"I meant..."

"I know. It was very thoughtful of you." Ada had to get Nathan back to his family, but if she didn't give her siblings cleaning instructions, the house would be an even worse mess when she returned.

"Hannah, hand Sadie the broom so she can sweep the floor, and give the twins clean rags to wipe the counter. Then you can dust off the table. Be sure to use dry cloths. Otherwise the flour will turn into a sticky mess."

A loud knock on the front door startled them. They all glanced at each other and the mess. No one was fit to answer the door except Hannah. She was shy and even hung back when her siblings played or got into trouble, which was why she was the only one not covered with flour.

When everyone's gaze fixed on her, Hannah's eyes widened and her lip quivered. She ducked her head. "I'll go," she whispered. Then with a bowed head, looking as if she were heading to be punished, she went to the door.

A man's deep voice carried down the hall, although Ada couldn't make out the words. Then heavy boots clumped down the hallway, and Ada panicked. They were in no shape for company. Why was Hannah bringing someone to the messy kitchen?

Hannah walked through the doorway followed by Josiah, and heat swept up Ada's neck and splashed across her face, leaving her cheeks burning. Of all the people who had to see her in such disarray, it had to be Josiah.

* * *

The young girl who answered the door had assured Josiah that Nathan was here, but he almost forgot about his son as he took in the scene in front of him. Flour everywhere, including on four of the children, broken pottery, and Ada stood in the middle of it, her cheeks rosy and her eyes apologetic, holding her little sister's hand. Her black dress and apron were spotted with flour, but laugh lines crinkled around her eyes. He had to stop staring, but he was mesmerized by her beauty, her calmness.

He cleared his throat. "Is everything all right? No one's hurt?"

Ada's laugh sounded embarrassed. "We're all fine. Just a bit messy. The girls were hoping to surprise me."

"So I heard." Josiah chuckled. "I see they succeeded."

"*Jah*, well, this wasn't the surprise they intended."

"That's good to know. I wouldn't want too many surprises like this one."

"It was an accident," Sadie, her face fiery red, said in a defensive voice.

"Accidents happen," Josiah said. "I've had plenty of my own." He smiled at her to assure her he hadn't intended to shame her.

"I, um..." He made the mistake of looking back at Ada and lost his train of thought. The sunlight streaming through the window highlighted the gold of her hair, and despite the mess surrounding her, her eyes twinkled. He could get lost in those eyes, which seemed to be staring back at him with equal intensity.

Sadie broke the spell. "Thank you for bringing us home earlier, Josiah."

What? Oh, right. He'd taken them down the shortcut, and...*Nathan!* For the first time, he glanced around the room. His son stood in the corner of a clean part of the room. As soon as their gazes met, Nathan stiffened and shrank back against the wall behind him.

Relief flooded through Josiah. His son was safe. He

rubbed the back of his neck to release the tension and unclenched his jaw. "You found him," he blurted out. "I searched everywhere."

The sympathy in Ada's eyes did strange things to his insides. "I slowed down near that tractor trailer accident and saw him standing beside the road, watching the lights. I was going to bring him straight home, but…" Ada's whole face and neck flushed a deeper shade of pink. "I was worried about my siblings, so I came home to check on them, and then I found this…"

"What she means is," Sadie interrupted, "she thought we were kidnapped." She smiled at Josiah. "By you."

"*Ach*, Sadie." Looking mortified, Ada gave her sister a warning glare, but Sadie only laughed. Then Ada turned to him. "I'm so sorry. I didn't really think that. I mean, someone from the road crew told me…"

Sadie jumped in again. "Some man told her you took us down a dead-end road, and they both jumped to conclusions."

"I don't want you to think…" Ada's already rosy cheeks darkened to crimson.

The more flustered she grew, the more Josiah wanted to take her hands and calm her down. To hold her close and reassure her. To keep his mind off those thoughts, he forced himself to concentrate on Sadie's words. "I see. I believe I know the man you're talking about."

"You do?" Ada pressed her hands to her cheeks, streaking them with flour.

Josiah swallowed hard. The flour on her face made her appear even more adorable, and he longed to brush it away by running his fingers down her cheeks. With his thoughts occupied by images of stroking the softness of her skin, he struggled to come up with a coherent thought. *The man. Concentrate on the man.*

"Um, yes," he finally croaked out. He fastened his gaze on the floor by his feet and forced himself to picture the SLOW sign—a warning he desperately needed right now—and the man who held it. "He was around forty with a black mustache and a sunburned nose, jeans and a white—"

Now it was Josiah's turn to color. With hot cheeks, he floundered for a substitute description. Like many *Englischers*, the man wore his undershirt under his safety vest, but the thought of saying that word to Ada and her sisters was unthinkable.

Ada broke the uncomfortable silence. "Yes, that's the man who suggested you were, um, kidnapping my siblings."

"He confronted me about that and threatened to report me to the police."

"Yes, he sounded ready to contact the police, but I'm sorry I let him put ideas in my head. Will you forgive me?"

"Of course." Josiah made the mistake of glancing at her. Even spattered with flour, her beauty shone through. He clenched his fists as he remembered the man's comments. She didn't deserve to be thought of that way.

"I didn't really think you were capable of being a kidnapper." Ada's voice shook a bit. "But I did worry about my siblings going down that road and not coming back."

"I understand. Most people don't know about the dirt path behind Zook's barn. I wouldn't either, except Jakob directed me that way last week." Josiah broke her gaze and concentrated on the floor. Counting swirls in the wood grain might keep his mind from straying to where it shouldn't go.

"Thank you for taking care of them," Ada said.

"It was my pleasure." And so was standing here talking to her. *Thirty-two, thirty-three...don't look up... thirty-four.*

Ada's soft voice interrupted his counting. "Are you all right?"

"What? Yes, yes, of course. Why wouldn't I be?" His answer sounded defensive, and he hastened to correct himself. "Thank you for finding Nathan and taking such good care of him."

The back door opened, and David, accompanied by an older boy, started to step inside.

"Wait!" Ada called, and both boys halted in the doorway. She softened her tone. "Noah, take David around to the front door."

Noah surveyed the kitchen. "What happened here? It looks like a winter snowstorm." He chuckled. "And Mary Elizabeth's a snowman. Or is she a snowgirl?"

Mary Elizabeth's lip quivered, and Noah held up a hand. "I was just teasing."

Josiah needed to collect Nathan and leave before he made a fool of himself. "I should be going, but thank you for caring for Nathan."

David's gaze, though, went quickly from the flour to Nathan cringing in the corner, and his eyebrows rose. He turned to Ada and signed furiously.

She signed back, and Josiah wished he knew more sign language so he could follow the conversation.

When it looked as if their conversation had concluded,

Josiah said, "Tell David I'm sorry I didn't listen when he tried to tell me about Nathan."

"Why don't you tell him yourself?" Ada suggested gently. "He reads lips."

Slightly exaggerating his lips as he talked, Josiah apologized and thanked David.

The small boy nodded. Then he signed to Nathan. After pointing to himself and then to the stairs leading to his room, he waited for Nathan's reply.

Josiah held his breath, wondering if his son would reply. He couldn't believe it when Nathan nodded and headed toward the stairs. And even more unbelievable, his son hadn't uttered a peep. No crying, fussing, or kicking. Maybe some of his tantrums came from loneliness. Josiah had kept him away from other children because he was afraid Nathan would hurt them, but it seemed he'd been mistaken.

Nathan's crestfallen look when David exited and shut the back door tore at Josiah's heart. But when David entered the front door, cut through the living room, and beckoned, Nathan beamed. He followed David to the stairs, scooting close to the wall, staying as far away from Josiah as he could. That niggling thought from earlier hit Josiah full force right in the gut. Nathan's tantrums might be his fault. His son almost seemed to hate him. But why? What had he done to upset Nathan that way?

Josiah pushed aside his own hurt and tried to concentrate on Nathan's sunny smile. His son hadn't been that happy and animated since…since…Josiah squeezed his eyes shut to stop the rush of memories. Nathan as a toddler curled up on Ruth's lap with a book. Laughing as she threw a ball to him in the yard. Kneeling beside her as she weeded the garden.

Then their world shattered. Hearing Ruth had cancer had ripped apart their happy lives. Although it had been heart wrenching, Josiah agreed when she wanted to try experimental treatments in Mexico, like others in their community had. Nathan was only two years old—too young to be separated from her. All Josiah wanted was to be with them, but he had to pay for Ruth's medical care, so he endured the three years of loneliness while they were gone.

By the time Ruth returned she'd been much too ill to lift her head from the pillow. From time to time, Nathan signed to her, and she'd try to sign back. Josiah wanted to learn more signs, but he couldn't tax Ruth's small store of energy. Other than a few basic signs, the only big ones he knew were *Mamm, Daed*, and *I love you*. He'd added the sign for *gone* after Nathan continually asked *Mamm where?*

"Are you all right?" Ada's question startled him.

"I'm fine," he croaked. He must have looked like a fool, standing there with his eyes closed. "I was remembering..." He couldn't say *my dead wife*, so he stumbled to a stop.

Ada waited for him to finish, but when he didn't say anything, she gave him an understanding look. "Memories can be painful sometimes."

His grief must have shown on his face. "They can be." To lighten the mood, he gestured toward the flour. "And they also can be frustrating, but situations like this create humorous stories later on."

With a bit of tartness to her tone, Ada replied, "Why

don't you ask me about this in a few weeks and see if I find it funny?" The quirk of her lips made it clear he hadn't upset her.

Josiah laughed. "I'll be sure to do that." He wasn't certain, though, that he'd ever find the memory of her dabbed with flour comical. For him, it would stir emotions better left alone. Emotions he shouldn't be having while he was still in his mourning period.

With a rueful glance at Mary Elizabeth, whose gaze ping-ponged back and forth between them, Ada said, "Well, we'd better get this mess cleaned up. I'm going to take Mary Elizabeth outside to dust her off."

"I'm sorry. I didn't mean to keep you. I'll collect Nathan and get moving." Josiah headed toward the stairs. "Would it be all right to go up to get Nathan? I have errands to run."

"If you have errands, why don't you leave him here until you're done? David doesn't often get to have friends, so it would be nice for him to have company."

Josiah was reluctant to leave Nathan, knowing his penchant for fits, but he acquiesced. "I'll be back in an hour, if that's all right."

Ada waved a hand. "Take as long as you need. I'm sure the boys will be fine."

"Nathan can be a problem." That was an understatement. When he was in full-blown-tantrum mode, he could be dangerous. "I worry he may hurt someone." *Like you. Or your brothers or sisters.* "If he gets in one of his moods, he might hurt David."

Ada only smiled. "David is the youngest of eight, he's used to roughhousing. I'm sure he'll be fine."

Was that a glimmer of uncertainty in her eyes? He

hesitated, but she waved him off. When one of the little girls emerged from the closet with rags and a broom, he backed up to let her pass.

"Let me help you with the cleanup," Josiah said.

"No, I'm a big believer in encouraging children to clean up their own messes," Ada said as Sadie started sweeping the flour into a pile, stirring up puffs of white powder.

Remembering all of the messes he'd cleaned up after Nathan fell asleep at night, Josiah squirmed. He hadn't been teaching his son about responsibility. Though if he were honest, he had no idea how to get Nathan to cooperate, something his teacher seemed to have accomplished in a short time. Unless, of course, this was only the calm before a major storm. For her sake, he hoped not.

Chapter Ten

Ada was relieved when Josiah finally left, although part of her still wished he had stayed. But she would rather he'd seen her looking neat and clean, with the kitchen presentable. She had an hour to restore everything to order and erase his negative impression of her and the house. Mentally, she scolded herself for caring what Josiah thought. She should have no interest in his opinion, except as it related to teaching his son.

Ada led Mary Elizabeth to the back door. "Be sure everything is spotless," Ada warned her other sisters.

Her jaw set, Sadie said, "You told Josiah children are supposed to learn responsibility. If that is so, what about her?" She pointed to Mary Elizabeth. "She's the one who made the mess by dropping the flour canister after I told her to leave it alone."

"Sometimes we all need to work together," Ada replied.

"Fine." Sadie swept so hard the broom sent plumes of white billowing into the air.

"Sadie," Ada snapped. "Doesn't God want us to help others?"

"I'm sorry," Sadie said, her eyes brimming with tears.

Ada wanted to hug her sister, but she and Mary Elizabeth were much too floury. "It's been a hard day for you, hasn't it?"

Sadie blinked back her tears, but spoke through gritted teeth. "We didn't get any lessons at school today, everyone teased me because I had a crybaby sister, I couldn't play with my friends at recess because of her. I had to drive the pony cart to your school because of her. Now I have extra chores because of her."

Ada sighed. Putting it that way, it didn't sound at all fair. "Would it help to know that Mary Elizabeth will be scrubbing and drying the floor when you're done? And washing all the countertops?"

Mary Elizabeth's eyes rounded, and she started to protest, but Ada silenced her with a stern glare.

"I guess," Sadie muttered, though she sounded far from mollified.

Ada herded Mary Elizabeth out the back door and shut it behind her. After leading her sister out to the grass, she took off Mary Elizabeth's kerchief and flapped it in the wind while her sister shook out her skirt. Fine white powder settled everywhere.

Mary Elizabeth giggled. "Noah was right. It does look like snow."

"Yes, we could use a little snow right now." The late afternoon sun still beat down and, combined with the high humidity, the day was uncomfortably hot. Ada stepped some distance away from Mary Elizabeth and shook her own skirt and apron, and then used her sister's kerchief to dust herself off.

Mary Elizabeth's giggles turned to belly laughs when Ada knelt to brush off her sister. "You have flour all over your face," Mary Elizabeth choked out between laughs.

"I do? All over, or just a few dabs?"

"*Neh*, it's everywhere." Mary Elizabeth took the kerchief and wiped Ada's cheeks and forehead.

How humiliating! She'd been talking to Josiah like that. He'd probably been snickering to himself the whole time.

Her embarrassment made her scrub a little harder than necessary at Mary Elizabeth's face and clothes. "We won't get all the flour out of the fabric." She sighed. If the other girls had flour on their clothes, it would add one more load to the wash. "You know," Ada said to her sister, "I think you should also do the extra load of laundry."

Mary Elizabeth's mouth opened and closed several times, but no words came out.

"I started doing laundry when I was six," Ada told her. *Mamm* had been sickly for several years before Sadie was born, which accounted for the large age gap between them. After each baby, their mother lost more strength. Ada shook off the memories of those years of drowning in chores, of all the responsibilities of caring for baby after baby, of raising her siblings, and of filling in as a parent. Heavy responsibilities she still carried, although her siblings were now old enough to help with some of the burdens.

Mary Elizabeth was still gaping at her.

"Sadie and Hannah both wash clothes. There's no

reason you can't do it. You just have to remember the most important rule: Keep your fingers away from the wringer."

"I can't do that." Mary Elizabeth's voice rose in a whine.

"You can and you will," Ada said in a firm voice. They'd all been babying Mary Elizabeth, not expecting much from her because she was the youngest girl and so overly emotional since *Mamm*'s death. David was a year younger, and no one coddled him. David helped Noah with all the outdoor chores without complaint. No wonder Sadie felt resentful. They were all grieving, but the rest of the family still managed to do whatever needed to be done.

"*Ouch!*" Mary Elizabeth wriggled away. "You're hurting me."

"Sorry," Ada said automatically, her mind busy planning how to implement the changes. She turned her sister around to brush off her back, but tried to be gentler. First, she had to let Mary Elizabeth know they'd be making changes and then find a way to ease her into it. "Now that I'm teaching, you'll need to help out more."

"I don't want you to teach." Mary Elizabeth's voice quavered. "I miss you."

"I know. I miss you too, but I have a job to do." Ada finished brushing off the back of her sister's dress and then took her hand to take her back inside. "And your job is to go to school." Although her behavior at school was another issue they needed to address, Ada was too exhausted to tussle over that now. She'd postpone it until after dinner. "Let's see if they've cleaned up the kitchen."

Most of the dust had been cleared by the time they returned, so Ada helped Mary Elizabeth fill the scrub bucket and set her to washing the floor. Then Ada hurried to her room to change into a fresh dress and apron. Her conscience whispered that changing clothes was *hochmut*, that it was vanity to impress Josiah. And a sin to be attracted to a married man. She attempted to quiet the still, small voice with the excuse she only wanted to look presentable, to make a good impression on the parent of one of her pupils. But no matter how she tried to justify it, deep inside she was aware of her duplicity.

* * *

As he was doing his errands, Josiah mulled over Nathan's behavior around Ada and David. Perhaps he'd been wrong to isolate his son, but he feared subjecting others to Nathan's outbursts. Seeing Nathan calm and interacting with others started an ache deep inside. How long had it been since he'd seen his son quiet, his face serene instead of twisted into a scowl or a screech? Even seeing him with his eyes open was startling; Nathan's eyes were normally squinched shut, his fists in tight balls, his mouth either pinched shut or shrieking.

After Ruth died, he'd been hard to handle. But since they'd arrived in Lancaster, his tantrums had increased. *Mamm* struggled with Nathan's crying; he pushed her away whenever she tried to comfort him. But he seemed to save his full-blown flare-ups for Josiah, which hurt deeply.

But what wounded him even more was the way Nathan had edged away from him this afternoon. Something was going on with his son, but he had no idea what. Even worse, he had no way of finding out when the two of them couldn't communicate.

Ada seemed to have bridged that gap in one short morning. If Josiah were honest with himself, he'd experienced a twinge of jealousy when she cuddled Nathan on her lap. His son hadn't kicked or shoved her away.

He mentally tried to forget that image by reviewing the list of items he needed at the hardware store, but nails and grout provided little distraction. Ada's tender expression, her gentleness, her... *Stop, Josiah.* With great effort, he pictured the repairs he needed to do in his mother's kitchen. Creating a checklist in his mind, he numbered and recorded each purchase. By the time he pulled into the hardware store parking lot and tied Silver to the hitching post, he'd almost—not quite, but almost—succeeded in banishing the images of Ada holding Josiah, of Ada covered with flour, of Ada's soft voice as she said good-bye.

By the time he finished his errands and made his way through rush hour traffic, several hours had passed. As he sprinted toward the front door, the older boy he'd seen in the kitchen opened the barn door and stepped out.

"Hello," he called. "Are you here for Nathan?"

Josiah nodded. "I'm sorry I'm late."

"David doesn't mind. He likes having a friend to play with." The boy headed his way and stuck out his hand. "I forgot to introduce myself. I'm Noah."

"Nice to meet you." Josiah shook his hand. "I hope Nathan hasn't been any trouble."

"Not that I know of," Noah said as they crossed the lawn to the front door. "Although I was out in the barn doing the milking."

Josiah breathed a sigh of relief. If Nathan had one of his fits, Noah would have heard him even in the barn.

Noah walked with him to the front door. "Go ahead

in. Everyone's in the kitchen. I have a few more chores to do before dinner."

"Thanks." Josiah hesitated on the doorstep. Entering the house of someone he barely knew made him nervous, but not as nervous as what he'd find inside. The only blessing was that he heard no noise. Josiah forced himself to turn the knob and ease the door open.

The first thing that hit him was the sense of peace in the entryway. Quiet voices came from the kitchen, and the tang of tomatoes, onions, and cooking meat drew him forward and made his mouth water. He crossed through the living room and stopped near the kitchen doorway, unable to believe the transformation. Except for several countertops filled with rows of gleaming glass jars of tomatoes, the room was spotless. Ada had changed into a clean dress and a black work apron. She was angled away from him, so he could barely see her profile, but she looked breathtaking.

His stomach growled as she bent to check the meatloaf in the oven. He and Nathan would be headed home to heat up chicken corn soup, followed by an evening of temper tantrums. What would it be like to eat dinner in this haven of peace?

Off to his left, Nathan had his back to the doorway, so Josiah could observe him without being spotted. His son and David were setting the table. David pointed to a fork and then signed something Josiah assumed was *fork*—two fingers in an upside-down "V," bouncing on his palm. Nathan attempted the sign, his hands clumsy. They moved to the next place, set down a fork, and David repeated the sign. This time Nathan's movements appeared to be closer to David's. With misty eyes, Josiah copied David's sign.

He stayed in the doorway, breathing in the homey smells, focusing on his son, who was intently watching David's every move. He studiously avoided staring at Ada. David repeated his instructions as he placed a knife at each place, and Josiah imitated the signs along with his son. Although he wasn't sure how the words *fork* and *knife* would help him, Josiah wanted to take whatever opportunity he could to communicate with Nathan.

When the boys rounded the table to place silverware on the other side, Josiah stepped back so Nathan couldn't see him. He'd never seen his son this content or interested. At least not since he was young and his *mamm* was still healthy. Josiah didn't want to do anything to disturb this tranquility.

In front of him, with their backs to him, Ada and Sadie were bustling from the sink to the stove. Mary Elizabeth turned, juggling a wobbly pile of plates. The top plate teetered, and Josiah dove forward, catching it before it could hit the floor. Then he put a hand on the stack to prevent the rest from falling and was rewarded by Mary Elizabeth's relieved smile.

"Steady there." Josiah tapped the plates into a neatly nested stack.

At the sound of his voice, Ada and Sadie whirled around.

Ada pressed a hand against her chest. "You startled me. I didn't hear you come in."

"I'm sorry. I didn't mean to scare you. Noah told me to come in."

"Of course, of course. You're more than welcome." She fanned her face, flushed with the heat of cooking.

"I should have let you know I was here, but I was

busy watching the boys." Josiah motioned to the other side of the room, where David and Nathan were so intent on their teaching and learning they hadn't noticed his arrival.

"David is enjoying showing Nathan some signs. He was doing that upstairs earlier." She beamed at him before turning her attention back to the boys.

Ada's smile took his breath away. To keep his attention off her, Josiah studied the large garden outside the kitchen window behind her. Plump green tomatoes blushed with red hung heavy on the branches. His *mamm* had a tiny garden out back, but his heart ached for the small plot in Ohio that he'd plowed before Ruth got ill. She'd loved working in the garden, but they'd had so little time together.

When Ruth learned she had cancer, he'd supported her decision to go to Mexico, where treatment was less expensive and more options were available. The loneliness of those years without her and Nathan, followed by her final months at home and the past nine months without her . . .

"Are you all right?" Ada's soft voice drew him back to the kitchen.

"What?" The swift move from past to present dazed him. "I'll be fine." *I hope. Perhaps, though, grief never ended.* With Ada staring at him, he fumbled for an explanation. "Your garden is lovely. It reminded me of my— my"—his throat spasmed—"wife's."

Chapter Eleven

Oh." A frisson of disappointment shot through Ada, a disappointment she quickly doused. Guilt over her attraction soured her stomach. *You already knew he was married. You have no right thinking about him like that.*

To conceal her feelings, Ada headed toward the boys. Catching David's eye, she signed, *Daed here*, and pointed to Nathan. Her brother's face fell, and he signed to say he wanted his friend to stay. Nathan studied the two of them while Ada told David to ask Nathan's *daed*. At the word *daed*, Nathan's frown of concentration changed to a scowl.

Ada was positive Nathan knew the word, yet each time he saw the sign, he had an odd reaction.

Nathan followed David's lead and turned around. He glanced toward the doorway, and his eyes widened. With a cry, he dodged behind Ada, grabbing a handful of her apron with one hand. She put an arm around him and gave him a brief hug. With so little sign language, this must be his way of saying he wanted to stay longer.

She turned to Josiah and shrugged. "I guess he's not quite ready to leave. And David's begging to have him stay. Maybe he could join us for dinner?"

"I think we've imposed on you for too long already."

Because Nathan could not express himself in words, Ada had to interpret his body language. With the way he was clutching her, he seemed desperate to stay, and her brother was staring at her with pleading eyes.

"I think he'd really like to stay, and we'd love to have him for dinner." When Josiah started to shake his head, she blurted out, "You're welcome to stay for dinner too." Then she wished she could cover her mouth. What was she thinking? "I'm sorry. I'm sure you have dinner waiting for you at home." *And a wife, Ada.*

"Not tonight. It'll only be the two of us. We're heading home to heat up some soup." Josiah gave her a dazzling smile. "All the more reason for us to get going, but thank you for your kind offer."

"If you're only having soup, why not stay? We have plenty to share, and the boys could have a little more time together."

"I don't think . . ."

"Please? Or at least let Nathan stay? I could drive him home after dinner."

Josiah shook his head. "I couldn't let you do that. Who would watch the children while you're gone?"

Ada gestured toward her sister who was draining the potatoes. "Sadie can see that they all get ready for bed."

The pot Sadie was holding clattered onto the counter, and her sister turned, arms across her chest. She didn't say a word, only pinched her lips shut and fixed Ada with a resentful glare.

Ada was taken aback. Sadie had always been helpful. She and Ada shared most of the housework, and Sadie always cared for her younger siblings without complaint. Yet twice today she'd been defiant. Ada had no idea what was wrong, but they'd need to have a talk tonight. After her talk with Mary Elizabeth . . . and after dinner, cleanup, baths, and bedtime stories.

Tiredness swept over Ada. Once all that was done, she still had lesson plans to do. Now that she'd met her scholars, she'd need to work out some tasks based on their abilities. And she wanted to read more about ways to handle the crying and acting out. . . .

"Ada, are you all right?" Josiah started toward her. "You've had a long day and must be exhausted."

"I'm fine." Except the kindness in his eyes was making her weak. She concentrated on the small boy beside her. As his father approached, his body tensed as if he were about to scream. With one quick movement, Ada knelt and wrapped her arms around him. Humming had worked that morning, so she tried it again. His clenched fists relaxed, and some of the rigidness drained from his body. When he seemed calmer, she pulled back a bit so she could sign the word *go* followed by a question mark. Nathan's head whipped back and forth in a definite *no*.

Josiah stopped suddenly, his eyes on his son. "He answered your question." He sounded disbelieving. "I've never seen him answer a question before, not since . . ." He shook his head and said in a voice clogged with tears, "If it's all right for him to stay—?"

"Of course. Will you be staying too?" Part of her

wished for him to say *yes*, but her conscience warned she
was asking for trouble.

"I don't want to make extra work for you."

"It's no trouble at all. It's only one extra plate at the
table." *It's more than that.* Ada ignored the warning of
the small voice inside, but she couldn't ignore the quick-
ening of her pulse as she waited for his answer.

"If you're sure…"

"I am. You're more than welcome." *Be careful, Ada.*
Worried she'd sounded overeager, she added, "David
will be thrilled." *And so will I.*

Now that she'd issued the invitation, it dawned on
Ada it wasn't proper to invite a man to dinner when
Daed or another adult wasn't here, especially one she
was attracted to. But they'd have seven—eight, counting
Nathan—chaperones.

Ada turned to David, who'd been watching them warily. "Two more," she said to him, making sure he could
see her lips.

Her brother beamed and held up one finger. Then he
pointed to the table, where he'd already set out silverware for Nathan. So her brother had been sure his friend
would be staying for dinner. David had given Nathan his
favorite spot on the bench beside her chair.

Her brother came over and took Nathan's hand, and
together they hurried to the silverware drawer. When
they neared Josiah, Nathan tugged David in a wide circle
far away from his *daed*. They returned with a fork and
knife for Josiah, and David placed them at *Daed*'s old
place, before leading Nathan to the opposite end of the
table.

Once again, Ada marveled at David's sensitivity.

Without his hearing, he'd developed his other senses more keenly, but his empathy seemed the most highly developed.

After motioning for Josiah to sit in the chair, she joined her sisters as they finished preparing the meal. Ruby filled water glasses and carried them to the table. Her twin, Grace, stood on a chair at the stove to stir the succotash. Ada put an arm around Sadie and, with a flick of her head, indicated her sister should sit at the table. Sadie's eyebrows rose, but her lips curved in a slight smile as Ada took over hand-mashing the potatoes. They were setting the serving dishes on the table when Noah opened the back door.

"Sorry, I'm late," he said as he rushed past them. "I'll go wash up."

He returned and slid into place as Ada carried in the meatloaf platter. "Chores took longer than usual without David's help," he said. Facing David, he said, "I missed you. I didn't realize how much help you give me."

David smiled back, so he evidently understood.

Noah turned to Josiah. "I unhooked your horse, rubbed her down, and fed her. I hope you don't mind."

"Thank you. That was very thoughtful of you." Josiah's cheeks reddened. "I'm sorry I didn't do it."

"It was no problem," Noah assured him.

As soon as Ada placed the last platter on the table and settled into her chair, everyone bowed their heads for silent prayer. She was pleasantly surprised to see Nathan participate. Teaching David had been difficult. She wasn't positive, but just before she closed her eyes, she thought Nathan's lips were forming words. She let go of the thought to concentrate on the Lord's Prayer, but after the prayer was over, Ada intended to find out more about Nathan's skills.

As they ate, David signed to Nathan. At times, Ada caught a glimmer of understanding in Nathan's eyes, but usually his brow furrowed as if he were concentrating hard, trying to figure out what the signs meant. Her brother was good about pointing out concrete objects, and he repeated the motions several times until Nathan was able to copy the signs well.

Ada turned to Josiah. "So how much sign language does Nathan know?"

Josiah shifted uneasily and stared down at his plate. "I don't have any idea."

Ada was flabbergasted. How could a father not know about his child's vocabulary?

Before she could voice her concerns, Josiah said miserably, "My wife took him along when she went to Mexico for cancer treatments. He was two and lost his hearing while they were gone. An infection or something. They weren't sure, and I didn't find out until...later." Keeping his head down, he pinched the bridge of his nose. "When she got too sick to care for him"—his words grew husky—"they came home."

Ada regretted starting this conversation and bringing up bad memories. If only she could reach out and comfort him.

"I wanted to return to Mexico with her and Nathan, but I had to work to pay the treatment bills," Josiah continued. "While she was home for those few short months..." His voice broke, and his Adam's apple bobbed up and down. He was silent for a short while, and when he spoke again, he choked up. "...she taught me a few signs, but most of the time, she was too weak." He shrugged helplessly.

"I'm so sorry. I didn't mean to bring up such painful memories." Ada wished she'd kept her questions to herself.

Josiah, his head still bowed, waved a hand, and it was obvious he was struggling for control. To give him time to recover, she turned to the children. "Would anyone like another slice of meatloaf?"

Noah, who always seemed to be hungry, licked his lips. "I would."

Ada served him and then turned to Nathan. She signed the question, but when he looked at her blankly, she pointed to the platter of meatloaf and mimed putting a piece on his plate. He ducked his head shyly before nodding. After she served him, he glanced up at her with a huge smile, a smile that warmed her heart.

Josiah lifted his head, and Ada motioned toward the meatloaf. He shook his head, and said in a choked voice, "I can't eat much more, but it was delicious. Thank you for letting us share your meal."

As soon as everyone finished, Sadie hopped up to gather the plates, but Ada motioned for her to sit down. "Mary Elizabeth will clear the table tonight and help with the washing up."

"Me?" her little sister squeaked.

"*Jah*, you," Ada said. Inwardly, she smiled at Sadie's bemusement.

Josiah slid back his chair. "I'm happy to help."

Ada shook her head. "Thank you, but I've decided it's time for Mary Elizabeth to take more responsibility." Perhaps if they stopped treating her like a baby, she'd stop acting like one. At least that was Ada's hope. Usually after Sadie cleared the table, she supervised Mary Elizabeth's bath while the others cleaned the kitchen and did the dishes.

Josiah stood and pushed in his chair. "Thank you for a delicious meal and the wonderful company. Much nicer than eating alone." He rounded the table and headed toward the sink. "Nathan and I should be going soon, but first I'd like to help wash the dishes."

Ada jumped up to intercept him and almost ran into him. He held out a hand to steady her, and the touch of his fingers on her shoulders set her heart pattering out of control. She'd never been this close to a man before, and being around one she was attracted to... One she had no business thinking about... She backed up and clasped her hands to keep from reaching out, pulling him closer. Lowering her eyes, she blurted out, "We don't need help. Mary Elizabeth and I can handle it." Then realizing how rude that sounded, she stammered, "I'm sorry. We appreciate your help, but you and Nathan are guests. I wish we had dessert to offer you, but that ended up on the floor earlier."

Mary Elizabeth bit her lip and then said in a teary voice, "It was an accident." The look of betrayal in her eyes stirred Ada's guilt.

Ada opened her mouth to apologize, but Josiah spoke first. "It's not easy being the youngest, is it?"

"But I'm not the youngest." Mary Elizabeth gave him a puzzled look. "I'm a year older than David."

"Of course you are," Josiah soothed. "I should have said youngest girl. I was the youngest boy, so I know what it's like. You're never old enough to do what the older ones do, and everyone always blames you for everything."

Gazing at him with adoring eyes, Mary Elizabeth agreed. "But you probably didn't cause accidents like I do."

"You'd be surprised," Josiah said. "Once when we were having church at our house, *Mamm* and my *aenti* had spent all week cleaning. *Daed* had set up the church benches, which extended into the kitchen from the living room. *Mamm* set a big bowl of chocolate pudding on the counter and then went to greet everyone. I wanted to sneak one little taste, so I slid the bowl to the edge of the counter. I could barely reach, and the bowl tipped."

"Uh-oh." Mary Elizabeth sucked in a breath.

"It shattered, and chocolate pudding flew everywhere. It dripped from the benches, covered the floor, and coated me from head to toe. *Mamm* and some of the ladies rushed around, trying to clean everything before the service started, but there wasn't time for me to change. I had to sit through church with hardened chocolate pudding on my hair and clothes. And we didn't discover until later that several people had been sitting in spots of pudding the ladies had missed."

Mary Elizabeth giggled so hard, she held her stomach.

Ada could barely contain her own mirth, but she could easily imagine his *mamm*'s distress. Having a clean house for church was so important. "Your poor *mamm*. She must have been so embarrassed."

"Yes, she was. And people never stopped talking about it."

"I'm glad ... I didn't spill ... flour before church," Mary Elizabeth wheezed out between chuckles.

"I am too," Ada agreed. She had enough people talking behind her back already. "Which reminds me, we need to clean the kitchen now."

As she started toward the sink, Josiah stopped her. "Please let me help. After all you've done for Nathan today, I'd like to do something in exchange."

"It was no trouble. I was happy to do it, and besides, you helped my siblings get home."

Josiah waved aside all her protests, and the next thing she knew, he was ensconced at the sink with Mary Elizabeth beside him holding the dish towel. Ada hovered nearby, busying herself with putting away leftovers and cleaning the counters and tables. She told herself all these chores needed to be done, but if she were honest, she did them because the work kept her near Josiah and gave her a chance to observe him without being obvious.

Ada had finished wiping the table—twice—and continued rubbing in circles as she eavesdropped on his conversation with Mary Elizabeth. From this spot, she had a good view of their faces.

"So how was your first day of school?" Josiah asked her sister.

Mary Elizabeth's eyes filled with tears, and she ducked her head. "Not good. I missed Ada."

"That's understandable. The first few weeks of school can be hard." He handed her a plate to dry. "Did you learn anything? Have fun at recess?"

Keeping her attention on the glass she was wiping, Mary Elizabeth said in a small voice, "No. I cried all day. And Sadie was mad at me because nobody could hear the teacher."

"Oh, that bad, huh?" When Mary Elizabeth nodded,

he said, "I guess I'm not the only one who made it hard for the teacher to give lessons on the first day of school."

Mary Elizabeth glanced up shyly. "You did?"

Josiah gestured toward the glass she was holding. "I'll wait until you put that away to tell you."

Mary Elizabeth quickly returned it to the cupboard and stared up at him with expectant eyes.

Josiah smiled at her before handing her another glass to dry. "I'm embarrassed to admit this, but I ran away from school the first day. I missed my *mamm*, so I ran home. The teacher chased me out to the playground, but she didn't catch me."

"*Ooo...*" Mary Elizabeth sucked in a breath and stared at him with wide eyes.

Ada clenched the rag she'd been aimlessly pushing around on the table. She hoped Josiah wasn't giving her sister any ideas. The last thing she needed was for Mary Elizabeth to run away from school.

Josiah nudged Mary Elizabeth back to work by handing her another glass. "It was the worst decision I'd ever made. I got in trouble with my parents."

Her sister's disappointed *oh* suggested she had been thinking of following his example. Then Mary Elizabeth brightened. "But I wouldn't get in trouble with Ada."

Josiah's eyebrows rose. "I hope you aren't thinking about following my example."

Mary Elizabeth shuffled her feet. "Well, maybe, a little."

"*Ach*, your sister will have my head."

"No, she won't." Mary Elizabeth giggled and looked over at Ada, who straightened up and tried to look purposeful.

But when Josiah turned in her direction and their

eyes met, the rag dangling from her hands fell from her nerveless fingers. Flustered, she bent to pick it up, but knowing he was staring at her made her movements awkward and clumsy. She breathed out a sigh when he turned back to the dishes.

"So what happened next?" Mary Elizabeth asked as he handed her a plate.

"My *mamm* marched me back to school. It was almost time for recess. I had to stay in the classroom and do chores while everyone else played."

Mary Elizabeth frowned, and Ada hoped that part of Josiah's story might be a deterrent. Her sister disliked chores, and losing playtime would be a major punishment.

Josiah washed the next plate slowly. "I thought about running away again, but when I glanced out the window, *Mamm* was standing at the edge of the playground with her arms crossed." He handed over the dish and started on another. "I tried running away the next morning, but one of my older brothers grabbed my suspenders and the other grabbed my arm. They didn't let go until I was inside the schoolhouse." He sighed. "It's hard to get away with anything when you have older brothers and sisters."

"I know," Mary Elizabeth agreed.

Ada had to smile at the sympathy on her sister's face as she commiserated with Josiah.

"But you know what was funny?" Josiah said. "Once I started paying attention to the teacher, I discovered I loved learning."

"You did?"

"I especially liked being able to read books for myself instead of waiting for people to have time to read to me."

"Ada likes to read too. She does it almost every night." Mary Elizabeth lowered her voice. "When she thinks I'm asleep, I sneak to the top of the stairs to watch her. When she's not quilting, she's reading. Read, read, read."

Ada couldn't hear Josiah's response, but from now on, she'd pay closer attention to her sister's breathing to be sure she really was asleep.

"So what are your plans for tomorrow?" Josiah asked Mary Elizabeth.

Ada had run out of chores to do in the kitchen, but she re-swept the kitchen floor. She told herself it was so she could hear his story, but she had to admit she was equally—or maybe even more so—interested in watching him.

Mary Elizabeth hesitated. "I want to be brave, but..." Her chin wobbled. "I miss Ada, and I miss *Mamm*." She put the plate in the cupboard and then swiped her eyes with her dress sleeve.

Josiah took his hands from the dishwater and wiped them on his pants. Then he squatted down in front of Mary Elizabeth and set his hands on her shoulders. "It's hard being brave."

She sniffled. "I know."

"When I want to be brave, I remember Bible stories. David must have been scared to fight that huge giant, but God helped him. Do you remember the story of Queen Esther? She was afraid, but she did what God wanted her to do, and her bravery saved her people."

Mary Elizabeth nodded, although her eyes were still damp.

Josiah smiled at her, a smile that made Ada swallow

hard and turn away. She headed toward the pantry, but stopped when Josiah started speaking again.

"Daniel was brave when he faced the hungry lions." He pinned Mary Elizabeth with a serious look. "Is Rebecca's class as scary as a den of lions?" He took his hands off her shoulders and curved his fingers into claws. When he growled, Mary Elizabeth giggled.

"No," she admitted.

"Then maybe tomorrow you could try being like one of them?"

"I—I guess." Mary Elizabeth's teeth clamped down on her lower lip. "I'll be Queen Esther"—her voice shook—"because we don't have any lions." A hesitant laugh followed her words, and she gazed up at Josiah adoringly.

As adoringly as Ada wished she could do for more reasons than just her attraction to him. Her heart overflowed with gratitude. Not only had he been gentle and understanding with her sister, he'd also taught her a lesson, which saved Ada from lecturing her tonight. Josiah's stories made a much stronger impact than her pleading.

* * *

Josiah's heart went out to this little girl. He understood what it was like being one of the youngest in the family and never being able to keep up with the others. It would be hard to leave her older sister when she was missing her *mamm*. But his conscience pricked him. He'd used Scripture to teach a lesson, to help her, but wasn't he a hypocrite if he couldn't trust God in his own life?

"We'd better finish these dishes," he said to Mary Elizabeth as he stood. "Everyone will wonder what took us so long."

She dried as fast as she could, but by the time Josiah finished washing, a mountain of dishes had piled up. He picked up a towel and helped. Ada had been hovering behind them doing chores while they worked, but when he turned in her direction, she scurried toward the pantry and stowed the broom. Then with a brief apologetic glance, she left the room. He stared after her until he realized he'd been scrubbing the same plate over and over.

Mary Elizabeth heaved a huge sigh after she put the final dish in the cupboard, but Josiah would have preferred to dawdle. He hadn't had a peaceful evening like this since before Ruth passed...

He shook off the gloom surrounding him. He'd just talked to Mary Elizabeth about being brave. Now it was his turn to face the lion.

Nathan hadn't made a peep since dinner. Josiah's tense nerves gradually unraveled, making him realize how tight his muscles and jaw usually were whenever he prepared for a confrontation with his son. Like he was doing now. Before Ruth's death, he would have prayed for courage, but now...

Now he had to depend on his own strength. A strength he wasn't sure he possessed. He suppressed a sigh as he strode toward the stairs.

When he reached the bottom of the stairs to call Nathan, Sadie was descending. She put a finger to her lips. "Nathan's asleep."

Josiah shook his head. *Nathan asleep? Impossible.* His son never went to sleep without a huge fuss. Never.

He still couldn't believe Nathan hadn't made a sound or had one fit since he disappeared upstairs after dinner.

Making exaggerated tiptoeing steps, Sadie motioned for him to follow her upstairs. She led him to the first bedroom on the right, where the door was almost shut. She eased the door open, and Josiah stepped inside to find Nathan curled up on the rag rug, wrapped in a quilt. Josiah's eyes stung. His son had never fallen asleep without screeching, usually for hours.

Sadie whispered, "I sent David to take a bath while Mary Elizabeth washed the dishes. When I came back, Nathan was asleep, so I covered him with a quilt."

"I'll try to pick him up without waking him, but first I'll have to unwind the quilt."

"No need to do that. Just take it with you," a soft voice said from the doorway.

Josiah hadn't heard Ada come up the stairs, but she stood right outside the room, making him nervous about lifting Nathan. "If he wakes, he might cause a ruckus."

"It's all right," Ada assured him. "No one's gone to bed yet."

"Are you sure?" Josiah hated to shatter the silence, but he needed to take Nathan home. After kneeling beside his son, Josiah hesitated. Nathan was cocooned in a cream-colored quilt with a complicated pattern of intertwined fans in variegated shades of pinks. "This quilt is so beautiful, I wouldn't feel right taking it."

"It's all right," Sadie assured him. "Ada makes plenty of them."

"You made this?" Josiah marveled at the intricate stitching. He'd grown up watching *Mamm* quilt, so he was aware of how much work went into those tiny, even stitches. "You quilt *plenty* of these? When do you have the time?"

Ada's cheeks matched the quilt. "I won't now that I'm teaching."

"But she used to," Sadie said. "She had to make money to feed all of us when *Mamm* was ill and *Daed* was out of work."

"Sadie!" Ada scolded in a low tone.

Despite his vow not to stare, Josiah's eyes were drawn to Ada. Not only was she beautiful, she'd sacrificed to support her family. And she'd been responsible for taming his son. She appeared flustered by his scrutiny, so he averted his eyes.

"I need to go," he said, scooping Nathan into his arms as gently as he could. His son kicked and muttered something in his sleep, so Josiah stood still until he settled. "Thank you so much for the delicious meal and for caring for Nathan today. It's been wonderful." Words could not express his gratitude for a warm meal and an evening of solitude without a screeching child.

"It was our pleasure. David enjoyed having a friend to play with. We should do it again soon."

Josiah nodded, afraid if he spoke, he might wake Nathan. Or reveal what was in his heart. Then he regretted agreeing to visit again. As much as he'd like spending time with her—and her family—it wouldn't be wise. He should avoid temptation.

Chapter Twelve

Josiah laid Nathan on the buggy seat in the back, and when his son remained asleep, he released the breath he'd been holding. After sliding the passenger door closed, Josiah strolled around the buggy and climbed in. Usually he dashed to the front and leapt in to stop the buggy from rocking and calm his son's screams. He couldn't recall the last time he'd been able to look up at the darkening night and appreciate the stars sprinkling the sky or enjoy the stillness of the night. Taking a deep breath, he sat for a few minutes in gratitude for the serenity.

The roads were deserted except for a few cars, their engines deafening as they zoomed past until the roar faded in the distance. The ride home went swiftly, and he was soon pulling into the barn. *Mamm* had left the barn doors open and the kitchen light on. Remembering the last time he'd been in the barn, his pulse raced as he slid open the buggy door to get Nathan. Relief coursed through him to see Nathan still curled up on the backseat.

He gathered his son in his arms as gently as he could, and Nathan barely stirred. A long day at school, followed by playtime with a friend, must have worn him out. Grateful, Josiah strode to the house, eased open the kitchen door, and stopped short.

Mamm sat in a kitchen chair, her face tense, her eyes closed, and her lips moving. She always went to bed early so she could get to Linda's restaurant before dawn to bake pies and cakes.

The lines in her face softened as soon as she saw him. "Thank the good Lord, you're home! I've been praying for your safety." She pushed on the tabletop to lift herself to her feet and hurried over to peek at Nathan. "Is he all right?"

"He's fine, *Mamm*. Just tuckered out." Josiah spoke softly so he didn't wake Nathan. "What are you doing up so late?"

"Praying for you," she retorted tartly.

Josiah almost asked why, and then it dawned on him. After discovering Nathan missing, he'd dashed off without leaving a note. No wonder *Mamm* had been worried. Frantic, most likely. "I'm so sorry. I had a bit of a scare with losing Nathan this afternoon."

"Losing him?" *Mamm* stared at him, then pulled back the quilt a bit so she could see Nathan's face. "What happened? You're sure he's all right? Where have you been?"

Josiah wished he could hold up a hand to stop her peppering him with questions. "Let me put him to bed. Then I'll explain."

For once, Nathan stayed sleeping when Josiah lowered him onto the bed. Maybe being bundled in the quilt soothed him. If it did, he'd pay Ada whatever it cost to keep this quilt. He left Nathan in his clothes for the night. Sleep was more important than wrinkled clothes. He lifted the covers to remove Nathan's shoes, only to discover his bare feet. Children usually played barefoot, but with Nathan having no friends and little playtime, Josiah hadn't thought to look for his son's shoes. It was too late to go back to Ada's now, but inside he was rejoicing that he had an excuse to return to her house.

Mamm was still in the kitchen doorway when he returned. "Did you have anything to eat? I saw you hadn't touched the chicken corn soup."

"We ate, thanks." While Josiah tried to organize the day's events into some semblance of order, *Mamm* bustled around the kitchen fixing him a snack. "I brought some of the leftover apple strudel from the restaurant," she said. "Do you want it warm or cold?"

"I don't really need a snack..." At her hurt expression, he amended his statement. "Cold will be fine." *Mamm* loved to feed people. So did his sister Linda— hence, the restaurant she ran with her daughter.

Mamm set a plate in front of him filled with a generous slice of strudel. Then she shuffled back to the refrigerator to pour a large glass of milk. Josiah waved to the chair near him, and she sank into it, staring at him with expectant eyes.

"I know you need to go to bed," Josiah said, "so I'll give you a condensed version." He proceeded to tell her of Nathan's meltdown at school, the teacher's calming ways, opening the buggy to find Nathan gone.

At his *mamm*'s sharp intake of breath, he stopped, but she waved him on. "I see you found him."

"Actually, his teacher found him. He'd crawled out at the accident site. I'm so grateful she recognized him. I don't know what would have happened if she hadn't."

"You'd still be out there searching."

Josiah nodded. "True." *Mamm*'s comment brought up the signalman's kidnapping charge, but he skipped over that for now. She might laugh about that later. But at the thought of someone kidnapping Nathan, Josiah's gut clenched.

Mamm waved an impatient hand. "The teacher found him? How did you know that?"

"The man who held the STOP sign described the woman who'd picked up Nathan. It sounded like Nathan's teacher. Anyway, I found Nathan at her house."

"And what time was this?"

"Sometime this afternoon," he mumbled. When *Mamm* motioned for him to go on, Josiah stumbled through an abbreviated explanation of Nathan's friendship with David and the dinner invitation.

"But you still should have been here when I got home from the restaurant." She crossed her arms and gave him a look that demanded an explanation.

"I'm sorry. I offered to help with the dishes."

"The dishes?" *Mamm*'s voice rose.

"I thought it was only fair after she'd cooked dinner and taken care of Nathan." Josiah wished he hadn't sounded so defensive. *Mamm* would probably read into that.

"Of course." A tinge of sarcasm colored her words. "You'd feel obligated to do that for your tired *mamm* at the end of a long day too?"

Josiah ducked his head so she couldn't see his expression. *Mamm*'s sharp eyes saw more than he'd like. It was obvious she sensed there was more to the story he wasn't telling. When he was young and she raised a questioning brow like that, he'd spill out the truth, every last detail. Tonight it took strength to resist. He couldn't confess he was falling for Nathan's teacher. Even though *Mamm* understood and sympathized with his loneliness after being without Ruth's companionship for years, Josiah already knew what *Mamm* would say; he'd been telling himself the same thing. Falling for someone while he was mourning was a big mistake.

*   *   *

Shrieking outside the window awoke Ada from her pleasant dreams to a hot, airless room. Strands of hair had pulled loose from her braid and clung to her sweaty forehead. She wiped her damp brow, burrowed back into her pillow, and willed herself to drift back into the cool woods she'd been exploring with Josiah. *He'd picked a wildflower bouquet…*

The shrieks grew louder and closer. So close they seemed to be coming from their front lawn. But that was impossible.

At a knock on the front door, Ada rolled out of bed. She couldn't go to the door in her nightgown. By the time she tucked her braid under a kerchief and threw on her spring cloak, Mary Elizabeth had dashed downstairs and opened the front door.

A man's voice drifted upstairs, but Ada couldn't distinguish any words. Fear for her sister's safety propelled her to move. Her foot caught in the nightgown hem as she raced down the steps, and she grabbed for the railing to keep her balance. She righted herself and resumed her rush to the door. She skidded to a stop. *Josiah? What was he doing here in the middle of the night?*

He glanced up, and her body temperature—already sweltering from the heavy cloak on this hot summer night—rose several degrees.

"Ada?" He averted his eyes. "I'm so sorry to disturb you."

He wasn't disturbing her. At least, not in the way he meant.

Footsteps padded down the stairs behind her, and her siblings crowded around her and Mary Elizabeth.

"*Ach!* I didn't mean to wake everyone in the house. I—Nathan—must have left his bunny here."

Noah rubbed his eyes and asked in a sleepy voice, "What time is it?"

Josiah hung his head. "Around three a.m."

"Will finding the bunny stop those screams?" Noah wanted to know.

"I hope so," Josiah said, but he sounded far from sure.

"Then let's all search. I'll check David's room." Noah pounded up the stairs.

"I'll look in the kitchen," Sadie volunteered, although she was swaying on her feet. Grace trailed after her.

Ada signed to David, and he rushed up the stairs.

"I hope he didn't lose the rabbit at the accident site. I have no idea what I'll do if he did."

"Nathan was sucking the bunny's ears while he watched the fire truck lights," Ada told him. She couldn't remember if he still had it when they arrived at the house. "Ruby, can you check the buggy?"

Josiah shuffled his feet. "I'm sorry to put everyone to all this trouble."

He looked so uncomfortable, Ada wanted to put him at ease, but she was unsure how to do that with all the noise coming from the buggy. "Would it be all right if I went out to comfort him?"

Josiah shook his head. "It's much too dangerous when he's like this. I'm afraid he'll hurt you."

"I'd like to try." Ada brushed past him with a battery-powered lantern and headed for the buggy.

Josiah hurried after her and reached for her arm. Even through the cloth, his touch sent sparks zinging through her. Ada drew in a breath and stepped back before he could see her reaction.

"Please, I don't want him to hurt you," Josiah begged.

Ada lowered her eyes. She didn't want them to give away the attraction she felt. Taking a deep breath to calm her racing pulse, she said, "I've dealt with many temper tantrums."

"Not like this you haven't."

"I'd like to try."

The buggy rocked back and forth so hard, she could barely slide open the door. Josiah lay on the backseat, shrieking and kicking. She climbed into the buggy and reached over the seat. Slipping a hand past his flailing arms, she laid it on his head and stroked his hair. His eyes flew open. He backed away from her touch, but then he turned his head to look at her. His mouth still open in mid-scream, he gurgled to a stop.

Ada, he signed.

Tears came to her eyes. She'd tried to teach the scholars her name sign and theirs today, but none of them seemed to comprehend. The only sign they'd all cooperated on was *cat*. Nathan must have been paying attention the whole time.

Nathan, she signed back, and his mouth snapped shut. He studied her hands as she made the movements for his name again and then pointed at him. His lips curved into a half smile.

Now that he was still, Ada folded down the front seat, made the sign for *come*, and held out her arms. Nathan stared at her warily for a few seconds before glancing around the carriage fearfully. When he looked back at her, she signed again, *Come*.

Nathan rose to his knees, but stopped as if undecided. He checked each window, then stood and leaned toward her. Ada slid her arm from the cape to wrap it around him and draw him close. In a heap in the corner lay the quilt she'd sent home with him.

They sat quietly for a few minutes, Nathan's head nestled against her. His eyes slid closed several times, but each time they did, he startled himself awake. His body started to soften and grow heavy against her, a sure sign he was close to sleep.

David came dashing across the front yard, swinging the bunny by its ears. He peeked into the buggy, and Nathan lit up. The two of them seemed to be sending messages through looks, and then David handed the bunny to Nathan, who gave him a tired smile, but his eyes conveyed his thanks.

David signed *good night*, and Nathan smiled again. Popping a bunny ear in his mouth, he leaned closer to Ada and closed his eyes.

Tell everyone to go back to bed, Ada mouthed to David.

He nodded, patted Nathan on the shoulder, and headed back inside.

This time, when Nathan's eyes closed, they stayed shut. As soon as his breathing appeared steady and even, Ada laid him on the backseat and covered him with the quilt. It was too warm for a blanket in this weather, but sometimes security overrode heat.

As she stepped from the buggy, Josiah reached out a hand to assist her. "I don't know what you did in there, but thank you. I stayed away from the windows in case seeing me started his crying again."

His eyes looked so sad and discouraged, Ada longed to reach out to him, but they were out here on the lawn alone—her in a nightgown, her hair undone down her back.

"I'd better go," she said, whirled around, and headed for the house.

* * *

Though he should avert his eyes, Josiah couldn't tear his gaze from her figure silhouetted in the moonlight. A sharp pang went through him. A pang of loneliness, of longing.

He waited until she'd gone inside and shut the door before climbing into the buggy. Blessed silence reigned as Silver trotted toward the road.

Ada was a miracle worker. Josiah could think of no other words to describe her. Well, he could, but wouldn't allow his thoughts to go there. She remained on his mind, along with guilt. He'd loved Ruth. During the mourning period, he should be honoring her memory, not letting another woman stir his emotions. Though he tried to push away the memories of Ada's gentleness and caring, they stayed with him the whole way home.

When he carried Nathan into the house, *Mamm* was already in the kitchen. He took his sleeping son upstairs, but instead of going back to bed, he went down to join her. A pot filled with water and canning jars bubbled on the stove.

"Isn't it too early for you to be up?" he teased. She appeared almost as tired as he felt.

"I couldn't fall back to sleep after Nathan started screaming, so I figured I'd do something useful." She gestured to the canning kettle before taking a mixing bowl from the cupboard shelf. "I forgot to tell you, I can't pick Nathan up at noon today."

Josiah stared at her. He couldn't ask for time off work again.

Mamm had her back to him, cracking eggs into a bowl. "Mary has a new baby and won't be back waitressing, so I'll be filling in at the restaurant."

"Will you still be doing the desserts?" When she nodded, he said, "But won't it wear you out to do waitressing too, especially with missing so much sleep last night?"

"I expect it will, but Linda needs help. Mary's replacement can't start for another week."

A week? Did she just say a week? "You're not planning to fill in the whole time, are you?"

"What else can I do? Linda can't hire someone for only a week."

Sinking into a chair, Josiah buried his head in his hands. A whole week. He'd lose his job if he took off that much time. If only he'd had some warning, he could have made plans. No, that wasn't true. He didn't know anyone who could or would handle Nathan. Except for Ada, but he couldn't ask her.

"What can I do about Nathan?"

Mamm stirred the eggs and poured them into the frying pan. The liquid hitting the sizzling butter hissed and spit. "I was worried about that, so I spoke to Betty."

The bishop's wife? But she had two children who needed her time and attention. Maybe she knew of someone who could care for Nathan, though.

"Betty suggested Martha. She said her daughter's quite good with special children. You'll need to ask Ada if Martha can stay in the schoolhouse for the afternoon. Betty wouldn't be able to transport him to her house. Not if he's acting up."

Josiah nodded. Martha had calmed Nathan yesterday. She might be able to handle him, but Josiah worried about her being in the schoolhouse alone. What would happen if she couldn't control one of his temper fits?

Mamm's timer ticked down and rang. She turned off the heat under the canning jars with one hand while lifting the skillet from the heat with the other. "Ready for some eggs?" she asked.

Josiah wasn't sure he wanted breakfast quite this early, but it had been a long night. "Sounds good."

He waited until *Mamm* had reset the timer and taken her place at the table. Then they both bowed in prayer. After they raised their heads, he expressed his concerns about Martha being alone with Nathan.

Mamm chewed for a minute before answering. After she swallowed, she said, "Why don't you ask Betty to stay with Martha?"

Chapter Thirteen

Ada struggled to get out of bed in the morning. After being awakened in the middle of the night, she'd had difficulty falling back asleep because pictures of Josiah kept running through her mind. She dragged herself downstairs to start breakfast.

Mary Elizabeth beat everyone else to the kitchen. Ada hoped Josiah's talk with her the night before had made an impact, but her sister ran over and hugged her legs, her eyes overflowing with tears.

Ada ignored the tears and said, "I'm glad you're here early. I can use help with breakfast. Why don't you drag a chair over, so you can stir the oatmeal?"

Her lower lip thrust out, Mary Elizabeth let go of Ada's skirt and folded her arms.

"You said you want to spend time with me," Ada reminded her. "Now you can."

Mary Elizabeth's sideways glance revealed her

doubt, but her sister climbed on a chair and started stirring vigorously.

Ada smiled at her enthusiasm.

By the time Sadie came downstairs, the oatmeal was almost ready, and Hannah had set the bowls on the table. Sadie raised her eyebrows when she spotted Mary Elizabeth on the chair, but a swift smile crossed her lips. Ada directed Ruby to get the milk and Grace to bring the maple syrup and applesauce to mix into the oatmeal.

"What am I supposed to do?" Sadie demanded.

"Why don't you call David and Noah for breakfast?"

"That's all?"

Ada smiled at her. "Did you want more chores?"

Sadie shook her head and backed away. Her belligerence of last night seemed to have lessened.

When everyone sat down to breakfast, Ada's gaze kept straying to the chair at the opposite end of the table where Josiah had sat last night. Today the chair seemed emptier than usual. Over the past few months, she'd come to accept that *Daed* would never be able to fill that space again; yet Josiah, so vital and alive, sitting in his place revived old wounds and ever-present guilt.

When he fit into that seat—and their family—so smoothly yesterday, his presence stirred other longings. Ones, she reminded herself, Josiah could *not* fill. Ada dreamed of marrying, of sharing a table with a husband and children of her own. But she had no one to court, no one to marry, no one to share her life.

Because *Mamm* had been so sickly, Ada had had no chance to attend singings or court like others in her buddy bunch. Then after the recent situation with *Daed*, she'd become the subject of gossip in their community. Ada had come to accept that no respectable man would be interested in dating someone with a reputation like hers. Once Josiah heard the story, he'd condemn her too. Besides, with seven siblings to raise, she had no chance of fulfilling those dreams.

Count the blessings you already have. She had her siblings and work to do. Ada forced herself to look away from the chair and concentrate on breakfast. As soon as the meal and kitchen cleanup ended, she rushed upstairs to grab the word cards she'd made last night. When she passed the girls' bedroom, Sadie stood in the doorway, hands on hips.

"Come on, Mary Elizabeth, it's time to go. If you don't hurry, we're going to be late."

Mary Elizabeth stood in her room, her fingers curled, growling.

Sadie blew out an exasperated breath. "What are you doing?"

"Practicing being brave."

Sadie huffed. "I guess that's better than crying."

Mary Elizabeth looked up, hurt in her eyes, and Ada hastened to intervene before the tears started. "Josiah gave you that idea last night, didn't he?"

When her sister nodded, Ada motioned to Sadie to follow her to the other bedroom.

Sadie's face revealed her displeasure. "We're going to be late for school."

"It won't take long." Ada ushered Sadie into her room and shut the door. "First, I want to say I know it's not fair how much responsibility you've had to take on while I've been preparing to teach. We need to talk about dividing the chores more evenly too, but we can talk about that tonight."

Some of Sadie's defiance faded, but she tapped her foot impatiently.

"I know Mary Elizabeth is a trial for you, but try to be gentle with her. Losing *Mamm* has been hard on her, and she's not used to being separated from me."

"She isn't the only one who's missing *Mamm*," Sadie burst out. "*Mamm* wasn't here yesterday for our first day of school. No one asked about my day." Tears trickled down Sadie's cheeks.

Ada held out her arms, and Sadie rushed into them. "I'm sorry. I didn't think..." Ada had been so busy with her own problems and concerns, she hadn't considered how hard the first day of school would be for Sadie and the others. She hadn't asked them how their day went, although with Sadie's and Rebecca's descriptions of the crying, they wouldn't have had much to report. Still, she should have asked.

Between sobs, Sadie choked out, "I always ran into *Mamm*'s room as soon as I got home from school. No matter how sick she was, she'd be propped up in bed waiting for me." Sadie drew in a shuddery breath. "I ran in there yesterday without thinking, and... and..."

Ada tightened her hug. She'd hoped to get to the schoolhouse early to set things out this morning, but comforting her sister was more important. She patted Sadie's back.

"The room felt so empty. *Daed*'s not there now. And you're always so busy getting things ready for school, you don't have time for us."

"*Ach*, Sadie, I'm so sorry." Ada blinked back tears.

Ever since the bishop had asked her to take over the special school, it had consumed her time and energy. She worried about not being good enough to teach her scholars, so she read and studied, planned materials, and fretted about how to deal with the students. In the process, she'd neglected her siblings.

Sadie pulled back, her lip quivering. "I didn't mean to hurt your feelings. I know you have a lot to do. And I know you love us."

"Of course I do."

Sadie gave her a quick, hard hug. "We need to leave." She rubbed at the wetness on her cheeks. "Rebecca's going to think we're a family of crybabies."

As her sister hurried from the room, Ada said, "About Mary Elizabeth. Josiah told her last night to think about Esther and Daniel being brave. I think she was being a lion."

Sadie snickered. "I wish she'd be Esther instead. It would be quieter." Before Ada could say anything, she waved a hand in the air. "I know. I'll try to be nice."

"Thank you," Ada called after her. Taking a deep breath, Ada searched on the desk for the cards she'd made, but some were missing. Finally, she found them on the floor under the dresser. She must have scattered them last night when she threw on her cape.

By the time she got downstairs, the others had left for their school in the pony cart. David sat patiently waiting for her with a pair of shoes on his lap. Ada signed for him to put them on as she rushed past him to hook up the buggy. When she pulled out front, David came out of the house with the shoes still in his hand. She started to scold him only to realize he had on

shoes. She pointed to the pair in his hand and signed a
question mark.

Nathan's, he replied.

Oh, right. Josiah had taken him home in the quilt. He
must have left the shoes behind.

She was grateful to pull into the school yard; the day
would prove a distraction from thoughts of Josiah. She
wished, though, that she'd arrived earlier. With only ten
minutes until school started, two buggies were already
waiting. The one parked at the far corner of the playground belonged to Josiah. The bishop's wife descended
from the other, followed by Martha.

"I'm so glad you're here," Betty said as she crossed
the yard. "Lukas has an appointment at the clinic this
morning, but I didn't want to leave Martha here alone."

"I'm sorry I'm late. We had a small crisis this morning."

"Mary Elizabeth?" Betty's tight smile added to Ada's
guilt. "I understand she had some difficulties yesterday."

Ada couldn't tell if Betty's tone was sarcastic or
rushed. "Yes, she did. I believe we've dealt with the
problem with some help—" She broke off abruptly before she added *from Josiah*. No need to start gossip that
might damage his reputation.

Josiah crossed the parking lot. "I had a question before I leave," he said to Ada. Then turning to Betty,
he said, "Thank you so much for agreeing to help with
Nathan. I hope he won't be too much trouble."

"I'm sure Martha and I can handle it." Betty headed
off with a quick wave.

Ada turned toward him. "Help with Nathan?"

"That's what I need to talk to you about," Josiah said.

"Let me unlock the doors first." Ada beckoned to Martha, who was still standing in the spot where her *mamm*'s buggy had been parked.

Martha limped over, smiling. "I can't wait," she said in her throaty monotone. "It will be a good day."

Ada's spirits lifted at Martha's cheerful attitude. She appreciated having an assistant who brought joy into the classroom.

Josiah waited until they entered the building, then he turned to Martha, making sure she could see his lips. "Thank you for watching Nathan today."

Martha's smile broadened. "It will be fun."

At Ada's confused expression, Josiah explained about his mother's work schedule and her plan to have Martha and Betty stay at the schoolhouse in the afternoon to watch Nathan.

"Of course. If you'd like, I'd be happy to watch him the rest of the week." Ada was a little hurt he hadn't asked her. Nathan had been happy at their house yesterday, and she'd been able to calm his crying last night.

"You have so many other things to do. Besides, we imposed on you too much yesterday."

"It was a joy"—Ada stumbled to a stop—"um, to have Nathan. David enjoyed his company and..." Now she was prattling to cover up her slip. "I'm sure David would be thrilled to have Nathan spend the afternoons this week."

Ada glanced around. "Speaking of David, where is he?" He hadn't followed them into the schoolhouse. "I'd better check on him."

"Don't worry. He's probably playing outside."

Though Josiah's voice sounded comforting, a quiver of concern underlay his words.

After yesterday's missing children incidents, they both remained a bit edgy. And lack of sleep didn't help. Even though everyone eventually turned up safe, it was hard to shake the nervousness.

When they got to the door, the playground was empty. So was Ada's buggy.

"Oh, no!" Josiah sprinted across the playground. The door to his buggy was hanging open. "I checked that door twice before I left," he said over his shoulder.

Three more buggies were coming up the driveway, but Ada kept pace with him. Had the boys taken off together? Or had Nathan taken off and David followed him?

Josiah reached his buggy slightly ahead of her and screeched to a stop. He held up a hand and backed away. "They're all right," he whispered. "David's helping Nathan put on his shoes. Why don't you peek in without letting them see you?"

Ada leaned forward so she could see. Her brother was twisting a shoe onto Nathan's foot. Nathan had his eyes scrunched up while pushing down. Ada couldn't help smiling. David's movements were making it impossible for Nathan to put his foot in the shoe.

She caught David's eye and mouthed, *Need help?*

David nodded and let go of the shoe. When it dropped, Nathan's eyes popped open, and David gestured toward the door. Cringing, Nathan glanced over his shoulder. His apprehensive look relaxed as soon as he saw her. Ada held out her arms, and he came to her. After motioning for David to carry the shoes, she picked up

Nathan, who scooped his terrycloth rabbit from the seat and clung to her.

To her surprise, Josiah was no longer behind her. In fact, she didn't see him anywhere, but with the other children and their parents heading into the school, she had no time to look. Nathan squirmed to get out of her arms, so she set him on the ground. After Ada helped him with his shoes, Nathan walked between her and David into the school building. Quite a difference from his arrival the day before.

Chapter Fourteen

Josiah stayed hidden on the other side of the buggy until Nathan's back was turned. As his son entered the schoolhouse, Josiah's heart ached. If things had been different, Ruth would be walking him to the door. Maybe the three of them would have walked hand in hand together. *Why, God, why?* It wasn't fair that Nathan had no mother. No matter how many times he repeated the assurance he'd heard since he was a child—whatever happened was God's will—his heart refused to accept it.

What hurt even more was Nathan's happiness around Ada. To see his son act lovingly and cooperatively with someone else, someone he'd known for only a few days, cut him deeply. Perhaps Nathan clung to Ada because he missed his *mamm. But why does he fight me? What have I done to make him react this way?*

If only he could ask for Ada's help in dealing with the tantrums and learning sign language, but he needed to spend less time around her, not more. Having his son push him away tore Josiah apart inside. Gloomy thoughts persisted as he headed to the job site. He was grateful Silver knew the way because he could barely keep his eyes open. The three a.m. trip across town with no sleep afterward and his early morning tussles with Nathan had shattered his peace of mind.

Josiah hitched Silver to a post some distance from the worksite and sleepwalked toward the house the construction company was building. He was roofing today, so he needed to stay awake and alert. He jerked himself awake several times, but the rest of the time his mind wandered.

"What's the matter with you, Yoder?" the foreman yelled up at him. Ralph paced around below him. He pointed to the small area of roofing Josiah had finished. "Your mind's not on the job today."

No, it wasn't. It was at the schoolhouse, wondering how troublesome Nathan was being, worrying if Martha and Betty would be able to handle his son this afternoon, wondering if he should have taken Ada up on her offer to watch Nathan. Josiah shook his head to dislodge this morning's picture of her tight golden blond twists disappearing under each side of her *kapp*, her sparkling blue eyes... Of yesterday with flour on her cheeks... Of the moonlight on her face last night... Of his last glimpse of her with her braid drifting down her back, her feet bare, the sheer white gown floating around her ankles...

The hammer slipped from his grasp and went hurtling through the air.

"Yoder!" Ralph's sharp cry jolted Josiah back to the job site. "That could have hit someone below. Like me."

Josiah tipped his head to see the ground below. Ralph's steel-toed boot connected with the hammer, kicking up a puff of dust and sending the hammer flying toward the nearby grass. Evidently, the foreman wasn't worried about it hitting anyone down there.

His fists bunched and face red, Ralph yelled, "Follow that hammer. Take your lunch break and do your day-dreaming then. When you get back, the only thing you'd better focus on is work."

His cheeks hot, Josiah climbed down the ladder. Grabbing his cooler, he headed to a nearby tree. He sank onto the grass under a leafy oak, opened the lid, and pulled out a thick ham sandwich on *Mamm*'s homemade bread. Eyes still closed after his silent prayer, he bit into the chewy crust and savored the smoky, salty taste with its sharp tang of mustard.

A hand knuckled his straw hat. "OK if I join ya, dude?" Marcus towered above him, the pink hard hat he had clasped in one hand almost hidden behind his back. The greasy smell of fries came from the fast food bag he clutched in his other huge hand.

Josiah motioned to the grass beside him. He'd been hoping for some peace and quiet, some time to think. He was so exhausted, though, he might drift off. Maybe company would keep him awake and prevent his thoughts from straying to where they shouldn't go.

Josiah gestured toward the hard hat. "Forgot yours to-day?"

"Yeah." Marcus's cheeks darkened.

Like many construction companies, Anderson & Sons handed out pink hats to those who came to work without theirs. The color was supposed to discourage workers from stealing them and to encourage them to remember their own next time.

Tossing the pink hat under the tree, Marcus set down a white bag with grayish grease spots. "Decided to take lunch early. I'm tired of all the *purty-in-pink* comments."

"I can imagine," Josiah said. The other guys whistled and catcalled every time Marcus walked by.

Marcus lowered his bulk to the ground. "Whatcha doing taking lunch so early, man?"

With a shrug, Josiah studied the house under construction. "Ralph told me to take a break."

"That 'cause you almost beaned him with that hammer you dropped?"

"I didn't know it almost hit him." No wonder the foreman had barked at him like that.

"Yeah, right. Sure ya didn't do it on purpose?" Marcus nudged him and winked. "Big mouth like him deserves it."

Josiah hoped Ralph didn't think he'd done it on purpose. "No one deserves to get hurt."

Marcus rolled his eyes. "Whatever." He opened his bag and shoved several fries in his mouth. After he swallowed, he said, "It's not like you to be so careless. What's goin' on?"

Josiah shrugged. Then worried Marcus might think him rude, he said, "Troubles with my son."

"Kids. They're trouble no matter what age they are. I oughta know." From the wild tales he told about his four boys, he'd had plenty of experience.

"Well, Nathan's only six, but he's—" How could Josiah describe Nathan's outbursts without making his son sound like a spoiled brat? "Well, he has crying fits, but he's grieving for his *mamm*."

"Give him time. It's not even been a year yet, has it?" Marcus unwrapped a fast food burger that emitted the sharp odor of pickle and onion. "Or if it's real bad, take him to a shrink." Mayonnaise oozed out as he picked up the loaded bun. "Or don't you people believe in shrinks?"

Josiah wasn't sure what shrinks were, but it didn't seem like a solution to Nathan's problem. "The problem is he can't talk."

"At his age?" Marcus said around a mouthful of sandwich. "I've heard of kids that don't talk until they're three or four, but six is kinda late."

"He lost his hearing when he was two."

Marcus munched for a minute, a thoughtful look on his face. "The kid's deaf? Aw, man, that's tough." Finishing his bite, he wiped his mouth with the back of his hand. "You know any of that sign language stuff?"

"Not much," Josiah admitted.

"So why not learn it? Although"—he pinned Josiah with a serious look—"once they reach a certain age, there's no communicating with them anyway." He popped several more fries in his mouth and shook his head.

Josiah leaned back against the rough bark and closed his eyes. Pictures of Ruth, weary and pale, demonstrating a few signs, faded to images of Ada, vibrant and lively, confidently signing to her brother. The other night he'd almost asked Ada if she'd teach him, but it would be much wiser to find another teacher.

"You sleeping?" Marcus's question dragged Josiah back to the construction site. After swallowing down the last of the fries, Marcus stood and crumpled the bag in his fist. "I gotta go. Me and Rodrigo are planning to sneak away from the old ladies this weekend. You know how it is." His grin faded. "Aw, sorry, dude." He cuffed Josiah on the shoulder. "Hang in there."

Josiah finished the rest of his lunch, stowed his cooler in the buggy, and trudged back to the job site. The clock was ticking toward noon, and Ada would be leaving work soon. Images of her swam before his tired eyes. Beautiful, serene, tired after a long day. Crossing the playground to get into her buggy. Behind her, Nathan's shrill screams echoed across the playground, while Martha and Betty, at their wits' end, tried to calm a kicking, screeching whirlwind.

His stomach in knots, Josiah reached the ladder and hauled himself up two rungs.

"Yoder!" the foreman yelled behind him.

Josiah jumped and almost lost his grip on the ladder. He swiveled his head toward his red-faced boss. Visions of Nathan and Ada faded at the sight of Ralph's scowl.

"You're usually my best worker," Ralph growled. "What's going on up there?"

"I'm sorry. I'll work harder this afternoon to make up for it."

"I wanna know why it happened in the first place."

Josiah didn't believe in making excuses for his behavior, but Ralph stood waiting, his arms crossed. "Rough night," Josiah mumbled.

"Thought the Amish didn't go on benders. Nice to know you're human." He clapped Josiah on the back. "Next time save it for Saturday night." His gruff voice softened a bit. "Now get up there and get to work the way you normally do."

Too tired to correct the misunderstanding, Josiah nodded and climbed the ladder to the roof. He forced his attention away from the schoolhouse and onto each nail. They needed to go in with precision so the roof didn't leak.

Whenever he caught himself worrying or daydreaming, he jerked his thoughts back to the roof. It wasn't fair to his employer to let his mind wander elsewhere— no matter how pressing his worries—when he should be concentrating on his job. He was being paid to have his full attention here; anything else was cheating his employer.

A white pickup truck emblazoned with the Anderson & Sons label pulled into the lot, and a man stepped out holding a thick stack of papers. He huddled with Ralph for a few minutes, and then the foreman blew a whistle.

"Finish what you're doing and gather round," Ralph called.

A flurry of hammering and sawing ensued before men clambered down ladders to surround Ralph and the man wearing a suit and tie.

Beside Josiah, one of the men scoffed, "Who's he think he's fooling? Look at his hard hat and shoes. Not a scratch on them." The man's gleaming hard hat and shiny steel-toed shoes contrasted with the crew's scuffed, well-worn clothing and equipment.

Ralph held up a hand, and the chattering ended. "I'd like to introduce the owner of Anderson & Sons, Mr. Lyle Anderson. He's come here from New York today to tell us about a special project."

"We're planning to expand Anderson & Sons across the country," Anderson said. "Our new head of advertising decided we should splurge on small, local projects that get free media coverage. And that's where you come in."

"He think we're gonna advertise for him for free after working for such low wages?" the man next to Josiah grumbled.

Lyle Anderson handed Ralph a stack of papers. "Pass these out so everyone can see what I'm talking about." He faced the men again. "We'd like you to come up with ideas for community service projects. Something Anderson & Sons can underwrite."

A small sheaf of papers made its way down the row, and Josiah took one and passed the rest on. He read the paper in his hand as Lyle Anderson droned on. The company directors would choose one project per region to fund.

"So," Lyle continued, "The finished project should be something with an 'aw' factor. Kids and animals are always a big draw for the media, so plan accordingly. Send us your best ideas."

Ralph thanked the owner and then yelled, "OK, back to work, everyone."

As the men dispersed, Lyle Anderson pointed to Josiah. "You, there, what do you do?"

"I'm a roofer, sir."

Anderson glared at the straw hat Josiah wore. "Where's your hard hat?"

"I'm Amish. We don't wear hard hats."

"Everyone wears a hard hat on Anderson sites. No exceptions." The company owner's voice grew shrill. "I'm not dealing with another lawsuit."

Ralph intervened. "The Amish don't believe in suing people, and they've been granted an exemption—"

"Not from me they haven't," Anderson snapped. "I will not have a worker on my property without proper safety equipment. Young man, I expect you to put on a hard hat immediately."

Although Josiah understood the supervisor's concerns, the rules of the *Ordnung* were deeply engrained in him. The hat represented his humility and separateness from the world. To remove it in public or wear a different hat than his brethren? *Neh*, he couldn't do it. Not even to keep his job.

"I'm sorry, sir. It's against my beliefs to wear a different hat than the rest of my community."

Hands on his hips, Lyle Anderson looked Josiah up and down. "You heard my ultimatum. Either that hat goes or you do." His face red, he spat out, "You understand?"

"I understand, Mr. Anderson. I'm sorry I can't continue to work here. I've enjoyed my job." Josiah turned and walked toward his buggy, his thoughts churning.

Behind him, Lyle Anderson's voice rose in disbelief. "He'd really lose a job over that foolish hat?"

"The hat is part of his religion," Ralph retorted. "I can't believe you just fired my best worker."

"Roofers are a dime a dozen," Anderson said. "Put an ad in the paper, and you'll have someone in place at the end of the day."

"You don't understand." Ralph was practically screeching. "He does more work than two men combined, always arrives on time, never stretches out his lunch hour, and..."

The voices faded as Josiah moved out of earshot. He untied Silver and slid into the buggy, the flyer still in his hand. He tossed it onto the seat beside him, picked up the reins, and headed toward the street.

Ralph waved him down, and Josiah pulled to a halt. "Anderson doesn't realize it's illegal to fire you over that hat," Ralph said. "OSHA regulations allow you to wear it. Might be best to go home now and take tomorrow off so I can sort this out, but report for work Thursday as usual."

Josiah appreciated Ralph's support, but Lyle Anderson, as the boss, had made it clear he was in charge. If Josiah had any questions about Anderson's word being law, the man's clenched fists and teeth as he stalked over to Ralph erased all doubt.

"You'd better not be rescinding my decision," Anderson thundered. "I own this company—lock, stock, and barrel. No one, not even legal, will reverse my decisions."

Ralph held up a hand in protest. "But the—"

"I should be going," Josiah said, flicking the reins.

Ralph mouthed *Thursday* at the same time Anderson said, "No hard hat, no job."

The horse picked up speed, carrying Josiah away from the arguing men. Ralph had told him to come back Thursday, so Josiah would obey his order. But he had no idea if he'd still have a job.

Chapter Fifteen

With Lukas absent and Nathan calm, Ada walked into the classroom with more confidence than she had yesterday. With no screaming children, she could do what other schoolteachers did—greet the arriving scholars by the door. Nathan clutched her skirt and shrank behind her when the next wagon pulled into the school yard. David stood on her other side, smiling. Martha stayed just inside the doorway, bouncing a little on her toes.

Leah hopped out and brought Lizzie to the doorway. Ada greeted both of them. Lizzie's head jerked to one side, then she flailed her arms. Several sounds issued from her mouth.

"Tell everyone about your surprise, Lizzie," Leah encouraged her.

Lizzie's tics increased, and she struggled to get out words between clicking sounds. "I have...a...baby...brother."

Ada squatted down to her level, and Nathan backed up and flattened himself against the door. "How wonderful!" Ada said. After signing the word *baby*, Ada pantomimed rocking a baby. Martha clapped and beamed, and Ada turned to David to mouth more details. Martha avidly watched Lizzie's and Leah's mouths as they discussed the baby.

Smiling, David studied everyone's faces and lips. He signed to ask the baby's name. Ada interpreted his request and followed up by translating Lizzie's spoken *Matthew* to the class, but Nathan stayed semi-hidden behind Ada, his body tense.

Before she left, Leah leaned forward to whisper to Ada. "The delivery went well, and I have some exciting news. I'd love for you to stop by the store today if you can." Giving everyone a brief wave, she crossed the yard to her wagon as Emily's mother pulled in.

Once Emily joined them, Lizzie shared her news again while Ada signed, eliciting a flicker of a smile from Emily. Grateful for the peaceful start to the day, Ada herded the children into the classroom. Will had still not arrived, but it was time for school to start.

Lizzie's announcement provided the perfect lead-in to the day's lesson—signs for family members. Ada gathered the cards she'd made last night after Josiah and Nathan left. She began with *baby*, and then *brother* and *sister*. Next she demonstrated the sign for *daed*. As soon as he saw the sign, Nathan shrank in his chair and glanced over his shoulder fearfully. He appeared on the verge of a meltdown, so she quickly switched to the sign for *mamm*.

Nathan squeezed his eyes shut and repeated the sign.

He'd evidently had a lot of practice with that one. A tear trickled down his cheek, and Ada regretted choosing that sign. He'd be missing his *mamm* while she was in Mexico. She wanted to reach out to comfort him, but didn't feel right singling out one scholar over the rest.

Opening his eyes, which were brimming with tears, Nathan signed *Mamm gone*. He repeated it a second time and burst into tears. Ada broke her rule about not giving a child preferential treatment and cradled him in her arms while he sobbed.

Miriam arrived with Will during Nathan's crying jag. Will covered his ears and balked when his *mamm* tried to walk him through the door. Ada, her arms full, smiled encouragement, but Will only planted his feet more firmly.

She pinched her lips together to hold back her sighs. The morning had begun so well, they'd actually made some progress on lessons before everything fell apart. Now they were headed back to yesterday's chaos. Lizzie's tics had slowed once they'd started the signing lesson, and Emily sat, still and silent, as usual. Martha hurried to the door and blocked Will's view of Nathan.

"Will can go for a walk," she told Miriam. Martha stepped outside and beckoned to Will. To Ada's amazement, he followed her. Bless Martha. She was a godsend.

While Martha walked Will outside, Ada rocked Nathan until his sobs quieted to hiccupping sniffles. She wiped his face and nose, gave him a tight squeeze, and waited until he had composed himself. Then she motioned toward his chair. He looked up and met her eyes, and she could read the longing in them. He wanted to be held and cuddled. Ada was as reluctant to let him go as he appeared to be. If his *mamm* was so ill, she might not be able to hold him when she was home. And it seemed she wasn't home now due to her treatments. The poor child seemed to be starving for affection and closeness. But she had a classroom to run, and it wouldn't be fair to hold one child and not the others.

Giving him another tight squeeze, she encouraged him to return to his chair. A few minutes later, Martha peeked her head in the door and, seeing that all was quiet, led Will into the classroom. Ada decided not to continue with family signs. They'd had enough drama for one day.

The rest of the morning went fairly well, with one major outburst from Will and, when Ada's back was turned, a sudden screaming session from Nathan. Ada had no idea what had prompted it, but she managed to calm him before the parents arrived.

Despite the morning being less hectic than the day before, Ada was drained by the time most of the students had been picked up. Even with no accident to delay her today, Will's *mamm* again breezed in fifteen minutes after school let out. Ada suspected Miriam was chronically late.

Betty had already arrived to help Martha with Nathan, and she eyed Miriam. "School is over at precisely noon. It is unfair to ask the teacher to watch Will after that time."

Miriam shriveled under her gaze. "I'm sorry," she said meekly. "I'll try not to be late again."

"Don't bother to try; see that you do it."

As she had that morning, Ada puzzled over Betty's sharp tone.

Shoulders slumped, Miriam approached Will and convinced him to leave his favorite windmill toy. Outside, in her family's buggy, Martha was dodging Lukas's kicks and flailing arms as she tried to calm him.

Ada stood in the doorway, ready to intervene if Martha needed help.

Betty came up behind her. "You're free to go."

"I was just waiting to see if Martha needed any help."

"There's no need." Betty's tone brooked no argument. "My daughter is perfectly able to care for Lukas."

"I wasn't doubting her abilities. I only wanted—"

"I'm tired of people underestimating her," Betty burst out. "She's capable."

Ada was taken aback by her vehemence. "I know she's capable. She's a marvel in the classroom. I couldn't teach without her help."

Her words seemed to mollify Betty, who sighed. "I'm sorry for being so *gretzy* today. Having two special children makes it hard to cope sometimes."

Ada reached out and touched her arm. "I understand." After being in the classroom for half a day, she could easily imagine the stress of dealing with outbursts all week long.

"Thank you." Betty motioned to Ada's buggy. "You can go. I'm sure the day wasn't easy. Martha and I will be fine."

"If you're sure?" Ada hesitated to leave until Lukas was calm and inside the schoolhouse. But when Betty shooed her toward her buggy, Ada turned and signed to David, who was building a block tower with Nathan. Her brother made a face, but stood and started heading toward her.

With a loud cry, Nathan grabbed David's leg and tried

to drag him back. David tumbled to the floor, cracking his elbow and scattering the blocks. He scrambled to a sitting position, cradling his elbow, and burst out crying.

Nathan looked startled and a bit uncertain, but when David's tears started, Nathan howled. Ada crossed the room, sank to the floor, and wrapped her arms around both boys. A commotion in the doorway drew her attention. Martha had been leading Lukas through the doorway, but all the chaos and noise set him off. Jerking away from Martha, he took off into the parking lot, and Martha ran after him.

What more could possibly go wrong? A scuffling in the doorway provided an answer. Josiah had arrived.

* * *

Josiah stood at the threshold, uncertain what to do, how to help. His predictions of Nathan hurting someone must have come true. Outside the schoolhouse, Martha was chasing a screaming Lukas who was probably running because of Nathan's cries. David was in tears, no doubt due to Nathan, and Ada was struggling to calm his bawling son. Josiah wanted to race over, grab Nathan, apologize to everyone, and escape.

Instead, he did what he had done that morning, moved to a spot where he could observe without being seen. As long as he stayed out of his son's line of sight, Ada might be able to calm him as she had before.

She sat on the floor, her dress spread around her, an arm around each boy. She tilted her head and rested her cheek against Nathan's hair, and Josiah's heart somersaulted in his chest. The sweet gesture was one a mother would make while comforting her child. A loving gesture Nathan hadn't experienced in almost a year. Nathan's sobs quieted until he was gulping breaths through his open mouth. When his crying ceased completely, Nathan tipped back his head and met Ada's eyes. A message passed between them. Then Nathan reached up his small hand and patted Ada's cheek. Through misty eyes, Josiah imprinted the picture on his heart.

Behind him, Martha had caught up with Lukas and wrapped her arms around him. The ruckus died down as Martha murmured softly to her brother.

Inside, Nathan knelt beside Ada as she examined David's elbow. She mouthed something to her brother that made him laugh. Nathan copied his example, then with a puzzled frown on his forehead, watched their mouths intently as they communicated. At each exchange, David's smile widened until he burst into laughter. Nathan joined in. Josiah's heart expanded even more. He'd dreamed of sharing moments like this with his son.

Wanting so badly to be part of the group, to share their mirth, Josiah stepped through the door. Ada noticed him first and, at the invitation in her eyes to join them, his pulse quickened. He crossed the floor toward them.

Nathan, who had scrambled to his feet when David did, had one hand resting on Ada's shoulder and his head thrown back in deep-throated giggles. Her arm encircled him, holding him close. David stood facing both of them, signing quickly.

Ada's face glowed, her lips curved in a delicious smile. "You're off work early."

Before Josiah could explain, Nathan looked over and saw him approaching. His son's mouth snapped shut, cutting off the chuckle, and he froze in place. His eyes wide, he ducked behind Ada. In one brief moment, his joy erupted into a fury of fireworks.

Shame heating his cheeks, Josiah strode over to pick up his son. Nathan reached out for Ada, as if begging her to save him. Josiah debated letting her try, but embarrassment and Betty's disapproving glare made him hasten out of the schoolhouse, carrying his squalling son.

* * *

Ada struggled to regain her composure as Josiah headed toward the door. She'd just managed to calm Nathan when his father's appearance set him off again. And Josiah's appearance hadn't only disturbed his son, it had created an equally intense reaction inside Ada. Guiltily, she glanced at Betty to see if the bishop's wife had noticed.

But Betty, her arms crossed, was glowering at Josiah. She harrumphed as he strode across the school yard. "That child needs more discipline."

Ada disagreed. She'd noticed Nathan's reluctance to be around his *daed* before. Nathan had gone out of his way to avoid Josiah at her house yesterday. He'd cringed when his father came closer. He threw tantrums when he was around his *daed*, but calmed when she approached. Something wasn't right. Yesterday Sadie had vented her irritation through sarcasm and defiance. But what if you had no way to express your feelings? Would the frustration build up until you exploded?

Chapter Sixteen

The whole way home, Ada mulled over Nathan's situation. If he had words to express his feelings, it might decrease his tantrums. The more his vocabulary grew, the better he could communicate. She'd work on some feeling words with him to see if that helped.

The only thing that baffled her was that Nathan never seemed to exhibit those outbursts around her, only his *daed*. Several times yesterday, that had been obvious. Maybe she needed to observe their interactions more closely to see what was causing Nathan to act out.

For now, though, she'd enjoy the rest of the day off. Beside her, David wriggled on the seat. He'd been trying to point out things they were passing, but she'd been too preoccupied to notice. She focused on her brother and let her worries drift away.

The minute they pulled in the driveway, Mary Elizabeth shot out of the house and across the lawn and hurtled herself into Ada's arms. Sadie, who had followed her out the door, walked at a more dignified pace.

"How was she?" Ada asked.

Sadie shrugged, but Mary Elizabeth bubbled over. "Rebecca said I did much better today."

Sadie flicked her eyes heavenward. "I guess you could call it better. She only cried three times."

"That's good, isn't it, Ada? Because I really, really missed you."

Ada had no idea how long the crying lasted or how much class time she'd interrupted. She'd need Rebecca's input on that. "It sounds as if you did better than yesterday."

"Ask her how many times she growled today." Sadie blew out an exasperated breath.

"Josiah told me to act like Daniel."

"Daniel," Sadie said in her superior-older-sister manner, "did not growl. The lions did."

Ada held up a hand. "That's enough. I'm glad Mary Elizabeth cried less today. Perhaps she could work on growling less. For now, I hope you'll be patient, Sadie." Ada pinned her sister with a look.

Sadie lowered her eyes and mumbled an *I'm sorry*.

Mary Elizabeth beamed. "I forgive you, Sadie."

"So who would like to go with me to the health food store today? Leah asked me to stop by." Ada tapped David on the knee and mouthed the invitation. He brightened, and Mary Elizabeth danced around.

"I'll go call the others," Sadie offered, and Ada gave her a grateful smile.

All of her siblings liked accompanying her to Leah's

family's store, because the neighboring farm had goats and a large playground for the kids.

When they arrived at Stoltzfus Natural Products Store, Ada pulled the buggy close to the fence by the goat farm, and everyone raced over to see the goats. Everyone but Sadie. Ada sighed internally. Her sister must be getting too old for goat-watching.

"Do you want to come with me?" Ada asked, but Sadie shook her head. "Will you keep an eye on the others then?"

Sadie dragged her feet on the way over to her siblings, who were standing by the fence calling to the goats.

When Ada walked into the store, the bells attached to the door jingled. Leah glanced up and smiled, but she held up a hand, signaling for Ada to wait as she tapped each small jar on the counter with a fingertip. Then she recorded the number in the open ledger beside her. When she was done, she looked up with her usual beaming face. "Sorry. I'm doing inventory, and if I lose count, I have to start all over." She closed the ledger with a snap. "This can wait. How are you? How is the teaching going?"

Leah's bubbly voice always made Ada's spirits rise. She tried to match her friend's cheery greeting, but the school day had drained her energy. "I'm fine."

"That bad?" Leah's sympathetic look made Ada feel guilty.

The day hadn't been that bad. The meltdowns had been minimal, and the children had learned a few things. Ada still wanted to do more to reach Will, Lukas, and Emily, but everyone had learned a little sign language, and they seemed to enjoy the math counters and patterns.

Leah waved a hand in front of Ada's face. "Are you all right? Tell me about it."

Ada had barely started when the bells jangled. She waited while Leah waved to the customer who'd entered behind her.

"Hi, Josiah," Leah gushed.

At the sound of his name, Ada turned, and her breath caught in her throat.

Josiah stood near the door, gazing out the glass. "Hello, Leah. And Ada," he said without turning toward them. "*Mamm* asked me to pick up her usual order. She also suggested I ask about any remedies for calming children."

Reaching onto the shelf behind her, Leah pulled down a bag. "Here are your *Mamm*'s herbs and teas. If you follow me, I'll show you our Added Attention Vitamins. They're right down this aisle."

"I hate to bother you, but could you bring it here?" Josiah flashed her a pleading smile and returned his attention to the parking lot. "Nathan's sleeping in the buggy. After his escape yesterday, I don't want to take my eyes off him."

"His escape?"

"I'm sure Ada will tell you the whole story. She was the one who found him." Josiah turned the full force of his smile in Ada's direction.

Ada worried she was grinning like a fool.

"Sounds like you two have been having some interesting adventures together." Leah raised her eyebrows at Ada.

It's not what you think, she wanted to tell her friend, but with Josiah standing there, she remained silent.

The bell on the door tinkled, and an elderly woman hobbled in. Josiah turned his heart-stopping smile in her direction and leaned forward to hold open the door, deflating Ada's excitement. She'd misread the warmth of his smile, a smile he seemed to bestow on everyone equally.

After Leah had waited on the customer, she disappeared down an aisle and returned with a white plastic bottle that she carried over to Josiah. "Some parents claim this works well."

He read the label between glances out the window. "That sounds good." He looked up at Leah with the same smile that had set Ada's pulse racing, and Ada's heart constricted at the sunny smile Leah returned. "How much do I owe you?"

"Let me go figure it out." Leah held out her hand. "Would you like me to put that in the bag?"

Josiah passed the bottle to her without glancing up. "Thanks."

Was it Ada's imagination, or did her friend look flustered? And had their fingers touched when Leah took the bottle?

As Leah sidled past Ada to get to the register, she gestured toward the board near the entryway where notices were pinned. "I thought you might be interested in that pink one, Ada. A lady from the *Englisch* school put it up a few days ago."

Ada walked over to the board, trying to calm her fluttering pulse as she stood only a few inches away from Josiah.

"Am I in your way?" He edged over to give her more room.

Not at all, she wanted to say. She mentally scolded herself for being disappointed. She had trouble paying attention to the corkboard instead of the tanned forearm so close she could reach out and stroke. *Ada Rupp! What is wrong with you?*

She turned her body until his arm, sprinkled with dark hairs, was no longer in view and searched for the paper Leah had mentioned. Amid notices about auctions, fundraisers, and specials on carpentry and woodwork, the bright pink flyer stood out. The heading, "New Strategies for Special Needs Children," caught her eye. Several specialists were speaking at a local school that evening. Ada sighed. She'd love to hear them.

Leah looked up from the register. "What was that sigh for?"

"The program sounds wonderful. It's about special needs children, so it would really help my teaching."

"I know. That's why I suggested it." The cash register dinged as Leah punched in numbers.

"I can't ask Sadie to babysit. Not at night." Putting everyone to bed was too much to expect from her sister even when things were going well, but with Sadie's recent attitude, it would be impossible. "I wish *Daed*..."

"I know." Leah glanced over with sympathy in her eyes before placing Josiah's bottle in the bag with his *mamm*'s order. "What day is it? Maybe I could babysit."

"I couldn't ask you to do that." Ada tried to keep the disappointment from her voice. "Besides, the program's tonight."

"*Ach*, I'm sorry. I should have mentioned it sooner."

Leah scurried over to Josiah with the bag and told him the price. "I'll be right back with your change," she said as she headed for the cash register with his money. She counted out some bills and coins before closing the drawer with a snap. "I wish I didn't have to work tonight, Ada."

"What time is the program?" Josiah asked, startling Ada so much she jumped.

"Seven to nine," she read from the flyer.

"I'd be happy to watch your siblings so you can go," he said.

Ada stared at him, speechless. What a generous offer. Finding willing babysitters for seven children was almost impossible. "Thank you," she finally stuttered out. "But I can't accept—"

"I promise I won't kidnap them this time." He glanced at her with a twinkle in his eye.

"I—I didn't think you would." Ada had never been so near him for this long before, and she couldn't seem to draw in a breath. That must be why she was so dizzy and lightheaded.

"I'll be there at six thirty, if that will give you enough time."

"It would be plenty of time, but I can't accept your offer." Ada managed to get out a whole sentence despite her shortness of breath.

Josiah looked hurt. "You don't trust me?"

"No, yes. I mean, I do trust you, but…" When he looked at her like that, Ada couldn't think, couldn't remember what she planned to say.

Leah stood transfixed looking from one to the other, her eyes wide and curious.

Josiah strode to the door and pushed it open. "If it's not a trust issue, I'll see you at six thirty."

"No, no, wait," Ada called after him. "It's too much to ask of you."

He pivoted, a smile crinkling the corner of his eyes. "I don't think so. Not after I woke you at three a.m."

Behind Ada, Leah sucked in a breath. The minute the door slammed behind Josiah, Leah clutched Ada's arm. "What is going on between you two?"

"Nothing," Ada answered, but the truth sent a pang through her.

"Ada Rupp, I don't believe you." Leah pitched her voice low and imitated Josiah's words, "*Not after I woke you at three a.m.*" Putting her hands on her hips, she said, "What exactly does *that* mean?"

"It's a long story."

Leah placed herself between Ada and the door. "I'm not letting you leave until you tell me every word of it." When Ada protested, Leah only crossed her arms and refused to budge.

So, between Leah's gasps and exclamations, Ada recounted yesterday's events.

When she finished, Leah shook her head. "You know he's—"

"Yes, I know." Why did everyone think it was their duty to warn her Josiah was married? *Perhaps because your attraction to him is so obvious.*

Leah exhaled loudly. "I don't see you for a few days, and all this happens. My news pales in comparison to that."

"Ada, Ada." The twins burst into the shop, both talking at once. "Mary Elizabeth fell on her head."

"Where is she?" Ada raced out the door, following the twins to the goat pen, and almost ran into Josiah. She held out a hand to avert a collision, and her hand accidentally bumped into his chest. Although she yearned to stroke the hard muscles her fingertips had encountered, she jerked her hand away, unsure if she was out of breath from running or from touching him. If she didn't get some air soon, she might faint. She gasped in a breath, hoping Josiah would think it was from racing across the parking lot.

He held a muddy Mary Elizabeth by the hand. "I'm sorry I didn't get to her in time to stop her tumble. I saw it but was too late."

"Oh, Mary Elizabeth." Yesterday flour, today mud.

"Thank you." Ada had been so focused on the spot her hand had touched on his chest, she'd missed the mud smeared on his pants and shoes as well as the arm and hand her sister was clutching. "I'm so sorry."

Josiah laughed. "A little mud never hurt anyone." Then he sobered. "Except for the ones who have to clean it up, I suppose."

Right now, that was the least of Ada's worries. Catching her breath was one of her major concerns, along with wondering if Josiah could tell what his nearness was doing to her.

He turned Mary Elizabeth over to her, and their hands brushed. Ada swallowed hard and concentrated on her sister. "Did you hurt yourself anywhere?" She wished her voice were steadier and stronger.

Mary Elizabeth shook her head, sending mud flying and spattering Josiah even more. Ada pinched her lips together and prayed for patience. She started to apologize, but Josiah waved it away.

He glanced down at his already muddy clothes. "It didn't hurt anything." Josiah turned toward the goat pen, where David and Nathan were hanging on the fence, side by side.

"Nathan got out?" Ada asked.

Josiah looked chagrined. "Last time he slipped out the driver's side. Despite all my careful watching, I didn't monitor the passenger door. I figured it would be too heavy for him. I suspect he had some help."

The only help would have been from her family. "I'm sorry."

"Don't be. It's good for Nathan to have friends, and they seem to be a calming influence on him. If only I could be too." Josiah heaved a sigh.

Ada's heart ached at the sadness in his voice. Teaching Nathan sign language might help eventually, but she wished she had a solution to help him now. She longed to offer to teach Josiah sign language too, but with her emotions ricocheting out of control whenever he was around, that wouldn't be wise.

"I'd better get going," Josiah said. "I'll see you at six thirty."

"No, I can't let—"

"I always keep my promises. I promised to be there, so I will." He headed toward Nathan, leaving Ada spluttering.

As soon as Nathan noticed his *daed* coming toward him, he cringed and opened his mouth as if to scream.

Again, Ada noticed his odd response. Was Nathan expressing his disappointment at leaving his friends, or was there more to it?

"Josiah," Ada called, "Why don't you let Nathan stay

with David? We'd be happy to have him, and it won't be for long if you're coming over soon."

Josiah halted and backed up a few steps. Nathan closed his mouth, but watched his *daed* warily.

Shoulders slumped, Josiah pivoted and walked toward Ada. "I don't want to put you to any trouble."

Ada laughed. "I'm offering to watch one child for a few hours, while you're going to watch seven extra in return."

At her teasing, some of the light came back into his eyes. "When you put it like that..."

As Josiah turned to go, Ada urged her siblings to get in the buggy. While they were clambering in, her gaze remained focused on his retreating back.

Once he pulled out, her breathing returned to normal. "I'm going inside to let Leah know Mary Elizabeth is all right." She turned to Sadie.

Before she could say a word, Sadie grumbled, "I know, I know. I'll watch everyone."

"I appreciate it," Ada assured her. "I'll try to hurry."

She crossed the parking lot and stuck her head inside the store. "Sorry, I have to go. Mary Elizabeth's covered in mud." At the questioning look in Leah's eyes, Ada added, "She fell over the fence and into the goat pen. She's fine, but her clothes are a mess."

"Oh, dear." Leah suppressed a laugh. "She does seem to keep you hopping."

"I wanted to hear your news, though."

Leah's eyes took on a dreamy look. "I helped deliver Lizzie's brother last night. Actually I did more than help. Sharon let me do most of it on my own." She leaned forward, placing her elbows on the counter, an excited expression on her face. "And she asked if I wanted to train under her."

"But you can't be certified." It would be a shame for Leah to put in all the training and then not be able to practice. Sharon Nolt, the certified midwife who delivered all the Amish home births, was a Mennonite.

"That's the best news of all. Sharon checked into state regulations, and uncertified midwives can deliver babies. So I'm going to be a midwife!"

The joy on Leah's face filled Ada's heart to overflowing. "I'm so happy for you!"

"I still have to tell *Mamm* and *Daed*, but I'll find a way to convince them."

Ada laughed. "I'm sure you will." As the youngest of eight, Leah managed to charm her parents the way she did everyone else.

Leah hugged herself, as if hugging her secret close. "Don't tell anyone yet, please."

"Of course not. I'm happy for you. I'll stop back another day to hear more about it. Right now, though, I'd better take my muddy sister home." *And prepare for Josiah's visit.*

Chapter Seventeen

On the way home, she told her siblings Josiah would be taking care of them that evening while she attended a meeting.

Once again, Sadie looked sulky. "I like Josiah, but don't you trust me to take care of everyone?"

If Ada hadn't been driving the buggy, she'd be rubbing her aching forehead. No matter what she did, she seemed to upset Sadie. Keeping her voice even, she said, "If you'd like the responsibility, I'll let Josiah know. You can take full charge, and he can sit in the living room in case anyone has an emergency. Is that what you want me to do?"

Sadie sucked in her out-thrust lower lip and stayed silent for a moment. Then she said, "No, I don't want to take care of everyone, but I wish you had asked me first."

"I see." Ada clenched the reins. She seemed to be

praying for patience fairly frequently the past few days and more so in the past few hours.

As soon as they got home, Ada assigned chores to everyone but Sadie and Noah, because her brother had to do the milking and care for the horses. "Can you hitch up the carriage?" she asked Noah as he motioned for David to follow him out to the barn.

"You left me out." This time instead of sticking out, Sadie's lower lip was quivering.

"I'm giving you a break," Ada said as she marched Mary Elizabeth off for a bath.

"But I wanted to do something for Josiah too." Sadie flounced past them. Her sister had evidently taken a liking to Josiah.

Ada rubbed her temples. The dull ache she'd had driving home had increased to a steady pounding. Not sure what would mollify Sadie, Ada racked her brains to think of something that might be more fun than work as her sister stomped down the stairs.

"Why don't you make a snack for him," Ada called after her, "but it'll have to be something that doesn't need flour." She wasn't positive, but Sadie might have snickered.

Once Mary Elizabeth was done with her bath, Ada had her pull up a chair and grease the casserole dish and shred the chicken. Hannah was busy chopping the onions, and the twins had started the noodles and peas. On the other side of the kitchen, Sadie was hunched over a dish on the table. When all the ingredients were ready, Ada helped Mary Elizabeth mix the casserole and put it in the oven.

By the time dinner was ready, David, Nathan, and the

twins were bathed and dressed in their nightwear. Ada had added all the muddy clothes, including Nathan's, to the laundry pile filled with floury dresses. Tomorrow this towering stack would provide Mary Elizabeth's first lesson in washing clothes. Nathan was dressed in Noah's outgrown T-shirt and pajama pants.

During the meal, everyone chattered about Josiah's arrival except Nathan. Sensing his friend's discomfort, David took him upstairs to his room as soon as dinner ended. Though her siblings begged, Sadie kept her special snack covered with a towel so nobody could peek before Josiah arrived. While the girls washed the dishes, Ada left the kitchen to freshen up and collect a notebook and pen. She could hardly contain her own excitement, although she'd be hard-pressed to say which elated her more—seeing Josiah or attending the class.

When the knock came at six thirty, all the girls were waiting by the door. David and Nathan remained upstairs. Noah was in the barn readying the carriage.

"Guess what, Josiah!" Mary Elizabeth bounced to the door. "I made dinner all by myself."

"It isn't all by yourself if everyone else cooks the ingredients," Sadie said dryly. Then she added, "Besides it's *hochmut* to brag about what you do."

Tears swam in Mary Elizabeth's eyes, and she ducked her head.

Josiah placed a hand on her shoulder. "The first time you make a meal is special, even if other people help."

Hannah, who rarely spoke, said softly, "Isn't it also a sin to judge someone else, Sadie?"

Sadie had the grace to look embarrassed, but then she brightened. "I have a surprise for you, Josiah."

"I can hardly wait," he replied, "but I want to check on Nathan first, and let's make sure Ada is ready to go."

Josiah's eyes met hers, and the room around her disappeared as she got lost in their depths. "I—I should go, so I'm not late."

"Drive carefully. I hope you enjoy your evening."

Ada clutched her notebook to her chest, struggling to hide her nervousness. "Thank you," she said as she headed for the door. Before she closed it behind her, she added, "And I hope you enjoy your evening as well."

Josiah chuckled. "I'm sure I will."

* * *

Josiah stared after Ada until a tug on his arm reminded him of his duties. Mary Elizabeth pulled him toward the kitchen. "Do you want some of Sadie's special dessert?"

"That sounds good." He allowed Mary Elizabeth to show him to a chair, the same one he'd sat in last night, except he missed seeing Ada's smiling face across the table.

She stood beside him, a serious look on her face. "You're sitting in *Daed*'s chair, but he won't ever sit there again."

"Mary Elizabeth," Sadie warned. "You know better."

When Sadie turned her back to get plates from the cupboard, Mary Elizabeth leaned close to his ear and whispered, "It's a secret because what Ada did to *Daed* was bad. Real bad." Mary Elizabeth straightened up as Sadie headed to the table.

Josiah sat stunned. He was unsure how much of a six-year-old's story he should believe and wondered what

Mary Elizabeth considered "real bad." The bishop had told him about Ada's *mamm* being ill and then dying, but he never mentioned her *daed*. Ada seemed too sweet and loving to hurt someone.

Sadie plopped a casserole dish on the table. "I'm sorry this is a no-bake dessert, but we didn't have any flour." She directed a pointed look at Mary Elizabeth.

Remembering yesterday's flour disaster, Josiah hid a smile. "This looks delicious. Should we call the others to share it?"

From the pained expression on Sadie's face, she hadn't planned to include everyone else, but she went to the stairs and called up. Seconds later, they all thundered down the steps. Josiah smiled to see Nathan all ready for bed and part of the group. Not only did David stand with him like a bodyguard, but Noah also laid a protective hand on Nathan's shoulder. Josiah's pleasure dissolved when he realized the person they were protecting him from was ... *Me. He's scared of me.*

David led Nathan to the far end of the table, where he'd sat yesterday. The whole time Nathan cast wary looks at Josiah. His son had trouble enjoying his snack because he kept glancing up to check Josiah's end of the table, as if worried Josiah would jump up and snatch him away from his friends.

I'm not an ogre, Josiah wanted to tell Nathan and his protectors. *I'd never hurt him. Never in a million years.* His heart heavy, Josiah ate two of the peanut butter bars. Judging by everyone else's expressions and requests for seconds and thirds, the dessert was a hit, but Josiah barely tasted it.

When the dish was empty, Sadie collected the plates

and ordered everyone to brush their teeth. She even supplied Nathan with a new toothbrush from the pantry. Josiah offered to help with the dishes and took advantage of the opportunity alone with her to build bridges.

"I understand you're the one in charge when Ada's gone," he began.

Sadie seemed to be struggling to hide a smile as she filled the sink with dishwater. "Not when you're here."

"The problem is," Josiah continued, "I have no idea what everyone's usual bedtime routine is, so I'll need your help. If you don't mind."

"I'm happy to help." Sadie flashed him a smile and plunged a stack of plates in the dishwater.

"That's a relief. I was worried about getting everything wrong." Josiah wasn't only saying that to make Sadie feel better. The pressure to do a good job weighed heavily on him. He already felt like a failure as a *daed*, and now he might have lost his job. He'd like to succeed at one thing today.

Sadie washed, he dried, and she put away. Meanwhile, the others brushed their teeth and got ready for bed. The household worked like a well-oiled laundry wheel. Josiah's eyes stung as they straightened their rooms and laid out their clothing for the next morning. The only bedtime routine he'd known for the last nine months involved kicking and screaming, tears and exhaustion. And after his son finally fell asleep, Josiah ended up on his hands and knees cleaning up things that had been flung or had broken.

"Before bed we have story time," Mary Elizabeth informed him.

Story time? Josiah's heart sank. He hadn't read a story

to a child since...He swallowed. Since Nathan was a toddler. There'd been no time for reading when Ruth and Nathan came back from Mexico—and he couldn't find a way to communicate the story even if there had been. "I'm not sure I'll be good at this."

"That's all right." Mary Elizabeth led him into the living room, handed him the Bible story book, and crawled into his lap. The twins crowded close to him on the couch, with Sadie on one side and Hannah on the other.

David pulled a reluctant Nathan into the room. Though David tried to get him to join the group, Nathan resisted. Josiah's throat constricted when his son crouched in the farthest corner of the room. David, his eyes sad, glanced at everyone sitting on the couch, but went over and sat beside Nathan. Noah followed them. Nathan, sucking on his rabbit's ear, stared at him with wide, fearful eyes.

"I'll sign for the boys," Sadie said.

A dart pierced Josiah's heart. He couldn't remember holding his son on his lap the way he was holding Mary Elizabeth. Not since Ruth died. His voice thick, Josiah asked, "What story shall I read?"

"Anything but 'Daniel and the Lion's Den,'" Sadie begged.

"You don't like that story?" Josiah asked. Maybe it was too scary for the younger ones.

"I like it a lot," Sadie said as she rearranged her position until she faced the boys. "We've just been having trouble with Mary Elizabeth growling all day."

The twins giggled. "She goes around like this." They bared their teeth and curled their fingers into claws.

Josiah squeezed his eyes shut, torn between laughter

and chagrin. Had she copied his demonstration from last night? He only hoped the lesson that went along with the growling had sunk in.

Mary Elizabeth sniffled. "They all make fun of me for trying to be brave."

Josiah tightened his arm around her. "Being brave is hard, but I'm glad you're trying."

She looked up at him with adoring eyes.

"It would be nice if she tried harder," Sadie said. "And stopped the growling."

To defuse the tension, Josiah held up the book. "So what story should we read?"

Sadie suggested Queen Esther, and everyone agreed, although Josiah suspected that Mary Elizabeth's older siblings were hoping she'd adopt a new model of bravery. Josiah stumbled his way through the story, while Sadie translated it into sign language. He glanced at Nathan surreptitiously from time to time, but from his son's frowning concentration on Sadie's hands, Nathan wasn't understanding much of the story.

When the story was over, they bowed their heads for prayer and then scattered to their rooms. David took Nathan's hand and led him upstairs. Later when Josiah slipped upstairs to check that all was well, the children were sound asleep, including his son, who was curled at the foot of David's bed, wrapped in another quilt, his rabbit clutched in his hand.

Josiah's eyes burned with unshed tears. His son had fit into this family after only a few short days, and he trusted them. Yet he distrusted his own father. Josiah had to find a way to regain that trust and become a family again.

* * *

Ada eased the front door open so she wouldn't wake her siblings and stopped dead. Josiah sat on the sofa engrossed in a book, the picture of domestic bliss. All of Ada's dreams came rushing back. To be married, to share a home with a man who loved her and cared for her. Though she had no right to do so, she let fantasy overtake reality.

And then he did look up. Only it wasn't her future husband, but Josiah meeting her eyes. A shock zinged through her as their gazes connected. She forced herself to lower her eyes, to fight her way through the confusion clouding her thoughts.

"Hi," she croaked. "How did everything go with the children?"

Josiah seemed as flummoxed as she was. "Um, fine." He blinked. "You've done a wonderful job of organizing your household. Everything ran smoothly, and the children all went to bed on their own. Even Nathan. He's sleeping at the foot of David's bed."

Ada blew out a breath. "I'm glad they didn't give you any trouble." She'd worried they might use her absence as an excuse to flout the rules.

"So how was your meeting?"

"It was wonderful. I learned so much," Ada enthused. "One lady runs a summer camp for children with autism, and she showed pictures of their play area with a rope the children scale to ring a bell, wide wooden balance beams, hammocks, net swings, and so much more. Wouldn't it be wonderful to have something like that for our school?" All they had were some balls and sidewalk chalk for recess.

"I'm sure the children would enjoy it."

"It's also good for them. Each section helps with different sensory and motor skills. And you wouldn't believe what they have indoors." Ada described the swings they used in place of desks. "There's so much I'd like to try."

The school held an auction every fall, but proceeds went for maintenance and other costs. She planned to buy picture boards and weighted neck rolls or blankets with the small amount she'd been allotted, but the rest of the equipment was only a dream. Like her dreams of the future.

*   *   *

Josiah had trouble following some of Ada's narrative because she recited the equipment and techniques so quickly, and most were new to him, but he was captivated by her flow of words, her passion. Josiah had always considered her attractive, but when she was animated like this, she was irresistible.

Her face grew wistful as she talked about sand tables, pet therapy, and slides for children in wheelchairs. The more she shared, the more Josiah wished he could fulfill her dreams. The crumpled flyer on the floor of his buggy mocked him. That Anderson & Sons contest might have funded a project like this one, but he wasn't sure if he was part of the company anymore.

Ada continued, "I also found out about a daycare program for special children that runs several days a week. They have one-on-one aides, and each child has an individualized program. Isn't that wonderful?"

What was even more wonderful was her enthusiasm and interest, her love for learning, and her glowing face as she spoke. Josiah couldn't keep his eyes off her.

"One of the volunteers invited me to come for a tour tomorrow afternoon, and I plan to take David. Would it be all right to take Nathan? I know you had asked Betty and Martha to watch him."

Josiah forced himself to focus on what she was saying. She'd asked about taking Nathan somewhere tomorrow. He wasn't sure where, but he needed to get his thoughts headed back to the conversation rather than on staring at Ada. He hoped lighthearted humor was appropriate with what she'd asked. "If I say it's too much to expect of you, I suppose you'll remind me I watched your siblings tonight."

"*Jah*, I would say that." Ada laughed, then turned pleading eyes to him. "Please let me take him along."

When she looked at him like that, how could he resist her pleading? "So where is this place you're headed?"

She gave him the name of the center and address. "They're open until six, so you could pick him up at the center after work."

Work. The word hit Josiah like a punch in the gut. He wasn't sure whether or not he'd have a job on Thursday.

Ada must have mistaken his silence for tiredness. "I'm sorry," she said. "I didn't mean to keep you up so late."

Josiah stood. "I'm sure you need your sleep after last night. I'll go get Nathan."

Ada reached out a hand, but stopped short of putting it on his arm. "He's sound asleep, isn't he? It would be a shame to wake him. Why don't you let him spend the night?"

"I couldn't do that. It's too much for you to do"—he waved a hand to prevent her from saying it—"even if I did watch your siblings tonight."

"Exactly."

He was too tired to argue. All the missed sleep from last night had caught up with him. He acquiesced. But one thing he knew for sure. He was treading on dangerous ground.

Chapter Eighteen

Ada could hardly wait for the school day to be over so she could visit the center. After four meltdowns (one for Nathan, two for Lukas, and one for Will) and one runaway (Lukas), Ada was exhausted and determined to try some of the equipment and techniques she'd learned about last night.

Hope Musser, the Mennonite volunteer she'd met last night, greeted them in the lobby and took them on a tour of the building. In the first room, a teacher and a young boy were working on matching handheld computers. "Katie teaches speech to hearing-impaired students," Hope said.

Ada had no idea how Josiah would feel about Nathan using a computer, but the boys watched in fascination. Hope herded them down the hall to the next rooms, while Ada made mental notes of activities she could try at school.

In the craft room, Hope motioned to the arts and

crafts activities and then indicated a central table, which held stacks of newspapers. Two children were tearing them into strips. "Children on the autism spectrum enjoy repetitive tasks like this. It's good for their fine motor coordination, but they're also helping the community. They stuff strips into waterproof plastic to create mattresses for the homeless."

"What a wonderful idea!" Ada said. She could try that with Will and Lukas.

They moved quickly through the academic rooms on each side of the hall and passed the lunch room, where a few children were eating with their aides.

When they reached the final room, Hope opened the door a crack and peeked in. "This is our MSE room, meaning multi-sensory environment. No one's in here now, so you can come in and enjoy it. Children who are out of control come here to calm down."

Ada stood in the doorway, stunned. Dark walls made the room feel like a cave; it was lit by only a small strand of pastel-colored miniature lights high on the wall. Giggling, Nathan and David dove into a pit filled with grapefruit-sized plastic balls. After throwing a few back and forth, they lay on their backs and closed their eyes. Nathan kept a tight grip on his rabbit, as if worried he might lose it in the ball pit. A net swing and a soft reclining chair offered other places to relax. Headphones allowed children to listen to music or block out noise.

"Oh, I wish I could have something like this at the schoolhouse," Ada said. It might have soothed some of the morning meltdowns.

"Looks like it calmed the boys," a deep voice said behind her.

Ada whirled and almost bumped into Josiah, who stood close behind her. "Josiah! I—I wasn't expecting you so early."

His face colored a deep crimson. "I finished what I had to do today, so I decided to stop by."

Hope cleared her throat. She handed Ada two booklets. "Here," she said. "These are the catalogs I mentioned last night. I have a student coming soon, but feel free to show your *friend* around." The way she emphasized *friend* implied a romantic connection.

Ada's cheeks heated. Had her interest in Josiah been that obvious? She took the catalogs, hoping her face didn't match the red adaptive tricycle on the cover. "Thank you so much for these and for the tour," she said to Hope, before turning to Josiah. "These catalogs have equipment in them. Some of the things I was talking about last night."

After Hope walked down the hall, Josiah leaned his head close to hers while she flipped through the pages, and Ada's hands shook as she found the page she was looking for. "I want swings like these for the classroom." She gasped as she read the price. "I didn't realize they'd be so expensive."

"They wouldn't be too hard to make," Josiah said.

"Really?" She made the mistake of glancing up at him and couldn't look away. Ada worried he could hear her heart hammering.

Josiah broke their eye contact and then nodded. "A lot of those materials could, um, be bought for less." He seemed a bit nervous, and Ada was afraid he'd read the interest in her eyes. Waving a hand toward the hallway, he said, "This place looks great, and Nathan seems to be comfortable here."

"I could continue bringing the boys in the afternoons this week, if you'd like."

Josiah hesitated, and she expected him to protest. He surprised her by saying, "I'd appreciate that."

He peeked in the MSE room where Nathan had now stretched out on the reclining chair. He had his eyes closed and his rabbit clutched to his chest. David looked up from the swing and waved.

"Would you like a quick tour of the other rooms?" Ada asked shyly.

Josiah nodded, and Ada confirmed with an employee that the boys could stay in the MSE room for a few minutes. Josiah seemed to be interested in the center, but maybe he was only being polite. He listened intently, though, when she pointed out things in each room she wished she could do at the schoolhouse. Just before they arrived back at the MSE room, Josiah stopped. "Would you mind if I waited outside in the parking lot? Just in case Nathan gets upset when he sees me? I don't want to disrupt the others in the center."

"Of course." Ada's heart went out to him. How hard it must be to have your son react that way. She waited until she was sure he'd reached the lobby before she entered the room. She breathed in the peaceful environment for a few moments and then tapped her brother on the shoulder.

David's face fell. *I want to stay*, he signed.

Ada ruffled his hair and signed that Nathan's *daed* was waiting. David sighed and went to get Nathan, who also looked reluctant to leave.

We'll come back tomorrow, she mouthed to both of them. David grinned and clapped. A puzzled frown

182   *Rachel J. Good*

creased Nathan's forehead as she spoke, but he followed David's example.

Ada reached for David's hand, and after a questioning glance, Nathan took her other hand. She smiled down at him and was rewarded with a brilliant smile. When they exited the center, Ada searched for Josiah and spotted him standing by his buggy at the far end of the parking lot, a great distance from where all the other buggies were parked.

She headed in that direction, both boys skipping along beside her until Nathan spotted his father. He stopped dead, dragging on her arm, as if trying to pull her back. Josiah took a few steps toward him, and Nathan ducked behind her, trembling. On her other side, David froze.

Ada turned and knelt to face Nathan. Throwing his arms around her neck, he buried his face against her shoulder, his whole body shaking. She hugged him close for a few seconds, then took him by the shoulders to look into his eyes. His gaze was riveted over her shoulder, and he grew increasingly agitated the nearer Josiah came. When Josiah lifted Nathan into his arms, the small boy let out a bloodcurdling scream and held out his arms to Ada, as if begging her to save him.

As Josiah crossed the parking lot to his buggy, Nathan's screeches increased, and he kicked and bucked in his *daed*'s arms. Ada and David stood rooted to the same spot until Josiah's buggy pulled out onto the road. Nathan's yells still split the air as the horse trotted down the road.

Sharp pains shot through Ada's stomach. Nathan had been begging for rescue, and she'd ignored his plea. The look in Nathan's eyes when he spotted his *daed* haunted her. Ada had seen it before, but today she'd finally identified it. A look of pure terror.

Chapter Nineteen

Once again, seeing Nathan with Ada raised Josiah's feelings of inadequacy as a parent. Last night while babysitting her siblings, he'd hadn't encountered any trouble, although that might have been due to Sadie's competence. He'd always wanted a large family, but he couldn't even deal with one child, let alone more.

After they'd traveled for a while, Nathan settled down, allowing Josiah time to think. He'd taken mental notes of the equipment that interested Ada. Most of it could be built pretty easily. A few pieces might need to be ordered, but even so, the projects could be completed for a small fraction of the cost. Now that he'd seen what some of the equipment looked like, he could draw up plans.

The only problem would be financing the projects. All his savings had gone toward Ruth's medical bills.

Josiah pulled into the empty barn. *Mamm*'s missing

wagon must mean she was working the evening shift. If he could get Nathan into the house without waking him, he'd have time to work on his plans. The whole time Josiah was taking care of Silver, he kept a close eye on the buggy doors. Then he reached into the buggy for the crumpled paper on the floor before carefully lifting Nathan and his rabbit.

He managed to get Nathan onto the bed and remove his shoes without waking him. He'd struggle with dinner and bath time later. Right now, he was eager to get to work.

Josiah sat at his desk and sketched plans, then made duplicates. By the time he'd filled out the required paperwork, Nathan was whining. The rest of the evening proceeded with the usual battles and yelling until Nathan fell asleep, exhausted. Josiah was equally as weary, and he tumbled in bed soon after, although fitful dreams woke him often during the night. Much of the time, he was racing after someone, but the person eluded him, leaving him bereft and lonely.

The next morning after tussling with Nathan, Josiah was so worn out all he wanted to do was fall back into bed. But he had a mission to accomplish once his son was in school. Peace reigned soon after they pulled out of the driveway when Nathan fell asleep. David came out to meet the buggy when they pulled in. Josiah opened the door and folded down the seat. Then he stayed hidden on the opposite side of the buggy while David climbed in to wake Nathan. Once again, after a few wary glances around, Nathan climbed out happily.

Gathering his courage, Josiah drove to the job site.

He swallowed back his embarrassment at being fired and stepped out of the buggy.

"Hey, man," Marcus called, setting down the level he was using. He hurried over. "How ya doing?"

"All right," Josiah managed to say. "Do you know who gets the applications for that advertising project?"

"You gonna put in a plan?"

"I'd like to." Although maybe he should find out if he still had a job.

Just then Ralph shouted, "Hey, Yoder, get over here."

Other guys stopped their work to stare down at Josiah as he crossed the construction area to meet Ralph.

"You planning to turn that in?" Ralph asked, waving at the application papers.

"I'd be happy to if I'm allowed."

Ralph reached for the sheaf of papers. "I'll mark you down as the foreman for the project." He shrugged. "No telling which one they'll choose." Then he wagged a finger. "Wish you had a phone, Yoder, 'cause I tried to get ahold of you yesterday. Called the phone number on your job application. Guy who answered ran over to your house and said no one was home."

That would have been Josiah's *Englisch* neighbor. "Sorry."

"Yeah, me too. Talked to legal yesterday, and they said, according to OSHA regulations, you're allowed to wear your straw hat. Those of us who work around Amish country know that, but the New York City guys didn't. So you're still part of the crew."

The worry that had twisted Josiah's stomach into knots slowly unraveled. He still had his job.

Ralph continued, "They agreed to pay you for the

time you missed yesterday. Least we can do after how he treated you."

Josiah shook his head.

Ralph's face fell. "You won't be coming back?"

"I'm happy to have my job, but I can't accept pay for hours I don't work."

"You're kidding me, right?" His boss's mouth hung open. "Nobody turns down extra pay."

"It wouldn't be right to take it." Rolling up his sleeves, Josiah said, "Do you want me to finish the roofing?"

"You're something else, man." Ralph slapped him on the back. "Yeah, get on up there." As Josiah walked away, he called, "Oh, and Yoder? No daydreaming up there."

"Yes, sir," Josiah said, but keeping his promise would be hard when Ada seemed to occupy almost all his thoughts.

* * *

Ada had tossed and turned most of the previous night because Nathan's eyes haunted her dreams. He was petrified by his father and had no way to communicate. Poor child. No wonder he exploded. But what was causing his fear? Could Josiah be abusing him?

She tried to reconcile that with the Josiah she'd seen. The one who'd offered to babysit. The one who'd listened and encouraged her plans after the meeting. The one who'd given Mary Elizabeth gentle and thoughtful advice as he helped with the dishes.

She shook her head. It didn't seem possible. Yet she'd read enough teacher training books to be wary. She questioned her judgment. She discussed Josiah and Nathan with her siblings at breakfast, without mentioning her concerns. Her sisters all agreed Josiah was wonderful. When she brought up Nathan's reaction to his *daed*, David immediately signed.

Nathan scared.

"Of his *daed*?" she asked, and he nodded vigorously. So her brother had come to the same conclusion.

Noah added, "He avoids his *daed*. At story time, he backed into a corner away from him. I sat with him and David because he seemed to need protection."

"Josiah would never hurt Nathan," Sadie burst out. "He's too nice."

Another conclusion Ada had reached. But the two conclusions didn't mesh. The only one who could explain Nathan's fear was Nathan himself. Ada vowed to give him a voice. She'd teach him to communicate.

Ada was so preoccupied with Nathan's situation while they cleaned the kitchen after breakfast, she missed Sadie's question until her sister tugged on her arm.

"I asked you twice already. What are we going to do about Mary Elizabeth?"

"Has she been crying or growling?"

"Some of both. Mostly growling, although not as much as before." Sadie waved her hand impatiently. "But that's not the big problem. She missed you yesterday afternoon. She fussed most of the time you were gone."

Ada sighed. Once again, she'd been so wrapped up with her teaching, she'd neglected her siblings. "I promised Josiah to take Nathan to the center again today. I could take Mary Elizabeth with me if you'll drop her off."

"What about the rest of us?" Sadie put the dish she was drying in the cupboard. "You don't ever spend time with us anymore."

"You're all welcome to come along." Ada wondered if the center would welcome seven extra children as visitors.

"I don't want to do that."

Ada bit her tongue to keep from lashing out. *What do you want, Sadie? Besides contradicting me on everything, that is.* Lack of sleep combined with Sadie's attitude and concerns about Nathan left Ada drained, and the day hadn't even started yet.

Ada arrived at school still in a sleep-deprived haze, the fear in Nathan's eyes constantly on her mind.

Josiah's buggy pulled into the school yard, and Ada beckoned David, who ran out to meet his friend. Josiah got out and stepped to the opposite side of the buggy before David clambered in to wake Nathan. The two boys walked toward the schoolhouse, with David signing and Nathan frowning at his hands.

Ada leaned toward Betty as she walked into the schoolhouse. "Have you noticed that Nathan cries a lot around his *daed*?"

"I certainly have. And I know exactly what the problem is." Betty glanced around, making sure no one was close enough to hear. "That child needs stricter discipline. Josiah is much too lax."

Betty's comment only added to Ada's confusion, and later that afternoon, when Ada spoke to Hope about the situation without giving Nathan's name, Hope encouraged her to call Child Protective Services.

Ada thanked her for her suggestion, but added, "We

don't like to involve outside services like that. I'll try talking to the bishop."

"I'll be praying," Hope told her. "You really need an authority to check into this, though. Children have been killed by abusive parents."

"I don't know that he's being abused." Although evidence seemed to point in that direction, Ada's mind and heart refused to tie together the words *Josiah* and *abuse*.

Chapter Twenty

Ada needed answers to her questions, answers only Nathan could give. Over the next week, she set aside part of each day to work alone with him at recess now that they had transitioned into full school days. Although she felt guilty about going behind Josiah's back, she needed to find out why Nathan was so fearful.

Nathan was a fast learner, for which she was grateful. In addition to what she was teaching, David shared many signs with him, and he and Nathan developed a combination of miming and signs that enabled them to communicate while they played.

She should be teaching Nathan basic words, but instead she was working on signs for *hurt*, *angry*, *sad*, and *scared*. When she'd given him enough signs for feelings and taught him to use the picture boards Hope had recommended, she was ready to ask the questions burning in the back of her mind.

She hated to think the worst of Josiah, but she needed to find out the truth and protect Nathan, if necessary. She'd been mistaken about Josiah before when she'd believed he'd kidnapped her siblings, and she hoped she'd made an error this time too.

She gestured for Nathan to stay behind as the others headed outside. He skipped over, which lessened her guilt about keeping him inside. Glad he trusted her, she started with some simple signs he'd been learning. When he played with David, *ball*, *truck*, and *book* showed up often. Her brother's name seemed to be his favorite, but she didn't want to remind him that David was outside playing while he was inside, so she skipped that.

Then she plunged into the inquiry she needed to make. She signed *Scare you* with a question mark, expecting him to point to one of the pictures on the board—spiders, snakes, dark steps to a basement, a tiger with a menacing set of teeth—so she could work the conversation around to the real topic on her mind. Instead, Nathan immediately signed *Daed*.

She double-checked his answer, repeating it back to him as a question. He nodded so vigorously when she asked if his *daed* scared him, Ada's stomach churned. She'd wanted to find out the truth, but knowing her suspicions were correct made her sick.

She asked her next question: *Daed hurt Nathan?* Rather than answering, he replied by pointing to himself and signing *Scared*. Ada had no idea how the two ideas connected. Did he mean he was scared of being hurt? Or scared to tell her?

She moved on to the picture card of a child. Pointing to one spot at a time on the front and back of the child, she asked if his *daed* hurt him there. Each time he shook his head. Now Ada was thoroughly confused. She drew a question mark in the air.

Nathan signed slowly as if he were struggling to share something for the first time. Tears in his eyes, he signed, *Mamm gone*.

Ada nodded to let him know she understood. Poor kid. He was missing her, but had no way to share his feelings. *Sad*, she responded.

His head bobbed up and down. He pointed to himself and added *Cry*. He followed with *Daed sad. Daed cry.* Yes, Josiah had gotten choked up when he talked about his wife.

Then five sentences came in rapid succession. *Daed hurt Mamm. Mamm gone. I scared. I gone.*

Ada struggled to interpret the meaning behind the sentences and tie them together properly. Nathan seemed to be accusing Josiah of hurting his mother. That much was clear. Was he scared about his *mamm* being gone? Or scared that whatever happened to his *mamm* would happen to him? Or did he want to go where she was?

She tried to clarify his statements by asking additional questions, but his knowledge of sign language limited his answers. Two things became clear: Josiah was not hurting him physically, but Nathan was frightened of his *daed*. He confirmed both statements multiple times.

Her head reeling, Ada racked her brain to think of other signs she could teach him to help her discover the truth. She didn't like to involve her brother, but Nathan and David communicated so well together, David might be able to find answers. She'd talk to him tonight after dinner.

* * *

Ada waited until everyone was in bed that evening before slipping in to talk to David. She sat on the edge of his bed, and he sat up, surprised.

"Do you know why Nathan is scared of his *daed*?" she signed.

When he shook his head, she asked, "Will you help me find out?"

David agreed, and from the other bed, Noah, in a sleepy voice, pledged to help too. Now that she'd enlisted her brothers' help, maybe together they could find answers.

At recess the next day, David sat on the playground in earnest conversation with Nathan. From time to time, Nathan chewed hard on his bunny's ears, but he also seemed to be responding. Ada hoped her brother could glean some more clues. Nathan bounded in from recess, but David followed, a frown wrinkling his forehead. Ada longed to know what they had discussed, but she needed to wait until she and David had time alone.

The school day passed slowly and was marred by several outbursts. Martha did her best to calm her brother, who seemed especially agitated. Ada decided to order some weighted neck rolls from the catalog Hope had given her. The books she'd read claimed weighted vests and neck rolls calmed children with autism. What she wanted most of all, though, was a multi-sensory room like they had at the center. She could use it herself right now. But that gave her an idea. Perhaps she could create a place in the classroom for peace and calm.

First, though, she needed to get through this day. With a grateful heart, she turned the scholars over to their parents when the school day ended. Ada couldn't look Josiah in the eye when he picked up Nathan, and she struggled to be civil. With a heavy heart, she let Nathan leave, when all she wanted to do was hug him to her. Until she knew more, though, she had no right to interfere. Even if she did, she'd have to leave discipline up to the bishop. Most of all, Ada couldn't let her attraction to Josiah blind her to the truth.

Then, her stomach jittery, she waited until Martha left before asking David about his conversation with Nathan. After her brother finished, Ada repeated the information back to him several times in both sign language and speech.

The final time David read her lips, he nodded impatiently and signed. *Can we go home? I want to play before chores.*

Ada nodded, but the whole way home, she mulled over David's information. She had to talk to Josiah as soon as possible.

The next morning she arrived at the schoolhouse early and waited outside for Josiah, who usually arrived first. She only hoped Betty didn't drive in and see her having a private conversation with him. As soon as his buggy pulled in, Ada hurried across the parking lot. David followed her to accompany his friend into the schoolhouse.

As usual, Josiah stepped out of the buggy and stayed out of Nathan's sight. While David climbed over the lowered front seat to wake Nathan, Ada rounded the buggy and almost plowed into Josiah's chest. She skidded to a stop, but her pulse continued its headlong flight.

"I need to talk to you," she said. "Could we meet here after school once all the pupils have gone home?"

Josiah's eyes widened, and Ada hoped he hadn't misconstrued her request. "It's about Nathan," she explained.

His forehead wrinkled. "Is everything all right?"

Ada was unsure how to answer that. "It would be best if I explained this afternoon."

"I'll come a little later than usual," Josiah said. "That way people won't wonder why we're, um, meeting."

"Good idea." Although Ada wished they were meeting for another purpose. She mentally shook herself and hurried to the schoolhouse door. She was a few feet away when Betty drove in. Ada slowed to a walk, hoping she was far enough from Josiah's buggy to allay Betty's suspicions.

The rest of the day inched along as Ada greeted her pupils, taught them some lessons, and mentally rehearsed what she would say to Josiah.

With great relief, she watched the last parent pull out of the parking lot at the end of the day. Josiah hadn't arrived yet, but when he did, no adults would be around to see them having a private conversation.

As soon as Josiah pulled in, she waved him over. He left the buggy and jogged in her direction, a bright smile lighting his face.

She turned her attention to David and Nathan who were playing together. "I thought we could sit at the picnic table." She motioned to the wooden table at one end of the building. "I'll let the boys know where we'll be."

When she returned, they took seats on opposite sides of the small picnic table. The broiling September sun had heated the wooden bench so it burned through the fabric of her dress. Ada *rutsched*, trying to get comfortable, but nervousness also made it hard to sit still. Being so close to Josiah, staring directly into his eyes, she almost forgot what she'd planned to say. *Think, Ada.* She lowered her gaze. *David. Nathan.*

"I think I've discovered why Nathan fusses when he sees you." She paused to draw a breath into her air-starved lungs. The summer heat made it hard to breathe, but so did the intensity of Josiah's gaze as he leaned forward, eyes focused on her.

"Why?" Josiah's desperate plea was like a drowning man begging for help.

Ada wanted to reach across the table and hold his hands, find a way to comfort him. "David talked to Nathan, and…"

"And?" Impatience seeped into his words.

Ada rushed out her words to give him his answer. "Nathan believes you took his *mamm* away, and he's afraid you'll do the same to him."

Josiah stared at her. "He's afraid I'll get rid of him?"

"Yes. He doesn't understand what happened to his *mamm*, why she's gone." Ada clenched her hands in her lap to keep from reaching out, wishing she could wipe the sorrow from his face.

"Nathan asks about his *mamm* every day." Josiah's voice grew husky. "I have no way to explain other than to sign *Mamm gone.*"

"Oh, Josiah, I'm so sorry. That must be hard." To be unable to communicate with your own son. To be so isolated. And poor Nathan. To have no idea why his *mamm* was gone.

"My signing only made it worse, didn't it?" Josiah lowered his head and rubbed his forehead. "I had no idea. I should have found some way to learn more sign language," he said, his voice raspy. "But even if I had, I couldn't teach Nathan. Not with the way he avoids me."

Ada laid a hand on his sleeve to comfort him, but wished she hadn't because she longed to stroke the powerful muscle under the cloth. But if she jerked away, he might wonder why. *Concentrate on his sadness, Ada.* She willed her fingers to remain still and focused on sending caring through her touch.

"I was so grateful he'd be learning it at school and hoped once he did..." Josiah gazed off into the distance. "All this time, I thought he understood what happened to his *mamm*." In a broken voice, he continued, "Maybe I made a mistake not taking him to her funeral."

What did he say? His words buzzed in Ada's brain. She must have heard him wrong. She'd assumed his wife had gone back to Mexico. Unlike the women in their community, who dressed all in black after a death, men didn't change their usual attire, so she'd had no clue his wife had died. Her thoughts ran wild, and she barely heard Josiah's next words.

"He wasn't there when..." Josiah choked back a sob. "I just assumed he understood..."

Josiah isn't married? He's a widower? All those times she'd berated herself for thinking about him... All those times she... As the load of guilt tumbled away, the feelings she'd suppressed rushed in, overwhelming her. She had to calm herself. Not let her attraction show.

Right now, helping Nathan—and his *daed*—should be her only focus.

"What have I done?" Josiah gripped her hands.

Relax, Ada. He doesn't realize what he's doing. He's grasping for something to hold on to in his desperation. Nevertheless, her heart pattered faster.

Josiah's anguished words poured out. "I've frightened my son every day for the last nine months. Every time I signed to him, every time I picked him up, every time I carried him out the door, every time I put him in the buggy, he must have thought..." He looked sick.

"Don't blame yourself. You didn't know."

His fingers tightened on hers. "How will I ever make it right? I can't talk to him, explain what happened. Even if I learned the signs, he doesn't know them. What am I going to do? How can I explain?"

Ada had no idea how to teach abstract concepts in sign language. For feelings, she could use facial expressions and pictures, but for *death* and *God* and *heaven*, she was at a loss. She tried to remember teaching David to understand some of those signs, but it had happened gradually over time, and she'd never analyzed how she'd done it.

Josiah glanced down at his hands, and redness suffused his face. "I'm sorry." He quickly withdrew the big, strong hands engulfing hers, leaving Ada bereft.

She moved her hands back to her lap, but the touch of his fingers remained. Ada struggled to gather her scattered thoughts.

Josiah cleared his throat. "Maybe I should ask the teacher at the center if she could teach me sign language."

Fierce jealousy gripped Ada at the thought of Josiah

working with the pretty Mennonite teacher. A jealousy she had no right to feel. "I'd be happy to teach you," she blurted out.

He frowned. "I don't think... That is..."

Ada's heart sank. He had no interest in working with her. She'd been foolish to offer.

"I wouldn't feel right taking up your time. You have so much to do with teaching and caring for your brothers and sisters."

Unsure if his response was a polite refusal or if he truly worried about overloading her, Ada paused before answering. She longed to say she'd love to teach him, to spend time with him, but she tempered her response. "I don't mind." Then worried that sounded too unenthusiastic, she added, "I'd be happy to do it."

"Thank you for the offer." Josiah stood. "I should pick up Nathan, although now that I know I'm scaring him..."

Ada longed to erase the misery on his face. No *daed* should have to endure such pain. "Why don't I take Nathan home with me," she suggested, "and you can join us there later? David and I can try to explain using sign language he knows."

A look of relief crossed his face, but then he stiffened. "No, it's not right that you should have to deal with our problems. You've done so much already."

"It's no trouble at all. David loves spending time with Nathan."

When he looked about to protest, she said, "You want this to be easier for Nathan, right? He should have some explanation."

"You're right. Nathan's needs are most important." He

glanced away and swallowed hard. "What time should I come for him?"

"Why don't you come for dinner?" Ada cut off his mumbling about being an imposition. "The girls enjoyed your company, and you can always wash dishes afterward," she said teasingly.

Josiah laughed. "Who could pass up an invitation like that? All right, dishes it is." He started to walk off but then turned toward her. "Thank you."

The look in his eyes took Ada's breath away. His eyes overflowed with gratitude. But his gaze contained something deeper, much deeper, she couldn't identify. As if they'd connected soul to soul.

Chapter Twenty-One

The enormity of his mistakes overwhelmed Josiah. He'd traumatized his son. No wonder Josiah clung to Ada. When he was with her, he felt safe. Safe from the father who would... *Who would what?* What did Nathan think would happen to him? Josiah wished he knew what terrors ran through his son's mind.

Even more, he wanted to alleviate them, to let Nathan know how much he loved him, to share a relationship with him like Ada had with her brothers and sisters, to do things together. For some reason, every activity he pictured doing with his son, Ada accompanied them.

His skin still registered her gentle touch, butterfly light, conveying caring and empathy. He couldn't forget the compassion in her eyes when he met her gaze. The softness of her skin when he gripped her hands. The emptiness inside when he'd forced himself to let go.

He replayed each touch, each gesture, each smile until

Silver trotted down the driveway and into the barn beside *Mamm*'s wagon. Then he shook away the thoughts and readied himself for his *mamm*'s barrage of questions.

As usual, she was in the kitchen, amid counters filled with canning jars. She greeted him, then stared at his empty arms. "Where's Nathan?"

"I'll be picking him up from his teacher's house later."

"I see. I did laundry this afternoon." *Mamm* pointed to a small, neatly folded stack of clothes and the quilt. "I didn't recognize those. I assume Nathan borrowed them?"

The clothes Ada had lent him. He'd take them with him when he went for dinner tonight. "Yes, he did."

Mamm's folded arms indicated she was waiting for an explanation, one Josiah didn't want to give, knowing it would only lead to more questions. "He wore them the night he stayed at his teacher's house."

Mamm raised her eyebrows. "His teacher seems to be taking a great interest in him."

Josiah couldn't tell if *Mamm*'s comment was neutral or if she'd included a note of censure. Curiosity underlay her words as well, but Josiah was unwilling to share too much about Ada because *Mamm* would read into it.

He needed to let her know they would be at Ada's for dinner and why, so he launched into the day's events, explaining what Ada had discovered and the plan for helping Nathan. By the time he finished, *Mamm*'s eyes were teary.

"The poor little boy." She reached into the pocket under her apron and pulled out a hankie. "No wonder he kicks up such a fuss."

"Yes, I'm sick inside thinking about what he's been

going through because of me." Sick didn't begin to describe the guilt that overwhelmed him at the thought he'd been terrorizing the son he loved more than life itself. "How could I not have known? Why didn't I pay more attention to the messages he was sending when he kicked and screamed?"

"*Neh*, don't blame yourself."

The same thing Ada had said, but Josiah did blame himself. He should have tried harder to find out the cause of his son's distress. He should have spent time learning sign language. He should have...

Mamm patted his arm, and Josiah flashed back to Ada's hand on his sleeve. He forced himself to return to the kitchen.

"I'm going to learn sign language. Ad— Nathan's teacher offered to help." He avoided saying Ada's name for fear *Mamm* might pick up clues to his attraction. Calling her the teacher helped put distance between them. Or was he only fooling himself?

The way *Mamm* was scrutinizing him, she'd detected some of the undercurrents he was attempting to hide. With a brief nod, as if satisfying herself about something, she said, "I'm grateful Nathan's teacher is so willing to help him."

* * *

As Josiah strode across the parking lot, Ada gazed after him until he climbed into the buggy. Then she hurried into the schoolhouse, worried he might have seen her in the rearview mirror, staring at him.

The air inside felt cooler, but it did little to temper

the heat that being around Josiah had created. When he'd reached out and gripped her hands, it had been only desperation on his part, but the sensations it generated were real. So real, her fingers remained warm from his touch. With seven siblings and the situation with *Daed*, she had no business yearning for the impossible.

Once she'd regained her composure, she locked the schoolhouse and called the boys.

"Nathan will be coming home with us. His *daed* will join us for dinner," she said to David.

He and Nathan both watched her lips intently, but only David jumped for joy. Nathan's face puckered at the word *daed*, and he glanced around. The lines on his face relaxed when he didn't spot Josiah's buggy. Ada wished she could explain he didn't need to fear his *daed*. Poor child. And poor Josiah.

Using sign language and their own private motions, David conveyed the good news to Nathan. His eyes uncertain, he looked up at Ada. She nodded and was rewarded with a broad smile.

Tucking his hand in her brother's, Nathan skipped along beside David and climbed into the buggy. He leaned against Ada as she drove. Several times he almost drifted off, but caught himself and jerked awake. David kept him busy by pointing out various things and demonstrating the signs, which Nathan copied.

When they arrived at the house, David and Nathan thundered upstairs. Ada had to talk to Nathan before Josiah arrived, but she wanted the rest of the family to understand, so she called Noah into the kitchen, where her sisters were making chicken pot pie.

Sadie was rolling out the dough and cutting it into

squares to drop in the boiling broth right before the meal was ready. The twins were washing and cutting up carrots and celery. Hannah emerged from the pantry with a jar of chicken breasts Ada had canned.

"You'd better get another jar," Ada told her. "Nathan and Josiah will be eating with us tonight."

"They will?" Rather than looking annoyed, Sadie reached for the ingredients to make more dough. "We'll need more pot pie squares then."

"First, I'd like to talk to everyone before Josiah arrives." Ada waited for everyone to gather around her and then explained why Nathan screamed for his *daed*. "Nathan only knows that his *mamm*'s gone, and he blames his dad. He's scared Josiah will get rid of him too."

Noah shuffled his feet. "Poor kid. No wonder he's so upset."

Tears in her eyes, Sadie said, "Poor Josiah too."

Mary Elizabeth sniffled.

"If any of you have ideas about how to explain this to Nathan," Ada continued, "let me know. For now, we just need to convince him his *daed* won't hurt him or get rid of him."

Everyone nodded, and Ada sent Hannah up to get the boys.

"David and I will talk to him for a little while in the living room. Then maybe all of you can join us. Dinner won't take long to cook."

David came down the stairs with Nathan. They sat next to each other on the couch, and Ada sat across from them. By the time the rest of her siblings joined them, Ada had begun the discussion about Nathan's *mamm*.

A wistful look crossed his face. *Want Mamm*, he signed.

You miss Mamm? Ada responded.

Nathan frowned at the sign for *miss*. Ada poked her chin with her index finger, wrinkled her brow, and made her face as sad and regretful as she could. Nathan imitated her. This time he bobbed his head up and down so vigorously, she had no doubt he understood.

His eyes grew misty, and he blinked. Then he signed, *I miss Mamm*, and tears rolled down his cheeks.

"Oh, Nathan," Mary Elizabeth gushed. She rushed over, swept him into her arms, and hugged him tight.

Nathan's eyes bugged out, and he seemed to be appealing for someone to save him. Ada tapped her sister on the shoulder and untangled Mary Elizabeth's embrace. "It was very thoughtful of you to care about Nathan's feelings, but he might be a bit overwhelmed right now."

"But I'd want someone to hug me tight." Mary Elizabeth's chin quivered.

"I know," Ada soothed. "Not everyone reacts the same way, though. Some people like to be alone when they're sad." She pulled Mary Elizabeth onto her lap. "Why don't we see what else Nathan has to say?"

But Nathan seemed to have been startled into silence. To give him time to recover, she directed her siblings to finish fixing dinner, then she and David did their best to communicate the idea that Nathan's *daed* wouldn't hurt him. Nathan looked skeptical, so she assumed he'd understood most of what they'd said. Ada suggested David take Nathan to his room and keep trying to convince his friend. She joined her sisters in the kitchen.

The broth was bubbling by the time Josiah knocked.

Sadie and Mary Elizabeth tried to elbow each other out of the way to be the first to reach the door. Ada put her hands on their shoulders to separate them. Then she walked between them, because, truth be told, she wanted to be the first to the door.

Sadie glared when Mary Elizabeth grasped the doorknob first. But her expression turned sunny when Josiah smiled and greeted both of them. Then he looked at Ada, and her heart stuttered. If Sadie hadn't invited him in, Ada might still be lost in his gaze.

Josiah held out a small stack of clothing and the quilt. "*Mamm* washed them, so they're clean."

As Ada took them from him, their fingers brushed. *Breathe. Act normal.*

"*Danke* for letting Nathan borrow them," he said.

"We're having pot pie tonight," Sadie broke in. "I made the dough squares."

"Smells delicious," Josiah said, and Sadie beamed.

Not to be outdone, Mary Elizabeth pushed in front of Sadie. "I buttered all the bread." She took his hand and pulled him through the living room. "Come out in the kitchen and see."

Josiah inspected the towering stack of homemade bread slices, alternating face up and face down, with a serious expression. "Very nice."

Sadie pulled out the chair he'd sat in the last time. "Have a seat."

"*Danke*." He smiled at her but turned to Ada, a question in his eyes.

She motioned toward the stairway. "The boys are upstairs. We did try to talk to Nathan. I'm not sure we convinced him, but I hope we made a start."

Josiah sank into the chair Sadie had pulled out for him. "It seems I've done everything wrong."

"You didn't know." Ada stopped herself from reaching out to comfort him. Having her sisters in the kitchen, keeping an eye on them helped keep her impulses in check. "How could you?"

"Still, to do this to my own son." He squeezed his eyes shut and pinched the bridge of his nose. "I wish..." His voice broke. "I wish I'd been a better father."

Mary Elizabeth rushed across the room and threw her arms around him. "You're a good *daed*." Then she stepped back, glanced over her shoulder at Ada, and asked, "Do you like to be alone when you're sad?"

Josiah glanced at her with startled eyes. "Being alone makes me sadder, I think."

Mary Elizabeth lifted her nose in the air with a sniff and threw Ada an *I-was-right* look. "Ada says some people like to be private."

"That's true," Josiah agreed. "Some people hide their feelings. They prefer to bear their burdens alone." He studied Ada with a thoughtful expression.

Sadie interrupted. "Should I put the pot pie squares in now?"

"They won't take long to cook," Ada said. "Maybe we should wait until everyone washes up and comes to the table." Ada sent Mary Elizabeth to call the boys while the twins set out the plates and Hannah filled water glasses.

As everyone filed to the table, Sadie dropped the dough into the pot and stirred to separate the squares.

Nathan skidded to a stop when he saw his *daed*. His face puckered, but David tugged at his arm. Nathan turned to face his friend. David signed slowly, reassuring Nathan his *daed* was not taking him away. Then David pointed to himself and Nathan and signed *friend*. A smile bloomed on Nathan's face.

Then, pointing to each person at the table, David interlocked his index fingers twice in the symbol for *friend*. Nathan nodded after each one. David saved Josiah for last. This time Nathan's face turned to stone.

Ada's stomach clenched at the pain in Josiah's eyes. She couldn't even begin to imagine how hurtful it would be to have your own son reject you. She whispered a silent prayer, *Lord, please heal Josiah's hurt and give us the wisdom to reach Nathan and reunite him with his father.*

Mary Elizabeth, her expression mirroring Ada's distress, signed to Nathan that his *daed* loved him and wouldn't hurt him. From the skeptical look he gave her, Nathan understood her. But he circled far around Josiah to get to his place at the table.

Josiah sat, his lips pinched together and eyes downcast, as David and Nathan settled into their places. They all bowed their heads for prayer, and when Josiah looked up again, his face appeared expressionless, though he glanced at Nathan with longing and regret throughout the meal.

Sensing Josiah's distress, her siblings told humorous stories, trying to include Nathan by adding signs, but he studied their hand movements, a look of confusion on his face. Whenever everyone laughed at the punch lines, though, he joined in.

* * *

A sharp pain shot through Josiah when a rusty laugh issued from Nathan's throat. The only times Josiah had seen his son happy and laughing had been here in this kitchen. Here, where he felt safe from his father. Safe and loved. Two of the most important needs of a child. And Josiah had failed to provide either.

Throughout the meal, Nathan avoided looking in Josiah's direction but engaged with everyone else. Now that he understood the reason behind his son's outbursts and avoidance, he had to find a way to reduce Nathan's fears and establish a loving relationship. Connecting with Nathan seemed to be an insurmountable barrier, but Josiah was determined to overcome that obstacle. With Ada's help, learning to communicate with his son now seemed possible.

After the meal and the final silent prayer ended, Josiah rose. "Time for me to keep my end of the bargain." He carried his plate and glass to the sink.

Scuffling ensued behind him, along with several squeals. Josiah positioned himself so he could observe the drama.

"I'll dry," Sadie announced, carrying a stack of plates toward the sink.

"It's my job." Mary Elizabeth scrambled to push in front of her sister, but Sadie maneuvered around her and reached the counter first.

Sadie set down her dishes and waved a hand magnanimously. "I usually wash, so I'll be kind and take your turn to dry."

Mary Elizabeth pouted. "I want my own turn."

"Girls!" Ada's voice cut through the bickering. "I'll do the drying if you can't settle this peacefully."

Josiah hoped a compromise couldn't be reached. His heart beat faster at the thought of touching Ada's soft skin while handing over wet plates, of feasting his eyes on her while she worked.

His hopes were dashed when Sadie became the voice of reason. "You did dishes with Josiah the last time, so I should get a turn. Then next time it will be your turn again."

"We could share," Mary Elizabeth said, her tone plaintive.

Sadie huffed. "All right. You dry the silverware, and I'll do the plates and glasses."

Sniffling, Mary Elizabeth agreed. Josiah alternated washing a piece of silverware with a dish or cup to keep the drying fair. As soon as they had settled into a routine, Ada flashed him a brilliant smile and headed for the stairs.

Josiah lost his grip on the glass he was washing, and it slipped into the sudsy water. It clinked against a plate, and he forced his attention back to the sink. Holding the glass up to the light, he examined it for cracks or chips and was grateful to find it intact, which was more than he could say for his nerves.

When he'd handed over the last plate, he drained the sink and dried his hands. "I'll take Nathan now, so all of you can get ready for bed."

"No." Mary Elizabeth rushed over and grabbed his hand. "You can read us the bedtime story."

"Please," Sadie pleaded. Both girls tugged him into the living room and toward the couch.

It warmed Josiah's heart to know they wanted him to stay, but he couldn't, wouldn't stumble over another

Bible story with Ada watching. "Your sister's here tonight. I'm sure she's planning to read to—"

His words died in his throat as Ada descended the staircase with David and Nathan, one boy on each side, grasping her hand. His son stared up at Ada, adoration in his eyes. Josiah only hoped he'd been masking his own feelings better.

When they reached the foot of the stairs, Nathan caught sight of him and backed up against Ada's skirt. She knelt beside him and turned him to face her. After mouthing, *It's all right*, she signed a few things that had the word *daed* in them, while David stood beside her nodding enthusiastically. Nathan looked from one to the other.

Just before she rose, Ada's hands formed words he knew so well, *Daed loves you*.

Nathan shook his head, and Josiah's heart sank. No matter what they told him, his son didn't want to believe them. Could he ever rebuild Nathan's lost trust?

Chapter Twenty-Two

Ada, Ada." Mary Elizabeth charged over, and Nathan backed up a few steps. "Josiah's going to read the Bible story to us tonight."

Eyebrows arched, Ada turned to Josiah.

He shrugged. "I planned to take Nathan home, but the girls insisted. I assume you'd prefer to do it."

One corner of her mouth quirked. "We'd all be honored to have you read."

"See?" Mary Elizabeth dragged him back to the couch and sat next to him. Sadie plopped down on the other side, holding the Bible story book.

The other children tromped down the stairs freshly bathed and in their pajamas. They gathered in the living room for story time, and Josiah stared around the room longingly. Being part of their bedtime routine stirred deep-down yearnings. For family. For togetherness. For a relationship with his son.

His gaze lit on Ada, who had settled on the floor beside his son. Nathan let go of her hand and signed something.

"What did he say?" Josiah asked Ada. "I saw the sign for *Mamm*, and he pointed to himself."

"He said he misses his *mamm*."

"Oh." Josiah's chest tightened and his eyes blurred.

"Show me that sign for *miss*, please." Josiah copied Ada's movements, trying to convey his own anguish through his expression when he reached the word *miss*.

I miss Mamm too, Josiah signed.

Nathan, eyes wide and uncertain, stared at him. He shrank back against Ada, and she lifted him onto her lap, her eyes sparkling with tears. Nathan cuddled against her, tucked a rabbit ear in his mouth, and closed his eyes. Ada brushed away his teardrops with her fingertip, then stroked his cheek, gently and rhythmically, until his face relaxed.

Sadie handed Josiah the book, and the pages fell open to the parable of the Lost Lamb. He blinked to clear his vision, but the printing on the page still swam until he could barely make out the words. His voice husky, he read the brief story of the shepherd who left all his other sheep to find one lost lamb.

"I'm glad he found it," Mary Elizabeth whispered.

So was Josiah. He too would give up everything to bring his own lost lamb back into the fold.

* * *

The interaction between Josiah and Nathan had touched Ada. Josiah, with his limited sign language, had bared his soul to make a connection with his son. A connection

Nathan severed. But for a few moments, he'd seen his *daed*'s pain. Someday soon, she hoped they'd both be able to share their grief.

Her siblings slipped out of the room and headed to bed, but Ada sat there, still stunned at the powerful emotions Josiah had brought to reading the book.

As if deep in thought, Josiah stood slowly and set the book on the nearby table. Then he turned to Ada, and his face softened as he stared down at his sleeping son. "He looks so comfortable," he said.

"He's asleep," she whispered.

A small half smile crossed his face. "I know from his breathing." He swallowed hard. "I've learned to tell, because the only time I can get close to him or sit next to him is when he's sound asleep."

"Oh, Josiah," Ada breathed. She almost added, *I'm so sorry*, but sensed he wouldn't want pity. Yet the picture of him so desperate for closeness broke her heart.

"We should go." Josiah crossed the room and bent to take his son from her arms, leaving her chilled where Nathan's small, warm body had nestled. "Thank you for the meal and—and this." He motioned with his chin toward the couch and Bible story book.

Before Ada could say anything, he continued, "Tonight and the night I babysat are the first times I've read to my son since—since..."

Ada pressed her lips together to prevent an exclamation of pity from escaping, but a small breath hissed out. How lonely he must be. "You're welcome to share story time with us anytime." *Oh, Ada, what are you doing?*

Josiah looked taken aback. "Thank you, but I don't think..."

Of course not. It wouldn't be appropriate for a widower to continue visiting her like he was tonight. Not while he was still in mourning. And not with all the children asleep and no one to chaperone.

Ada hung her head and mumbled, "I'm sorry."

"Nothing to be sorry for. Your invitation was kindly meant." A note of yearning underlay Josiah's words. "I wish I could take advantage of the offer, but..."

"I know." Ada couldn't meet his eyes.

Josiah shuffled his feet. "Well, thank you for dinner. It was delicious." He started toward the door.

"Oh, I thought we could talk a bit about how to tell Nathan." She tried to keep the disappointment from her voice.

Looking torn, Josiah glanced down at Nathan. "I should get him home."

"If he's getting heavy, you could put him on the couch." Why was she trying to get him to stay, when she should be encouraging him to go?

Josiah shook his head. "I shouldn't." Yet instead of continuing toward the door, he moved toward the couch and lowered Nathan onto it.

Ada's heart skipped with joy.

Josiah stood, his back to her, bent over his sleeping son. With one hand, he smoothed down Nathan's bowl-cut bangs.

Did he plan to stand that way while she spoke? "You could have a seat," she said softly.

To her relief, he lowered himself onto the sofa beside Nathan. Ada chose the wooden rocker for its safe distance from the couch. That way, she wouldn't reach out and touch him, no matter how much she was tempted.

He went back to running his hand over Nathan's hair. "I can't do this when he's awake, so I have to take advantage of it when I can."

"I understand." It must be painful not to be able to touch his son lovingly during the day. Ada felt guilty about her exasperation with Mary Elizabeth. She should be grateful that her sister clung to her.

"I appreciate you doing this for us. To think I might be able to communicate with him and have him understand, I can't thank you enough."

"I'm happy to do it." Seeing Josiah and Nathan rebuilding their relationship would be *wunderbar*. "There is one thing I've been thinking about. After I've taught Nathan enough sign language and words like *heaven*, *God*, and"—she hesitated a moment—"*death...*"

Josiah winced and rubbed his forehead, shading his eyes from view.

"It might be good," Ada said gently, "to have a psychologist or grief counselor present when we tell Nathan the news."

"*Ohhh.*" Josiah sounded as if he were in pain. Burying his face in his hands, he mumbled, "I've been living with the pain for all this time, but it will be the first time he's heard."

"I know." It took a great effort not to scoot the rocker closer, not to reach out and put a hand on his arm. Her heart longed to comfort him, but her conscience won. She gave him a few minutes to absorb the information before offering, "Would you like me to teach you some of the signs I'll be teaching Nathan?"

In a choked voice, he said, "Yes, if it's not too much trouble."

"Of course," she said in such an inviting way, her cheeks burned.

"It shouldn't take long," he said eagerly. "At least I hope not. I'd really like to know a few signs that might make it easier for me tomorrow morning."

A few signs wouldn't take long. Part of her wished for an excuse to keep him here longer. "What ones did you want to learn?"

"Would Nathan know the word for school?" Josiah glanced down at his sleeping son, and his jaw tensed. "I thought it might ease his fears when I take him out of the house in the morning."

"Oh, that makes sense. I did try to teach the scholars the word *school* from the first day, along with their names."

"So he'd know David's? And yours?" Josiah's eyes searched hers. "He likes to be around you, so if he knows he's going to see you, it might calm him."

Ada nodded. "He knows both our names." She demonstrated the sign for *school* first, and then their names.

When Josiah had mastered those, he stood. "These should help, and maybe as I learn to communicate with him"—he lifted Nathan gently without waking him—"he'll understand I'm not as awful or scary as he thinks I am."

"I'll work to teach him the concepts he needs to know. Once Nathan knows the truth, he'll realize he has nothing to fear."

But he would have much to mourn.

Chapter Twenty-Three

The construction crew was wrapping up at the end of the day on Friday when a white pickup pulled up and Lyle Anderson emerged. Ralph called the crew together. Josiah stayed near the back of the group, so he didn't call attention to himself.

"The project winner for this area has been chosen," Anderson said, "and I'll be announcing that shortly. First, though, I hope we'll have many willing volunteers who'll donate time to the special project."

"Huh? They expect us to work for free? After a long day on the job?" Clint spat out. "He's got to be crazy."

Marcus sidled up next to Josiah and jabbed him with an elbow. "Bet you'll volunteer, won't you?"

"If I can," Josiah replied. If he didn't have Nathan to care for, it would be easier, but he'd try to give as much time as he could, no matter what project had won.

"What for?" Clint demanded.

Marcus leaned past Josiah to address Clint. "The Amish believe in helping others. Isn't that what God wants you to do?" He nudged Josiah, who nodded.

Clint circled his index finger around beside his head. "Crazy, man."

Lyle made a show of opening the envelope and unfolding the paper. "The advertising department chose"— he paused as if expecting a drum roll—"playground equipment for a special needs school."

Josiah sucked in a breath. No one else would have submitted a request like that, would they?

"This project was submitted by"—Lyle's face twisted as if he smelled fresh manure—"Josiah Yoder." He singled Josiah out in the crowd and added an insincere "Congratulations."

Marcus whistled and clapped Josiah on the back. "Way to go, man. At least you'll be donating your time to a project you chose." He shuffled his feet in the dirt. "You can count on my help."

"Thanks." Josiah grinned at him. He could hardly wait to tell Ada the good news.

Lyle Anderson called for volunteers and several men, including Marcus, stepped forward.

Clint grumbled, but then said, "If you were willing to help people out, I guess I should too. Besides it's for little kids." He walked up to stand beside Marcus.

After dismissing the other men, Lyle turned to the volunteers. "Here's how this will work." He outlined the plan and then passed out work schedules. "As you can see, we're planning to start tomorrow and get this done as quickly as we can, so we'll devote the next few weekends to it."

Then he sobered. "We do have some wringer washers and gas-powered refrigerators."

Ada smiled to let him know she wasn't offended by his earlier joke. "Actually, I'm a teacher, and I wondered if you had any empty refrigerator cartons. I'm hoping to do a project with my class."

"Of course. Let me check in the back." He headed toward the stockroom, but called over his shoulder, "How many do you need?"

"Two would be good."

He returned dragging two large cartons and helped her load them in the wagon and even tied them down. Ada thanked him and, with Mary Elizabeth dragging on her apron, crossed the street to the hardware store for duct tape and a craft knife.

"What are you going to do with these?" Mary Elizabeth asked as they climbed into the wagon.

"You'll see," Ada said, and drove to the schoolhouse.

When she pulled into the driveway, she jerked her horse to a stop. Large trucks filled the school yard, and men were unloading wood and metal.

"What's happening?" Mary Elizabeth asked.

"I don't know." If the bishop or school board had planned any renovations, they would have told her. And they'd use Amish workers. These men were all *Englisch*, except for one man with his back turned who was wearing a straw hat.

That back looked familiar. *Josiah.*

Ada clucked to the horse and moved the wagon off the driveway and onto the grass. Then she tied the horse to a tree, told Mary Elizabeth to stay in the wagon, and marched up the driveway toward Josiah.

Whistles and catcalls followed her progress through the school yard, and Josiah spun around.

"Ada? What are you doing here?"

"I could ask the same thing." She waved a hand at the trucks and men. "Why are they here?"

"I, um, well, it's a long story." Josiah rubbed the back of his neck. "You mentioned you wanted a special playground for your scholars, so I drew up some plans based on what you described."

"You're building a special playground?"

When he nodded, she could have kissed him. Well, maybe not kissed him. That would never be appropriate. Reluctantly, she pulled her gaze from his lips. But definitely hugged him. If that were allowed. Which it wasn't.

"You were listening when I spouted off about all the things I wanted for the schoolhouse?" Ada couldn't believe he'd actually paid attention.

"Of course, and the pictures in the catalogs too. I tried to find a way to get them for you. I told you they could be made for a lot less money."

Ada sucked in a breath. "You're paying for all this?"

"No, no, my company is. They had a contest, and I submitted plans for the playground. My plans were chosen just yesterday, so I didn't have a chance to tell you."

Ada stared at him dumbfounded. "This will all be free?"

"Yes, all you have to do is keep the children away from the construction area for the next few weeks. I wouldn't want to see anyone get hurt."

"I see. That should be easy to do."

Ada was at a loss for words. All around her men were carrying huge wooden beams, unloading equipment. For a playground. *Her* playground. One she'd only dreamed about. "Oh, Josiah, thank you. You don't know how much this means to me."

She blinked back the wetness in her eyes and gazed up at him. A mistake. Even blurred by moisture, he looked good. His rugged face, broad muscled shoulders... *Ada, stop!* She forced herself to stare at the ground by her feet.

"You're welcome," Josiah said, his voice husky. "I hope the scholars enjoy it. I know you said it would benefit their sensory motor skills."

He'd even remembered that? She'd prattled on and on that night and at the center, excited by all she'd learned. And he'd cared enough to pay attention to everything, even the small details.

"So what are you doing here on a Saturday?"

Josiah's question startled Ada. What was she doing here besides entertaining thoughts about him that she shouldn't? "I, um..." *Think, Ada. The wagon. The appliance store.* "I planned to work on a project," she said in a rush, gesturing toward the refrigerator boxes. "I'll do it at home instead."

The tilt of his head invited her to explain more, so she added, "I wanted a multi-sensory room like they have at the center, but that's impossible. So I'm going to cut one side off each box and duct-tape them together. With a small door cut in it, it'll make a little hideaway."

"What a great idea," he said. "Very clever and inexpensive."

Inside, Ada was preening, but she needed to deflect his praise and rid herself of *hochmut*. "It was nothing," she mumbled. "I want to help the students learn."

"You do a great job of that. Nathan has learned so

much. And you've gone beyond your duties in offering to teach me sign language."

"We should start your lessons. Could we meet after school on Monday?" Ada hoped she didn't appear over-eager.

"That would be *wunderbar*." The smile that accompanied his words flipped Ada's heart upside-down.

"Hey, Yoder," one of the men called. "Stop flirting and get over here to help."

A scarlet flush swept across Josiah's cheeks. "I apologize. I'd better get back to work. Our company has a tight deadline for finishing."

"I understand. Thank you so much for doing this." Ada hoped she didn't sound like she was gushing. "I'm so glad the bishop approved of the project and..." Ada's words trailed off as a sickish look crossed Josiah's face. "Are you all right?"

"The bishop," he croaked. "I forgot to ask him."

"Oh, no." Ada took in the trucks, equipment, and supplies. "You can't ask everyone to wait while you get his permission."

"No, the boss set a strict schedule. And I can't leave until we're done. By then it'll be too late."

"I drive right past his house on the way home. I could stop and tell him you need to talk to him and give him some insight as to why the playground will be so helpful to the scholars."

"That would be wonderful, thanks," Josiah said, a worried look in his eye.

Ada turned to go, but said over her shoulder, "And thank you for doing this." Their eyes met, and Ada almost stumbled under the intensity of his gaze.

Turning her head, she forced herself to focus on the wagon. Now that she knew Josiah was a widower, she had difficulty reining in her emotions. All the feelings she'd tried to deny, to push under the surface, came bubbling up, increasing her attraction to him. But she had no business thinking about him in that way. He was still in mourning. But she couldn't help clinging to hope for their future.

*   *   *

Josiah tried not to stare after her as she walked down the driveway to her wagon. He couldn't believe he'd been so focused on surprising Ada, picturing her thrilled face when he told her the news, he'd completely forgotten about getting permission from the bishop and the school board.

"About time, Yoder." Marcus slapped him on the back. "Thought you were gonna spend all day talking to that girl." His lips curved into a sly smile. "Not that I blame you. She's... *Wow* is all I can say."

"That yer girl, Josiah?" Clint asked as he grabbed the other end of a thick wooden support beam Marcus had started unloading.

"Just because she's Amish doesn't make her my girl," Josiah growled, checking the plans to direct the placement.

Clint laughed. "Wasn't just that she's Amish, man. She eyed you up pretty good. And I'd say you were doing the same."

His face burning, Josiah hurried over to help Rodrigo with the unloading. He wished he hadn't been so gruff with Clint, but his coworker had exposed his secret desire.

* * *

The minute Ada got back to the wagon, Mary Elizabeth bombarded her with questions. Ada tried to answer patiently, but her sister's chatter distracted her from replaying her conversation with Josiah and from picturing his face, his...

She jerked her mind back to the road and to Mary Elizabeth's incessant questions. They'd almost driven past the bishop's house when Ada remembered she was supposed to stop. She jerked on the reins and pulled the horse to a halt on the side of the road.

Mary Elizabeth stopped mid-question and switched to a new one. "Why are we stopping?"

"I promised Josiah I'd tell the bishop about the playground." Ada turned into the Troyers' driveway.

"Oh, can I play with Martha?" Without waiting for an answer, Mary Elizabeth hopped out of the wagon before Ada had stopped completely and headed for the door.

Ada was still tying up the horse when her sister knocked. The bishop's bushy eyebrows rose as Mary Elizabeth danced from foot to foot and asked to play with his daughter. At his nod, she brushed past him and darted into the house.

He held open the door until Ada reached the porch. "Come in, come in."

Ada hoped he'd maintain his cheery demeanor once she'd explained about the playground. Her sister had disappeared, so she must have gone in search of Martha.

He motioned her to the couch in the living room. "Have a seat. You're here to see Betty, I presume."

With a twinge of guilt, she stopped him. "Actually, no, I'm here to see you."

The bishop still stood, his eyebrows arced in a question.

"It's about Josiah." When the bishop's eyebrows shot up even more, she hastened to explain. "I just came from the schoolhouse. I was taking over some supplies, and I met Josiah there. I mean, he was already there."

At the bishop's skeptical look, she hastened to explain why Josiah had been at the schoolhouse on a Saturday. "His company plans to fund a playground for the school. I saw the plans, and they'll be wonderful for the scholars. Not just our present scholars, but future ones. Everything is wheelchair accessible, and the rubberized ground cover will provide a soft, spongy surface if anyone falls."

Bishop Troyer only frowned, so Ada hurried on. "The therapy swings will cradle the children, and they're especially beneficial for children with autism." She hoped that might sway the bishop, whose expression darkened.

"The motion is calming and makes it easier for students to learn. The swings also stimulate children's senses and improve coordination and motor skills." Ada's explanation trailed off as the lines around the bishop's mouth tightened.

"Josiah should have asked permission first. This is something the school board needed to discuss and approve."

"He didn't know until yesterday that they'd chosen his project."

"He still should have talked it over with us before he

submitted the plans." The bishop's tone brooked no argument, and his lips thinned even more.

Ada hated to see Josiah get into trouble for his generous gift. "Can't you forgive him?"

"First I need to see what he needs to be forgiven for." The bishop jumped up and jammed on his hat. "Excuse me. I need to discuss this with the school board. Then we'll meet with Josiah." His words sounded ominous.

Ada sat there staring after him, wishing she'd presented the situation better. She'd hoped for a better reception and had tried to justify the need for a playground, but the bishop seemed more concerned that Josiah hadn't asked permission. Ada hated to think of Josiah getting in trouble for his thoughtfulness.

Slowly, she rose from the couch, wondering where to find Mary Elizabeth.

A stern voice spoke behind her. "Ada, I'd like to speak with you." Betty headed toward a chair opposite Ada.

"Of course." Ada sank back onto the couch.

"It has come to our attention"—Betty's tone sounded ominous—"that you had a male visitor last night."

"Josiah Yoder came for dinner because I was watching his son." Ada hoped the gossip making the rounds wouldn't damage Josiah's reputation.

"It was a rather long dinner." The disbelief in Betty's voice indicated she believed more had happened than a simple meal. "The Scriptures do warn you to stay away from all appearances of evil."

Ada gasped. It wasn't anything like Betty seemed to be implying. Well, she did have thoughts about Josiah that she shouldn't, but... "He's learning sign language. We're trying to find ways to help Nathan."

"There's no reason that can't be done during after-school hours."

"Yes, of course." Ada stumbled over her words. They should meet in public places. She'd been foolish to encourage Josiah to stay later at her house.

Betty stood. "I hope you'll take my advice."

"I certainly will." Ada rose, called for Mary Elizabeth, and headed for the door. As much as it pained her, Ada would confine her meetings with Josiah to brief teaching sessions after school when others were around.

Chapter Twenty-Four

On Monday morning Josiah prepared for the usual outburst when he woke Nathan. As soon as his son opened his eyes, he shrieked and jerked away. Josiah took a few steps back.

If his son was scared of him, picking him up would only increase his fear. Josiah's chest tightened as he remembered the way he normally swept Nathan into his arms. All that time he'd been terrifying his son. As hard as it was to wait, he'd give Nathan time and space, letting his son come to him when he was ready.

Josiah braced himself for Nathan's daily question, *Mamm where?*

Instead his son signed, *I miss Mamm*, and tears rolled down his cheek.

The thickness in Josiah's throat made it hard to swallow. He responded, *I miss Mamm*, but Nathan stared at him suspiciously. When he added his daily *I love you*,

Nathan shook his head and shrank back. That denial hurt more than pounding fists and sharp kicks.

In some ways, Nathan's outbursts were easier to bear than these silent tears, because Josiah had no way to reach out and comfort him. Although Nathan had clawed and hit and struggled to get away, at least they'd had some physical closeness, even if it was negative. But now, Josiah hesitated to touch his son. He longed for the relationship Nathan had with Ada. To do that, he needed to communicate and find a way to gain Nathan's trust.

Josiah walled in his pain and determined to start a new routine, one he'd decided on after seeing Ada's siblings take responsibility for cleaning up their messes. Rather than dressing Nathan, he pointed to the clothes he'd laid out, then pointed to his son. He followed up with the word *school*.

Nathan's face brightened, but he backed up to the opposite side of the bed when Josiah pointed to the clothes once more. His son opened his mouth to scream, but rather than picking up Nathan to dress him, Josiah strode out the door and closed it behind him. He was tempted to peek in to see his son's reaction but instead headed for the kitchen to start breakfast.

Ten minutes later, Nathan shuffled into the kitchen. Josiah avoided looking in his direction and busied himself with dishing out scrambled eggs and bacon. He risked a quick glance as he set one plate at each place. Nathan had twisted suspenders, his collar caught inside his shirt, his shirt buttoned crooked, and his shoes on the wrong feet. But he had dressed himself. Josiah's heart did a victory dance, and he resisted the urge to fix them.

Nathan climbed into his chair, bowed his head for

prayer, and ate everything on his plate. Josiah set a tooth-brush and hairbrush on the end of the table and cleared the plates. When he turned his back, Nathan slipped off the chair, pick up both brushes, and left the room.

Josiah didn't inspect Nathan's grooming and kept a large distance between them as they headed to the barn. Usually the buggy rocked back and forth with Nathan's screams. This time, Josiah slid open the buggy door be-fore hooking up Silver. By the time he had finished, Nathan had folded down the front seat and climbed into the back. He lay on the seat, sucking on his rabbit's ear.

After Josiah lifted the seat in place, he signed the three words Ada had taught him last week—*school*, *David*, and *Ada*. Nathan pretended to ignore him and closed his eyes when Josiah tried to sign again, but his lips curved up. For the first time in nine months, Josiah started the buggy with no shrieks, kicks, or tantrums.

* * *

Ada arrived at school early to find barricades enclosing the construction site. Heavy support beams had been dri-ven into the ground and were held in place with cement. David bounced on the wagon seat and signed that he couldn't wait to play on the playground with Nathan. Ada couldn't wait either. She wanted to encourage the others to use the equipment once the playground was completed. Her heart overflowed with gratitude for Josiah's thoughtfulness.

She unlocked the schoolhouse door and returned to the wagon for the refrigerator-carton hideaway she'd cre-ated. As she and David maneuvered the large cardboard structure from the back of the wagon, Josiah pulled into the school yard.

He hopped out and hurried over. "Let me help you with that." Turning so David could read his lips, he said, "Can you hold open the schoolhouse door?"

David nodded and raced over. He flattened his back against the door so they could enter. After they set it on the floor, Josiah asked David to wake Nathan, and David flew out the door, leaving the two of them alone together.

Remembering Betty's warning, Ada hurriedly adjusted the cardboard hideaway. "We—I should get outside to greet the parents."

"This is such a clever idea." Josiah opened the small door she'd cut in the cartons. "The children will love it."

"I hope so." Ada stood and smoothed down her skirt. They had to get outside before other parents arrived. She started for the door, and Josiah followed her.

He pushed open the door and stepped back for her to exit. Brushing past him made Ada's breath catch in her throat.

"I tried something new with Nathan this morning," he said.

She turned toward him and regretted it when her pulse jumped, but looking away would be rude. Even if she could manage to do so. The excitement on his face made that impossible.

"I let him take responsibility for dressing himself and getting into the buggy. We didn't have any outbursts. *Danke* for the signs you taught me."

"How wonderful!" Ada's stomach somersaulted at the way his eyes crinkled when he grinned. The sensation almost made her forget she needed to put distance between them before anyone arrived. Gathering her wits, she managed to reply, "You're welcome. And thank you for the playground." *Leave, Ada.* But she couldn't break eye contact.

They were still gazing into each other's eyes when Betty drove up, and Ada's heart sank. She rushed past Josiah and toward David, who was helping Nathan out of the buggy.

Across the parking area, Martha exited her *mamm*'s buggy and, with a bounce in her step, started toward the playground.

Josiah came up beside Ada. "I'm glad the school board decided to approve the playground, and that I can help build it. You've done so much for the scholars. And for me."

If they'd been alone, Ada would have basked in the compliment, though it was *hochmut*. But worrying about Betty watching made her edgy. She had to find a way to get rid of Josiah politely when he seemed determined to continue the conversation.

Josiah pointed to where his son and David stood. "I'm afraid Nathan may need a little straightening. I tried not to touch him this morning after he got dressed. I hoped it would help with his fear."

Ada couldn't help smiling at Nathan's twisted suspenders and crooked collar. "That was wise. I'll be sure to get him untwisted." She didn't glance at Josiah; she couldn't risk locking gazes again.

"It isn't only his suspenders. His shoes are on the wrong feet, and his shirt is buttoned..."

Any other time she'd be delighted to talk about anything to spend time around him, but right now all she wanted to do was escape. She cut him off mid-sentence because the bishop's wife was beckoning her. "I'd better see what Betty wants." Ada had a pretty good idea, though.

Martha approached and gaped at the beams.

"I'll see you after school," Ada said to Josiah, and moved over to join Martha.

"It will be beautiful," Martha breathed, reverence in her tone.

"Yes, it will," Ada agreed. "When you're done looking, could you take the boys into the schoolhouse?"

When Martha nodded, Ada crossed the parking lot, dreading the lecture she'd have to endure.

* * *

Josiah walked over to the wooden beams and shook them. They all stood firm. He inspected the work the crew had done on Sunday without him there to supervise. Everything appeared sturdy and ready for the next phase.

He used his inspection to sneak peeks at Ada as she stood beside Betty's buggy. The sharpness of Betty's tone carried across the parking lot, but Josiah couldn't distinguish the words. From Ada's slumped shoulders and bowed head, it seemed as if the bishop's wife were scolding her. But for what? Josiah's protective instinct urged him to cross the school yard to defend her, but the voice of reason held him back.

Ada nodded and backed away, but Betty shook a finger at her.

What in the world had Ada done to deserve Betty's wrath?

While Betty was pulling out of the parking lot, Josiah hurried over. Ada looked on the verge of tears, but when he tried to talk to her, she waved him away.

Hurt, Josiah stood there staring after her as she hurried into the building. They'd had such fun together last week. Had he said or done something to upset her? Josiah replayed their conversation this morning. Her face glowing in the morning sunshine when she stepped outside the schoolhouse. The way she'd turned to look at him when he spoke. She'd gazed up at him with… *With what? Gratitude*, he decided. *Yes, it must have been gratitude. Anything else had to be a trick of the sunlight.*

* * *

Ada stood outside the schoolhouse door to greet the remaining scholars as they arrived. Some of the children had difficulty adjusting to changes in the environment, so she wanted to reassure them. She also needed to let parents know to keep their children and younger siblings away from the construction, and she described the future playground equipment to satisfy everyone's curiosity.

Inside Martha was fielding questions and introducing the students to the cardboard hideaway. The refrigerator boxes proved invaluable for calming Will and Lukas several times that day, and Ada was grateful she'd made the hideaway. Despite its soothing effects, she was exhausted by the end of the day.

All weekend she'd been looking forward to working with Josiah, but knowing Betty would be supervising them dampened her excitement. She dreaded telling Josiah they'd have a chaperone.

When he came through the door to pick up Nathan, Betty was already waiting, leaning against the far wall, arms crossed.

At Josiah's broad smile, Ada's tiredness disappeared, and fresh energy surged through her.

He crossed the room. "Would it be all right if Nathan and I stop by tonight for a half hour or so after dinner?"

Conscious of Betty's eyes on them, Ada said stiffly, "I'm not sure that's a good idea." At the look of hurt in his eyes, she tilted her head slightly in Betty's direction.

Josiah gave a barely perceptible nod. "I see."

"Betty suggested we meet after school."

"So she can chaperone?" He turned his back to Betty, hiding his grin from the bishop's wife.

"It seems so."

"All right, teacher, where should I sit?"

Ada hadn't thought about that. She tried not to giggle as Josiah lowered himself onto a student chair. Then she sobered. Not only was Betty glaring at them, but the small chair emphasized Josiah's broad shoulders and long legs. She averted her eyes. "Maybe Martha's chair would be better."

"I don't think that would be wise. Then we'd be sitting next to each other."

"I, um, meant you could pull it to the other side of the desk."

Josiah did, but having him sitting across from her reminded Ada of the picnic table, and her mouth went dry. She struggled to speak, and her demonstrations of the signs were stiff and awkward. After six signs, she gave up. "Maybe Nathan could come to my house after school tomorrow, and when you pick him up..."

"That sounds like a good plan." Josiah jumped to his feet, seemingly as eager to get away from Betty's scrutiny as Ada was. "I'll see you tomorrow," he said quietly.

Although she shouldn't be defying the bishop's wife, Ada was looking forward to teaching Josiah in a more relaxed atmosphere tomorrow. Or as relaxed as she could be, feeling the way she did about him.

* * *

Yesterday Josiah had been glad to end his sign language lesson, but today, despite a promise to himself to only stay a short while, he had trouble tearing himself away. Ada had taught him several signs and reviewed some others.

Sounds of a scuffle came from the kitchen. "I can do it myself, Sadie," Mary Elizabeth yelled.

Ada jumped up. "I'll be right back."

Josiah rose too. "I should be going." But he followed Ada to the kitchen, where Mary Elizabeth was trying to wrestle a knife from Sadie.

"Stop!" At Ada's sharp command, both girls froze.

When Sadie noticed him behind her sister, crimson flooded her cheeks. "I didn't want Mary Elizabeth to cut herself."

"I see. That was wise." Sadie beamed, but Mary Elizabeth glowered.

Josiah couldn't help feeling sorry for her. He knew what it was like to have older siblings. Somehow the younger ones always landed in trouble.

Ada turned to Mary Elizabeth. "I chopped vegetables

when I was your age. There's no reason why you can't, but for now, I only want you to do it while I'm supervising. Why don't you wash the vegetables, and Sadie can chop."

Mary Elizabeth looked slightly mollified. Then she smiled at Josiah. "Are you eating dinner with us?"

He shook his head. "I've been here too long already." He met Ada's eyes and her disappointed expression. He felt the same, but if Betty had anyone monitoring their behavior, he needed to leave.

"Yes, we don't want another reprimand." Ada turned to her sister. "Can you run up and get Nathan?"

When Nathan came down, David walked him out to the buggy, and Ada helped him into the backseat before Josiah got in. It was such a relief to not have his son screaming.

"Thank you," Josiah said to her.

"It was a pleasure." Her broad smile seemed genuine. "Why don't we plan to do this twice a week? I'll teach Nathan after school, and then I can share the signs with you when you pick him up?"

"*Jah*, that sounds good. Do you think we should do a bit at school so Betty doesn't get suspicious?" He wanted to learn as much sign language as possible, so he could communicate with Nathan. If he were honest, though, spending more time with Ada was also a motivating factor.

"That makes sense. Maybe it would be a good time to review. I have trouble thinking when Betty's staring at me."

"I do too."

Josiah's heart sang as he drove home. For the first time in a long time, he had hope that he could establish a relationship with his son. They'd come a long way, thanks to Ada. And he'd get to be with her every day.

Chapter Twenty-Five

H ere's what we have planned for the media events." Lyle Anderson eyed Josiah. "I scheduled everything on a Friday or Saturday, so I don't want to hear any excuses." In a falsetto tone, he mocked Josiah, "I can't miss church."

Marcus nudged him. "Just ignore him, man."

"I'm fine," Josiah assured his friend. Plenty of people made fun of the Amish for their beliefs and old-fashioned dress, so he was used to it. But being singled out or having the whole schedule rearranged to suit him made him uncomfortable. He was grateful, though, they'd eliminated any Sunday plans.

"So here's the schedule." Lyle passed out half sheets of paper. "As you can see, this Saturday our publicity department will do a photo shoot of the empty playground and equipment from different angles. Then they'll take pictures of the crew. You all need to be here at eleven a.m. for that."

Josiah stared at the paper in his hand, his stomach

queasy. He hadn't realized the publicity department intended to take photos. Should he speak up now or wait and talk to Mr. Anderson privately?

"What's the matter, man?" Marcus whispered. "You look sick."

"I can't do this."

Marcus's eyes grew round. "You can't defy him on this or else..." He sawed his hand back and forth under his chin.

"I know." Josiah decided approaching Anderson afterward would help the boss save face in front of the crew, but the roiling in Josiah's stomach increased as the owner detailed the rest of the plans.

Anderson waved his half sheet in the air. "Listen up," he yelled, staring at Marcus and Josiah. "Friday, we have statewide media coverage for the grand opening. They'll take pictures of the children using the equipment."

Marcus groaned. "Oh, man." He closed his mouth when Anderson scowled in his direction, but as soon as the boss looked away, he muttered, "You guys don't believe in pictures, do you?"

Tight-lipped, Josiah replied with a terse *no*. Anderson would go ballistic when he discovered the children couldn't be photographed.

"So remember, Saturday at eleven here at the playground. Wear decent clothes, but something you could work in and your hard hats." He shot a sour look at Josiah. "And you," he said, singling out Josiah, "the publicity department wants some individual shots of you with the equipment because this was your idea." His disgruntled expression made it clear he didn't agree with their plan.

As the men were dispersing, Josiah whispered a

prayer for courage before he approached the boss. "Mr. Anderson, we have a problem with the photo shoot."

Anderson held up a hand. "You're not going to blow this. We have it all set to release to media outlets across the country. They even have some TV commercials lined up. The company has put a huge amount of money into this project, so they're expecting big returns."

Josiah clutched his suspenders. "The Amish don't believe in having their pictures taken. So neither the children nor I can be at the photo shoot."

"I don't care if you're in the pictures or not," Anderson said through gritted teeth. "But those children had better be there." He got into his pickup. "That's all I have to say." He slammed his door, cutting off Josiah's protest.

"They won't be." Josiah stood staring after the pickup as it zoomed away. He had to find a way to stop the photo shoot.

His first stop on the way home from work was Ada's house. Protecting her and the children was his main priority.

Ada came to the door, a kerchief tied on her head. She must have been cleaning. Seeing her, all words fled.

"Josiah?" For a moment she stood there as if stunned, then she said, "Come in, come in," and opened the door wider.

He could do this better if he weren't facing her, staring at her. He passed her and headed toward the sofa. "I have a problem, a big problem, and wanted to let you know first."

Ada sucked in a breath and lowered herself into the wooden rocking chair across the room from him. "Nathan? Something's happened to Nathan?"

She looked so distressed, he wanted to reach out and comfort her, put his arms around her, hold her close. Clenching his hands in his lap, he forced himself to study the rag rug on the floor. "Nathan's fine. He's with *Mamm*."

"So what is it?" Ada sat on the edge of her chair, leaning forward.

"It's about the playground," he started.

"Oh, no, was there an accident?"

"No, everyone's fine." *Everyone but him, that is.* "The company wants to do some photo shoots of the playground."

"That'll be nice," she said. "It's looking wonderful, and maybe it will help other special schools with ideas."

"No," he said, his voice tight. "They don't want to just shoot the equipment. They want pictures of the children using it."

Her sharp indrawn breath increased the ache in his chest. He should have taken more time to find out the company's plans before he submitted the application.

"I'm heading over to talk to the bishop now. The company intends to send photographers to the school next Friday." Josiah stood. "I'll stop back to let you know what the school board suggests."

"Why don't I go with you?" Ada suggested.

As the teacher, she should be there. But Josiah hesitated. Sitting so close to her in the buggy would be torture. A torture he longed for but needed to avoid. "Maybe we should drive separately."

"*Jah*, of course." Ada appeared as flustered as he was. "Let me tell Sadie, and I'll follow you."

* * *

Ada went in search of Sadie. "I need to go talk to the bishop about the playground," she told her sister. "I don't know how long I'll be gone, but you may need to start dinner if I'm not back in time."

Her sister grumbled under her breath.

"Please, Sadie, Josiah's waiting. He has a problem we have to figure out how to solve."

As soon as Ada mentioned Josiah's name, Sadie sat up straighter, and her pinched-up expression smoothed out. "If it's to help Josiah, I'll do it."

"I appreciate it." So Sadie would help Josiah, but not her own sister?

Instead of leaving while she was gone, Josiah had hooked up her buggy and parked it in the driveway behind his. She called out a thank-you, and he waved. As they drove, he slowed at all the turns to be sure she was following. When they reached the bishop's house, Josiah waited for her to accompany him to the porch.

Betty opened the front door, and her eyebrows rose when she saw the two of them together.

"We need to talk to Laban," Josiah said.

She looked at him askance. "I don't think this is a good idea."

"It's about the playground."

"Oh." She flushed and stepped back. "Come in and have a seat. He isn't home yet."

Ada and Josiah sat on opposite ends of the couch. Betty's eagle-eyed scrutiny kept Ada from even glancing in Josiah's direction. She clenched her hands in her lap and concentrated on the pattern of a quilt draped over a nearby chair to avoid thinking about Josiah.

When the bishop arrived, Betty waved in their direction. "Josiah and Ada are here to see you."

Bishop Troyer took a seat opposite Josiah as Betty exited the room. He nodded at both of them. "So what brings you here?"

Josiah explained about the photos of the playground and the children.

"*Ach, vell,*" the bishop said, stroking his beard, "we can't deny them access to the playground or school building because all the equipment belongs to them. It was built with their money and supplies."

"Right," Josiah agreed. "And their whole purpose was for an advertising campaign, so not having the children will be a problem. I wish I'd understood more about their plans before I submitted the application."

"Don't blame yourself," Ada blurted out. She wished she could erase the lines around his eyes and mouth. That led to a desire to glide her fingers along his strong cheekbones, to stroke his beard . . . *Ach.*

"I thought," Josiah said, "you and the school board might give the children a day off that Friday."

Laban leaned back in his chair and stared at the ceiling. "I don't want one school to have a day off and not the other."

Forcing her thoughts from the softness of Josiah's beard to the conversation, Ada said, "Most schools take field trips to visit other classrooms. Could my students visit the other school that day?" The thought of taking trips with her scholars had never occurred to her. They were only beginning to adjust to the classroom, which meant they might have meltdowns in a new environment.

Bishop Troyer tapped a finger against his lip. "Hmmm . . . That might work. I'll contact Rebecca."

Ada regretted her hasty suggestion. "I should have thought about Rebecca and the disruption to her school day."

"I'm sure she'll be happy to help. Most of your students have brothers and sisters in her classroom who can assist." The bishop smiled at Ada. "A good solution to our dilemma, but"—he turned to Josiah—"that doesn't solve your company's advertising problem."

"I know." Josiah leaned forward, his hands on his knees. "I'd better contact them to let them know."

"That would be wise." Laban rose. "I'll speak with the school board and talk with the parents."

The next morning at work, while Josiah explained the situation to Ralph, Marcus passed them and stopped short.

He swatted Ralph on the arm. "Man, you look like you're about to toss your cookies." He gave Josiah a questioning look and flicked his head in Ralph's direction. "You say something to him to make him look so sick?"

Ralph only groaned.

Then Marcus studied Josiah. "Actually, you don't look so good yourself. You OK?"

"It's the photographs," Josiah muttered. "I need to let the advertising department know our schoolchildren can't be photographed."

"Oh." Now it was Marcus's turn to look worried. "That bites. Wish I could help." He gave Josiah's shoulder a squeeze and walked on past. A few yards away, he halted and turned to Josiah. "Here, man." Marcus tossed him a cell phone. "You can use my phone to call."

Josiah caught it. "Thanks."

Ralph dug through an accordion folder stashed behind the backseat of his truck. "I'm guessing you don't want to call Lyle direct."

Josiah winced. "I'd rather not. Is there someone in advertising I can talk to?"

"Here ya go." Ralph handed him a tattered paper. "This is a list of all the departments at corporate." He tapped a finger on a number. "Want me to read it to you?"

"Could you put it in for me?" Some of the men in his community secretly used cell phones, but Josiah never had.

Ralph snorted. "You don't know how to use one of these?" He tapped the screen multiple times, then held it to his ear. "It's ringing. When you're done, hit this."

Josiah nodded and pressed the phone to his ear. When a voice answered, he stammered out his problem. They connected him with someone else, who passed him on to another department. Josiah listened to tinny music while he waited. It was a wonder *Englischers* got anything done if they spent all this time waiting. Better to do it the Amish way—face to face.

By the time he finally spoke to the person in charge of the project, he'd almost forgotten why he called, and he'd lost an hour of work. The man spent the first few minutes yelling and threatening, but when Josiah returned a soft answer for wrath, the advertising executive calmed down.

"We need kids," the executive insisted. "Amish kids. That was the hook we used to reel in the media. It's a big part of our SEO."

Josiah had no idea what SEO was, and the word *hook* made it sound like the man was going fishing, but Josiah could see how advertising was like fishing. Both had the same goal: to trap the unsuspecting.

"Are you still there?" the man demanded.

"Yes, I am. I'm so sorry to upset your plans." Josiah wished he could suggest an easy solution to the problem. "But we can't allow the children to be photographed."

"I get it, I get it. It's just that I didn't need another headache with this project." He was silent for a moment. "We'll have to hire models. Borrow or buy clothes."

Josiah didn't know how the bishop would feel about loaning clothing to *Englischers* who didn't follow their faith. It seemed a mockery of their religion. But he couldn't stop the advertising executive from purchasing clothing from local resale stores to dress up children. Would the community be upset with him for the false advertising?

"Josiah?" the man said. "Thanks for the heads-up. We'll run way over budget on this. Costumes, model fees, and who knows what else." He blew out a breath so loud it hurt Josiah's ear. "But at least we won't get there to find a deserted building."

Josiah apologized again before hanging up.

"Everything OK?" Marcus asked when Josiah returned the phone.

"I guess. I'm not sure the bishop will appreciate *Englisch* models impersonating our community in front of the school building, but I imagine he'll say we can't judge others."

And thankfully, when Josiah told Laban later that day, he echoed Josiah's words.

Chapter Twenty-Six

Josiah pulled into the schoolhouse parking lot on Thursday afternoon, hoping to catch Ada before she took Nathan and David home. *Gut.* She was still here. He strode to the door and knocked to alert her to his presence before opening it a crack.

"Josiah?" Ada pressed her clasped hands against her chest. "You startled me."

No doubt that explained the pinkness of her cheeks. "I'm sorry. I knocked to let you know I was here." Josiah clutched at his suspenders to keep from reaching out to soothe her. *Soothing her is all you had in mind?*

"What are you doing here?" Ada shot him a questioning look.

Hoping to see you, spend time with you. Josiah tamped down his wayward thoughts. "I, um, need the key to the schoolhouse for the photo shoot tomorrow." He could have asked Laban for the key, but he'd make any excuse to see her again.

"The key?" Her voice almost squeaked.

Had he frightened her that badly? "I need the key so I can let the media inside for pictures." He had an ulterior motive, but he wanted to surprise her. He'd already cleared it with the bishop.

"I—I wasn't sure if they'd be coming inside, so I've been *redding* up." Ada turned her back and gathered her cleaning supplies.

She brushed past him on the way to the cloakroom, and Josiah gripped his suspenders even tighter and fought the overwhelming urge to take her in his arms.

"Yes, they'll be coming inside." When she passed the cardboard boxes he'd helped her bring in earlier in the week, he asked, "Should we move the cardboard hideaway into the cloakroom?"

Her voice muffled, she said, "I guess that would look better for pictures."

He couldn't tell if his suggestion had hurt her. He hadn't meant to, but he did need the boxes out of the way for his surprise. "It'll make more room. I have no idea how many reporters will come."

"True." Ada emerged from the cloakroom with her hair smoother, her kapp straighter, her skirt brushed clean of dust, and her cheeks even rosier.

Josiah wished she'd preened for him, but she most likely would have done it even if he hadn't been here. "Let me help you with that," he said as she dragged the boxes across the floor.

She laughed. "I think I can manage two cardboard boxes."

He rushed over and grabbed the opposite end. "The duct tape might pull apart." *That's only an excuse for getting near her.* To cover up, he asked, "Did your multi-sensory room help?"

"It's been *wunderbar.* Will and Lukas calm down quickly after they go inside." She backed into the cloak-room. "Will sometimes goes inside and does his lessons in there. He seems to like being cocooned."

Ada's brilliant smile almost caused him to drop his end of the hideaway. He couldn't wait to see her face when he revealed the surprise.

"I'm so glad it's helpful." He'd have to find a good place for the hideaway if the children used it. But not until after the photo shoot.

"Thank you for your help." Ada scurried to the door. "We—I'd better go." Lately she seemed to be avoiding him.

"Can I ask you something?" He waited until she'd stopped and turned toward him. "Are you running from me? Did I do anything to offend you?"

"No, no, of course not." She flapped a hand, dismissing his concerns. "But we shouldn't be here together."

"I'm sorry. I forgot about Betty. I should have thought about your reputation." He walked over and held open the door.

She hurried through. "I'm more concerned with yours," she said as he exited after her. She bent to lock the door, then handed him the key.

Their fingers brushed as he took it, and he sucked in a breath. Was her rapid breathing because she'd been rushing? Or was she equally as affected by their touch?

His heart still pounding, Josiah waited outside the

schoolhouse until Ada and the boys had driven away, then he unlocked the door and went inside. He moved all the extra student desks into the cloakroom, flipping some over to stack them on top of each other.

Half an hour later, Marcus and Clint pulled their trucks into the school yard, and all three of them unloaded the additional equipment. Josiah directed them where to place things, and they assembled everything.

"Looking good," Marcus said as he lugged in the final bag of sand. "Hope your girl is impressed with the changes."

"She's not my girl." Josiah tightened the last wing nut in place and stepped back to view their work.

Marcus laughed. "But you'd like her to be."

Josiah wanted to deny his friend's words, but honesty wouldn't let him.

* * *

On Friday morning, Mary Elizabeth jumped up and down. "Ada's coming to our school today," she sang over and over at the top of her lungs.

Ada snatched the stack of plates from her hands. With her sister's bouncing around, the dishes were in danger of smashing. She set the plates on the table and then placed her hands on Mary Elizabeth's shoulders. "I know you're excited, but you need to calm down before we have an accident."

As soon as Ada let go, Mary Elizabeth twirled around in a circle, her arms wrapped around herself. "I can't help it. I'm so excited I get to see you today."

"You see her every day." Sadie's sarcastic tone and

superior glare made Mary Elizabeth shrivel for a moment.

Then Mary Elizabeth thrust out her chin. "But I never see her when I'm at school." She didn't add *so there*, but her tone implied it. She went back to setting the table and singing her song, but this time in a quieter voice.

"You do realize," Sadie said, "that Ada won't have time for us. She has to take care of her scholars."

"I know." Mary Elizabeth sounded on the verge of tears. "But she'll be there."

"*Ach*, Sadie," Ada said, "I'll make time for all of you too. Several mothers will be coming to help, so I'll have more time to spend with you." Once again, Sadie had made the point about Ada's scholars being more important than her siblings.

Sadie's comment pricked Ada's conscience. Ada and her siblings had reached Rebecca's classroom at their usual time, but her students wouldn't be coming until a little later to give Rebecca time to get everyone settled and ready for the guests. Ada stood at the door, tense and worried, hoping the visit would go smoothly. She also worried about Josiah, who planned to report for the photo shoot but avoid the cameras.

Betty pulled up first, and Martha tugged Lukas toward the door, a huge smile on her face. But Lukas refused to sit in the chair Rebecca pointed out. He flattened himself against the back wall of the classroom, and Martha stood close to him. Ada's other scholars arrived in a flurry, and older siblings claimed Lizzie and Emily, taking them to their desks. Lizzie's *mamm* sat in one of the visitor's chairs in the back of the room. Will's *mamm* came slightly late, but since Betty's scolding she'd been closer to punctual. Will joined Lukas along the back wall, and his *mamm* took a chair nearby.

Josiah, appearing frazzled, stuck his head in the door and beckoned to Ada. Screams came from the parking lot. Ada jumped up and went outside. Josiah's buggy was rocking back and forth.

"Nathan was fine until we turned away from the schoolhouse." Josiah rubbed his forehead. "I tried the signs I knew, but I wasn't sure how to let him know he'd still be seeing you and David. I'm sure he thought I was lying and I was heading somewhere to get rid of him."

Poor Nathan. And poor Josiah.

"I was hoping seeing you would calm him." Josiah slid open the buggy door, folded down the seat, and stepped back.

Though every nerve in her body was dancing at Josiah's closeness, Ada brushed past him and reached into the buggy to stroke Nathan's forehead. He shrieked louder and bucked away from her touch. She tried again, and this time his eyes flew open. He swallowed his scream, and his mouth opened in an *O*. Then he flung himself into her arms, almost knocking her over.

If Josiah hadn't caught her, Ada would have fallen. But now she was in even more danger of collapsing. He'd wrapped his arms around her to support her, and her body pressed against his hard chest; the warmth of his body heat penetrated the back of her dress. Ada's legs trembled, and with a sigh, she melted in his arms.

The thought of Rebecca and the scholars staring out the window snapped her back to reality. On shaky legs, she took two steps forward.

"Are you all right?" Josiah sounded winded, but he

didn't let go of her arms. "He's too heavy for you to carry."

Keeping her back turned to hide her burning cheeks, Ada forced herself to answer calmly, but she couldn't hide the breathiness of her voice. "I'm used to carrying children." With Nathan in her arms, she stepped away from his supporting hands, but the warmth of his touch still lingered. "I need to get inside." She set Nathan on his feet, took his hand, and turned to head back into the schoolroom, hoping Josiah hadn't noticed the rapid pattering of her heart.

"I know." He sucked in a deep breath. "And I need to get to your schoolhouse. I hope I can avoid the media frenzy."

"I'll pray for you."

A strange expression flashed across Josiah's face but disappeared before Ada could identify it. Desperation? Regret?

"Thank you," he said finally. "I'll need all the help I can get."

Ada started toward the building but stopped. "Oh, I forgot. If it's all right with you, David would like Nathan to come to our house after school again today." And she'd enjoy teaching Josiah more sign language, even if their time together had to be brief.

"Nathan will enjoy that," Josiah said. "But could you come to the schoolhouse this afternoon? Would Sadie be able to watch everyone for a short while? I wanted to get your opinion on something, and I can give you back the key."

With Betty's lecture ringing in her ears, Ada hesitated. But it wouldn't take long to give an opinion and hand over a key, and they'd be outside. "I guess so," she said finally. If she told Sadie she had to meet Josiah, her sister would be happy to watch everyone for a short while.

Josiah looked a little hurt by her lackluster response. "Thanks."

Ada wished she could correct what she'd done, but she had no idea how to do that without giving away her real feelings. "I'll see you this afternoon. I hope everything works out all right with the advertisers." She hurried off.

When they reached the schoolhouse door, Nathan glanced over his shoulder to watch his *daed*'s buggy leave and released a slow breath as it turned onto the main road. Ada ached for both of them. She needed to stop letting Betty's paranoia prevent her from helping Josiah and Nathan communicate.

Once Ada entered the schoolroom, Rebecca said, "Now that everyone's here, we'll get started."

Although Rebecca hadn't meant it as a rebuke, Ada was self-conscious about how long she'd been outside with Josiah. From the back of the room, she couldn't see out the windows, but Rebecca and her scholars could. Had they seen the embrace? It had only been assistance to prevent her from falling, but it may have looked different to everyone else.

Nathan wriggled off the chair beside her when David beckoned to him. Sadie slid her chair over to make room for Nathan to sit beside David. Rebecca waited until Nathan had settled into place, then she motioned for her scholars to come to the front of the room.

"We planned a special greeting for you today," Rebecca announced.

Ada's heart swelled as her siblings' voices rang out loud and clear in a welcome song while Sadie signed the words. What a thoughtful gesture! Or it would have been if Lukas hadn't cringed and backed against the wall and Will hadn't covered his ears.

The rest of the day went surprisingly well, with only a few meltdowns. Her students participated in several of the class activities, and Rebecca assigned one scholar to play with each of Ada's students during recess. Despite it being a busy day, most of Ada's thoughts centered around Josiah. She prayed about the playground, but most often, she drifted into daydreams about Josiah's embrace.

* * *

Josiah arrived before the photographers and unlocked the schoolhouse. He strolled through the buildings and the grounds outside to be sure everything was in place.

Lyle Anderson got out of his truck. "Well, at least you showed up." He glanced around. "Where are the kids?"

Josiah had been dreading this. Evidently, the advertising department hadn't told Lyle about the change in plans. Josiah could stall until the models arrived, but his conscience urged him to tell the whole truth. Taking a deep breath, he said, "The children won't be here today. They're visiting another school, but—"

Face red and eyes bulging, Anderson leaned into Josiah's face. "I told you not to mess this up," he screamed.

"I let the advertising department know." Josiah kept his voice quiet and calm.

Anderson adopted a fighting stance, legs spread and fists clenched. "You contacted them without telling me?"

"I'm sorry," Josiah said. "I shouldn't have."

Lyle swore. "You certainly shouldn't have. We can't have the shoot without kids." His voice rose to an even higher pitch.

"The man I spoke to said they'd bring in models."

"Do you know what models cost? We're already way over budget." Anderson stomped off muttering.

Josiah headed after him. "Mr. Anderson?" The boss kept his back turned and ignored the call, but Josiah caught up with him. "I realize my misunderstanding cost the company money. Please take any extra expenses from my pay."

Anderson snorted. "You think your paltry salary could come close to what they'll be paying the models? They'd be docking your pay until Christmas of next year." He turned and faced Josiah. "You rich enough to afford that?"

"No, but it's not fair for the company to lose money over my mistake. Whatever it costs, I'll pay." Even if it meant getting a second job.

"Forget it," Anderson growled. "You know what a headache that would be for accounting? More trouble than it's worth."

While Anderson directed traffic to a grassy area opposite the playground, Josiah hung the special cocoon swing he'd bought beside the swings the company had provided. It had been expensive, but he wanted to contribute something special. This was his way of showing his appreciation for all Ada had done for Nathan.

"Hey," the boss bellowed, "don't get dirty footprints on the rubber."

Josiah tested the swing to be sure it was secure. Then he bent and wiped away the faint impressions his shoes had made on the blue rubberized ground cover under the equipment.

Soon after Marcus and Clint pulled in, the child models, dressed in Amish clothing, piled out of a van, and the driver sent four of them into the schoolhouse. One small girl waited while the driver unloaded a wheelchair. Then she hopped in, and he pushed her toward the building.

Josiah held open the door and asked as they passed, "She doesn't really need that wheelchair, does she?" After he said it, he worried his question might be rude, but he was curious.

"Of course not," the man replied. "She'll just use it for the pictures."

"Isn't that dishonest?"

"Huh?" The man looked at Josiah as if he were crazy.

But Josiah still puzzled over it after the photographers arrived and the girl posed on the special wheelchair slide and ramps. Why would they let the photographers believe a lie? Didn't it bother their consciences?

As Anderson led the photographers and reporters around, he pointed out all the special features of the playground, quoting some of the articles Josiah had read about the benefits. He also took credit for the cocoon swing outside and the equipment Josiah had built and paid for inside, while sending Josiah a *don't-you-dare-contradict-me* glance.

Marcus started to interrupt until Josiah stopped him. "But it's not fair," Marcus muttered. "It's your work and your money."

"I didn't do it for credit." Josiah wanted no part of

showing off, bragging about accomplishments, being in the limelight. Besides being *hochmut*, it diminished the real purpose of the work—being of service to others. Although, if he were honest, he'd also had another motive. Pleasing Ada.

Josiah again had to deflect attention from himself during the photo shoot of the crew. He requested the photographers not snap pictures of him, and he stayed out of the group shots of the crew. And when the company photographer insisted on a picture of the "idea man" behind the playground, Josiah motioned to Lyle Anderson.

"He's the real head of the project," Josiah insisted.

Anderson's mouth dropped open. He stepped closer to Josiah and said in a low voice, "Everyone wants credit. Go get in the picture."

Josiah shook his head. "I don't."

After the photographers and reporters left, Anderson called the crew together. "Great job, guys. Thank you for all your hard work. This publicity will help the company and attract new business. So you helped save your jobs." He dismissed the men, but told Josiah to wait.

Marcus clapped Josiah on the shoulder. "Good luck, man," he whispered. "I doubt he'll fire you after this success."

Josiah wasn't so sure. Dread pooled in his stomach as he headed toward Anderson. Marcus had no idea how much Josiah's mistake had cost the company.

A slight flush stained Anderson's cheeks. "Look, I know I've come down hard on you for your religion. Although I don't agree with any of it"—he avoided Josiah's eyes—"I do admire people who stick up for their beliefs. You showed yourself to be the better man today."

Josiah stood there, shaking his head, as Anderson walked off. His boss saw everything—even morality—as a competition. Josiah had no desire to be a better man than anyone else. He'd been raised to be the best person he could be in God's sight.

* * *

When Ada turned into the schoolhouse drive that evening, the only vehicle parked on the playground belonged to Josiah. The photographers must have gone, which was a relief. She hoped Josiah had avoided them. He climbed out of his buggy as she drove into the lot.

He hurried over. "Before I return the key, I wanted to show you something." Ushering her toward the schoolhouse door, he said, "I'll go in first, but please don't look yet."

Ada glanced behind her, almost expecting to see Betty behind her, frowning. By the time she turned around, Josiah had slipped through the door and closed it so she couldn't see inside. When he opened it, she'd insist on standing out here to view whatever he had in mind.

The door creaked open, and Josiah stared at her. Ada forced herself to break eye contact. Then she stood there transfixed.

The desks were missing. In their place were therapy swings. *Therapy swings.* Ada forgot her vow about not entering the building and rushed toward them. She slid her hand down the slick coolness of one of the metal supports, then pushed the mesh seat until it swung back and forth, as she imagined Will and Lukas cradled in these cocoons. Her heart filled to bursting, she barely heard Josiah's soft words.

"There's more behind you," he said.

Ada let go of the swing and spun around. "Is that—?" She pressed a hand against her mouth. *A sand table.* She took a few steps toward it and stopped. Turning toward Josiah, she said, "You didn't tell me about the interior plans."

"I wanted it to be a surprise. I hope it's all right."

All right? It was more than all right, it was so amazing she couldn't put it into words. She nodded.

Josiah studied her, lines of anxiety around his eyes. "Are you sure?"

"Very sure," she managed. She wanted to fling her arms around him and hug him. She clenched fistfuls of her apron to keep herself in check. "It's *wunderbar*." Her eyes stung, and she spun away from him and headed for the sand table.

She needed to do something with her hands to prevent them from touching Josiah. Picking up a handful of sand, she let the grains run through her fingers. "Oh, oh, oh."

"Is something wrong?"

"No." She gestured toward the sand toys at the other end of the table. "I just saw those. They're perfect." Measuring cups, spoons, pitchers, funnels, shapes, animal molds. "How did you know?"

"I ordered them from one of the catalogs you showed me. And this table can be used for sand, beans, and water, so"—he knelt and pointed under the table—"you can open it under here to drain the sand or water into this container."

Ada longed to kneel beside him to study how it

worked, but she didn't dare get that close. Her heart was already beating double time. Instead, she waved a hand that encompassed all the equipment. "You did all this?"

"No, no, two of my coworkers helped." He got to his feet.

Ada backed up a bit to increase the distance between them. "And your company paid for all this too?" she asked, her voice shaky. The company's generosity and Josiah's nearness both overwhelmed her.

He shuffled, and color crept up his neck and spread across his cheeks. "They paid for some, but most came from another donor."

"Who? What a generous gift! I'd like to thank him. Or her?"

Josiah didn't meet her eyes. "He prefers to remain anonymous."

He seemed to be hiding something, but Ada had no time to find out. "Please convey my thanks. I'll have the children write thank-you notes. Perhaps you'd be kind enough to deliver them." She could barely breathe with him in touching distance. They'd been in the schoolhouse together much too long. "We should go."

Josiah only nodded.

As they reached the door, Ada turned for one last look at the newly furnished room. *First the playground, now this.* Everything she'd dreamed of having for her students. Her eyes blurred. "Thank you," she whispered, although the words proved inadequate to express all the gratitude in her heart.

* * *

Ada's soft words touched Josiah, constricting his chest in exquisite pain and longing. He forced himself to wrap his fingers around the doorknob, and the cool metal warmed rapidly from the heat of his hand. He determined not to look at her as he opened the door, but as she passed, he lost the battle. Her gaze locked on his, and he drowned in the crystalline blue of her eyes.

A click startled them. Josiah jumped in front of Ada to shield her from the photographer and held a hand in front of his face. The camera clicked again.

"Please," Josiah said, turning his back. "Don't photograph us."

Josiah stood inches away, so close he feared she could hear the rapid staccato of his heart. So close the swift fluttering of her breath lifted the hairs of his beard. So close he could sweep her into his arms. Her wide eyes reminded him of a doe startled by a hunter.

More clicks propelled him into action. He reached for her and turned her so her back faced the camera. Then sheltering her with his arms and body, he gently guided her into the building and slammed the door.

Still breathing hard, he released his hold. "I'm so sorry. I thought all the photographers were gone for the day."

"Don't blame yourself."

But he did. For this and for her trembling. It was his fault the photographer had startled her like this. "I should never have submitted that grant application without checking all the requirements."

"I'm still glad you applied," she said, her words unsteady. "If you hadn't, the scholars wouldn't have all this wonderful new equipment."

"That's true." But was it worth the problems he'd created? "Why don't you stay in here, while I try to reason with the photographer?"

Tilting his hat as far forward as he could and blocking his face with his hand, Josiah slipped out the door and approached the young man. "The photo shoot was this morning."

"Yeah, I know. I accidentally deleted some of the photos I took when I tried to send them."

"You're welcome to take as many pictures as you'd like of the playground, but please don't take any pictures of us or use the ones you've already taken."

"Aren't you being hypocritical, dude?" the photographer asked. "You let them photograph the kids this morning."

"Those children weren't..." He'd promised Lyle he wouldn't tell anyone.

"Oh, wait a minute, I get it. It isn't the photos you're worried about." The young man leered. "That girl in there isn't your wife, is she?"

The question caught Josiah off guard. "No, no, she's not."

"So you're cheating on your wife?" At Josiah's shocked look, he continued, "I live around here, so I know what your beard means. You're married."

In truth, Josiah was cheating on his wife, but not in the way the photographer meant. Everything he thought and felt when he was around Ada violated his mourning period. "It's not like that."

"Yeah, yeah, that's what they all say. When someone else does it, it's evil. But when you do it, it's somehow different." He shook his head.

To justify his actions would be *hochmut*, but he couldn't allow Ada to suffer for his mistakes. "Please don't print any pictures of Ad—the teacher."

"Ah, so she's the teacher. Pretty great set-up you have going." In a falsetto voice, he mocked, "Sorry, honey, I have to work late on the playground tonight."

"That's not—"

"Save it." The young man raised his hand. "Besides, I don't have any say on which ones they'll print. That's the layout department's call." He walked off, leaving Josiah buried under a load of guilt.

Chapter Twenty-Seven

The next morning when *Mamm* came home from baking desserts at the restaurant, she marched over to where Josiah was mucking out the horse stalls.

Slapping a newspaper against her hand, she demanded, "What is this?"

The rake slipped from Josiah's hands and clattered against the side of the stall. Pictures of him—and Ada—were splashed across the front page of the local newspaper. Having their pictures taken was bad enough, but what those photos showed was even worse. Ada exiting the schoolhouse while Josiah held the door, their eyes locked. Josiah facing Ada to shield her, making it look as if they were in an intimate embrace.

"Where did you get this?" Josiah asked.

"At Linda's restaurant. I picked up the bundle of daily newspapers she has delivered for her customers, and those"—she stabbed a finger at the offending pictures—

"were on top." *Mamm* skewered him with a look that demanded an explanation.

Any explanation he gave would be incriminating. But Ada deserved no blame. "I know what they look like, but our meeting was innocent." *Well, maybe not on his part, but for sure and certain on Ada's.* The angle of the photographer's shot, though, made it appear they'd both been gazing longingly at each other. Only a trick of the light.

"Please tell me you weren't alone in that schoolhouse with her," *Mamm* said, "so I can at least stop some of the gossip."

"I wish I could say we weren't." The nausea in his stomach increased. He'd ruined Ada's reputation. "I only wanted to show her the new equipment and give back the key."

"Oh, Josiah." *Mamm* passed a shaky hand across her forehead. "You do realize it's not quite ten months since…"

"I know." His words sounded sharper than he'd intended. He shouldn't be taking his guilt out on *Mamm.* "I'm sorry," he mumbled. "It's not you who's making me upset."

His main concern was Ada. Had she seen this yet? If she hadn't, he wanted to warn her, but going to her house on a Saturday would only add to the gossip. Perhaps not many people would see it. Most of the *g'may* read the Amish newspaper, *Die Botschaft*, but some also took the *Englisch* paper. Those who read the *Englisch* paper would condemn them both.

Mamm threw the offending newspaper in the trash, but Josiah fished it out when she wasn't looking. Alone in his room, he pulled it out and allowed himself to fantasize that Ada gazed at him with the same intensity as he'd stared at her. No wonder the *Ordnung* forbade photographs, calling them a form of idolatry. Pictures also posed another danger. Josiah lost himself in daydreams of his lips on hers. He forced himself to bury the newspaper under some clothes in his dresser drawer and tried to forget the images, but they haunted him.

*   *   *

"Ada, Ada, wake up!"

Still groggy, Ada waved a hand to stop Mary Elizabeth from shaking her and to prevent the images of Josiah from disappearing. She'd spent the last two nights in the dreamland of his arms. They were outside the schoolhouse with no photographer, only Josiah's arms around her, his head bent close, their lips . . .

"We're going to be late for church!" Mary Elizabeth shrieked.

With a groan, Ada let the picture of Josiah fade and rolled out of bed. She followed her sister downstairs to rush through breakfast. Then she and Sadie sat the girls facedown at the table one by one to pull their hair back into neat bobs and pin on their prayer *kapps*.

Despite their late start to Ada's morning, they arrived at Leah's house early, and everyone but Sadie tumbled from the buggy to watch the goats.

"Don't get dirty," Ada warned. "And come inside in a few minutes."

With a pained expression, Sadie trudged toward her siblings. "I'll watch them. I'm sure you'll want to help Leah get ready for the service."

Church benches lined the barn, and only one other buggy stood in the lot. The Troyers'. Ada headed for the house and found Leah and her mother scurrying around the kitchen.

Instead of her usual cheery smile, Leah frowned when she spotted Ada. "Betty's waiting in the living room. She wants to speak with you before the service." From Leah's pained expression, Betty's summons wasn't for a friendly conversation.

Ada's stomach roiled as she entered the room, where Betty sat stiff and upright, frowning at a newspaper in her lap.

"I'm disappointed you didn't heed my advice." Betty tapped her fingers on the paper. "If my previous Biblical warning to avoid 'all appearance of evil' didn't influence you, perhaps this one will: 'Be sure your sin will find you out.'"

"I—I don't know what you mean." Or maybe she did. Betty couldn't know about the schoolhouse, though, unless... *The newspaper?* Josiah had asked the photographer not to print those shots.

"Perhaps this will refresh your memory." Betty shoved the newspaper under Ada's nose.

Oh, no! Ada's shaky legs refused to hold her. She sank into the nearest chair, the paper rattling in her trembling fingers. She closed her eyes, hoping to block out the images, but every detail of the pictures had been burned into her mind and memory. In the photo, she'd been staring at Josiah as if... *Did he see these? How can I ever face him again?*

Betty's scolding came to her through a haze of shame. Having their pictures in the paper was bad enough, but even worse, the photo had captured her longing. Surely Josiah had seen it. And now, so had the rest of the community. Or they would soon. This paper would circulate through the *g'may* as rapidly as the gossip.

Leah poked her head through the doorway. "The service will be starting shortly." After Betty left, she shot Ada a look of sympathy.

The women, who congregated in the kitchen before services, had already headed to the barn. Ada hurried from the room before Leah could question her. Then keeping her eyes downcast, she crossed the parking area to gather her siblings. She couldn't bear to look anyone in the eye as she herded her family together and started toward the barn.

David tugged on her apron and pointed to Josiah's buggy just pulling into the parking lot. Ada wanted to hustle him along, but David had been helpful at keeping Nathan quiet during church. She shouldn't allow her own embarrassment to stop her brother from helping others.

Other than the clip-clopping of hooves and rattle of wheels, Josiah's buggy was silent. Either Nathan had fallen asleep, or he'd stopped fighting his *daed*. Ada nodded for David to meet his friend, but she kept her back turned and pretended to watch the goats with Mary Elizabeth while she waited for Nathan to join them.

Ada couldn't resist one peek at Josiah, who stepped aside so David could crawl into the wagon. Josiah's gaze swept the parking lot, and when it rested on her, he tensed and his jaw clenched. He pivoted so his back faced her.

Ada's spirits plummeted. He'd seen the pictures and realized how she felt about him, putting him in an awk-

ward position. If only she'd stayed outside the schoolhouse, this never would have happened.

Nathan still stayed far away from his father, but
he no longer screamed. Once David and Nathan had
joined her, Josiah strode off toward the circle of men
without once glancing at her. After a brief nod in
Ada's direction, Josiah's *mamm* trailed behind David
and Nathan. Ada's face flamed. What must his *mamm*
think of her?

Ada slid onto a bench on the women's side with Mary
Elizabeth on one side of her and David on the other.
Nathan sat beside him, and Josiah's *mamm* took a seat
at the end of the row. Ada stole a quick glance across
the room to find out where Josiah was seated. He was
directly across from her on the men's side facing her.
Though she yearned to study him, she avoided looking
in that direction. Throughout the sermons, she fixed her
gaze on the ministers who spoke. When Bishop Troyer
talked about sin, Ada squirmed, wondering if he was directing his message toward her and if his wife had any
input in the topic.

After the service, Ada went to the kitchen with the
other ladies. She took a job in the back corner of the
room slicing snitz pie instead of serving the tables in the
barn. But she couldn't help hearing the whispers behind
her, and conversations stopped when she passed by to
hand full platters of pie slices to the servers.

Leah's *mamm* tapped her shoulder. "I'll finish the
pies. Could you take another platter of meat and cheese
out to the barn? Leah said they're running low."

Ada longed to make an excuse to stay in the kitchen.
Instead she ducked her head to acknowledge Anna's re-

quest and picked up the tray. Keeping her head down, Ada trudged toward the barn.

* * *

Throughout the service, Josiah gripped the *Ausbund* and concentrated on reading each word whenever they sang. Then he gave each minister his undivided attention. Not looking at Ada during the service was difficult. He avoided glancing at Nathan for fear people would mistake the direction of his gaze.

Afterward, while he helped Leah's *daed* convert the church benches into tables, Josiah allowed his tense muscles to relax. Ada had gone into the kitchen with the other women to prepare the meal, so he didn't have to be vigilant again until she brought out the food. Once she started serving, he'd need to be careful not to look at her. He took a seat with his back to the buffet table, but each swish of a passing skirt behind him invited him to swivel his head.

One of the school board members, Merv Fisher, set down a plate filled with pickles, red beet eggs, and a thick Lebanon bologna and cheese sandwich. Taking a seat across from Josiah, he asked, "So how is the playground coming along?"

All the chatter around them fell silent, and most men's eyes fixed on Josiah. Evidently Merv hadn't seen the newspaper story. Josiah ignored the raised eyebrows on either side of the table.

Josiah cleared the thickness from his throat to answer the innocent question. "It's finished now," he told Merv. "You should stop by to see it. The sand table and therapy swings are also set up inside the schoolhouse." His words conjured up the memory of Ada's surprise—and joy—as she'd seen them, and Josiah had trouble bringing himself back to the conversation.

Merv smiled. "I expect Ada is happy with the improvements."

Ada's name hit Josiah with a jolt. He could only return a sickly grin.

One of the men nearby snickered. "I'd say she appeared overjoyed."

The snide comment brought suppressed chuckles, but Merv missed the undercurrents. Heat flooded Josiah's cheeks.

"Oh, *gut*, *gut*," Merv said. "I read more from those articles you gave us about how the playground equipment would help the students, and I think we—the whole school board—made the right decision."

Josiah mumbled a thank-you and shoved the last bite of his Lebanon bologna sandwich into his mouth. He stood so abruptly the bench rocked. "I need to check on Nathan." Though he could flee from the table, he couldn't escape the speculative looks or the embarrassment.

In his haste, he nearly barreled into Ada. She squeaked out a breathless sorry, and the tray in her hands tipped. He grabbed it to keep the meats from tumbling to the ground. Fighting the urge to look at her, he steadied the tray, and their fingers brushed. A tingle shot through him. He lost his inner battle and lifted his gaze. Once again, her eyes mesmerized him.

Long seconds passed before he managed to break their gaze. By the time he did, they were caught between the men streaming past and the women heading to the barn for the second seating.

Any denial he'd make now about the newspaper photographs would ring hollow. In ten seconds he'd undone all the damage control he'd tried to accomplish during the three-hour church service. Tight-lipped, he turned his back and searched the yard for Nathan, but his mind and body remained focused on the softness of Ada's fingers and the beauty of her eyes.

* * *

Ada returned to the kitchen, her legs and hands still trembling from running into Josiah.

Before she could compose herself, Leah sidled up to her. "I want to talk to you later."

The last thing Ada wanted was to discuss the newspaper photos and her feelings for Josiah. "Once we've eaten, I should get my brothers and sisters home."

Hands on her hips, Leah asked, "Are you avoiding me?" When Ada didn't answer, Leah said, "It's a lovely day outside. The children will be fine playing or watching the goats after the meal."

"I know." Ada bit her lip.

Leah laid a hand on Ada's arm. "I'm your friend, remember?"

To Ada's relief, Leah's *mamm* called her to take another platter of desserts to the barn.

After everyone had eaten, Ada helped with the dishes and *redding* the kitchen. She turned to leave, but Leah blocked her way.

"Look out the window," she said. "They're having a

good time. We can go upstairs to talk, or we can slip into the health food store to be alone."

If Ada had a choice, she'd prefer neither. "The store," she replied through stiff lips. At least there nobody could eavesdrop on their conversation.

Leah led her down the narrow hallway connecting the house to the shop. She opened the door, ushered Ada inside, and pulled two stools together. After motioning for Ada to sit on one, she settled onto the other.

"So what is going on? You two looked like"—Leah paused, as if picking her words carefully—"you've been courting."

"Those photographs made something from nothing." No matter how compromising they appeared.

"You're sure?"

"He's still in mourning, and I, well, I can't court anyone. Not with having my siblings to take care of, and not after what happened with *Daed . . .*"

Leah nibbled at her lower lip. "I'm sorry. I didn't think about that."

Neither had Ada. Not while she stared into Josiah's eyes.

*   *   *

Though it ripped him apart inside, over the next two months, Josiah did his best to avoid Ada. He stayed in the buggy while Nathan climbed out and went into the school with David. And when he picked Nathan up he kept his distance.

He wished he could keep learning sign language with Ada, but he needed to protect her reputation. Instead he drove to the center and asked if someone could teach him and Nathan. Together they planned additional words to add to Nathan's vocabulary so Josiah could communicate better. Nathan waited in the multi-sensory environment while Josiah had lessons, and his son emerged from the room calm and cooperative as long as Josiah kept his distance and allowed Nathan to go in to the teacher alone and get in the buggy by himself.

At church Josiah went out of his way not to get near Ada or even glance in her direction, but he paid a price for respectability. No more spending time with her. No more visits to her house. No more gazing into her eyes. But it also meant no more temptation and no more idle gossip.

Chapter Twenty-Eight

On Thanksgiving morning, Ada crunched across the light coating of frost shimmering on the grass. Nearby fields sparkled as the icy surfaces of chopped-down cornstalks reflected morning sunlight. Pulling her cloak tighter to ward off the chilly air, she slipped inside their neighbor's phone shanty. She'd hoped to have a holiday surprise for her siblings, but a few minutes later she returned to the house, the words *not yet* echoing in her ears.

When Ada opened the back door, the smell of roasting turkey filled the air. The warm, homey aroma brought up a wave of sadness.

Sadie glanced up when Ada entered the kitchen. She must have guessed Ada's destination because her sister's eyes asked a silent question Ada didn't want to answer. She shook her head, and Sadie, her mouth pinched into a firm line, returned to chopping onions.

"I'm sorry, Sadie." Ada scraped the slush from her

shoes before removing them and placing them on the wooden shelves *Daed* had built by the back door.

"It's not your fault." Sadie's words were clipped and bitter.

Ada worried she'd made a mistake in planning a big *Englisch*-style Thanksgiving this year. For the first holiday without *Mamm* and *Daed*, she'd hoped it would cheer her brothers and sisters, but instead she'd emphasized their loneliness and loss.

And the plans she'd hoped to announce for the afternoon had been scuttled. With a heavy heart, she basted the turkey.

Mary Elizabeth sniffled as she crumbled bread. Heads down, the twins chopped celery. Hannah stared off into the distance as she diced the potatoes to include in the filling.

Last year *Mamm* had been too ill to join them, but *Daed* had one of his good days and sat at the head of the table like old times. Although they didn't know it then, that would be the last holiday they'd all spend together.

Although they were all feeling the loss, Ada struggled to shake off her gloomy thoughts and concentrate on cooking. By the time they sat at the table for the meal, Ada was exhausted both physically and emotionally. Her parents' bedroom door remained closed, and her siblings glanced at it from time to time with tears in their eyes. Ada tried to make the meal as festive as she could, but heavy hearts made it difficult. And every time she glanced at the empty chair at the head of the table, her sorrow increased. *Daed* would never again take that place.

The last person to sit there had been Josiah. And that brought a different kind of pain and loss. If only . . .

Ada shook herself. Everything that happened was God's will, so she needed to accept it. Though she struggled with sorrow, she should be an example to her siblings. One of the best ways to overcome gloom was to help someone else. "I have an idea. You know how we used to take pies to Linda Beiler's restaurant in the afternoon? Why don't we do that today?"

No one wanted to leave *Mamm* last year, but every year before that, they'd participated in the Beilers' special event. On Thanksgiving the Beilers opened their restaurant to serve free dinners to the lonely, needy, and homeless. All of the Beilers' relatives and friends picked up members from the surrounding *g'may*s who had no family nearby and brought them to the restaurant.

Many members of the Amish church districts in the surrounding areas came to share pies and chat with the visitors. *Mamm* had always insisted they bake extra pies, and she'd send all of them, even during the years she'd been too ill to get out of bed. Last year had been the first time they'd missed.

Sadie blinked back tears. "*Mamm* would want us to go."

The others nodded, and Ada's spirits brightened a little. Despite their loss, they had much to be thankful for. "Let's go around and list our blessings," she suggested.

One by one, they shared their joys from the past year. When David signed his gratitude for his friendship with Nathan, Sadie jumped in and mentioned the fun they'd had with Josiah.

"Why doesn't he come over anymore?" Mary Elizabeth demanded. "We miss him."

So do I, Mary Elizabeth. So do I.

* * *

Josiah had risen early on Thanksgiving morning. *Mamm* left before dawn to help at the restaurant, but she'd left a long list of people Josiah needed to pick up and bring to the restaurant. First, though, he needed to drop Nathan at the restaurant to play with his cousins.

Today should be a day for counting his blessings, but for the past four years, he'd been without his wife. For three years she'd been in Mexico with Nathan, so he'd been all alone. Those last few months in Ohio she'd been too ill to lift her head from the pillow. This year she was gone. Nathan should have a *mamm. Why, God, why?*

He'd lost so much this past year, including his own son. Nathan still shied away from him—though he was gradually getting better. And the past two months of staying away from Ada had added to those losses. Not seeing her smile except in the newspaper photographs had cast a pall over his days.

His mourning period would end soon, and he could finally consider courting. As much as he'd like to ask Ada now, Josiah hesitated because people in the community would judge them for getting into a relationship too quickly. If he waited a few months, he'd protect her reputation and prevent gossip.

Although Josiah never again wanted to go through the pain of losing someone he loved, he saw something in Ada that made him believe they might have a future. And for that he was thankful.

He hurried to Nathan's room. He'd dawdled so much, he'd need to rush to get all his pickups done. His son lay sleeping peacefully, the stuffed terrycloth rabbit clutched to his chest. So innocent, so precious.

Today is a day to be grateful.

Josiah shook Nathan and stepped back from the bed before his son's eyes opened. Despite his distance, Nathan shrank back. Each time that happened a part of Josiah died. He pasted a loving smile on his face to cover his hurt and pointed to the clothing.

Nathan brightened. *School?*

Josiah hesitated to say *no*. Instead he used the new signs Katie at the center had shown them. *Thanksgiving. Cousins. Pie. Faithe.*

The last word made Nathan smile. He'd started clinging to his cousin Faithe since they hadn't been spending time with Ada. He needed a mother figure in his life, and eighteen-year-old Faithe enjoyed playing that role.

After Josiah took Nathan to Linda's, he drove down country lanes and assisted elderly people into his buggy. When the seats were filled, he headed back to the restaurant and started another round. The driving and conversations kept his mind occupied.

After his final round, he entered the kitchen to help, and Linda handed him heavy trays to carry out to the buffet. When the table was full, a local Mennonite minister offered a blessing, followed by silent prayer for the Amish. Then the hordes descended on the food. Josiah and his relatives carried plates to those who had difficulty walking. Soon everyone was seated at tables. Street people in their ragged clothes, some clutching trash bags of possessions on their laps, chatted with elderly Amish ladies in starched and pressed dresses.

Josiah leaned against a wall, his heart full.

Faithe passed him, carrying a water pitcher. "Aren't you going to eat?"

"I'm not hungry." He waved toward a table where an Amish widower leaned over to help a small girl cut her turkey slice. Opposite him a mother with four children communicated with Nathan using gestures and pointing. Once again his son had gravitated to a mother figure. "This was a wonderful idea you had, Faithe."

His niece smiled. "I'm glad we're able to help the community like this every year, but it wasn't my idea, it was God's."

Josiah's *of course* rang hollow in his own ears, but Faithe had moved on.

After they cleared the plates, the Mennonite minister led some hymns. Several Amish men followed with some songs from the *Ausbund*. During the singing, the door opened, bringing in a chilly gust of air, and Josiah looked up. Right into Ada's eyes.

* * *

Ada stopped so suddenly Sadie plowed into her, almost knocking her off her feet. She struggled to regain her balance and keep the pie carrier from overturning. She hadn't expected to see Josiah. He'd never been here before. But, of course, he was Linda's brother. So it made sense.

Josiah came to her aid. He reached out a hand to steady her. She trembled at his touch, and the pie carrier threatened to overturn. To her disappointment, he let go of her arm to grab the pie carrier and then glanced down at her.

Dazed, Ada stared into his eyes until Mary Elizabeth whined, "It's cold out here."

Ada broke the connection, and Josiah stepped back. Her siblings rushed through the door and crowded around him, peppering him with questions.

"Where have you been?" "When are you coming to visit?" "Where's Nathan?" "Will you come to read us a Bible story?"

Josiah laughed and held up a hand. "One question at a time, please."

David went first and asked where Nathan was. Josiah surprised them by answering in sign language. David's face lit up, and he rushed over to join his friend.

"You learned more sign language?" Ada asked.

A group of people tried to enter the restaurant but couldn't get past their small crowd.

"Maybe we should move out of the way so we're not blocking the door." Josiah pointed to a quiet corner in the crowded restaurant.

They retreated to the area he suggested, and the questioning continued. Ada was as eager to hear his answers as her siblings were. She waited until they'd completed their interrogation and had scattered to sit with friends. Then she asked again about his sign language.

Josiah stared at the floor. "I'm, um, taking lessons at the center."

"I see." She hadn't meant to let her hurt filter into her words, but the thought of him learning from someone else… "From Katie, I suppose." This time her tone sounded snippy.

He lifted a startled gaze to her face, and blood rushed to Ada's cheeks. As if the newspaper photo hadn't made her crush on him clear, she'd just betrayed her feelings again.

"*Jah*, Katie's been teaching me signs to use with Nathan. I could even tell him what we were doing today, which staved off a temper tantrum."

Was it her imagination, or were Josiah's face and words brimming with enthusiasm? And was his excitement about working with Katie or communicating with Nathan? The crack that had opened in her heart at the thought of Katie and Josiah together widened to a fissure.

Faithe came up behind Josiah and nudged him with her elbow. "We could use some help with dessert, *onkel*."

"Sorry," Josiah said.

"You should be," she teased. "I've been doing all your work while you've been hiding out in this back corner." She wiggled her eyebrows at him. "Why don't you wait until everyone's gone to spend time together?"

"We weren't..." Josiah shuttered the warmth in his eyes.

With an apologetic look, Faithe said softly, "I was only teasing."

With a sickish look on his face, Josiah mumbled a quick good-bye to Ada and headed for the restaurant kitchen.

Ada stood, alone, staring after him. Pretty, vivacious Katie was teaching Josiah. Ada's foolhardiness had cost her that opportunity. If she'd stayed outside the school-house that September day, she and Josiah could have remained friends. She would be the one teaching him sign language and spending time around him. Instead he'd been going out of his way to ignore her.

After Josiah disappeared into the kitchen, it dawned on Ada that secluding themselves in this dark corner probably undid Josiah's efforts to be circumspect. She'd managed to cast doubt on his reputation again.

She headed toward Mary Elizabeth, who was chatting with an elderly man leaning on a walker, but Leah waylaid her.

"You said nothing is going on between you," Leah whispered, "but you don't make it easy to believe."

If Leah had come to that conclusion, so had many other people. Ada shook her head and repeated the same excuse as she had before.

"Exactly," a sharp voice said behind her.

Ada whirled to face the bishop's wife.

The deep lines incised on Betty's forehead compressed into a formidable frown. "You're taking advantage of the fact that men in mourning are lonely and vulnerable."

Ada sucked in a breath. She had no such intentions. Contradicting Betty would be *hochmut*, so Ada stared at the floor.

Couldn't Betty see how Josiah usually went out of his way to avoid her? Besides, no matter how much she pined after Josiah, she could never marry. Not him or anyone. With the way the community had condemned her over the situation with *Daed*, what man would want to court her? And she couldn't ask anyone to take on the responsibility of raising her seven siblings.

Chapter Twenty-Nine

On Saturday afternoon when all the chores were done, Ada invited her siblings to accompany her to Stoltzfus Natural Products Store. "It's chilly out, so you'll need to bundle up."

Everyone but Sadie rushed to put on coats, scarves, and gloves. "I'll stay here," she said in a superior voice. "I'm sure the *little* ones will enjoy the goats." Her emphasis made it clear she didn't include herself among the younger children.

The snide comment gave Ada some insight into her sister's recent attitude problem. Sadie wanted to be considered grown-up, yet she resented the responsibilities that went with it. Or maybe she felt she already bore many of those responsibilities without being recognized as grown-up. Ada did tend to group all the younger children together. Perhaps if she included Sadie in more of a leadership role, her sister's resentment would lessen. Ada mulled that over as they drove to the store.

As the children piled out and headed toward the goats, Ada entered Stoltzfus Natural Products.

Leah looked up with a wan smile. "Oh, Ada, it's good to see you." Her cheerless tone didn't match her words.

"What's the matter?" Ada asked.

Her friend's morose face alarmed her. Leah exhaled a long, extended breath that seemed to rise from deep within her soul. "November is always a hard month for me."

Ada suspected she and Leah had the same inner pain: wedding season was difficult. A few of their friends married in other months, but most kept to the traditional November Tuesdays and Thursdays for their weddings. Going to weddings several times a week had only reinforced their singleness.

Picking up a box of small bottles, Leah motioned for Ada to follow her down a nearby aisle, where she sat on a low stool to straighten messy shelves and line up the new bottles. "The rest of the year, I can stay busy and push the sadness aside, but November is a constant reminder I'm destined to be an old maid."

"You don't know that," Ada said. "God may already have the perfect husband picked out for you. You have to wait for his timing." She automatically copied Leah's motions, moving items into neat lines on the shelf near her.

"If it's God's plan for us to marry, then why doesn't He send us husbands? I pray every day, but I'm still waiting for an answer."

Ada sympathized, but she'd given up her dream of

marriage. "It's painful to watch all those happy couples, knowing I'll never have a chance to court."

Leah's sly sideways glance indicated she didn't believe Ada's protests. "You and Josiah—"

Ada cut her off with a wave of her hand. "People are mistaken about us. Those newspaper photos made it look different than it really is."

"I'm not referring to those pictures. On Thanksgiving it was pretty obvious."

On my part, maybe.

The bells on the door jangled, and Leah hurried to the front of the store. When she greeted the customer, her perky voice had returned. "Hello, Josiah."

* * *

Josiah worked to keep his smile and attention trained on Leah, but from the corner of his eye, he caught a glimpse of Ada.

Leah's cheerful smile was accompanied by bubbly words. "What can I help you with today?"

"I, um, don't need anything. Nathan and I were passing by, and he spotted David climbing the goat farm fence, so of course, we needed to stop. I only wandered inside to warm up a bit." He rubbed his slightly chilly hands together to make his excuse appear authentic.

Leah leaned over and pulled a bottle out of a nearby box. "We just received a shipment of these." She turned the bottle so he could read the label. "It's a new product that's supposed to help calm children."

Josiah bent closer, but he had little interest in reading

about the tonic. "Hmm." His new position allowed him to see farther down the closest aisle. A flash of black gave him hope Ada was in that aisle.

"Would you like to try a bottle? We're giving a ten percent discount until the end of the month."

"What?" He'd been so focused on hunting for Ada, he'd tuned Leah out. She'd said something about a discount. "Thanks, but actually Nathan's much better. Ada discovered the problem, and we're working to communicate."

"Ada did?" The tilt of her head and eyebrows indicated she suspected something.

He attempted to make his voice as noncommittal as possible. "Yes, she's a good teacher. Very observant."

Leah made a face as if disappointed. "Yes, she's a wonderful *gut* teacher and sister and friend and person and—"

Her gushing made Josiah nervous. "I'm sure she is."

At his clipped answer, Leah's face reddened, making Josiah regret his sharpness.

"If you're only staying warm," Leah said, "feel free to browse the store, and let me know if I can help you with anything." She waved toward the aisle where Josiah had glimpsed the black fabric. "I'm stocking shelves back there. With Ada."

Had she emphasized those last two words on purpose? Or had they only stood out in his own mind? Leah seemed to have guessed his true purpose.

Not wanting to appear overeager to see Ada, he strolled each aisle in turn, starting with the one farthest from where Leah and Ada were stocking. For two long months, he'd barely glimpsed Ada, but running into her yesterday had brought all the feelings he'd struggled to bury back to the surface. It might be foolishness on his part, but he couldn't resist seeing her, talking to her, being around her. Especially now that he'd reached the end of his mourning period.

His heart started beating double time before he headed into the aisle where she was working. And when she turned and stared at him, he hoped Leah had some remedies for heart palpitations because his hammered so hard against his chest, his ribs hurt.

"Josiah?"

Her soft, breathy voice set all his senses skittering. And left him speechless.

"Are…we in your way?" She slid the stool from the center of the aisle to make more room.

"Ne…" He stopped himself before he said *never*. "*Neh*, of course not." Had that sounded too emphatic?

"We can move," Ada offered.

The only place he wanted her to move was into his arms. He gripped his suspenders to prevent himself from issuing that invitation.

"No need to move. I'm only—" What was he doing besides staring at her? He struggled to gather his scattered wits. "I, um, came in to warm up." *And see you.* "I can walk in a different aisle."

She moved closer to the shelf to widen the aisle, and Josiah imagining brushing past her, feeling her body heat. "No, no, I'll go the other way." He turned so abruptly he almost knocked over the cardboard display at the end of the aisle.

He held out a hand to prevent the tiny bottles of aromatic oils from tumbling. Once he secured them, he left the aisle on legs as unsteady as the still-wobbly display. He'd been foolish to come inside. "Maybe I should check on Nathan," he said as he hurried down the far aisle and out the door.

* * *

"Now what was that all about?" Leah asked as she eyed Ada. "Try telling me again there's nothing between you two."

"Leah, stop, please." Ada couldn't bear to have her deeper feelings exposed to scrutiny, even from her best friend.

"Did you see how flustered and embarrassed he was?"

Jah, he stopped dead as soon as he saw me. And he couldn't get away fast enough.

As much as Ada wished Leah's interpretation were correct, with the way Josiah had avoided her since the newspaper photos, she had no doubt he wanted nothing to do with her. Ever.

"Well, did you?" Leah demanded.

Ada straightened another row of jars to avoid Leah's piercing gaze. "Anyone would have been startled if they turned the corner to find us blocking the aisle."

"You think so?" The disappointment in Leah's voice revealed she'd been hoping for agreement and even a confession.

Ada refused to give her either. Any feelings she had for Josiah would remain tucked away inside, never to be shared.

To avoid more questions, she said, "I should take my brothers and sisters home."

Leah pushed her lip out in a pretend pout. "Already? You only stayed a short time."

"It's cold outside, and I only came to buy vitamin C. And to make sure you were coming to the Christmas cookie exchange."

Pushing herself to her feet, Leah sighed. "I guess it's that time of year again. We go right from a month of weddings to the buddy bunch cookie exchange." She walked into the next aisle and returned with a bottle that she handed to Ada.

"I know." Although they both loved their friends in the buddy bunch and the group had been together since they were sixteen, going to the annual Christmas cookie exchange became harder each year. Their friends had married or were engaged, and many had little ones already.

Leah led the way to the cash register. "It's difficult enough seeing everyone married or engaged, but the sympathetic looks they give us make it even worse."

Ada paid her and took the small bag. "I agree." And this year she'd need to endure speculation about Josiah.

"Do you want to ride together? I could pick you up on Saturday."

"That would make it a bit easier." Ada pushed open the door, and a gust of cold wind nearly blew her off her feet. "*Ach*, it's freezing out here. I shouldn't have left everyone outside so long."

"See you at nine," Leah called before the door jangled shut behind Ada.

Bent against the wind, Ada trudged toward the goats but stopped partway there. Josiah stood by the fence talking to her siblings.

One foot resting on the lowest wooden fence rail and an arm resting on the top one, he appeared unaffected by the cold as he gave Mary Elizabeth his undivided attention. Waving her arms and babbling, her sister seemed to be animating a story. When she ended, Josiah laughed, a low, throaty sound that started a tingling in her stomach, which spread through her body and made her legs weak.

Then he turned and looked at her, and her trembling increased.

* * *

The words he'd been about to say died on Josiah's lips. Ada, her cheeks pink from the cold, met his eyes, and once again he was drowning. Everything around him faded to fuzziness, the children's chattering receded. Only Ada stood before him in sharp clear focus.

Josiah tried to form a coherent thought. "I decided to stay—" *So I could see you.* He needed an excuse and seized on the first one that came to mind. "To be sure nobody landed in the goat pen." He *had* worried about that, but his conscience jabbed him for his dishonesty.

Ada's unsteady chuckle made him wonder if she'd seen through his half-truth. "That was thoughtful of you." But then, with a sincere smile, she added, "I appreciate it."

Josiah mentally exhaled. It seemed as if she'd accepted his hasty excuse.

David tugged at his arm and signed, asking if Nathan could come to his house. Josiah hesitated. *Mamm* was at the restaurant today, helping with an *Englischer*'s Christmas party, so they'd be alone for the evening. When he picked up Nathan, it would be close to dinner time, and Ada might feel obligated to ask him to stay. As much as he'd love that, he wasn't sure it would be wise. Not only because he'd spend the mealtime wrestling with his feelings, but also because his buggy would be parked outside her house. Linda had scolded him for the way he'd stared at Ada during the restaurant's Thanksgiving dinner.

David repeated his question, and Ada said aloud to her brother, "Josiah may not understand the signs. Why not ask him?"

"I did understand," Josiah told them, being sure he faced David, so the small boy could read his lips.

"That's right. Katie is teaching you."

The way Ada emphasized Katie's name made it sound as if she were upset. Had he hurt her feelings by learning from someone else after she'd offered to teach him? "Yes, she is, but she isn't nearly as good a teacher as you."

That earned him a slight smile. Perhaps he'd been right that she was bothered by Katie teaching him. "I wish you were still teaching me," he said wistfully. "I miss our time together." He probably shouldn't have admitted that, but he was glad he had when her whole face brightened.

"I do too. We'd love to have Nathan, and when you come to pick him up, we could spend a little time together"—her cheeks darkened to a deep plum color—"um, learning signs."

It seemed those last few words had been tacked on as an afterthought. Did she mean she enjoyed spending time with him, not just teaching him? Instinctively, he leaned closer, drawn by the look in her eyes.

A buggy pulled into the lot, and Josiah took several steps back. The bishop's sister and her husband emerged and waved. Had they seen how close he'd been standing to Ada? With the way gossip traveled, Betty would probably hear about it by nightfall.

David danced on his toes with impatience and tugged on Josiah's sleeve. Ada signaled for him to calm down, but he ignored her and signed a question mark in the air.

"I'm sorry," Josiah said with great reluctance. "Not today." As much as he wanted to, he had to protect Ada's reputation. He wasn't sure how to sign that, so he only did the double motion for *no*.

David ducked his head, and his lower lip wobbled. The excitement in Nathan's eyes died. His son's disappointed expression mirrored the one Josiah hid in his own heart.

Chapter Thirty

On Monday, Sadie came home from school with a large bolt of fabric. "Rebecca said you should get this first because you have six outfits to make. Plus you're working."

Ada had been so busy, she'd forgotten about the Christmas program. Teachers always bought fabric so parents could make matching outfits. Now she'd have to add sewing outfits to her already busy schedule. She sank down at the kitchen table and put her head in her hands. All the schools had Christmas programs, and she hadn't planned one. Nor had she bought fabric for the parents. What could she do with her scholars when most of them couldn't or wouldn't speak?

"It's all right. I can help with the sewing," Sadie said.

Ada's head shot up. *Sadie? Offering to help?* "That would be *wunderbar*. I'm also worried about what my scholars can do for their program."

"That's hard when most of them don't speak." Sadie's tone was a cross between flippant and understanding.

Ada smiled at her. Her sister seemed to be trying to make amends, but evidently, it was a struggle. "Yes, and many of them are shy or scared of people. Why don't we think about it while we sew tonight? I'll need to pass this fabric to one of the other *mamm*s soon."

That evening while they measured and cut fabric, Sadie said, "What about a pantomime for your students?"

"That would be perfect! Thank you, Sadie."

Her sister ducked her head shyly, but not before Ada caught the broad smile on her lips.

After weeks of rehearsals, everyone seemed to know their parts. Ada hoped they'd be able to execute them tonight in front of an audience. Unlike her siblings' Christmas program with its lively skits, songs, and poems, her class would reenact the nativity scene in silence.

After an early dinner, the whole family went to the school to set up for the program. As Ada pulled into the parking lot, David bounced excitedly and pointed to Josiah's buggy already waiting. He hopped out and ran over to greet his friend.

Josiah met Ada at the schoolhouse door. "I thought you might need some help setting up. I can unbolt the swing frames to collapse them, so you have room for the chairs."

"Oh, that would be *wunderbar*," Ada said as she unlocked the door. She hoped her response didn't sound too gushy. "I wasn't sure how many chairs we could fit in."

While Josiah took care of the swings, her siblings set

up chairs. Ada tried to keep her mind on setting up the props, but she kept sneaking peeks at Josiah. His shoulders so strong... *Was his mourning period over yet?*

Mary Elizabeth caught her attention when she twirled around in her angel costume, overjoyed at being part of the program.

"Help me set up your message cards so they're in order," Ada said, dragging the desk her sister would use to the front of the room. Then Mary Elizabeth flipped up each card, while Ada set up the new cut-open refrigerator carton that would serve as the backdrop. Will had meticulously colored it to look like a stable.

In front of it, she placed a small wooden feeding trough filled with straw and hollowed out a spot for the doll that would serve as baby Jesus. All the costumes and props were ready. Ada and Mary Elizabeth laid out the name cards and special papers for the end of the program by everyone's spot.

Lizzie and her *mamm* arrived first with the new baby. "Lizzie wanted to make the nativity more authentic tonight, so we had a few ideas," her *mamm* said. "We wrapped Matthew in swaddling clothes so he can go in the manger." She held out her three-month-old son.

"Oh." Ada stood dumbfounded. "That's sweet of you, but—"

"Don't worry. He's just been fed, and he's a wonderful *gut* sleeper."

While Ada stood there, opening and closing her mouth, trying to frame an objection, Lizzie's *mamm* marched over to the cradle, spread a blanket over the straw, and laid Matthew down. She and Lizzie looked so happy, Ada didn't have the heart to object. And Matthew was sleeping soundly. She only hoped the change in plans wouldn't upset Will, who was playing Joseph.

She had no time to think about that because the scholars were arriving and needed to get into costumes. Ada and Martha assisted the parents as they dressed their children in robes. Ada put weighted neck rolls under Lukas's and Will's robes, hoping the pressure of the rolls would keep both boys calmer.

After everyone had arrived, Ada stepped to the front and welcomed the families. "Because noise bothers some of our scholars, I'd like to ask everyone to be especially quiet and not to clap at the end."

People in the audience nodded, and Ada announced Mary Elizabeth as the narrator.

Pointing to her wings, her sister added, "I'm an angel too."

"Not always" came a quiet voice from the front of the room.

Mary Elizabeth frowned at Sadie.

Ada's face grew hot as people tittered, and she shot a quick warning glance at Sadie, then turned to the audience. "If you'll give us a few minutes to get set, we'll start."

Martha herded four of the children out the door, while Ada helped Emily into place. The small girl stood as placidly as usual by the manger. In her blue robe, she made a serene Mary. Miriam ushered Will to his place on the other side of the manger and handed him his staff. Ada had suggested he might like to tap the staff on the floor, and the repetitive movement helped to calm him and keep him still.

Once Mary and Joseph were in place and their live

baby Jesus slept peacefully in the manger, Ada signaled Martha to send in the shepherds. David and Nathan entered first, carrying their staffs, and headed toward the manger. Then Lizzie stepped through the door, and Ada clapped a hand over her mouth. Lizzie was supposed to carry a stuffed lamb. Instead a live lamb gamboled along beside her.

Mary Elizabeth gasped. "A real lamb. She's not supposed to..."

Ada waved frantically to get her sister's attention, and Angel Mary Elizabeth lifted her first sign: *Glory to God in the highest, and on earth peace, good will toward men.*

The shepherds approached the manger slowly as Ada had instructed them, but the lamb spotted the straw and broke away from Lizzie to nibble it. Before anyone could grab her, the lamb nosed the baby, who began to cry. Will dropped his staff, which clobbered Lizzie on the shoulder, and startled the lamb, who raced around the room. Lizzie and the baby were both bawling. Will covered his ears and backed into the stable backdrop, knocking it to the floor. The ripples of laughter drifting through the audience were quickly stifled.

Ada could have cried as she rushed to the rescue. The play was in shambles. David and Nathan were chasing the runaway lamb, Miriam was calming Will, and Lizzie's *mamm* was rocking Matthew. Between cries, Lizzie's arms and legs flailed, her head jerked, and she emitted clicking noises. Ada tried to calm her.

With Josiah's assistance, the boys cornered the lamb, and Lizzie's *daed* took it outside. Ada picked up the cardboard backdrop Will had flattened. When she set it up, it listed to one side. Matthew quieted, and his *mamm* laid him back in the manger. Miriam adjusted Will's weighted neck roll, led him back to his place, and handed him his staff.

Lizzie's *daed* came back in with the stuffed lamb they'd used during rehearsal, and shepherd Lizzie clutched it by one ear as her arms spasmed. Along with David and Nathan, the third shepherd knelt by the manger far enough away that her flailing limbs didn't hurt anyone. Soon some of Lizzie's tics calmed, and she hugged the lamb to her chest. Beside her, Nathan clutched his rabbit.

When all the children were in place, Mary Elizabeth helped Ada replace an end-of-program paper in front of each child. Then Ada signaled to Martha, who entered with Lukas, both dressed as wise men. Lukas carried a stuffed camel, and Ada sighed in relief that it hadn't been exchanged for a real camel. They carried fancy boxes that they placed beside the manger.

The original plan had been for three wise men, but Lukas had a fit whenever anyone else joined him. He stood quietly beside the manger with Martha by his side.

After everyone was in place, Ada's eyes stung. The backdrop might be crooked, one shepherd might be cradling a bunny, and one wise man towered over everyone, but they all looked so sweet up there. The program, which only a few short minutes ago seemed to be heading for disaster, was now back on track. Ada clasped her hands together and pressed her knuckles against her mouth. *Please, Lord, let the ending go well.*

Ada signaled to her sister, and Mary Elizabeth held up a sign and read it aloud: "What will YOU give to Jesus?"

Then in unison, all six children and Martha signed, *I give...*

All the rustling in the audience ceased, and all eyes were on the children as they bent down and picked up papers by their feet. Nathan fumbled with his, and all the scholars waited. He couldn't pick it up with two hands unless he dropped his rabbit. Reluctantly, he let go of the rabbit and lifted his paper.

As Mary Elizabeth changed the sign to say, *I give Him my*, all the children stood and held up hearts.

Soft *oh*s and *aah*s breezed through the room as the children stood holding the hearts they had colored. A tear trickled down Ada's cheek. They'd done it. Put on a program, and it had ended well despite the hitches.

Suddenly Nathan bent down, dropped his heart, and picked up his rabbit. Tucking his rabbit between his shoulder and cheek, he tilted his head to keep the rabbit in place as he signed, *I give...* Then he walked over to the cradle, hugged the rabbit one last time, and placed it beside baby Jesus.

At that impromptu ending, there wasn't a dry eye in the house.

* * *

Josiah stood, his back against the wall as the other families claimed their children, his heart too full to speak. When Lizzie's mom collected her baby, she tried to hand the rabbit back to Nathan, but his son only shook his head and pointed at the baby.

His throat tight with unshed tears, Josiah stared at the sign Mary Elizabeth had propped on the table. *What will*

YOU *give?* a still, small voice asked. In this Christmas pageant, his son had shown him the way back to God by giving his most prized possession to Jesus. In that silent, dark corner of the room, Josiah's soul wrestled until he'd made peace with God.

He might never understand why Ruth had been taken so young, but being angry with God wouldn't bring her back. By focusing on his loss, he had ignored his blessings, many of them here in this room tonight—his son with a generous heart, his caring *mamm*, a wonderful teacher, and even her seven siblings who had somehow wormed their way into his heart.

While he stood there, the last of the families departed. Ada knelt at the front of the room and signed to his son. Tears running down her cheeks, she wrapped Nathan in a hug. *Mamm*, still sitting on her folding chair, dabbed at her cheeks. Then Ada signed, *Daed where?*

Josiah's gut clenched, dreading the meltdowns that occurred whenever Nathan looked in his direction. He reminded himself that for the last few months, his son had started to come willingly without a fuss, but old habits still made him flinch.

Ada's searching eyes discovered him first, and inside him, a spark ignited. Her eyes, so soft and radiant, sparkling with tears, fanned the embers into flames. Flames that threatened to burn out of control. Powerless to break the connection, he remained lost in her gaze until she looked down to sign to Nathan.

He made his way forward and managed a few clumsy signs to tell his son he liked the program, but he had no way to share all that was bottled up inside his heart and soul. Words failed him too when he turned to Ada.

She also seemed to be at a loss for words.

He had to say something to let her know how powerful the program had been. "Tonight's pageant was"—he fumbled for a way to describe what it had meant to him—"meaningful, touching." No, it had been more than that. It had been transformative.

"I'm glad." The glow in her eyes added to the happiness filling his heart. Ada ducked her head. "I—I should finish cleaning up."

He wished he could stand there all night, staring into her eyes, but he nodded. "I'll put the swings back together." Such mundane words after a life-changing experience. If only he could express all that tonight had meant to him. She'd had no role in the program tonight, except as director, but if he'd had any say, he would have cast her as an angel. The angel who'd touched his and his son's hearts.

Chapter Thirty-One

When Ada pulled up to the schoolhouse on the Friday morning before Christmas vacation, buggies filled the playground. All her students had arrived before her. She panicked. She was late. The battery-powered clock in the kitchen must have been wrong.

"I'm so sorry," she babbled as the parents and students surrounded her. She fumbled trying to unlock the door. "I didn't mean to keep everyone waiting."

Josiah laughed. "You're not late, but don't go inside yet. We have a surprise for you, so we'd all like to enter first. Oh, and no peeking."

His dazzling smile left her brain so muddled, she couldn't come up with a coherent thought. She stepped aside so everyone could filter past.

"You look *ferhoodled*," Betty said as she herded Martha and Lukas through the partially closed door. "You know parents always give the teacher a Christmas gift."

Her Christmas gift? The last person who entered shut her outside. Even David had slipped inside. Ada stood on the doorstep, shivering. Then Josiah opened the door, and the heat that swept through her at the sight of him warmed her from head to toe. His mischievous half smile left her wondering if they had a prank planned, but she followed him into the building.

He ushered her toward the cloakroom, which confused her even more. All the parents and children stared at her expectantly. Martha was jumping up and down, clapping her hands silently so she didn't disturb Lukas. Beside her, Lizzie was windmilling her arms. Even Betty's recently dour and pained expression had lightened.

Ada passed them all and stopped dead. Someone had put a door on the cloakroom and totally enclosed it.

"Merry Christmas from all of us," Josiah said as he opened the cloakroom door. "Step inside."

Ada did and burst into tears.

The long narrow room had been totally enclosed and painted navy blue. Strings of tiny battery-powered lights hung along the walls, and the far end of the room held a small ball pit. A hammock hung from the ceiling. A reclining chair took up much of the rest of the tight space. Headphones lay on the shelf, along with two weighted blankets.

Ada had no doubt whose idea this was, and she wanted to hug him. If so many people hadn't been standing there, she might have, even though it was completely inappropriate.

She couldn't have asked for a better gift.

She turned and, in a tear-choked voice, whispered a

thank-you. Then she signed one. Several children appeared alarmed at her tears, so she explained they were happy tears.

Miriam handed her a card. "The *daed*s helped with the room, so the *mamm*s wanted to do something as well. Thank you for taking such good care of our children."

Ada opened the envelope to find a beautiful handmade card signed by all the children and their parents. Tucked inside the envelope were four slips of paper. Although she could barely read them with tear-blurred eyes, each one was handprinted by a different mother: *Good for one full day of childcare along with a dinner.* They'd each chosen a Saturday in January or February. What a generous and thoughtful gift! They all had homes and large families of their own to care for, so this was a major sacrifice.

Ada's throat clogged so she could barely speak. "I don't know what to say. Thank you all so much."

* * *

One look at the tears shining in her eyes, and all Josiah's lost hours of sleep on Friday and Saturday nights faded to nothingness. And when she met his gaze and whispered another thank-you, he was lucky they were surrounded by parents filing out of the schoolhouse, or he might have been tempted to sweep her into his arms and kiss away each tear.

Ever since the playground was completed, Josiah had toyed with the idea of building her a multi-sensory environment. During his sign language lessons with Katie, he'd seen the room's calming effect on Nathan. When he built the therapy swings and sand table, he'd looked at the cloakroom. It seemed a shame for it to contain only six coats and safety vests. The schoolhouse had once been filled with students, but they'd built a new building, and this older building had become the special school.

This time, before going ahead with the project, Josiah had discussed his idea with the school board. Although they'd been reluctant at first, Martha and Betty's high praise of the center's MSE room helped Josiah convince them. Ada's reaction today made that triumph even sweeter.

Her smiling face and tear-filled eyes stayed with Josiah throughout the weekend and on Monday as his family gathered at the restaurant for Christmas dinner. For the past twenty years, Linda had closed the restaurant on Christmas Day and on Amish Second Christmas the following day. Eating at the restaurant allowed the extended family to gather in one place. Each of Josiah's six older siblings came from Ohio, along with their spouses and large families. His oldest brother already had two grandchildren. Along with aunts, uncles, and cousins from both sides of the family, the room was bursting with energy and laughter.

Josiah had been a few years older than Nathan his first restaurant Christmas. Like his son, he'd trailed behind the older cousins, hoping to join their games and fun. Josiah and Nathan didn't attend last year; instead they'd stayed in Ohio to keep Nathan's life as normal as possible after Ruth's passing. But Nathan seemed to be enjoying himself today. Unfortunately, his son remained distant with him. Laughter and lively conversation flowed around Josiah, but even as he participated, his sense of aloneness and isolation increased.

His older brother Paul, carrying his two-year-old granddaughter, clapped Josiah on the back. "So how's that girl of yours?"

"What?" Josiah regretted his snappishness when a hurt expression crossed his brother's face. He shouldn't have been so curt, but Paul's question conjured up a picture of Ada that Josiah had to banish.

Paul frowned. "I heard a rumor you were courting the teacher from the special school."

"I'm not courting anyone." Josiah tried to keep his tone even.

Shifting his granddaughter in his arms, Paul sank into the chair next to Josiah. "I'm sorry." Rose laid her head on Paul's shoulder and sighed as he patted her back. "I can only imagine how difficult it must be." He directed a look of sympathy at Josiah.

Josiah squeezed his eyes shut for a moment. Having his brother pity him bothered Josiah. If he and Paul had been somewhere other than a crowded room, Josiah might have confided some of the rawness and pain. But a festive Christmas dinner was an inappropriate place to delve into such sadness.

When Josiah didn't answer, Paul cleared his throat. "So I was mistaken about you and the schoolteacher? *Mamm*"—he glanced around and located her on the other side of the room, cradling an infant—"seemed worried about a budding relationship a few months ago."

"A lot of people were, but it was based on mistaken information." He pulled the two newspaper pictures from the drawer from time to time. A few glimpses of her when he dropped Nathan at school. Her angelic face at the Christmas program. The joy on her face when she saw the multi-sensory room.

Paul waved a hand in front of his face. "Are you all right?"

"*Jah*, sorry." Josiah gestured around the room at the chattering crowd. "This time of year, being here alone..." *Wishing he were at Ada's table celebrating with her and her siblings.*

"It must be hard." Paul rose and squeezed Josiah's shoulder. "I'll be praying God sends you someone special."

"Thanks," Josiah managed to say. The problem was he'd already set his heart on someone special. But was Ada in God's will for him?

* * *

Unlike the *Englisch* who put up flashy outdoor lights and adorned trees with ornaments, the only decorations Ada and her siblings hung were strings of Christmas cards from friends and distant relatives. They also draped a garland of greens across the fireplace. Beside the hearth, Ada placed a small stack of gifts—one for each child. A rather lumpy package lay next to the larger pile.

For their first Christmas without *Mamm*, Ada tried to keep all the same holiday traditions, starting with homemade doughnuts on Christmas morning, followed by reading the Christmas story from *Mamm*'s worn black Bible. Ada shared the reading with Sadie, and her sister smiled in appreciation. After they sang a few Christmas carols, Ada let Sadie distribute the gifts, and Sadie surprised Ada by handing her the oddly wrapped package. They took turns opening the gifts, going from youngest to oldest.

Despite the package's unpromising outside, Ada's gift contained a book on teaching special students. "Thank you so much. I've been wanting to read this."

"I know," Sadie said. Though her sister tried to act matter-of-fact, her lips curved in a half smile when Ada exclaimed over the gift again.

Everyone spent time with their new presents before the afternoon meal. Though no one mentioned *Mamm*'s name, the silent sideways glances and choked voices made it clear when someone was remembering her.

"I don't suppose..." Sadie glanced at her siblings seated around the table and shut her mouth.

Ada guessed what her sister had been about to ask. Tomorrow was Second Christmas, a time to visit relatives. "Not today."

The next day, Second Christmas went similarly to the day before, except without opening presents. The roads were much too icy for travel, and Ada was grateful when Sadie didn't ask again. They'd made it through the first major holidays alone.

* * *

Josiah finished his lesson with Katie and headed out the door.

"Josiah?" Katie said, her voice gentle. "I think Nathan has the vocabulary he needs to understand about his *mamm*. I talked to the grief counselor, and she can come on Thursday, if you're ready."

If he was ready? Was anyone ever ready to tell a child his *mamm* has died? Josiah managed to keep his voice steady. "I'll plan for it." But his back to her, he squeezed his eyes shut as he fumbled for the knob and stepped into the hallway.

A soft hand collided with his chest. "Are you all right?" Ada asked, concern in her eyes. "I almost ran into you." With a nervous laugh, she removed her hand.

Her touch stirred him, and he could barely breathe. He wanted to keep her hand pressed against his thumping heart. First he'd almost run into her; now he stood tongue-tied. *Say something, Josiah.* He blurted out, "What are you doing here?" Then regretted it when she looked taken aback. "I didn't mean that the way it sounded. It's just that I was startled to see you here."

"I'm surprised to see you too. I came to pick up some books Hope has on autism. She's been a big help with lesson planning. But what are you doing here?"

"Taking sign language lessons."

"With Katie?"

"Yes." If he wasn't mistaken, she winced. Could she be jealous of his time with Katie? If so, she had nothing to worry about. He'd never be interested in anyone who wasn't Amish, especially not when he had eyes only for her.

"How is that going? I've been impressed with Nathan's growing vocabulary."

"It's been going well. Katie wants to schedule the grief counselor. When I first started working with her, I told her about your suggestion, and she agreed it would be wise."

"No wonder you look so upset."

"It'll be on Thursday." Josiah pinched his lips together so he didn't beg her to come.

Ada appeared as upset as he was. "Poor Nathan. And it must be so hard on you. Would you like me to be there?"

"Yes, I'd appreciate it. I didn't want to ask, knowing how busy you are." He needed to stop babbling. "I have to go, but thank you." He crossed the hall to the multi-sensory room to pick up Nathan.

The days dragged toward Thursday, each one endless minutes filled with dread. At last the hour arrived, and Josiah entered Katie's office to find everyone already assembled. Katie sat in her usual chair with a stranger beside her she introduced as the grief counselor. Ada sat on a thick mat on the floor holding Nathan. She'd agreed to drive him over after school to lessen the tension between him and his son before the session.

"We wanted the floor padded," the counselor explained, "because Ada mentioned Nathan's tantrums."

Josiah nodded. That was wise. Ada sitting on the floor rather than the chair made sense too. Although Josiah would have given anything to hold Nathan while he told him, he had to face his son to make the signs. Pushing aside his own heartache, he knelt before his son and swallowed hard. He signed the word *Mamm*.

Nathan's eyes opened wide, and he backed away, cuddling closer to Ada. *Mamm where?* he responded.

Clamping his teeth on his lower lip, Josiah readied his hands to tell his son the truth, but how could he inflict this pain on a little boy? Would Nathan understand?

He began with facts Nathan knew. *Mamm sick* and

train and *Mexico*. Ada reached for papers beside her and handed him pictures of the interior of a train and of the clinic in Mexico. Katie had shown Nathan the pictures when she taught him the words.

Nathan's brow wrinkled, but he nodded.

Josiah went on with the story. He explained about *Mamm* getting sicker. Each step closer he came to the end, the harder it became to continue, and he could barely hold back his tears.

"Don't be afraid to cry," the counselor said. "Seeing your sadness will show him it's all right to express his feelings."

A tear trickled down Josiah's cheek as he reached the words, *Mamm dead*.

Nathan did not react. He stared straight ahead, past Josiah or maybe through him.

Had he seen the words? Understood them? Josiah had no idea what to do. Repeat the words? The words were too difficult to sign again, so he moved ahead with the signs he had rehearsed: *Mamm go heaven. Mamm with God.*

Again Nathan sat still and silent. Then without looking at Josiah, he signed each word slowly. *Mamm... come back... when?*

Josiah choked back a sob and signed the word *never*.

Nathan shook his head wildly, then wrenched himself from Ada's arms and launched himself at Josiah, pummeling with his small fists.

Too overcome by his son's grief to stop the blows, Josiah sat there, stoically taking each hit both inside and out. Ada tried to intervene and stop him.

"It's all right," Josiah said. "He's not hurting me." At least not with his fists.

His anger spent, Nathan crumpled to the ground, wailing and throwing a fit.

"Let him go," the counselor said. "He needs to express his grief."

"Is it all right if I touch him?" Ada asked her.

"As long as he allows it."

Ada sat on the floor a safe distance from Nathan's kicking and pounding limbs, stroking his back. Josiah couldn't bear to sit there without responding. Josiah sat opposite Ada, who lifted damp eyes to meet his. The message of caring and sympathy on her face breached the dam of emotions he'd been struggling to control. A strangled sob escaped his lips as he reached out to lay a comforting hand on Nathan's head.

Why, why did Nathan have to go through such agony?

The minute his hand touched Nathan's hair, his son bucked away and batted at his hand. Josiah let his hand fall to his lap. To be so close but unable to touch Nathan was unbearable. He needed to do something to ease his son's pain.

After what seemed like hours, Nathan's cries subsided to whimpers, and he lay still. Ada reached out as if to gather him close but first glanced at the counselor. At her nod, Ada cradled Nathan close, and he slid his arms around her neck and snuggled against her shoulder.

Josiah ached to wrap his arms around both of them, hold them close, never let them go. If he'd done anything right today, it was inviting Ada to join them. She'd been a Godsend.

The lights flickered, signaling the center would soon be closing. Ada rose, still holding Nathan. Josiah reached for his son, but Nathan shrank away.

"I'll help him get his coat on," Ada offered, "and carry him out to the buggy."

The counselor stopped Josiah as he started out the door after them. "He may blame you for his mother's death. It's not uncommon. Give him some time to work it out. And don't be afraid to show your own emotions. It can be helpful for him to realize you're grieving too." She handed him a booklet titled *The Stages of Grief*, stages Josiah already knew intimately. The subtitle indicated it would help children, but how could he help Nathan when his son wanted nothing to do with him?

Chapter Thirty-Two

Josiah, his eyes stinging and his throat tight, leaned his head against the bedroom door as Nathan cried himself to sleep for the fifth night in row. All he wanted to do was cradle his son in his arms and comfort him. He'd tried the first night, but Nathan bit and clawed and kicked until Josiah left him alone. The second night Josiah entered the room determined to weather any storms, but the minute Nathan glanced up, he'd shrieked and signed, *Go away. Go. Go. Go.* As soon as the door closed behind Josiah, Nathan's shrieks ended, and the sobbing began. Sobbing that lasted for hours.

Nathan picked at his food, refused to participate in class, and stopped playing with David. He cried and clung to Ada after school and kicked and screamed when she placed him in the buggy. The few strides he'd made with Nathan during the school year had been lost in the storms of grief.

Josiah went to bed exhausted and woke discouraged. On school days Nathan dressed and crawled into the buggy, but his movements were listless and his face despondent.

When Josiah woke on Tuesday morning, two feet of snow covered the ground. *Mamm* took one look at the weather and went back to bed. Josiah let Nathan sleep in. The roads hadn't been plowed, so today would be a snow day.

Nathan woke and padded down to the kitchen looking confused. He barely glanced at Josiah, but he signed *school*.

Josiah pointed out the window. Nathan's eyes widened, and he pressed his face against the glass. He'd spent years in Mexico and last year indoors with *Mamm*, so snow was a new experience for him. Josiah set Nathan's heavy coat, snow pants, gloves, and boots on the bench near the door. Then he pointed to them, turned his back, and donned his own outer garments as slowly as he could. By the time he reached the door, Nathan had his winter gear on.

The two shovels Josiah had leaned against the side porch last night had frozen against the wooden wall. While Josiah chipped the ice to free them, Nathan took off one glove, scooped up a handful of snow, and screamed. Shaking and blowing on his hand, he jumped up and down on the porch. Josiah wished he could take his son's hand in his and rub it warm. Instead he kept his distance and signed *cold* and *snow*.

With a barely perceptible nod, Nathan rubbed his red hand against his jacket and donned his glove again. Josiah took the large shovel and left the smaller one on the porch. Nathan ignored Josiah as he started shoveling the path to the barn. A little while later, though, metal scraped on concrete behind him. Trying not to be obvious, Josiah turned his head far enough to see from the corner of his eye. Nathan was copying his movements, so Josiah left a bit of snow on the walkway as he shoveled, and Nathan scooped it up and tossed it onto the piles Josiah made.

After they reached the barn, Josiah fed and cared for the horses as Nathan peeked from behind the buggy. While Josiah fetched water, Nathan petted each horse in turn, but he disappeared as soon as he spotted Josiah returning. Having Nathan imitating his movements was exciting, but Josiah still longed for the normal father-son relationship of sharing chores, communicating, having fun together.

A long day stretched ahead of them. Josiah had an idea, but he wasn't sure he could convince Nathan to try. He headed back to the house with Nathan trailing behind. His son imitated Josiah's shuffling steps to avoid slipping and falling on icy patches.

The aroma of warm cinnamon rolls greeted them as he opened the back door. Josiah breathed in the heavenly aroma as he hung his wet coat and snow pants up to dry. Once again, Nathan copied his every move, although his face remained pensive.

Mamm smiled. "Looks like you had a helper today."

Turning so Nathan couldn't see his lips, Josiah said, "He followed me and tried to do what I was doing."

"*Wunderbar.*" *Mamm* smiled at Nathan and offered him a cinnamon roll. She laughed when he snatched it and wriggled onto a chair to stuff it into his mouth. "Would you like one too?" she asked Josiah.

"Shortly. I wanted to check the attic for something first."

When he returned, slightly dusty, about ten minutes later, he carried his childhood toboggan. "I'm hoping I can convince Nathan to try it. What do you think?"

Mamm's eyes got a faraway look in them. "You always loved sledding down that steep hill at Miller's farm when we visited Linda. He probably will too."

Outside snow plows rumbled by, clearing the roads. *Mamm*'s words gave him an idea. Miller's farm was only a short distance from Ada's. Perhaps having David along would convince Nathan to try sledding. And it would give him an excuse to see Ada.

* * *

Enjoying the peace of the snow day, Ada curled on the couch to read the book her siblings had given her for Christmas. A knock on the door interrupted her. She hurried to answer the door, unsure who would be calling in this weather.

"Josiah?" Ada stood dumbfounded for a minute before realizing he was standing outside in drifting snow and freezing temperatures. "Come in."

He shook his head. "I don't want to track snow into your house, and Nathan's all wrapped up in the buggy with blankets and a hot water bottle, so I need to keep an eye on him. I came to see if David wants to go sledding with Nathan." He cupped his hands and blew into them. "If it's all right with you, of course."

"It's fine with me. I'll call him." She turned and called up the stairs to Noah, "Please send David down." Icy wind blew in the door, and she shivered.

"I'll shut the door," Josiah said. "I don't want you get-ting chilled."

"Nooo…" Ada pressed a fist to her mouth. That had almost sounded like a moan, like she was begging him not to go. Too embarrassed to turn around, she waited for David to descend and signed Josiah's message.

David danced up and down while signing thank-you to Josiah.

Ada signed for him to hurry and get into warm clothes. As they waited, she said wistfully, "What fun! I remember being David's age and going sledding."

"You haven't been sledding since then?"

"Not that I remember. *Mamm* was too ill. *Daed*, well, he didn't have time for that. And there was always too much work to do." Ada had missed out on a lot of the play and fun other children had while caring for her *mamm*.

"Why don't you come along?"

"I couldn't. I don't like asking Sadie to watch the others."

"So bring them all. Miller's farm isn't far from here. We can all walk over together."

"You're serious."

"Of course. You work hard and deserve some fun. And Nathan will be delighted to have extra friends."

Ada studied him to be sure he meant the invitation be-fore turning to call her siblings. They all rushed to get ready, and soon everyone was trooping through the snow to Miller's Hill. Sadie took David's and Nathan's hands to help them over the drifts, and Noah helped Mary Eliz-abeth. The twins and Hannah walked in a line behind them, leaving Ada and Josiah to bring up the rear.

Nathan watched intently as Noah pushed off and jumped on behind Mary Elizabeth. Then the three other girls took a turn. The next time David hopped on and patted the wood behind him. Nathan, a look of fear on his face, stepped back and shook his head. Sadie hopped on behind David, and they sailed down the hill. Nathan watched them with a wistful expression.

The next time it was David's turn, Ada took Nathan's hand and led him to the toboggan. He cooperated until she tried to get him to sit, but with David's encouragement, he took his place on the toboggan. Instead of pushing off, Sadie climbed on behind him and wrapped her arms tightly around both boys.

"Can you give us a small push, Ada? I don't want to go too fast for his first try."

"Good idea." Ada leaned over to push, and the toboggan took off slowly.

Stepping back, Ada stumbled, and Josiah took her elbow to help her regain her balance, but he didn't let go. Although the rest of her was frozen, the place where his hand touched stayed warm, or perhaps it was only her imagination.

At the bottom of the hill, Sadie helped Nathan off the toboggan. David walked up the hill beside Nathan, whose eyes were shining. For the first time since the grief counseling session, he smiled.

When Sadie reached the top, Josiah took the rope from her. "I think it's time your sister had a turn." He motioned to Ada, then took her hand to help her onto the toboggan.

Ada was convinced his body heat penetrated through her thick gloves. And the sparks he generated when he set his hands on her shoulders to push the toboggan warmed her from head to toe. He took a running start, leaped on behind her, and wrapped his arms around her. The exhilaration that filled her was partly the excitement of zooming down the hill, but mostly it was from having her back pressed against his chest, his arms cradling her.

Wind whistled past her face, stinging her cheeks; snow sprayed as they slid, icing her eyelashes. Ada gasped for air as the toboggan swooped down the hill. Both her heart and the sled were racing out of control.

At the bottom of the hill, they stayed pressed together, Josiah's arms encircling her, catching their breath. Although Ada had no idea how she'd ever catch her breath while she was so close to him. She relaxed back into his embrace, and he seemed as reluctant to let her go as she was for him to release her. She'd have been content to stay there for hours, if the children hadn't been clamoring at the top of the hill.

"My turn," Mary Elizabeth shouted.

"No, it's not," Sadie countered. "Nathan should get another turn. He only had one turn. Everyone else had two."

"Hurry up," Noah called.

Josiah sighed and stood. He reached down to help her to her feet, and as their hands interlocked, she tilted her head to look up at him, and their eyes met. She stood only inches from his broad strong chest, and his gaze moved to her lips. Her stomach swooped with the same exhilaration as whooshing down the hill, leaving her breathless.

"Adaaaaa!"

Mary Elizabeth's scream broke the spell. Josiah shook

his head and bent to pick up the toboggan rope, leaving Ada bereft.

He took her hand to help her up the hill, and Ada clung to that connection, but she couldn't help wondering what might have happened if her sister hadn't interrupted. The rest of the afternoon, they let the children take turns. When it was almost time to go, Josiah caught her eye and motioned toward the toboggan with his chin.

Ada yearned for one more ride with him, but knew she shouldn't. Reluctantly, she shook her head.

* * *

As Ada shooed her siblings toward home, Josiah could barely mask his disappointment. He'd had so much fun this afternoon, and so had Nathan.

Although his son had steered clear of him, he'd taken his first ride down the hill sandwiched between David and Sadie. After that, he'd gone eagerly. During one of his rides, Josiah stood at the bottom of the hill and mentally snapped a picture of Nathan's happy face and tucked it into his heart. His son's eyes and mouth wide, his scream of excitement as they hit a bump and almost tumbled off. Sadie righted the sled by tipping in the opposite direction, and they made it safely down the hill.

Josiah wished the day would never end. For the first time in years, he felt whole. The ache still remained, but joy had erased the sadness and pain.

After Ada supervised the groups and started them on the trail homeward, she waited for him to catch up. Although it wasn't right, he almost hoped she'd stumble so he'd have an excuse to take her arm or hold her hand. To his dismay, she stayed surefooted the whole way home.

When they reached the house, she turned to him. "Would you like to come in for some hot chocolate?"

An eager *yes* almost jumped from his lips, but he managed to contain it. "I'm sure Nathan would enjoy it." *And so would I.*

"Oh." If he wasn't mistaken, she appeared disappointed at his response.

"I'd like it too," he added, and was rewarded with a sunny smile. So she hadn't asked only out of politeness. She wanted to be around him the same way he desired to be near her.

Ada directed everyone to the basement to take off their snow-caked clothes. Then they all trooped up to the kitchen. Sadie put milk on to boil, Hannah got down mugs, and the twins scooped cocoa into the pot. Ada measured out sugar, and Mary Elizabeth went to the pantry and returned with a bag of marshmallows. Each move seemed carefully orchestrated.

The warmth of the kitchen thawed his frozen fingers, while the warmth of her presence melted his frozen heart. When he was around her, his loneliness disappeared, and his heart filled with a longing never to leave. That desire had overwhelmed him on the slopes today when she'd stared up at him with dazed eyes. He'd almost made a fool of himself. If Mary Elizabeth hadn't startled him with her yell, he'd have lost control and kissed her. What would she have done? Would she have returned the kiss?

"Would you like a slice of snitz pie?" Ada's soft voice jerked him back to the kitchen.

He blinked. *Pie?* His eyes focused on the lips forming the words, but his imagination struggled to make sense of them. Somehow *pie* and *kisses* and *lips* had all jumbled in his brain.

Ada leaned closer and stared at him in concern. "Are you all right?"

"What? Oh, yes, I'm fine." More than fine. All his senses buzzed with her nearness, but he needed to give her a coherent answer. "I'd like...um, pie." He'd almost said he'd like to kiss her, but stopped himself in time.

A vision of loveliness, she flitted about the kitchen. Josiah couldn't take his eyes off her. A piece of snitz pie appeared before him. When she set a mug of steaming hot chocolate in front of him, he inhaled the sugary scent overriding the bitter cocoa, the same way her sweetness had overcome the bitterness in his heart.

* * *

The weather hadn't improved much when Miriam showed up that Saturday as her part of the Christmas gift of service. Ada found it hard to believe someone else would be doing all the cooking, cleaning, and childcare. She had no idea what to do with her free time.

"I'll put this casserole in the oven for your dinner," Miriam said. "Now go and have fun."

Ada had forgotten the mothers were babysitting so she'd have free Saturdays. She'd made no plans for the day. "What about your family?"

"My *mamm* and Levi are caring for the children, and I made a casserole like this for our dinner. It was no trouble to make one more." She made a shooing motion with her hands.

"Thank you so much." Ada hadn't had a break from childcare for years, except for the night Josiah had watched her siblings. *Josiah.* They'd had so much fun sledding earlier this week. If only they could spend today together. She'd thought several times he'd been about to ask about courting—especially now that his mourning period was officially over. The way he'd stared at her every time their eyes met. She hoped she hadn't been reading into those looks, the accidental touches.

Ada slipped on her coat. The only place she could think of to go was Leah's store. Her friend had guessed Ada's feelings for Josiah; she'd be the perfect person to tell about the sledding adventures. Leah would be honest too and tell her if she was making too much of the looks and touches.

Trucks had plowed and salted last night, so the roads were a mix of melting snow and ice. Her horse kicked up the gray slush, splashing it back toward the buggy. Leah's brothers must have started early because they'd cleared the parking lot, the long driveway back to their house, and all around the barns. Two buggies and a car were parked in the lot.

Ada stepped carefully from the buggy, watching for patches of black ice. She made it to the door as an *Englischer* exited, and he stepped aside to hold the door open for her. She stepped inside, and the door jingled shut behind her.

Across the room, Leah was balancing on a stepladder, her back to the door, struggling with a heavy box. Ada was about to call out to her when Josiah stepped out of the aisle near Leah. Ada's voice caught in her throat as she drank in his broad shoulders, his...

"Here, let me help you with that." Josiah's muscles rippled under his blue shirt as he reached for the box and took it out of Leah's hands. "I can hold it while you set out the stock."

Leah responded with effusive *thanks*.

Although Ada could barely see her friend's profile, Leah's brilliant smile and breathy voice sent warning signals. Ada didn't want to jump to conclusions on such flimsy evidence. Leah flashed her wide smile at everyone. And she might be out of breath from climbing the ladder with a heavy box. Josiah could be the cause, though, because Ada's lungs were struggling to draw in air, and she hadn't been climbing ladders.

Josiah stood beneath the ladder, holding the heavy box with ease. Leah reached in and put items on the shelf. They worked together smoothly. Josiah seemed to know when and where to move the box to prevent Leah from straining. It almost seemed as if they'd done this together before.

After Leah had arranged several bottles on the shelf, Josiah looked up at her. "So as I was asking before that customer came in"—he shifted the box again so Leah could access it more easily—"do you want to go to the Sweetheart Dinner?"

Ada's heart contracted in her chest. She'd thought... she'd hoped... after sledding together, she'd been so sure he'd ask to court her. She'd spent so many nights dreaming of them doing things together, having fun. And she'd even imagined their wedding. A wedding that could only ever be a fantasy. She couldn't marry, not with so many responsibilities. But deep inside, she'd been holding out hope Josiah would embrace her *and* her siblings.

Ada pinched her lips together to keep from crying out. She had to flee, to get out of here, but her legs, her whole body had turned to ice. She stood frozen, waiting for her friend's response.

Leah pushed a few bottles over to make more room and then looked down at Josiah, her expression serious. "You know I do."

Ada uttered a small cry as her dreams shattered, and the other two turned to look at her, their faces surprised. Shocked. Worried.

She turned and fled then, slipping and sliding across the parking lot, fumbling to untie her horse. Behind her, the door banged open, and Josiah called her name. But Ada leapt into her buggy and urged her horse into a trot despite the danger.

"Adaaaaa!" echoed across the parking lot as Josiah chased after her. The buggy's rearview mirror framed him and the frantic look on his face. In the background, Leah stood in the doorway, gaping.

Heedless of oncoming traffic, Ada turned the buggy onto the road, sending the wheels spinning and sliding. The horse strained to regain his footing as the buggy fishtailed, splattering slush. Once the buggy righted itself, the horse picked up speed, and they left Josiah far behind. But no matter how quickly she went, she couldn't outrun the pain of betrayal.

Chapter Thirty-Three

Josiah pushed past Leah and grabbed his coat from the counter. "I have to go after her."

Throwing on his coat, he raced across the parking lot and jumped into the buggy. Although he wanted to speed after her, he forced himself to drive with caution. If he were in an accident, he'd never be able to help her.

In addition to scanning for black ice, he watched for buggies that had skidded off the road. Although he kept his horse under control, he couldn't rein in his thoughts. He hadn't heard Ada come into the store. If he had, he would have waited to ask Leah his question. Or at least tried to explain the situation with Leah first.

He made it to Ada's without incident. She must have also because he hadn't passed her, but he'd knock on the door to be sure. Maybe she'd even allow him to explain about Leah.

He knocked, and the door opened. "I'm sorry about—"
Miriam? What was she doing here? Had she come to visit?

Josiah stood on the porch, cold seeping through his
coat, his toes numb. Now what?

"Josiah?" Miriam stared at him the way he'd been
staring at her.

"I, um, stopped by to tell Ada something. It won't take
long. Is she around?"

"Not today. I'm babysitting and fixing dinner. It was
her Christmas gift from the *mamm*s at the school."

Oh, that's right. The *mamm*s were taking turns
babysitting. He'd forgotten. "Do you have any idea
where she was headed?"

"Sorry, I didn't ask."

Josiah didn't want Miriam to get the wrong idea. "I
suppose it can wait." He wanted to do it as soon as possible, though. He needed to make things perfectly clear.

* * *

Once Leah's store was no longer visible in the rearview
mirror, Ada turned the nearest corner and slowed her
horse to a walk. She'd been foolish to speed in this
weather, but her only thought had been to get away. She
wandered aimlessly down a narrow lane. All she wanted
to do now was head home and burrow into bed. Hide
under the covers and never come out again. But she
couldn't. Miriam expected her to stay out all day.

All her dreams smashed. Her best friend with the man
she loved. She wondered how long they'd been together,
and why Josiah had invited her sledding. Ada groaned.
He'd asked her along because she'd sounded wistful, and

he was kind. He hadn't come to the house to see her; he'd come for David. And she'd pushed her way into the invitation. He'd extended the same invitation to her siblings.

No matter how many romantic fantasies she wove, she had to be honest. He had never asked to court her. She'd built that illusion from the looks they'd shared, random touches that may have been accidental, and her own budding attraction. She didn't want to admit it to herself, but she'd fallen in love with Josiah. A man who loved someone else.

Ada couldn't face the questions Miriam would ask if she returned so early. She had to find some place warm to stay until dinnertime. She turned down the next road and headed toward Naomi's Re-Uze-It, the Amish resale store run by one of her buddy bunch friends. She could pretend to shop for a few hours.

The shop was a few blocks off the main road, and when she pulled in, only two other buggies waited in the parking lot. Ada didn't want to speak to anyone, but she readied herself to greet Naomi and face a barrage of questions.

To her relief, Naomi wasn't at the counter. Her friend's voice carried from upstairs as she and a customer discussed whether it was too early to buy toddler sizes for a newborn. Because the building had been converted from a house, it had many rooms. Ada slipped down to the basement where Naomi sold used furniture. She settled into a rocking chair in the back corner of the dim room where a tall cupboard hid her from view.

The gift of a free day from the schoolhouse parents seemed more of a burden than a blessing. It made her realize how alone she truly was. She had nowhere to go, no one to visit. And now she'd lost Leah. It would be too painful to spend time with her best friend since she'd be courting Josiah.

She'd still have to see Josiah at the schoolhouse, which would be painful, knowing he was promised to someone else. Unlike the *Englisch*, who dated around, the Amish waited until the couple had feelings that could lead to marriage before courting, so Josiah asking Leah to the Sweetheart Dinner meant a serious commitment. A commitment that could last a lifetime.

As the shop's four o'clock closing time neared, Naomi crisscrossed the floor overhead, and the stairs creaked to the second floor. Ada tiptoed up the basement stairs, and while Naomi closed doors and straightened merchandise on the second floor, Ada eased the outside door open and crossed the parking lot to her buggy.

Cold, gray dusk closed around her as she drove the long, lonely road home. She pulled into the barn, un-hooked the buggy, and took care of her horse. Then she made her way to the house.

Miriam met her at the door. "Did you have a good time?" Before Ada could answer, she rushed on, "You have such wonderful brothers and sisters. I really enjoyed spending time with them. Dinner's in the oven, and I need to hurry home to cook mine."

"Thanks so much," Ada managed to get out. Grateful that Miriam hadn't questioned her about what she'd done, Ada started to close the door.

Miriam called over her shoulder, "I forgot. Josiah Yoder stopped by. He didn't say what he wanted."

Ada stood with the door hanging open, staring after Miriam. Why had Josiah come here? Maybe he'd been worried about her safety after she'd driven away so recklessly on an icy road, so he'd come to make sure she made it home safely. Slowly, she shut the door. At least she'd been spared the humiliation of facing him. From her reaction, both he and Leah probably figured out why she fled.

"Ada, you're home!" Mary Elizabeth flung herself at Ada's legs, hung on tight, and burst into tears. "I missed you."

"I missed you too." The only thing Ada had wanted today was to come home. Her life revolved around her siblings. And it was destined to stay that way.

Ada only picked at the casserole Miriam had left. Her stomach hurt, and she could barely finish the tiny amount she'd taken. Although her siblings polished off large portions, Ada found each bite tasted dry and flavorless. They had just finished their meal when someone knocked on the door.

While the twins cleared the table, Sadie went to answer the door. Leah's voice floated down the hall, and the roiling in Ada's stomach increased. She'd hoped to avoid Leah until the pain was less raw.

Sadie called down the hall, "Ada, Leah's here to see you."

Ada had no choice but to go. Leah was seated on the living room couch, so Ada took the rocking chair opposite her. The wooden slats against her back kept her upright when all she wanted to do was curl into herself.

Leah gave her a tentative smile. "Josiah came by to talk to you earlier?"

"Yes." Ada took a deep breath to steady her voice, but before she could say she hadn't seen him, Leah rushed on.

"So you know about the Sweetheart Dinner?"

Ada pushed the word *yes* from between clenched teeth.

Leah studied Ada's face. "I thought you'd be happy for me. I've waited so long to date."

If her friend were dating anyone other than Josiah, Ada would have been overjoyed. Although it was one of the hardest things she'd ever done, Ada forced a half-hearted smile. "I am happy you've found someone to court." *I only wish it were someone else.*

Leah twisted her hands in her lap. "I'm so scared and nervous. What if I'm making a mistake?"

Ada wanted to say, *You are*. But she couldn't let her own unhappiness influence Leah's decision. Would Leah change her mind about dating Josiah if she knew Ada's feelings? She longed to tell Leah, but that wouldn't be fair to Josiah. He had chosen Leah. And she loved Josiah enough to want his happiness.

Another knock at the door sent Sadie scurrying down the hall with Mary Elizabeth close on her heels. Ada sat with her back to the door, and Sadie's cheerful greeting froze Ada in place.

"Josiah," she squealed. "Come in."

Mary Elizabeth jumped up and down so hard the floor shook. "You're going to read us a bedtime story again?"

"I'd be delighted."

Leah leaned forward and whispered, "He's a wonderful father, isn't he?"

A picture flashed through Ada's mind of Leah and Josiah reading bedtime stories to Nathan and their children, and she wanted to bolt from the room, burrow under her bedcovers, and let the tears flow.

Leah jumped up from the couch and hurried to the door. Ada stayed where she was, her back to them. She couldn't bear to see their expressions when they greeted each other.

"I was just leaving," Leah said. "I just came by to discuss things with Ada."

"Drive carefully, Leah, and watch for black ice." Josiah's bass voice touched a chord deep within Ada. His words, though, were directed at someone else. He cared about Leah and wanted to keep her safe.

Leah's soft *danke* conjured up a picture of them staring into each other's eyes, reluctant to part. Maybe Ada could excuse herself by saying she was ill, which was the truth.

Before she could get up, Sadie led Josiah into the living room. Ada's pulse raced as he passed her chair, and she issued a stern warning to herself. He belonged to another woman. She might not be able to rein in her physical responses to him, but she kept her gaze fixed on the needlepoint wall hanging to avoid temptation.

Josiah settled onto the sofa in the exact spot where Leah had been. "So Leah explained?"

Ada couldn't push words past her closed-up throat, but she tipped her head up and down once. Oh, yes, Leah had explained. Josiah didn't need to add his interpretation. He and Leah acted solicitous about Ada's feelings, but she wished they'd leave her alone to deal with her feelings in private.

Sadie returned with David. "Hannah and the twins are finishing up the dishes. They'll be here shortly."

David signed, *Nathan where?*

Josiah signed back, *Bed* and *sleep*, and then turned to

Ada. "I wanted to come earlier, but I decided it would be best to wait until Nathan was asleep."

"How is Nathan doing?" Ada managed to ask a question that didn't sound too shaky.

"The crying has decreased. He's also been following me around more and copying what I'm doing."

Ada pushed aside her own sorrow to respond, "That's *gut.*"

"It is," he agreed, but his eyes held deep pools of sadness. "If only he'd trust me enough to let me get close."

Mary Elizabeth bounced into the room carrying the Bible story book and plopped down beside Josiah. Sadie sat on his other side. A short while later, the others joined them. Mary Elizabeth chose the story, and Josiah began reading.

For a short while, Ada fantasized they were a couple, but reality sliced through her. Her eyes blurred with tears, and the words faded into buzzing.

When the story ended, Sadie hustled her siblings off to get ready for bed, and Ada was alone with Josiah.

Josiah cleared his throat and then said, "I wanted a chance to talk to you about what happened in the health food store."

Why? So you could be the one to drive the knife deeper into my heart?

"I'm sorry you had to hear my question to Leah. If I'd known you were there, I would have explained first."

His apologetic glance only added to her growing agony. Josiah cared enough about her feelings not to hurt her. If only he cared enough not to court someone else.

"After what happened between us on Miller's Hill"— Josiah appeared to be studying every detail of the wooden floorboards—"I didn't want you to think I, um…"

So she hadn't misinterpreted his looks? He'd been as attracted to her as she'd been to him? That made this whole situation even harder to bear. Ada lowered her gaze, hoping not looking at him would lessen some of the pain, but it didn't help.

"When I suggested the Sweetheart Dinner, I wasn't sure Leah would agree, but she did. She was hesitant, but that's understandable."

No, it's not. Ada's heart twisted. *I wouldn't have hesitated for even a second.* She glanced up, but wished she hadn't. It reminded her of all she'd lost.

When she didn't answer, he continued, "I hope she'll be happy."

One part of Ada hoped so too, but the other part…

"Now that Leah's explained, I hope we can go back to being"—he swallowed hard—*"friends."*

Under the circumstances, Ada didn't feel it would be appropriate, but to say *no* might mean cutting Josiah out of her life completely.

When she didn't answer, he continued, "I hope things will work out for Leah and Ben."

"Ben? Who's Ben?"

Josiah gazed at her, a question in his eyes. "Leah didn't tell you?"

"Not about Ben." Ada struggled to make sense of the conversation. "I thought the two of you…"

"Oh, Ada." Josiah's words were anguished. "All this time, you thought Leah and I—?"

Yes, she had. Was he trying to say he and Leah weren't together? "But you asked her to the Sweetheart

Dinner?" She'd heard those words coming out of his mouth, and she'd heard Leah's answer.

"No, I didn't. I mean, yes, I did, but not for me. My cousin Ben is visiting from Ohio, and he's been picking up *Mamm*'s orders at Stoltzfus's store. He's interested in Leah, but he's shy. He wanted me to ask her in case she said *no*."

"You were asking Leah to the dinner for someone else?" Ada tried to wrap her mind around his explanation.

Josiah nodded. "You couldn't think I'd ask anyone else out after... after the other day?"

"I'd hoped not," she said shyly, "but when I heard—"

"I'm so sorry you walked in right then." He reached across and took her hand. "I never want to hurt you."

The caring look in Josiah's eyes melted Ada's heart. He caressed the backs of her hands with his thumbs, sending warmth cascading through her.

"Ada?" Josiah hesitated, and she waited breathlessly for him to finish. "Would you like to go skating next Saturday?"

Yes, yes, oh yes! Ada danced inside but managed to answer demurely. "I'd like that."

Chapter Thirty-Four

The week dragged for Ada, but finally Saturday morning arrived. At the loud knock on the door, Ada flew down the steps. Josiah was early. Betty had arrived only a few minutes ago. Ada yanked open the door, and the welcoming smile she'd planned for Josiah slid into confusion.

Marcy Givens, her *Englisch* neighbor, stood on the doorstep, holding out her cell phone. "You have a call."

A gust of frigid wind blew through the open door. "Come in, come in," Ada said. She slammed the door shut behind Marcy and held the phone to her ear. "Hello?"

"Is this Ada Rupp?" a woman's voice demanded.

"Yes." Who would be calling her?

The woman identified herself and explained she was calling about Ada's *daed*.

Dazed, Ada handed the phone back to Marcy.

"Is everything all right?" Marcy asked.

"Yes, but I need to leave right away. Thank you so much for coming all the way over here with the phone, especially in this weather."

Marcy smiled. "It's no trouble."

Ada appreciated Marcy's kindness, and when she returned, she'd drop off a few loaves of the homemade bread her neighbor loved, but right now she had to rush out the door.

The next few minutes were a flurry of activity as Ada explained to Betty, threw on her cloak, and raced out the door. She was racing for the barn when she stopped.

Josiah. He was coming soon to take her skating. She had to let him know she couldn't go with him. She dreaded telling Betty that Josiah planned to come calling, but it had to be done. She was halfway to the door when Josiah pulled into the driveway. She raced toward his buggy.

When he stepped out, she hurried into an explanation. "I'm so sorry," she said, her voice trembling. "I can't go skating with you today. I just had an emergency call, and I need to leave right away."

Josiah took her arm. "Wherever you're going, I'll drive you. You're much too shaky to be on the road." He led her around to the passenger side and tucked blankets around her. He turned his horse around. "Which way should I go?"

"You don't need to do this." She should go by herself. Once he saw where they were headed, he'd lose all respect for her.

"I want to do it," Josiah assured her. "Should I turn right or left?"

Her hands clenched in her lap, Ada directed him at each intersection until they reached the last street. "It's the last building on the left."

Josiah slowed as he reached the driveway and looked at her with a question in his eyes. "Here?"

She nodded, and he pulled into the parking lot. Shame overwhelmed her, and she couldn't bear to look at him as she mumbled, "My *daed*'s here." No decent Amish family would ever put a parent in a nursing home. Although the previous bishop had encouraged her to do so, the rest of the community had condemned her. She feared Josiah would too. What man would want to court a woman who left her father's care to strangers?

"You were with me for Nathan, so I want to be here for you."

As soon as they walked through the door, a woman in a flower-printed dress with a white lace doily covering her bun approached them. "I'm Faye Hess. May I help you?"

"We're here to see Ezekiel Rupp"—she lowered her voice—"in the dementia unit."

"I'm so glad you made it. I understand you wanted to be called whenever he's having a good day so you can visit." She motioned for them to follow her down a nearby hallway. "I'm sorry it took so long to get the meds adjusted. I do want to warn you, though, that his mood may change quickly."

Ada had seen that happen. That was the reason he'd been admitted.

"Whatever you do," Faye said, "don't contradict him or upset him. If he says it's summer, agree with him and talk about warm weather. If he says the sky is green, tell him it's a lovely color."

Ada nodded. She'd learned that the hard way.

"I don't know how long he'll stay lucid, so if his mood changes, press the call button immediately and get out of the room. We keep his door locked so he doesn't get out, but we'll leave it unlocked in case you need to escape."

"Escape?" Josiah repeated.

"Hopefully, it won't be necessary," Faye said. "But I always warn people, in case." She motioned for them to step back before she unlocked and opened the heavy metal door, with torn padding on the back of it.

Josiah's fingers tightened on Ada's as they followed Faye down the hall. She stopped at another door and unlocked it. She opened it wide enough to stick her head inside.

"Are you ready for visitors this morning, Ezekiel?" she asked.

"It's afternoon now, but I'm happy for visitors."

At the sound of *Daed*'s voice, tears sprang to Ada's eyes, and her gut twisted. Why had she agreed to put him in a home? She should have kept him at home. He sounded fine and so...normal.

When she stepped through the door, *Daed* looked up from the open Bible spread across his lap. "Ada, it's about time. You've finally come to bring me home?"

She'd like nothing better, but she had no idea how to undo what she'd done. "We've missed you."

His voice husky, *Daed* said, "I've missed all of you." Then he turned to Josiah. "Do I know you?" His glance fell to their entwined hands. "You're married?"

"Not yet," Josiah said smoothly, "but we'd like to be. We came to ask for your blessing."

Ada stared at him in shock. Then she recalled the nurse's words. *Oh, of course.* Josiah was playing along.

Her *daed* stroked his beard. "You'll take good care of her?"

"Yes, I love her, and I'll do my very best to care for her."

Ada's heart ached. The words she'd always dreamed of hearing were flowing from Josiah's lips, but only as playacting.

"Ada, you'll be a good wife?" *Daed* asked.

"Oh, yes, *Daed.*" She hadn't meant for her voice to come out so breathy and filled with yearning.

"Then I give my blessing." The broad smile stretching across *Daed*'s face warmed Ada's heart. He set his Bible on the bedside table and stood. "We should leave now so we're not late for the wedding."

"The wedding's not yet," Ada said.

Daed's face darkened, and she realized her mistake. "The celery still needs to be picked," she said hastily.

His tense shoulders relaxed. "Of course. I should have thought of that. Tell your *mamm* to hurry." He tottered a few steps toward the door. "Better yet, I'll tell her myself."

Ada panicked. They couldn't let him out of the room.

Josiah stepped in front of her. "Why don't we go get everything ready, and then come back for you?"

A look of confusion passed over *Daed*'s face. He glowered at Josiah. "Who are you?" he thundered. "Get out of my house!" He picked up the Bible and hurled it at Josiah, who pushed Ada behind him and spread his arms wide to protect her.

The Bible hit Josiah squarely in the chest and bounced to the floor. Behind him, Ada scrabbled for the doorknob.

The door opened behind her. "It's time for meds," Faye said in a cheery voice. She stopped short at the scene in front of her. "Your Bible, Ezekiel?" Faye said sternly, scooping it off the floor. "I know you didn't mean to throw God's Word. I'll keep it for you until you're ready to treat it properly."

She ducked when he swung a hand as if to slap her. With one swift motion, she pushed Ada and Josiah out the door, pulled it shut, and locked it.

Ada's heart pounded so hard her chest hurt. "I'm so sorry he almost hurt you."

"I'm used to it. He doesn't know what he's doing, poor man." Faye hugged the Bible to her chest. "I'll lock this up until he's lucid, and I'll let you out before I give him the meds." She escorted them to the metal door, unlocked it, and closed it behind them.

At the click of multiple locks, overwhelming sadness swept through Ada. Deep inside, she'd always held out hope they would be able to bring *Daed* home someday.

Josiah wrapped his arms around her and hugged her right there in the hallway. "I'm so sorry you had to go through this." He shook his head. "Losing your *mamm*, dealing with your *daed*, taking on the responsibility for the household, caring for your brothers and sisters."

Ada relaxed against him. If only she could stay here forever in his strong arms, safe and secure.

Locks clicked, and the heavy metal door creaked open. Josiah released her before an aide stepped into the hallway. Without his arms around her, Ada felt lost and lonely.

Visiting *Daed* had made it clear he would never recover. Her heart ached to know they'd never have him back home again. Even with the best medical care, it wouldn't be safe.

As if sensing she needed time to think, Josiah remained silent for the first few miles, and Ada was grateful. Lost in her thoughts, she tried to come to terms with losing *Daed*.

"I'm sorry about your *daed*. It must have been a difficult decision to make."

"It was." Ada had agonized for a long time. "I wanted to keep him at home, but his rages were dangerous. Most people in the community, including Bishop Troyer and Betty, believe I made the wrong choice."

Josiah's brow knotted into lines of concern. "Are they aware he can be violent?"

"I'm not sure. The previous bishop witnessed a few of *Daed*'s outbursts, and he suggested—insisted, really—on us placing him in a nursing home. Before Bishop Zook had his stroke, he and his wife helped me choose the Mennonite home." Every time she remembered that time, the guilt came flooding back, and Ada's stomach clenched.

"The staff seem compassionate and competent. I'm sure he gets good care." Piled-up snow blocked much of the shoulder, but Josiah pulled over as far as he could. Several cars passed, spattering slush on the horse and buggy.

"It's hard, though, having him away from the family."

"I can imagine. If there's anything I can do to help, please let me know."

"Thank you. I also appreciate you driving me to the nursing home."

"You're very welcome." In spite of the frigid weather, Josiah's smile set her heart ablaze.

When they pulled up to the house, he said, "I know today was hard and you might not be ready to talk about anything else right now, but since I already invited Leah to the Sweetheart Dinner…"

Startled, Ada turned toward him. The twinkle in his eye indicated he was teasing, but she could barely manage a wan smile.

"I'd like to issue another invitation to the person I'd been planning to ask all along. Would you do me the honor of going to the Sweetheart Dinner with me?"

How could she say no? But she must.

Being together today had been magical, but on the way home, thoughts of *Daed* and her siblings kept intruding. Taking a deep breath, she forced the words through her lips. "Now that you've meet *Daed*, you can understand why I can't court. Not you, not anyone."

Josiah stared at her as if her words made no sense. "You don't want to date me?"

Ada had to be honest. "I want to, but I can't. I have seven siblings to care for. I'd always hoped *Daed* might get better, and I'd be free to marry and start a life of my own." She blinked to hold back the tears. "Seeing *Daed* today made me realize it will never happen."

"What if I told you I consider courting you part of a package deal, and I like the whole package? And that I meant what I said when I asked for your *daed*'s blessing?"

Ada managed a half smile. He really meant that? Her seven siblings didn't scare him off?

"I have a son who needs more time and attention than all seven of your siblings put together," he said.

"Nathan's not a problem."

"Then it sounds as if we're in agreement about accepting each other's families. Will you go to the Sweetheart Dinner with me?"

"Are you sure?" After all he'd seen today, he still wanted to be with her?

"I've never been more sure and certain in my life."

Ada blinked back tears. She thought she'd never find love, yet she'd found someone who not only wanted to marry her, but someone who accepted her siblings too. And someone she loved with all her heart.

"Then the answer is YES!" The last word reverberated around the buggy, echoing many times over, the same way her heart kept repeating an unqualified *yes!*

Chapter Thirty-Five

Two days before the Sweetheart Dinner, Ada floated around, still feeling Josiah's arm around her.

Loud knocking stirred her from her reverie. She longed to stay in Josiah's imaginary arms, although she'd prefer his real ones, pressing her head against his strong chest, his heart beating in her ear.

The banging increased. Ada hurried to the front door.

"Ada," Leah burst out, and practically fell into Ada's arms.

"What's wrong?" Ada opened the door wider so her friend could enter. After shutting the door, she took Leah's arm, led her into the living room, and seated her on the couch. Then Ada sank down beside her.

Leah's lips were pinched together, and her eyes swam with tears. "It's Ben." Her voice shook. "He came calling the other night, but I'd rushed off to help Sharon with a delivery. I forgot all about our date when I heard Esther's labor had begun. I didn't tell Ben that, but I think he sensed it."

"Oh, Leah…" Ada laid a hand on her friend's arm, wishing she could erase the guilt in her eyes.

Leah hung her head. "I apologized, and he said he forgave me, but it's driven a wedge between us. I don't know what I'm going to do."

"Maybe the two of you should talk it over. If you tell him how much you love being a midwife and explain you can be called away suddenly…"

Leah clutched so hard at Ada's arm, her fingers pressed into the skin. "He wants to talk about our relationship tonight. What will I do if he asks me to stop attending births?"

Ada gently pried up her fingers, and Leah's eyes widened when she saw the marks on Ada's arm. "I'm so sorry. I didn't mean to hurt you."

"That's all right. You're upset." Ada rubbed her forearm briskly until the red marks disappeared. "As for Ben, he'll understand. If he doesn't, maybe he's not the right man for you."

Leah laughed shakily. "He's the only man who's ever shown any interest in courting me. If I give him up, I'll lose my chance of a future, of having a family." Her eyes filled with tears. "Besides, I already care about him."

Ada's chest tightened. Assisting at births meant so much to Leah. Surely Ben would understand, but would he be flexible enough to adjust to Leah's last-minute changes of plans? Ada wasn't sure. "What will you do if he doesn't agree?"

Leah sat lost in thought for several minutes. "I'll have to follow my heart."

"I'll support you whatever you decide," Ada said, "and I'll pray for you as you make the decision."

Leah leaned over and hugged Ada. "Thank you for listening and for being such a good friend. I hope your relationship with Josiah is going well."

Ada couldn't bear to share her own happy news when Leah was so troubled, so she tucked her memories of Josiah into the secret recesses of her heart. Perhaps after the Sweetheart Dinner, they'd both have wonderful *gut* news to share.

Each time Ada thought of that day in the store when she'd mistaken Josiah's question and Leah's answer, her heart clenched for a moment before returning to its joyful staccato beat.

Because all she could think about was love, Ada taught her students to say *I love you* to their families. First she taught it in sign language. Nathan, David, Emily, and Lizzie did well with the signs. Then she taught Will and Lukas on the letter boards. The two boys concentrated so much better when they were in their therapy swings, and after several tries, they could point to the letters in order. Ada used thick cardboard to make them take-home letter boards so they could share the message with their families.

The day Ada sent the messages home, Josiah arrived for Nathan. Ada tried to stay professional and limit the amount of time she spent staring into Josiah's eyes. Today she waited to see if Nathan would give his *daed* the heart he'd colored.

Nathan started toward Josiah, but as he passed Ada, he placed the heart in her outstretched hand.

*   *   *

On Saturday night Josiah prepared for the Sweetheart Dinner, his heart bursting with excitement. He'd have a chance to spend time with Ada alone. Seeing her every day at school made his heart trip faster, but they barely had time to exchange greetings and glances. She had, however, resumed teaching him sign language at her house when he picked up Nathan, but he'd been circumspect and kept the lessons brief. Every day, though, it grew more and more difficult to end the sessions.

Lizzie's *mamm* had agreed to come in the evening rather than during the day, and Nathan was spending the night at Ada's because *Mamm* was helping at the restaurant. When Josiah came downstairs, Nathan was already sitting by the door in his pajamas, clutching a small bag with his clothes for the next day. His eyes were shining, and he was so thrilled, he flashed Josiah a smile.

Although Nathan returned to his somber expression whenever Josiah looked at him, his face grew animated as he looked out the window. The minute they arrived and Josiah slid open the passenger door, Nathan jumped out of the buggy and raced to the front door. Josiah couldn't blame him; he wanted to do the same.

Nathan banged on the door, and Mary Elizabeth opened it, her smile as wide as Nathan's. Nathan dashed inside, but Josiah stood on the doorstep, mesmerized as Ada descended the stairs. Until tonight, he'd only ever seen her wearing black because she'd been in mourning for her *mamm*. Now she was dressed in teal. Other girls in their *g'may* wore that color, but he'd never seen anyone who looked as beautiful in it as Ada. The pink that splashed onto her cheeks when she caught sight of him contrasted beautifully with the dress. Then she smiled, and Josiah's breath caught in his throat.

Staring at Ada had warmed him so much, he'd been standing there with the front door wide open without feeling the icy winds whipping behind him until Ada shivered. "I'm so sorry." Tearing his gaze from her, he stepped inside and shut the door.

Nathan stood in the hallway, surrounded by Ada's siblings, and Josiah and Ada joined the circle. Nathan looked up at Ada with adoring eyes and signed, *I love you*. Josiah wished he were brave enough to do the same.

Then, one by one, Nathan went around the circle signing *I love you* to each of the children. He stopped when he reached Josiah. Ada laid a comforting hand on Josiah's sleeve, filling his heart with happiness, but nothing could touch the empty hole created by his son's rejection.

Then each of Ada's siblings took turns going around the circle signing *I love you* to each person, including him. That, too, helped to ease some of the pain. They all loved him, even if his own son didn't.

Ada signed to each of her siblings and Nathan, then turned to him, and her eyes said what her fingers didn't. Josiah swallowed hard and could barely tear his gaze away to do his own signing.

He went around the circle of children and ended with Nathan, but after he signed *I love you*, he spread his hands apart for *very much*. Then he turned to Ada, but before he could decide what to do, Nathan stepped between them. His back to Josiah, he signed to Ada. Gazing down at Nathan's hands, Josiah tried to decipher the signs. He recognized *you* and *Daed*, but the sign in the middle was unfamiliar. Nathan added a question mark at the end.

Ada appeared flustered.

"What did he ask?" Josiah asked.

Her cheeks grew even pinker. "Um, he asked if I'd"— she ducked her head—"marry you." She mumbled the last two words.

Josiah set a hand on Nathan's shoulder, and for once, his son didn't flinch away. "That should have been my job, buddy, but thanks," he muttered, although Nathan couldn't hear him. Then he looked at Ada. "You didn't answer him."

Ada gazed at him, her eyes wide and starry, and then her lips curled into a mischievous grin. "Fine, I'll answer him."

Josiah sucked in a breath and waited for her answer. An answer he hoped would be *yes*.

Instead she signed, *Ask your daed*, and flashed Josiah a sideways glance that set his blood zinging.

Nathan's face scrunched up the way he did when *Mamm* gave him a spoonful of cod liver oil. He faced Josiah but didn't meet his eyes. *You marry Ada?*

This was not how Josiah had imagined proposing to Ada. He'd pictured the two of them alone together in a buggy with stars overhead, not in Ada's front hall surrounded by a crowd of onlookers.

Josiah took Ada's hands in his and, encouraged by the love sparkling in her eyes, he asked, "Will you marry me?"

She gave that small breathless *oh* that always set his pulse thrumming, and then her *yes, oh yes* filled his heart to bursting.

Her siblings' cheers reminded him he wasn't only marrying Ada, he was marrying a family. His hand entwined in hers, he faced the circle of children to find Nathan signing to each one, *You my brother? You my sister?* Although they wouldn't technically be brothers and sisters, it touched his heart that Nathan wanted to make them part of his family.

* * *

Ada's eyes brimmed with tears as Josiah and Nathan questioned her brothers and sisters. She wanted to pinch herself to be sure she wasn't dreaming. Josiah had asked her to marry him! She'd always thought she'd never have a husband or a family, but now she'd be blessed with both. And the handsome man standing before her not only loved her, he loved her siblings too. God had answered her prayers in the most thrilling way possible. Giddy with joy, Ada whispered a prayer of thanksgiving for this wonderful blessing. This dream come true.

Her siblings then signed the question to Nathan, who broke into a wide grin. When he had answered *yes* to everyone, Nathan whirled around and launched himself at Ada's knees.

He hugged her hard and then pulled back to ask, *You my mamm?*

Ada thought her heart couldn't get any fuller. She nodded and let go of Josiah's hand to kneel and sign, *I love you very much*. Then she wrapped her arms around Nathan and held him close.

When she stood, Josiah, grinning and misty-eyed, slid an arm around her and drew her to his side. Ada leaned her head against his chest, reveling in the rapid beating of his heart. She laid a hand on Nathan's shoulder to bring him closer, and her siblings smiled.

"It's bedtime," Sadie said, and she herded everyone to the stairs.

Nathan dashed over to David and pointed to himself and then David before signing, *Brothers*. David's grin revealed how thrilled he was. The two of them started up the stairs together, but Nathan looked back over his shoulder at Ada and his *daed*.

He hurried back downstairs to Ada and signed, *I love you very much.*

After she smiled, Nathan stepped in front of Josiah and stared at him for a long minute. Then his hands swished into motion. *I love you, Daed.* He stood still for a second before widening his arms to add, *Very much.*

As Nathan scampered back up the stairs, Josiah, his eyes wet with tears, stared after his son until he disappeared. Then he swept Ada into his arms. "Thank you," he said in a choked voice before pressing his lips to hers.

Above them a snicker was accompanied by muffled giggles and shuffling feet. They stepped apart to find all eight children on the steps, staring down at them.

Josiah sighed. "I suspect we'll always have an audience."

Ada hid a smile. "That should keep us circumspect."

"To bed, everyone," Josiah said, and pointed to the second story.

After all the children scrambled upstairs, he turned back to Ada. "Now where were we?"

"Right here," she murmured as she wrapped her arms around his neck and drew his head down for a kiss.

Leah Stoltzfus is dedicated to both her Amish faith and being a good midwife. It certainly keeps her thoughts from straying to the handsome *Englisch* doctor—until a blizzard shows them both that feelings can run as strong and deep as faith. But can they have one... without sacrificing the other?

A preview of
The Amish Midwife's Secret
follows.

The phone rang as Kyle was rushing out the door. He didn't recognize the number. Probably a telemarketer, but just in case it was work-related, he hit the Answer button, tucked the phone between his ear and shoulder, and shoved one arm into his coat before saying, "Hello."

Slamming the door shut behind him by hooking it with one foot, he repeated his hello. Definitely an automated call. He should hang up now, but he was busy shrugging his other arm into the sleeve. If traffic was heavy, he was going to be late. He sighed loudly.

A voice on the other end quavered. "Kyle?"

It sounded like a human, but some of those telemarketing outfits managed to make their robocalls sound real. "Yes?" he answered cautiously. He wasn't interested in a time-share or a free cruise or...

"Kyle, it's Dr. Hess. I have a question for you."

Dr. Hess? Name doesn't sound familiar. Not one of the doctors I work with at the hospital.

"Yes?" he said again as he clicked open his car door and slid into the seat.

"I'm not sure if you remember me, but you and your brother used to visit my office. And I took care of your parents when…"

The words hit Kyle like a fast, hard gut punch. He froze with his hand on the door handle, but couldn't move to close it. Old memories came flooding back. Memories he'd pushed down under the surface. Memories he'd hoped never to dredge up ever again.

His "I remember" came out shakily. Why would the doctor be calling him? Had something happened to his brother? They hadn't spoken in years. A flood of guilt hit him. If Caleb had been hurt or was dying, could he go back and face him? And what about the twins and— No, he never wanted to see Emma again.

"Is everything all right? Has something happened to Caleb or—?"

"No, no, I didn't mean to alarm you. This isn't a medical emergency. Well, it is in a way. But it's my own emergency."

It dawned on Kyle he'd been sitting there unmoving. He'd forgotten all about being late for his shift. He yanked the car door shut and started the engine.

"I have some friends at the hospital who've been keeping tabs on you," Dr. Hess continued. "They've been telling me you'll go far in the medical field."

"Thanks." Although if he were honest, the thought of someone checking up on him gave him an uncomfortable feeling in the pit of his stomach. Had Caleb asked their old family doctor to do this spying?

Kyle whipped his car into traffic and pressed his foot

on the accelerator to shoot around a slow-moving truck. The minute he did, the old demons haunted him. That was one memory he wished he could erase. Speeding had destroyed his life and cost him everything he'd always wanted. He lifted his foot and let the car glide to a safer speed while Dr. Hess prattled on about his retirement dreams.

Biting back a sigh, Kyle tuned out the old man's words as he maneuvered through heavy rush hour traffic. He regretted not grabbing a cup of coffee to wake him up, because the drone of Dr. Hess's words was lulling him to sleep. Surely the doctor hadn't called a relative stranger to discuss his future plans. Kyle wished Dr. Hess would get to the point.

"So I considered shutting down the practice, but I'm one of the few doctors in the Lancaster area who still makes house calls. People have come to expect it. I've been in a quandary. That's where you come in."

"Me?"

"Yes, you. Seems to me you'll soon be needing a place to work after your residency. I'd be happy to turn my practice over to you if you'd help me out for the next year or two. I'd like to cut back to part-time hours."

Kyle slammed on the brakes before he ran a red light. "Take over your practice?"

"Yes, I thought Esther and I could move to the retirement village she's been talking about. You could live in the house so you'd have the office right there."

Kyle pictured the huge old farmhouse set on a country road with the office attached to one side. It was a far cry from his future aspirations, which included working at a major medical center in a large city. Country life wasn't for him.

"It's a great offer," he said, planning to let down his old family doctor gently. "I'll, umm…"

"Esther and I prayed about it, and we both felt led to give the practice to you."

"Give?" Kyle said faintly.

"Yes, *give*. We have plenty of money to buy a home in the retirement village and to live comfortably. With no children of our own, we thought it would be nice to help another young doctor starting out. The mortgage is paid off, and you'd be responsible only for the bills once I leave the practice."

Kyle pulled into a parking space at the hospital. *The man was giving away his practice and his home?* "That's a mighty generous offer. I, um, need to get in to work now. If I don't, I'll be late. But I'll think about it."

"Don't just think. Pray about it."

Kyle choked back the negative retort that sprang to his lips. You wouldn't catch him praying. Not for any reason at all. "Um, yes. I have to go, but I'll let you know my decision." He said a hasty good-bye and ran for the staff entrance door.

For a resident drowning in med school debt, that was a tempting offer. But it would mean returning to a place he'd left years ago and vowed never to return. A place where he'd have to face all the demons of the past.

* * *

Leah waited for Dr. Hess to get off the phone. Usually his wife, Esther, acted as receptionist, but he was sitting in the outer office, which meant she couldn't help but overhear his conversation.

"You're finally getting some help?" she asked when he hung up.

Dr. Hess laughed. "Esther convinced me it's time to retire, but I can't go until I'm sure I have a good replacement who will do everything I do."

"Someone like that may be hard to find."

"True, but I'm hoping to convince a young medical student to move back to the area. He grew up around here, and his mother was—" Dr. Hess ran a hand through his silver hair. "Esther tells me I ramble too much, and she's right." He leaned forward, all attention on her. "What do you need today, Leah?"

"I have an expectant mother I'm worried about, but she refuses to come to the office. She says she can't leave the children. I suspect it's money." Leah pulled out some ten-dollar bills and held them out.

Dr. Hess waved them away. "I have more than enough money. I can certainly afford to do some free visits."

"Yes, but—"

The doctor interrupted her. "What's her name and address?"

Leah gave him the information and tried once again to give him the money, but the doctor refused to take it.

He rose and picked up his medical bag. "I'll head over there now."

"Thank you so much. I'm praying for a healthy delivery for her." Leah followed him to the door. "I must admit I'm curious about this medical student. You said he was from the area?" As a midwife, she'd have to work closely with him.

Dr. Hess stopped beside his car. "His name's Kyle Miller."

Leah gasped. "Caleb Miller's brother?"

With a quick nod, Dr. Hess slipped into the driver's seat. "I'm hoping everyone can let bygones be bygones."

The Amish community had forgiven Kyle, but having him back in their midst as a doctor might dredge up old hurts. And for Leah it meant confronting a secret she thought would stay hidden. A secret she'd concealed for years.

ABOUT THE AUTHOR

Rachel J. Good grew up near Lancaster, Pennsylvania, the setting for her Amish romances. Striving to be as authentic as possible, she spends time with her Amish friends, doing chores on their farms and attending family events. Rachel loves to travel and visit many different Amish communities. She also speaks at conferences and book events across the country and abroad.

When she's not traveling, she spends time with her family and writing. In addition to her Amish novels, she's written more than forty books for children and adults under several pen names.

Learn more about Rachel at:

www.racheljgood.com
Twitter @RachelJGood1
Facebook.com

Fall in Love with Forever Romance

USA TODAY BESTSELLING AUTHOR

HOPE RAMSAY

The Bride Next Door

"Every story by Hope Ramsay will touch a reader's heart."
—BRENDA NOVAK, *New York Times* bestselling author

THE BRIDE NEXT DOOR
By Hope Ramsay

Courtney Wallace has almost given up on finding her happily-ever-after. And she certainly doesn't expect to find it with Matthew Lyndon, the hotshot lawyer she overhears taking a bet to seduce her. Matt never intended to take the bet seriously. And moving next door wasn't part of his strategy to win, but the more he gets to know Courtney, the more intrigued he becomes. When fun and games turn into something real, will these two decide they're in it to win it?

Fall in Love with Forever Romance

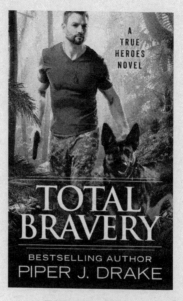

TOTAL BRAVERY
By Piper J. Drake

Raul's lucky to have the best partner a man could ask for: a highly trained, fiercely loyal German Shepherd Dog named Taz. But their first mission in Hawaii puts them to the test when a kidnapping ring sets its sights on the bravest woman Raul's ever met...Mali knows she's in trouble. Yet sharing close quarters with smoldering, muscle-for-hire Raul makes her feel safe. But when the kidnappers make their move, Raul's got to find a way to save the life of the woman he loves.

Fall in Love with Forever Romance

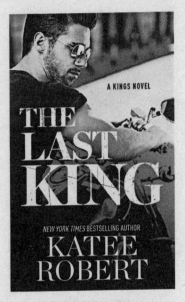

THE LAST KING
By Katee Robert

The King family has always been like royalty in Texas. And sitting right at the top is Beckett, who just inherited his father's fortune, his company—and all his enemies. But Beckett's always played by his own rules, so when he needs help, he goes to the last person anyone would ever expect: his biggest rival. Samara Mallick is reluctant to risk her career—despite her red-hot attraction—but it soon becomes clear there are King family secrets darker than she ever imagined and dangerous enough to get them killed.

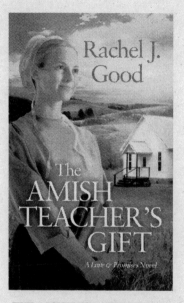